Darkness

A NOVEL

DAVID ADAMS RICHARDS

ANCHOR CANADA

Anchor Canada paperback published 2023
Doubleday Canada hardcover published 2021

Anchor Canada and colophon are registered trademarks of
Penguin Random House Canada Limited. Distributed by
Penguin Random House Canada Limited, Toronto.

Library and Archives Canada Cataloguing in Publication
Title: Darkness / David Adams Richards.
Names: Richards, David Adams, author.
Identifiers: Canadiana 20210131489 | ISBN 9780385690225 (softcover)
Classification: LCC PS8585.I17 D37 2022 | DDC C813/.54—dc23

Cover design: Andrew Roberts
Cover images: (tin interior) mdbildes/Shutterstock;
(tin lid) Zerbor, (paper) enviromantic, both Getty Images

Printed in the United States of America

Published in Canada by Anchor Canada,
a division of Penguin Random House Canada Limited,
a Penguin Random House company

www.penguinrandomhouse.ca

10 9 8 7 6 5 4 3 2 1

This book is humbly dedicated
To that sixteen-year-old girl
From Blackville, New Brunswick,
Who begged her dad
Stop and give me a drive
On a dark November afternoon;
Seven poems stuffed in my pockets,
And at eighteen hitchhiking
Toward a destiny I did not know

*The only difference between the saint and the sinner
is that every saint has a past,
and every sinner has a future.*

—Oscar Wilde

So the academics don't like you?
My dear, dear boy,
Can you imagine just how terrible it would be if they did?

—Mary Cyr speaking to Orville MacDurmot, July 1988

It is November
And almost always like November
The naked trees are waiting winter
The naked ground of autumn
And the fruit
Laced with worm holes
Fallen and Forgotten
And our Naked River—

—Poem fragment by Miramichi writer
Written in pencil, found in Gaby May Crump's possession

1.

A SYMPOSIUM ON JOHN DELANO WAS HELD AT BEAVERBROOK House in Newcastle, on March 26, some three years three months after his death, with the intention of celebrating his cases by illuminating his most unusual case, which happened some years before; a symposium about John Delano's investigation into rehabilitating the memory of a famous man from here, Orville MacDurmot.

Our local enthusiasts showed up with their own memories and descriptions of both men. They were now held in some esteem, even by those who did not like them as youth. The townspeople came in looking quite astute and grave in the pale, cold spring, as if they had been selected to perform some secret duty. Many did not look at anyone as they took their seats, again as if something important would be disclosed to a select group. Well maybe something would be.

The house, no longer a library, still had the antiquated dust of a century of bygone hopes and dreams, of a once-proud people, and a once-great river. A river now splayed out in a certain fashion to be almost a redundancy of strip malls and car dealerships.

The people, however, were of a type knowledgeable about the world yet isolated from it—having grown into middle age, or older than that, slower as well than what they had been, they moved through the spaces of the house as if the old Lord Beaverbrook himself would have known them all. They were the middle-class harbingers of a now-lost town. They were growing old and their children were gone to Alberta. They sat on seats looking solid and solitary and then, after a time, giving a nod to certain others there. Then they became quiet and respectful as the talk began, but not so quiet so as not to introduce their own thoughts on the matter. Then they became louder. And although there were not fistfights, there were accusations about who did what and when they did it.

That is, many who had had nothing to do with either John Delano or Orville MacDurmot now said they did. They said it in the way selective memory always manufactures a best-plausible scenario for the person remembering. It is a remarkable trait to have.

The preamble was set for nine that morning, and a late storm had closed the walkway and made the white building seem more white, more isolated. The entire town now seemed isolated, a spot on a map on the north side of the world. An old man, white too, with a white knit hat, blue jeans and short leather boots, wet with snow and water, was out shovelling at seven that morning and managed to make a pathway down to the road. He, Mr. Covney, had lived his whole life within two blocks of the great old house, and the goings-on in those rooms, and the history those rooms held, were as remote to him as Jericho. Except that now and then over the years he would say something quite surprising about the need for money to do something for upkeep, which no one else seemed to be aware of. He would have it worked out on a piece of paper and show it to the manse board. Then he would go away again, and do his job in silence.

About twenty people showed up. More came and some left during the day.

This was the story:

John Delano was approached by one Cathy MacDurmot, former girlfriend whom he had not seen in over thirty years. It concerned the death of her once-esteemed brother, the famed visionary archeologist (or so some called him), and the horrible accusations against him, of which we are all fairly familiar now. It was done as a last hope by Mrs. Trent—that is, Cathy MacDurmot—to try to free her brother from the allegations that had so joyously damned him. And now, in this quaint house, off the main road of life, we the grievers realized how we were at least in part the participants of this ungodly tragedy, which we now know was as farcical as it was preventable. But—and this was the most damning part—did any of us wish to prevent it at that time?

So we came here in the storm to find out about John Delano's report to Cathy MacDurmot. (Since she is known to us as MacDurmot and not Trent, we will use this name.) That was why the stiff formality of the attendees may have had a certain deliberating cause. That is, many of them felt that accusations were about to fly their way, or if not, perhaps a few accusations should.

The report by John Delano was filed almost a year later than Cathy had hoped it would be, but it did give her in the end some semblance of closure—that horrendous word that drifts about the law courts and police stations with an almost Luciferian air. After people are shot, incarcerated, drowned or bodies found. I have many times believed that the more we think Lucifer is not present, the more he smiles in irony from somewhere across the room. That he is, as Orville said, present in all things except joy. But so many of us do not know really what joy pertains to—joy is not happiness; sometimes joy has nothing to do with what brings happiness. Orville's joy was of that kind. It was the kind that sustains one throughout the darkness of the world—in the murk of night a light far away, a small craft on the sea that propels in us at moments a wild ecstasy, the kind that some artists or poets had, the great musician struggling at the end against loneliness and longing to produce the song of joy itself. This is then the most great promise that comes from God—or I believe it has to. For this too was the joy given to John Delano at the end of his life: to work hard, travel long and do something for a woman he had once betrayed—to make it up, so to speak. My God, what could be a greater joy than that?

So then this was and is still John's report, which is probably known to you all by now. It was told to Cathy MacDurmot in this very place; that is, upstairs on the third floor, in the old French room, where the poetry of Villon and others slept. There was snow falling, large flakes, and yet in spite of the flakes being lazy and large it was quite cold outside; a stale air transferred this cold, ridges of ice sat along the sidewalks, icicles hung from the eaves, and Cathy met him there, her hair now greying and her face thinning, which made her look like a sad, sweet bird. He shook her hand in some kind of apology, which he did not know how to express. He simply shook her hand—squeezed it just a tad and asked her if she had ever heard of a man named Dr. Milt Vale, a university English professor of some gravity. A man who had come from Illinois when young and settled in Fredericton. He posed the question with his eyes resting softly upon her, and with an indication by his look that he did not expect she would have. Now she had not, and asked him what this man had to do with her brother, with his death. He said, "Perhaps a great deal." She said, "Do you think my brother was innocent of these horrendous crimes?" and he said, with the air of a person who realizes he had not only made her suffer with his unthinking youth, but had also tormented her brother, that her brother was in his estimation completely innocent, and that if Orville had not had the amount of fame he had at the time (his picture was once on the cover of *Archeology Today*) he may—*may* was the word, though—not even have been charged. Or at least, such conclusions not so easily arrived at. His fame did work against him in the end.

John looked very serious and, somehow—perhaps by the way he dressed—detached from her, a rather officious public personage who was saying somewhat private things to her, which seemed to cause her alarm. For where was he going with all of this, and perhaps more importantly, where had he come from? Still, when he did smile, it was warm and entreating.

"I thought his being well-known would help?" Cathy asked. But she asked it as if she already knew the answer to come.

"Well, he was well-known by a variety of people in a variety of ways. At the last he wasn't known as an archeologist who tried to discover and protect priceless art—but as a problem, a vagary upon us. He was born here—with a cancer in his eye—at seven he lost this eye and became the one-eyed child; most of the river would never tease, but there were others. And those others found him, and took it upon themselves to torment. In his youth his poverty went against him also—though he was not poor, but he was outclassed by many of those in town, the doctors' sons and dentists' sons, and sons of others, and daughters too—and he arrived to school too soon, a year or so younger because of his brightness, so much promise.

"Orville was a rural boy too and had made few friends where he was from, so when he went to town in grade nine imagine how much of a hick he was, for all those who celebrated themselves as being sophisticated with their slightly more up-to-date sayings and concerns. After high school he goes away—then he comes back as an unusual presence in our lives—a brilliant Bobby Fischer, a dark eminence who tells us to go to hell. Not at the first—at the first blush people here wanted to be known as his friend—only he was by now no good at being friendly. They had ridiculed him once too often, and he no longer seemed to know quite how to react."

He told her Orville's death might have been caused by that kind of chatter, that kind of substance. Orville was unlike them—worse, he was someone they had to pay attention to after they'd strafed him with so much mockery in his youth. It was the worst kind of humiliation for them to endure—unspoken as it was. It made for a potent cocktail.

"Do you understand what I am saying? They had to acknowledge him, he whom they had all loitered in the hallways of the school to torment. This was a torment now visited upon them, those who lived and worked here, trying to plan for a retirement, a cottage by the beach . . . It created a maelstrom."

"I don't know," Cathy said, truthfully—for she did not know the bent of the conversation yet—and had little idea that the conversation would take this bent. What she saw in John Delano's eyes was a kind of insistence about who her brother was that unsettled her. A kind of settling of scores against the world and saying her brother needed his score settled.

He let it settle for a moment, until Cathy whispered it back to him, almost as a plea, "Maelstrom? The maelstrom against him—in what way?"

"Orville maintained that there was no progress until it was in that place we once naively called the soul. I think he had fought against saying this for some years. Then it was revealed to him in a certain way. So you see how he would fare in this world, especially with the way he looked—dressed in old grey suit pants, a plaid shirt, a dark tweed jacket that he never seemed to take off? The mockers once again had a chance to mock. In a way they were let off the hook."

Again John let this settle. He then mentioned Eunice Wise's name, but under his breath, as if he was trying not to mention it right away.

"One of the women here who continually seeks knowledge and will never know the truth," John said.

"Oh," Cathy said, "I knew her when she was a little girl—she sent away for a spy kit for her birthday and wanted to take my finger-prints." Cathy smiled. "Because someone had picked up her new tin dollhouse, and she was sure it was me. The only thing I remember is she got ink over my new dress—and Mom couldn't get it out."

"Did you?"

"Did I what?"

"Pick up her dollhouse."

"I'm sure I did since I never had one myself."

"He was very brave, your brother. Don't you think so?"

"Perhaps—do you think so?" she said. She had a very good mind, but no mind for where he was going. And he realized this, and it made him even more insistent, more determined to make her see Orville the way he did now, as a heroic figure—but not in quite the same way she saw him as one. Orville was the one who stayed in the woods, the boy who lived by himself in his bedroom as a recluse—the one who was pale and sandy-haired and silent—the brother who was odd. "Does everyone have one?" she wondered.

He saw her shudder suddenly because of this tack he was taking, which she was hearing for the first time. She did not like to hear it, and he did not want to tell it, but she had to hear and he had to tell.

But John also thought it strange he had alarmed her—for the outcome that had come from Orville's philippics against many things was dire enough.

So John said, trying to take another tack:

"Your brother travelled—he would leave in late fall or after Christmas and come back home in the spring. But then, about two years ago, he came home and redirected his efforts to his secret twenty-year-old dig on the shoreline that sits down from his property.

It was something that Eunice Wise first applauded—his dig, years before, when she touted him as special and her friend—but he would not tell her what the dig was for—and after she had her falling out with him (something that was bound to happen) she was determined to prove herself by stopping this dig—but I am getting a bit ahead of myself . . ."

"That is the dig Eunice contested—I mean the shoreline," Cathy said simply. "Not only her dollhouse." She said, brightening up, finding this quite amusing, "But her little clubhouse—she said I had tied a rope to the door so she couldn't get out. She said I was a barbarian—it was the first time I had ever heard that word. She also said that I hung around with the 'Indians' and told her real friends I did. So she wanted to take my fingerprints over that as well."

"Over what?"

"Tying the rope to her door! The kit she had was called I Spy Private Eye. Do you remember them?"

"No," John said.

"Well, she had one," Cathy said. "I was quite jealous. And she was always proving herself as a spy—especially against 'those awful MacDurmots'—strange, isn't it?" Then added:

"I would like to see Eunice again," she said. "See what she looks like now. Orville used to snare rabbits to sell, to get money to go to town— she would see him, and be revolted by him, by his blind eye—by our little means—strange she would say she was his best friend later on."

"Yes," John said, "of course—and a best friend of the First Nations as well. She was always quick to claim victory even if she had to attach herself to someone else—and anyone who does so can turn on you in a second."

"She had my friends turn against me—invited them into the clubhouse—they called themselves 'the Smart Swallows.' Of course she only got them in there to boss them about—she was president and CEO—and Sharon and Jane, the little dweebs, went right along with her—and I suppose always would do anything to belong—but soon they were all fighting, squabbling and calling each other names. Eunice pulled Sharon's hair, which I was extremely glad about. However, I never did get to be a Smart Swallow. I was jealous of them. I wonder where they are now."

Cathy nodded to herself at all these strange and melancholy memories. It was a different world now. She told John that she thought a lot about Orville—his childhood, their father, Maufat, and their mother, Irene—their kindliness and goodness. And they so hoped for their children but that they had little to offer their children except love. Eunice Wise seemed so important a person to her during those long-ago days, the first girl she knew who had her own fur stole and a father who was an MP.

"Orville had so little chance—but they so underestimated him," she said. "They truly underestimated him. They never forgave him for underestimating him, did they?"

"And you too, Cathy—they underestimated you as well."

"Ah—me," she said, gazing at him for a moment. "I've had my life—I mean I lived it—as well as I could, I suppose."

He stared at her a long moment, as if he wasn't certain how he should respond or what it was she meant. But then he continued.

"I saw him in the holding cell that morning when I came into court with Elvis."

He said it so Cathy imagined the man in his white jacket with the diamond implants, and she looked at him with a searching smile:

"Elvis?"

"Oh, yes—Elvis Turnaround, from the reserve near here."

"Oh?"

"Orville was about to be charged with the deaths of two people. It came because of that dig, which he had clandestinely done because he was told to leave Eunice Wise's land, which, when she first got to know him, she'd invited him to dig upon—she loved him to dig upon it—she insisted and promoted it. But then came the dispute. Such a bitter one—I believe she must have thought he should love her. Or honour her. It is what I am now thinking. She believed he owed her a great deal and expected things from him because she was supposedly as wise as he. At least she liked to infer that she was. I do not think he expected anything from her. At least not in the way she expected things from him. Or perhaps he did expect one thing that she did not give him—to be treated honourably. So now, there he was. He sat in the holding cell in a chair near us. The whole town was abuzz—like-minded in their revulsion. Only professors could be as like-minded as that little internecine mob. Little girls on street corners wearing army jackets with colourful patches, boys with tattoos on their necks spoke out in the park against Orville. Preaching about God when he was the one to kill those people. There is truly something hideous about finding graves. That was it as much as anything. So there was no excuse for a man like him. Their anger of course was that they had made something of him, spoke as if they cared for him, because he had made something of himself. They now realized they had been deceived. And that was even worse."

"Why—why did he seem so unconcerned about it all?" Cathy asked.

"I was not at all sure at that moment. I am now—I have come to tell you about how it is solved—in his favour."

She looked at him strangely. John continued:

"So I said hello. At first he did not recognize me; he looked at me quizzically, as if he wanted to know what kind of man I was—not what kind of officer, that did not seem to matter—the perplexed look was about me as a man. But it was an unsettling gaze that some famous people get after a while—so much more is known about them than the person they are talking to.

"'It's John Delano,' I said.

"'Ah,' he said, and was silent. Then he looked up at me again, somewhat astonished by all of it. That is when I realized that what he had written in one of his articles long ago was true: the past never goes away from us, and things that seem lost can come back in an instant. He of course was talking about a certain artifact that had been buried for three centuries, which was discovered in Virginia by a group of students he was with, and he wrote about this in *Esquire* magazine, when he was commissioned to write these tidbits.

"But by the glance he gave, I think he was remembering the harm I did to you when I was your boyfriend. Those days in the late sixties when we were young, listening in the half dark to the Beatles and Doors and Rolling Stones, and I suffering my rebellion against the world on those lost, snow-covered streets. It was when I was your boyfriend and Orville was a young boy and saw how I harmed you."

"But you did me not a bit of harm," Cathy said.

John nodded quickly. He had distanced himself from her by that reverie even as it incorporated her past, and he came out of his musing with a start. He looked at her, and smiled slightly—somewhat incomprehensibly. Then he straightened himself in his chair and continued.

"But I realized Orville had grown old. Though his look was startlingly grand. That is the only way I can describe his look. He was dressed as a countryman—a rural man, which in fact he had been all of his life. He had grown his beard. He had a brown-coloured shirt and tie. There seemed to be a little dust on it. He had black shoes—which seemed too large—on his feet, and his black pants were stovepipe-straight. But none of this lessened his grandness—his grandness came as it always does, from a sense of self. A certain facing of the world alone.

"So I let the 'ah' settle into my mind—it was in a way damning, as if to say, 'How can you now hold me here?' It was as if he was saying,

'I have important work to do, you know this is all nonsense, I did not kill a soul—I know my neighbours think I am mad—but so what? Let them think what they wish—I did not kill anyone—and they haven't as yet told me whom it is I have killed.'

"I caught this all, of course, in hindsight—reflecting upon it later. And I believed even then that he did do important work, but work that for most of us on the river would not figure much in our day-to-day lives. That he became famous because of it was true. But that was years before. In the last years people considered him obsolete. He simply wrote about our obligation to the soul. But being slow on the uptake we did not know it was a transformation; we thought it was all the same—that he was the crazy local man who was once revered with a certain number of honorary doctorates, accolades from universities, but he had never liked us here, criticized us too much—and was wholly secretive, so we were free to dislike him. In fact, 'free' is not the primary word here—I think we were *obligated* to dislike him. And then to find bodies of two people whom he had known. The people none of us cared about, because no real searches were carried out for them—and yet now the bodies were found. It made the world hysterical—and Eunice an oracle. Does this seem true?"

"Yes, I suppose it does."

"Orville stared at me, as if wanting to investigate me in some way. But his look said, 'I have lived a solitary existence far away from the limelight, but in some way my life's work will be known.' Of course I only think this now. The look was wonderful in a certain way—it could have been the beginning of a renewal of something between us. We could have been friends. But only if I took the time to apologize to him. I knew as much. Then, in that look I realized his life was one of intrinsic suffering. I say intrinsic because it was an internal matter—it was or seemed suffering of the soul. And sometimes great suffering, which I will try to explain here. However, he simply stared at me a moment, looked toward the corner of the office. He took out his old pipe, battered and bitten at the stem, and placed it in his mouth. But he did not light it. All that former fame and adulation, and afterward a slow and solitary and almost humorous decline into the abyss."

"Humorous?" Cathy asked. "You said *humorous* decline?"

"It must have been for some, don't you think? A man who wrote about our spiritual obligation after being an atheist? Making light of what he called 'the prevalence of silliness and superstition . . .'"

"Perhaps."

"Anyway, that day Elvis looked as harmless as a child. Except it was his sixth arrest. He kept breaking into houses. Sometimes he would take nothing more than a ham sandwich—and leave the mustard out, with the top off. Other times he would take a tin or two of dog food. So I knew we were looking for a thief who liked ham sandwiches and had a dog. That pointed clearly to my young friend from the reserve here, a likeable, childlike man, who never in his life fed in the trough of grievance while wearing a suit to a committee meeting—who never marched or plotted or ployed, and never received compensation from such actions. When I arrested him he asked if his dog, Bouncer, would face charges as well. Or maybe a firing squad. I told him a firing squad might be overdramatic. So Elvis said, 'Maybe you could put him under house arrest.'

"'Whose house?' I asked.

"'Maybe your house,' Elvis said.

"So I put Bouncer under house arrest—so for the time Elvis was in jail, Bouncer sat at my house on his own big blanket beside a tin dish.

"The day we went to court Orville was there as well—in the holding cell on the second floor. I gave Elvis a coffee and a cigarette. And he sat on the chair in his cell and asked Orville questions about the case, about the woman, and about the First Nations boy—'All we want to know is why you did it,' Elvis said, 'and then I will forgive you.' It seemed little Elvis was completely serious. He wanted to forgive Orville for this horrendous crime. Or crimes.

"At this time Orville was thought to be very prideful by me and others—and I apologize for saying so. He also looked slightly deranged. Still, I felt at once he never believed he needed to ask forgiveness, for he felt—in fact knew—he was being miscast by us."

Then John paused a little bit.

Cathy did not answer John—and he reflected on her own weight-bearing forgiveness. That she, Cathy, had had to forgive John—and worse, that she had in a way that was unspoken, which made his guilt seem present between them, for he had not asked. But he did not tell Cathy that he felt Orville wanted forgiveness too, if for nothing else for being misunderstood, after years of notices in the press—and after, on occasion, acting very uncivilly himself.

"But what had your brother said in the last fifteen months of his life? Nothing so terrible. He said that sin was infectious and would kill the world."

"There was some truth to it . . . there had to be some truth?"

"Oh, yes—more than some, I think. They thought he was an angry prophet who was casting aspersions on his former town. I now doubt that was the case. He was saying that the freedom we had achieved was bogus—I think this is what he was saying, at any rate."

"But that was preachy," Cathy said.

"Yes. Still, was it so damning? In a way, though, it allowed the idea of an obsolete notion."

"Notion?"

"Of evil—many people believed we had overcome evil. We thought that people could be all brought to the table, and reach a consensus, if they simply said that evil did not exist."

Cathy did not respond to this—it was striking but she had not known Orville's philosophy, so she was startled—it wasn't a weight upon her, but a thin sheet of air seemed to tingle on her skin. She looked away from him and remained silent.

John left that for the time being.

So he said:

"Orville did not answer Elvis. He simply looked at him and looked away. And I saw in Orville's face a rather gravelly, hardened look that I may have mistaken as callous. But now I think not—I think it was only his life abroad in Africa and Eastern Europe that made him seem so. That he was able to say, to Professor Milt Vale, 'Your Fabergé is fake,' without batting an eye, showed he did not stand on much decorum."

"Was it—fake?"

"I will come back to that later."

"But, a short two hours later, Orville was shot trying to run away. Why? Why did he do that—like a common criminal everyone assumed he was?" Cathy MacDurmot asked. Her voice had changed—that is, when she had first arrived, the traces of Miramichi accent were not as noticeable as now, and though she no longer used "ain't," which she did way back as a girl—in a precocious way—she refrained from that—but the lilt of our beautiful river was still there.

"Everyone said that he was trying to get away," John continued, "and people will believe it until tomorrow. Then I will make my report public. Even if he was trying to escape, he must have known his chances were minimal at best. Orville stood, looked around, threw two people off him as if they were children—and then Stevens pulled his gun, closed his eyes and fired. The impact made your brother fall through the window, but the report said he was shot as he tried to jump through the window—another rather easy miscalculation of his intention. That is, I know now that suicide was never in his nature.

"When we went to the ground floor we saw that he had not moved since he had fallen. The first snowfall of the year came down on his face, which looked entirely at peace. I believe *you* did not come down until a coat had been placed over him."

"Whose coat was it?" Cathy asked now.

"Mine," John said. "And I believe he was at peace—finally at peace, entirely so. I too initially thought he was trying to escape. Then I thought he may have been trying to commit suicide. And Constable Stevens could not be blamed. However, Elvis said, later that day, when his court appearance was postponed, 'I know when a man wants to kill himself and I know when a man wants to get away. That man seemed to not know who he had killed. He seemed suddenly to not know what was happening. He stood up and threw people off because he had been told a terrible thing that he could not believe. It put him in a state where he was no longer certain of what was happening.'

"'What do you mean, Elvis?' I asked.

"'I mean he did not want to escape, and did not want to die—he just wanted an explanation.'"

John continued:

"That struck me as one of the more brilliant and thoughtful moments in little Elvis's life. And I began to remember all that was said in the holding cell, and in the courtroom before that moment. Yes, a security guard and the sheriff's deputy did try to stop him, and there was a shot, and then a sudden crash through the upstairs glass. Could I have prevented it? I do not know. Still it was surreal to me!

"For some reason I began to investigate the case. First because I believe no constable would have pulled his gun if it wasn't for Orville having such a bad reputation. Worse, some of his reputation was promulgated by the fact that he wrote that evil actually existed. For if he believed in it, perhaps he was motivated by his insane belief, to show himself as evil."

"He never was!" Cathy said, in a hard, insistent tone. "That's nonsense!"

"I know that, Cathy. I do know that. But I heard these arguments against him for two weeks, and thought it was a waste of time—still, I owed it to him to at least look into it, into who he was, and what he had become from the time I knew him as a schoolboy. And then you asked me. And I owed it to you as well. And because of his death it began to open for me. That is, his very extraordinary life. His work in archeology. People at first celebrating him grandly, and then finding a way to deride him. It's what was allowed in their condemnation that struck me."

"'Allowed'—in what way do you mean?"

"Well, everything is allowed and nothing is, depending on who a person is. A man here steals a million, has people fear him, cheats his partners, and everyone simply shrugs. Another fights over the rights to access to his beach so he can continue his research, and is considered shameful.

"At first, even when you asked me to investigate, I was not going to act on it at all. I thought I had nothing to give. But I went on Facebook and saw over a thousand comments of celebration about his death from the people of his own river. Then, a day or so after he died, I was surprised to see the *Telegraph* interview his neighbour and former friend Eunice. She spoke about him as if she had *valiantly* tried to help him. She simply had to show that she was . . . that she was—"

"*Virtuous.*"

"Yes. That she was virtuous."

"And that bothered you?"

"Oh yes—something egregious about using this moment to shine forth, her face like a new penny."

"Did you know her before this?"

"Yes, a little. Not when she was taking fingerprints and had the dollhouse, not that long ago." Then John paused and said, "I suppose it all comes down to our obsession with beauty—all our sins. Eunice felt this was a beautiful moment for her to be interviewed—certainly an opportune time to make a statement. She had to feel that she did not want to, but was compelled to—by truth—and so she did. And that, my dear Cathy, was the beauty of it."

"Beauty?"

"He believed that man's consistent search was to find true beauty."

"Yes," Cathy said, but as if to herself. And she looked out at the day.

"Yes what?"

"Simply yes," she said, looking quickly back at him with the implication that she would not say any more.

So he continued:

"At any rate, two evenings later, I went down to his great house, closed up at the end of a long drive. It was a large, dark, rather imposing place, like a silhouette on a dark canvas, off the river by a mile or so, surrounded by trees and small outbuildings—sheltered on the north by a large fence, having a paddock for his horse—a house that seemed to sit under an uncertain tumultuous sky. A garden that ran on the east end, covered in frost, and sitting back. He had two tractors, and he had built up a redoubt, like a colonel ordering a defensive position against great odds. It ran about five feet high and for four hundred yards along his west side, to separate his land from another's. He did that when the dispute with his neighbour Eunice Wise first began. He did it shovelful by shovelful and stone by stone.

"There was at one time no reason to build up a redoubt, but their relationship turned sour. That it had gone on so long and had become so bitter had been terrible for them both, but he had done very little to exacerbate it. He perhaps wanted to, but did not know how to fight back without losing his sense of integrity. This will be proved as I tell the story. But at the last she was proven right about the land dispute. Or at least for the time being the court decided the land was in her domain. I do feel there was something opportune in their decision, some prejudice against him that made them sign off in her favour, but I cannot be really sure. I have seen great judges and bad judges, and justice, as finely tuned in our books as it is, is still a tad personal. After the court's decision he wrote her a quick note saying he would appreciate it if she let him dig there into the spring. She wrote back a decisive and definitive *no*. So he was compelled to stop his work, or face a fine. The idea that he wished to dig there until spring became a fact used against him.

"So I sat out front for a moment and thought all of these things through. Then I decided that he did not have much going for him at this moment. There is nothing quite so revolting as a Christian nowadays. Even though he never really said he was one. Not in so many words. I looked across the back field toward Eunice's. I became aware of a sensation. I gathered this sensation up, and let it settle. Eunice was our new rural phenomenon, one who provided us with constant visionary thinking. She was always telling us what we were doing wrong. She was so enthused about new answers to old problems.

"Perhaps she was civic-minded because after her divorce she needed something to draw her apart from others. The beauty Orville said people searched for, no matter where it took them—like taking fingerprints as a child. I have seen them on her wall, little prints of fingers of former friends, even yours, that she kept and guarded for years—they were placed on the wall of her den in small picture frames. Often when Orville spoke to her he would try to dissuade her from being so helpful. Still back she came to invent his need for her."

"Until one day there was an argument," Cathy said.

"Yes—there was. He told her to go. She became a friend of his enemies, and realized to her surprise that he had so many, many enemies; that they had all belonged in his shadowed past from his youth.

"All of these things were curiosities to me," John continued. "They seemed to reflect some intention on her part—like whom you intentionally do not mention or befriend on Facebook. That is, all of those she befriended were people who thought less of him as time went on. He himself was not on Facebook—or ever much on his computer.

"So I walked into Orville's back porch. His doors were never locked, for no one ever visited him, and anyone could have broken in. His house was still, the light came through white cotton curtains, and there was a smell of earth in pots throughout the porch that startled me, and when I went inside I saw his large kitchen open to a small den with grapevine chairs and small, wood-carved lamps and orchids and bookshelves, a place of immense greeting where no one came. The only one who had come there at one time was Eunice Wise. She had come often, and stayed long, until he told her to go home. I thought of her sitting in that chair in the kitchen, revisiting her problems, while he sat in the chair by the stove, with his pipe in his mouth, which he was too polite to light while she was in his presence. I think he may have cared for her quite a bit more than she cared for him. This tolerance of his was an offset to what people often thought of him, as being mean-spirited and abrasive. He listened as she spoke, and he was kind. He made her tea, even had her for supper. But beyond her quest for freedom, her showing herself to him as an example of what a woman could achieve and saying that she did so in such a backward, paternalistic place as the Miramichi, he had little to say to her himself. Or he would say:

"'Yup.'

"'My, my.'

"'Yup.'

"Once, when she said, 'I have something for you, will you sign it?' he said, 'Bring it and we will see.'

"That was all—that, in fact, was what he should not have said.

"Besides, he had liked her ex-husband, and was reserved about her divorce. He was reserved about taking on men like her husband as the enemy. She said she had outgrown this husband of hers— that she was disappointed in him. I watched them both, in my mind's eye, for some time before I moved on from the kitchen into the inner rooms. I watched them, I listened to her and I made no comment either.

"I walked though to the living room, having the broad window that looked down over his land. The grand front door *was* locked. The grandfather clock had stopped.

"He had concerned himself with the discovery of rock paintings and bones—the dust from history's traffic, beautiful as ochre sunsets over some darkening water. *Fool's gold, pyrite, is so beautiful, it catches you off guard*, he once wrote. But it is not only pyrite that catches us off guard—it was for him all the various emblems of splendour over five thousand years, vases and statues, containers, icons, heads, all impossible to take our eyes off, all priceless to us.

"I discovered, walking through the house, that in the last three years of his life he had sold off his belongings, one artifact at a time. Even a painting by Tom Thomson that was catalogued as his, he had sold to a doctor in Saint John. He gave most of the money away to various societies and organizations to help the poor. So I began to see who he was, and what his world was about. How different it was than what people thought."

"The sacrifices he made?"

"The sacrifices he made, yes. And how these sacrifices allowed him to speak of our celebrations in the last two years of his life—"

"What celebrations are those?" Cathy asked. "I don't understand."

"Good and evil," John answered, quickly. "Good and evil, which he feared the modern world had given up examining but were actual phenomena in our world, as real and as incredibly important as neutrinos. Suddenly, when he came back to his hometown a few years ago, he stated that God existed. I don't at all care that he said this, I only wondered why."

"When did you learn this?" Cathy said.

"Almost four months ago."

"But I don't know where this leads us," Cathy said.

"Well," he said, a little too flippantly, "It leads us to his martyrdom."

She looked up sharply when he said this, as if he were teasing, like he knew how to do. She seemed cross at him, as she was years ago when they broke up. And they had broken up in such a desperate way, a way she thought would never be able to heal. The same feeling entered between them for a moment or two because of the licence he'd seemed to take. That is, she felt he was being too flippant while showing his own worth.

He realized this, and nodded apologetically.

"So thinking this I walked upstairs, where the bedrooms were. I sat for a moment in the small alcove on an upholstered chair listening to the sounds of Eunice—that is, imagining her speaking to him about her . . ."

"Suffering?" Cathy asked, when John became stuck suddenly.

"Yes. So after a while I stood and walked around. I saw the grand desk in one corner of a large open space where he had his active books, the ones he referenced and read."

John told her he gave in to his curiosity, searched for a key, found it positioned in the side drawer and opened the tumbler at the top of the desk.

"Letters fell at my feet, of all shapes and sizes, from all corners of the world. From Australia, Nigeria, South Africa, Russia and so on,

and I spent a good part of a quarter of an hour cursing my curiosity and picking them up. To me, who was not an investigator in the
arrest and charge, this was a serious misstep."

"Misstep?"

"In that these letters were not confiscated—his room was not
searched better than it had been. So I looked through the letters and
one name struck me. And I read the correspondence.

"His name was Han Woo Lee. Orville said nothing to anyone
about Han Woo Lee or the letters. Perhaps he forgot. Perhaps by then
he had dismissed us and refused to comment. I began to look about
the floor for letters from Han Woo Lee.

"I read his letters while sitting in a chair, smoking a cigarette, and
wondered about—well . . ."

"About what was written?" Cathy asked.

"No, about the man, your brother, Orville MacDurmot," John
declared. "An arrogant, self-obsessed, at times self-righteous genius—"

"He was that?"

"Oh yes—there was no doubt. So I began to think of him as I
smoked my cigarette. That is, could a rural, solitary man, suffering
an injury to his eye and face, mocked in his youth, left alone, suddenly
famous and admired, and just as suddenly fallen, berated by those in
his vocation, having a hundred enemies and almost no friends, commit an atrocious crime when people no longer thought him valid?
Go to a monastery to live and meditate, and picket abortion clinics
because people said he had become mad, and then murder a young
girl he had himself impregnated? Of course, we know he could. That
is, his life, in a strange way, pointed to it. But then, you see, many
people have gone to that monastery to meditate—people not entirely
religious—secular men going through divorces, businessmen who
live in the workaday world and are suddenly troubled, students and,
yes, people who are seeking something else. Still, everyone, myself

included, thought he did what he had been accused of doing. For he rose the stakes against himself at every conference he attended in the previous two years."

"How?"

"By saying he had seen evil, and that if you destroy your soul, you destroy your life. And when they questioned him and asked him where he had seen evil, he said he had seen it in—a child murdered."

"The wrong thing to say," Cathy said.

"Yes. But then, looking through his papers, I saw something—I saw a trust fund set up for this very girl sitting in the small shelf at the top of his desk—for 175,000 dollars, ready to mature in a year, dollars to be given to her and no one else when she turned twenty-five. Who would do that, who would pay that, and then murder the beneficiary? Well, yes, he could have—but the senselessness of it left me cold, a chill swept up from my feet—I had discovered something—but I was unsure of what. For why would he faithfully continue to pay it, after she was dead, if he *knew* she was dead? The last payment was written out just a week before he himself died. So then, holding certain pieces of papers in my hand, sitting there and listening to the wind pick up outside, I tried to think things over.

"You see, one day when Eunice was speaking to him, he caught in her eyes something—a small drift in her mind, as if she was posturing in order to impress him. She had made a comment at supper that he should have preserves—that it was not a Maritime table until there was a bottle of preserves on it. She said this with her face shining suddenly, as if she had been taught to say this, and said it in an unnatural way; as if she was an academic learning social custom. This is finally what troubled him; he felt that everything she said was imprinted with false learning.

"This was some years ago, but I think it is important to bring up. She had taken his fingerprints too, you see, to make him *conform*—and she when younger had obfuscated at certain times about those awful lower-class MacDurmots, and how they had raided her clubhouse when she was young, and how her pretty dollhouse was upset by one Cathy MacDurmot—and then, well, then, Orville became rather well-known suddenly—when she was in the midst of taking a correspondence course in Native Studies at university. He was now suddenly acceptable—he had proven himself. But I will come back to the bottle of preserves in a moment—here—let me look . . ."

John attended to his collection of notes, his bits of paper, the articles he had collected—looking down at them and then glancing at her, as if asking her to bear with him. In her purse was a cheque for two thousand dollars, which she wanted to give him if he exonerated her baby brother. She had no idea if he would do so. But she knew he would never take the money.

"No, I will come back to Eunice's preserves later." He said, "I discovered that night in this study that Han Woo wrote a letter about ice cream and a young girl about the same time Eunice brought her bottle of preserves over. A few weeks later, if I remember. The letter warned Orville not to have this young girl in the house, because bad things might be thought about him, construed about what he was up to with that child. He lived alone, and even he said people were frightened of him. So do not bring children into the house!

"This letter, along with the trust fund that he had set up for this girl, actually became one of the major finds in the case, and it wasn't even found until after the case was over—or at least his life was over. I reflected on the trust fund, and I read the letter over and over, looking for something. What was it? Well, Orville might have abused the child. But the more I thought about it, the more I realized that Han Woo Lee was warning someone who was most likely an innocent— who did not know the gravity of giving ice cream to a young girl and inviting this little girl alone into his house with no other adults around, because he hadn't the slightest notion of doing anything to her. So another idea was formulating about something else going on—that all the evidentiary reports, if looked at from another angle, might show *virtue* rather than *vice*, and that we must find the guilty party. For the guilty party is still somewhere partying away—"

He might at this moment have been a little bit happy at the way he was able to impress his former girlfriend. He was, in the remotest of ordinary ways, jealous she had married a somewhat successful businessman who had looked down upon her family. A man who owned three car dealerships, who had the advertising slogan: *If you want a pal, come see Al.*

How could she have married him, John often thought. How in God's holy name could she have given herself to him! The triangular celebratory flags waving over the hoods of repossessed cars on a late hot August afternoon—yes, John had taken a trip to Toronto and had made a point of seeing them. He had seen the sterile yard, the small flags gone limp in the drenching, suffocating heat—the awful window glaring in the sun—and yes, he had seen her as well, Cathy MacDurmot, seated at a large desk, a too-large desk for her, in the drab, flak-green office. He did not go inside—he did not speak. He simply turned and walked away.

But he was also slightly happy, in the remotest of ways, that the marriage had not gone well because this man had looked down upon her rustic New Brunswick family who had nothing to give each other but love. And had looked most of all down at Orville.

But there was no doubt that Al too was now happy that this had happened to her infamous brother, because was Al now not proven right? Was the callow boy not deranged? Was the reason Orville had not come from his room that long-ago summer afternoon to shake his hand, when Al stood there in a Hawaiian shirt and soft yellow loafers, with a sun-drenched, sweating face, the fact that Al had detected some prurient motive from that violent boy, and that Orville knew it?

"I don't know what's wrong with him—Cathy tells me he had a mix-up at school?" Al had said. He'd looked sadly at Orville's father, Maufat, as if it was his fault. Al's pants pockets bulged with his black wallet—all their finances were in one account, and he held the credit card and chequebook. He had brought enough beer home for himself and Cathy, showing that he was a man who didn't want to be used. That was the real reason Orville had sat alone in his room. So this was one more motivating factor—John told her he was *going to prove the Als of the damn world mistaken.*

Cathy blushed suddenly, crimson, and looked at him sharply. He realized she wanted him to know, to feel the presence of the unspoken accusation in her bright eyes; that in some way the pathetic union between her and her former husband was the result of her fleeing from John himself—finding herself in a secretarial position in a strange, haphazard lake city and Al was there, selling repossessed cars, yes, a life that to him must have been so very superior to hers. The Maritimes—yes, he could exert a tremendous influence over her—and he set out to do so. He bullied her by small-minded commerce. And her plight was to be seduced not so much by Al, but by the loss of John himself.

Then both of them understanding this, by an almost indiscernibly fleeting glance, he quickly continued:

"So that night, as the rooms of your brother's house got quieter and by incremental degrees darker, I realized that something just might be very wrong here. Or at least wrong enough for me to take a second look. The house darkened little by little—the brass on the fireplace screen seemed to be a constant reflector of pale, after-rain light; the sun then flared against it and the damp, cold shreds of snow in the yard, the sun diminished, and a quietude overcame the inanimate objects about me. The chair, the desk, the books, the built-in shelves, the grand fireplace, all darkening in the grave room. One book more than others caught my attention. *The Seven Storey Mountain*. I picked it up and looked at it for a while. I reflected on what he had acquired—the china cabinet downstairs, with its china cups, its scent of oak wood, its expensive crystal wineglasses that he bought for a celebration that never came. The great house. He had intended to leave it all.

"The approaching darkness gave me a new source of resolve. Why had this man died—for what insane reason? He said the soul was great and one destroys their soul only by their own design—*that was the only proof that we were all equal*, there was no other proof of our being equal than our fight against evil—that is what he said, nothing much more. He said you could not have equality by social justice, for it was like a tipping canoe—the shifting of weight would always toss someone out. He said out loud that our souls throughout our lives chose our outward appearance, in order to prove to those we wished to influence exactly who we were. This to me was not just metaphysics, but a mirror into our own reality. In fact, for the first time I became aware he was telling us the truth. So I tried but I could think of nothing else that made him suddenly so objectionable. Was he in the end like a scientific holy man, scapegoated because he had disobeyed a convention? Perhaps. He certainly was as angry as John the Baptist, that man crying in the wilderness—he certainly was as unstable as that man. But this was in a way all coating—all varnish—it did not really say who he was. So I began to look into it, to look at the murdered young woman's life—at the life of the First Nations boy Danny John—and I found things out, until it became clear—it will all be revealed and we will know soon how these aspects, which played such an enormous part in his life, were but a token of his sometime greatness."

He said this in a fashionably antiquated way in order to please her.

"'Sometime greatness'?"

"Oh—well, yes, I think so."

"So you solved it?" she asked.

"Oh yes, I have solved it. We have solved it. It has been solved in a way to absolve him, but not at all to prevent the tragedy that he worried about; that is, of men and women destroying their own souls by searching and ascribing to a beauty that is unreal, and ignoring the beauty that is."

"And he is not guilty."

"No—he is not guilty—I am saying he was a visionary."

"A visionary who they called a racist."

"Oh, but they made a huge mistake in calling him that."

"How could they have made such a mistake?"

"Because like our news broadcasters, quick to exalt and quicker to condemn, they were filled with the orthodoxy of the moment—"

The room became quiet, and she looked serenely capable at that moment—it seemed her family, after all was said and done, did have a trait toward immortality that went far beyond the dollhouse she had tried to pick up and the fingerprints she offered as a peace offering to her young neighbour. And this immortality came because of the most damaged of them all; the one whose face had been shattered and was missing an eye. It seemed suddenly to bring grace down—that is, down from heaven. It was the first time in a while that Cathy MacDurmot had thought of heaven.

"I want to tell you what some on the river thought," he added after a moment. So that her face changed. He hesitated before he continued.

"Eunice decided to befriend him. They became true friends for a while. For a while she told people that he relied upon her—that she lived near to him, and kept an eye on him—understood him.

"After the falling out, however, she claimed all the great lower fields that joined their properties, she claimed one of his sheds, she claimed the large oak tree where he had a swing. She went about marking things with great swaths of red paint. She was a Wise—they came from Wise Point and Wise Point was quite near his land. Her father was once an MP. After the falling out—when she no longer called him her 'brave young boy'—she became a stalwart, vigorously against him. She had been kind to him, but now she wanted him to know: the shore road was hers, and she had let him use it because of her good nature. Once she decided he was not to be trusted she could no longer allow it.

"So one day some years ago she decided she wanted the land for herself because she wanted to sell it. But Orville was doing an archeological dig there. The man who had hired Orville to do his dig was Chief Amos Paul, who had died. The band council no longer wished him to continue on this dig. He refused to listen to them.

"It was then that Eunice became a compatriot of the First Nation band. So she hired Danny John, a First Nations man, to guard the shore road and keep Orville off the shore. Orville, for his research, had to get to that shore. He simply told people this. Danny John was sent down there to keep an eye on it, but from what I know he never bothered Orville and Orville doing his careful digs never bothered him.

"One day, five or so years ago now, Danny simply disappeared. There was a search but he was never found."

Cathy tried to reconstruct something and then asked if the idea formulated in the paper, that Danny John had come upon an act of murder being committed by her insane brother and had heroically tried to intervene, was flawed. John said yes, it was very flawed—"ludicrous, when you know what I now do," he answered.

"Who was the First Nations boy whose remains they found?" she asked finally.

"I will tell you in time," John said. "The worst of it was, Orville decided to defend himself in court—that was preposterously silly. But it is what he decided. 'The sooner I get this over with the sooner I get back to my work,' is what he told me," John said, "—the final thing Orville said to me as he was preparing to leave the cell. In a certain way he seemed to taunt me with that statement—just a little, as if my policeman's conduct was a channel for retarding his more important work."

"He was delusional." Cathy said. "That's what they said for three weeks in the paper—and even before this happened. That he had become delusional."

John thought a moment and then comforted her with:

"Our paper has a habit of saying what they learn from some source the night before. However, just because the world does not believe you doesn't make the world wise. Yet his last sentence to me was not that of a man about to try to escape—unless he was trying to deceive me, which I do not think he was—but his action the day of his death was of a man who'd just discovered something he could not comprehend."

Cathy looked at him as if he was about to reveal to her a secret.

"Why did he, then? Run? What couldn't he comprehend?"

"Because," John continued, "I believe he discovered who the remains of the woman were only in the courtroom when he was being indicted. I believe from what I found in his desk that he did not know until then who it was. For if the prosecutor's case rested on the premise that he killed this woman because of who she was, he could not have killed her without knowing who she had been. They had held off telling anyone who this woman was for the very grand effect on the public it would create—that was the prodigious moment. But in the end his reaction proved to me that Orville had no idea himself. He, in a nearly oblivious state, needed to leave the courtroom, tried to do so and was killed."

He looked at Cathy, at her comeliness, her decency, her "truth," as she sat before him, and wondered about her life, how insignificant it might have seemed to some—but how precious it actually was to the world. She never tried to become significant by holding on to the right theories. She never went to university or became involved in the trendy activism that enveloped so many. No, she took a job far away, on hot summer city streets, and lived in a small one-bedroom apartment. She was alone. Yet in that her glorious beauty shone. He realized too that his faithlessness when they were young had been involved in all her earliest decisions. In a way she was running from him. But back then people from her world so rarely went to university. He had more feeling for her now than he ever had before.

So he softly spoke about their time together—were they not once young and crazy? To think that they could ever be together—everything pointed against it. But he knew that what he spoke was a way to mitigate his culpability, and they could have been together forever if he had been as brave then as he was now.

So he clarified:

"Like me, Orville was not very good with love. I don't think he had anyone at the last—and I had far too many—but it all comes to the same thing in the end, loneliness and sorrow," he said.

"One begins to realize when a man is innocent," John told her. "Orville's look was one of disbelief—of actual horror—and it was not because he was being charged, or even what he was being charged with; to him that was all nonsense and could be easily explained—but unexpectedly, suddenly, it was who she was that he was being charged with killing that came as such a blow. You see, his life's work in a way presupposed the mistakes of the crowd, who had tormented him for years. He was like a Louis Pasteur, holding the vial to cure what the vile said it might cause. He expected to weather this storm easily or at least weather it in the end, once they knew whom the bones belonged to. He was so sure he himself knew! But everything aloof about him changed in an instant. He became a man struck as with apoplexy. It was as if all of his work was for nothing—everything he'd managed to achieve was lost. Then he simply stood up and began to toss people away—he was easily three times as strong as I ever was. It wasn't the young constable's fault—he had no idea that morning he would ever have to pull his gun at an enraged bull of a man, who then went through a window. But your brother's look was one of complete bafflement. This is what bothered me. For I recognized in that look utter human despair about someone he had loved, who he may have thought or must have thought was still alive. Someone everyone, even her brother, thought had done with all of us here, and had gone to Montreal five years ago. Someone Orville was certain he would leave his legacy to—that in the end he would give her some great gift! So then he had no idea whose remains it was he had found down at the bottom of his land. He had made a simple and a drastic mistake. But this simple yet drastic mistake worked to everyone's benefit. I thought of that a little, when I was at your brother's house.

"Later—a week or so later—I was transporting Mr. Elvis Turnaround to jail, and Elvis was speaking of the poor man who had been shot while going through the upstairs window.

"He was saying, our Elvis was, that a person must be forgiven for being ill—that we must all of us forgive. If he spoke about God and then went deranged and killed, well, God might be the best one to know what it was all about. Then I had the first cold shudder that the river might be—"

"Wrong?"

"Yes, wrong!" John whispered harshly. "Almost, in this case—if I can say it—demonically wrong. That they had spent their time hoping to discredit a man who was far more innocent than they could ever imagine.

"So I began to talk to Elvis about your brother and I asked him if he thought Orville was innocent or guilty. I believed Elvis just might be as good a judge of character as anyone.

"'That is a terrible crime,' Elvis said. 'However,' he said, 'Danny was six foot one—and maybe what they say in the paper makes that boy they found about five foot six—you know the editor of our paper is such a silly man he says only what he feels will make him look understanding.'

"That came as a complete surprise to me. First of all I thought it was only me who thought our paper's editor and columnists were frivolous—I didn't know Elvis thought so too. But he did, and he seemed almost contrite because of it. But I did not know something until then either. That is, that Danny was in fact six foot one. But Elvis said he was—that when the two of them tried to squeeze down through the co-op roof to steal cigarettes, Danny was tall enough to land on the insulated pipe almost six feet below them.

"'Why didn't you say something?'" John said he had asked.

"But Elvis said he believed they knew what they were doing, and they always told him he didn't know what it was he was doing, so he kept quiet, letting them do what they thought they must."

Then, looking up quickly, John told Cathy, abruptly, as if he had just thought of it (but of course he had been leading up to it) that Elvis asked if he could pee, and John pulled his car under the small underpass near the river where he could do so.

"So," John said, "we can thank Elvis. We can thank Elvis for a good deal."

"Thank Elvis?"

John said, more to the point, "Be grateful that Elvis had drunk two cans of pop. For it was under the underpass where I saw, in the upper corner, an unimaginably exquisite tag."

"A tag?" Cathy said. "What is a tag?"

"Graffiti."

He told Cathy that when he stopped for Elvis he saw that *OBA* was painted on a cement underpass a mile or so away from Orville's property. They just happened to be at that point in the journey when Elvis asked him to stop.

"And what did that graffiti mean?" Cathy asked.

He said it made him wonder about something.

"What did you wonder about?"

"The tag," he answered.

"I know, for Godsakes, John—but what, what *about* the tag?"

"If it was not so beautiful I would not have remembered it. But I had seen an almost identical tag before—somewhere, either in Fredericton or Saint John, I wasn't quite sure, but it struck me. I looked at it, and it came back to me—that is, the impression of it seemed to make my eyes dilate suddenly—a sudden intensification in my eyes, a sudden remembrance, an association from a few years before—that is how it struck me. I kept trying to remember where I had seen something so similar; so beautiful. It was more like a painting on the side of the wall!

"Then I thought of a small cement wall—a side lane or street—and an old wooden apartment building. I remembered I had gone to question a witness about a robbery some five or six years ago—nothing to do with this case—or at least nothing directly . . ."

"Okay . . ."

"Anyway, one night, about three weeks later, I went back to take another look at the graffiti. I felt it might help my memory. Besides, this tag, I felt, might be relevant to the case against your brother."

"Why?"

"I was not sure. But as I say I had seen that tag before somewhere. I wanted to see if it was the same kind of graffiti, the same tag. It might have had nothing to do with anything—yet perhaps this bit of graffiti was a long way from home—and so close to the discovery of the bodies. Is there a coincidence like this that ever remains a coincidence?"

"You remember things like that?"

"Yes, I do—I remember things like that. And that is in some way a terrible thing for me—that I remember many things. For instance I remember the stones on the ground, the night you fell on the church lane, when we broke up. I have never forgotten them."

There was a silence. He seemed to make the silence worse by look-ing down at the floor. Then after a moment she said:

"I remember them as well. So what about the tag?"

"Well, something really startled me. When I went back to the bridge to take another look it had been completely painted over with white paint—almost angrily painted over. I might say the anger with which it was done struck me in a very profound way. It was com-pleted in a hurry, or seemed to be, and huge amounts of white paint spilled haphazardly over it to block it from view."

"What would that mean?" Cathy asked. "And why did you say 'profound' way?"

"Well—it was just a thought. But here it is: I was thinking that the tagger remembered he had tagged and came back here one night and took time to paint over it. At first I told myself it was nothing important. But then after a time I thought, what if—that just per-haps it had something to do with the remains of those people being found—the tag had been there for a time—and then so soon after the remains were found, the subsequent death of your brother—the tag was erased? Over the next while it stuck with me. As I ate lunch, or sat by myself at Tim's, I began to believe the beautiful tag might be relevant to the murders—and so, in that way, to Orville's death."

"That was not much to go on, was it?"

The light shone on the books. There was a sound of cracking in the old house—far away.

"No, not so much. Yet I began to think our artist had learned that a woman's remains had been found. So he, OBA, must get rid of evidence that he had been here four years before, just in case."

"Four years?"

"The woman was murdered four years before the time I first saw the graffiti under the bridge, or close to it—*OBA* had been tagged four years before, *OBA—2004*. Of course I remembered that—but the date had been painted over as well. Still, it bothered me—it was so beautifully done—how could an artist just erase it?—maybe, maybe someone else had done so, it was done so roughly—and if that was the case—perhaps I was wrong."

"I see. So back to square one," Cathy said.

"I was not sure at all. But it began a process of investigation— OBA, the letter from Han Woo Lee, the trust fund paid faithfully even over the last four years to this woman who was murdered, and the look of disbelief on your poor brother's face. That led me over time not to the Miramichi but to Fredericton."

"*OBA* tagged, what does that mean?" Cathy inquired after a moment.

"It is, I am afraid, a longish story," John said. "And," he added rather happily, "it involves many, many, many clandestine things."

————

So John Delano began to tell the long story, as he had reconstructed it over the last year.

"I wondered," he said, "who had helped him decorate the house—this large grey house sitting back from the road that towers up toward the Maritime sky in splendid isolation and—well, sadness, of a sort that still brings a sense of awe or hope, in a fleeting way, when you think of Orville himself. I do—that is, I think it brings a sense of awe—when I think of him."

"Did you find out—who had helped him decorate?"

"Oh, yes, it was her—in happier, more friendly times. That is, Eunice—she had the run of the house when he travelled, and he was often away—lecturing here and there, or finding enough money to go somewhere and do his digs—and she was ecstatic to help him. That is, the name Wise allowed her to move into his world and inhabit it—because all of a sudden she could be a companion—or, more importantly, the only companion he needed. So she always felt comfortable going in and out of his place.

"He himself was reclusive and shy of people, and she became a kind of older sister figure who was often telling him how to improve. She was not that when he grew up—when he was a boy and had a tumour, losing his eye at that young age, operated on by Dr. Hennessey to save his life on a storm-filled night in February of 1959—when he was shy and lonely—and thought of as not 'quite right' because of his strange ways.

"Once she realized he was *the* Orville MacDurmot, the one in the paper, she was the first to knock on his door—and soon she had the run of the house, and helped him buy his china cabinet, his furniture and his desk upstairs. She would turn up every day in an all-weather coat, a pair of bright yellow rubbers, a quaint rain hat, some mittens, with a list of things he might need, and her hair cut as she had it from the time she was eight or nine, the bangs short, and looking like a yeowoman in her appealing colours."

"Like the actress she was," Cathy remarked.

"Sudden friendship was self-endorsing—but he did not quite catch it, for he was simply too innocent.

"She came with an article he had published in *Science Today* and wanted him to sign it—get his autograph. He did sign it, and she went away ecstatic after she had a cup of tea. She told people this. And let her ex-husband, Calvin, know that she had a new friend, a friend who respected her very much. That would change with time, of course—with time she would not love Orville so very much."

"Just as she did not love the MacDurmots so much in that former time," Cathy smiled.

So John nodded, paused, and then went back to that former time.

2.

"ONE DAY, WHEN ORVILLE WAS IN HIGH SCHOOL, HE MET A girl named Brenda. She sat two rows over and one seat down in class. She was a girl from town. He was struck by her like some terrible affliction. He could not look at her without awe. He wondered if he would ever be able to speak to her at all. This happened a year after you went away. What could he ever say to her? How could he convince her that beauty was inside him?

"After some weeks he started to hitchhike the twenty miles just to see her on Saturdays—not to speak to her, just to see her walking by with other girls on some errand of some importance, the warm drafts from store doors opening dissipating in the cold white air. He always had some money in his pocket in case she wanted a Coke. He tried to hide from himself how he actually looked to others. Did she notice him? And what might she think if she did? He came around the corner by Henry Street late one afternoon and felt the fleeting swish of her shoulder by accident, and was amazed that they had actually touched. But it was just her coat's shoulder pad.

"When he got the courage he began to ask her to let him take her to a dance, with notes he put into her locker. Cathy, you did not know this then. But this girl was going to be his girlfriend, his saviour. He would have a girlfriend too—that was it, you see. He waited for her in the hours after school, and missed his bus to see her walk down the long lane to the bottom of town. Then, after dark, he would make his way home alone, walking along the broken road leading out of town.

"And on those long journeys he would think that he too would have a girl. And she would be pretty, to offset who he was, or that he was not—pretty. To him girls were kinder and more forgiving than boys—and he believed in her as something like a saviour, I think. She would forgive his look and see his soul. He believed then that women would save the world. That is why his disputes with women later became such an anomaly and so harsh. Or I should say disputes with certain women. And perhaps add, in parentheses, that what he said was not so utterly false—though it was taken so by people who rarely think for themselves, which is the grand majority.

"At any rate he believed that Brenda's beauty was the good kind— the kind that could save him. Later he would write an essay on the idea that beauty would save the world. But it had to be the right kind of beauty. When I read that essay things became much clearer about his visiting the monastery in Rogersville. But I don't think she was as interested in how he thought as he speculated she would be in private.

"Still he continued to ask her out through these notes. And to her credit she did say yes. She did respond to these notes in a kind way, she said yes—and it too was written in a note, and placed in his locker, with *yes I will* encircled by a small heart. Much later he was to find out the note was placed in his locker by other girls whom she had told and who had played a trick on her. But still, once she found this out, she said yes to him.

"The problem was, she had to sanction it with her boyfriend, a boy named Junior Barker, from Derby. You might remember Barker Construction. He was the son. Yet Orville did not know this was a factor in her acceptance; and that she was simply honouring a trick played upon her.

"Junior Barker was furious over this trick, and he planned to go to the dance to chaperone from a distance. He was furious because it was shameful for his girl to be thought of as dating material by someone as deformed as your brother. He was also furious that she had accepted! People would make fun. Certainly they would make fun of him if he did not take charge.

"Orville worried for days how he would speak to her, how he would walk her home, what money he might have on him to do so. But she was incredibly nice to him. Met him at the door of her small house on George Street, introduced him to her parents—all the things young ladies with still budding bodies are supposed to do in these circumstances, and away they went—he more loftily anticipatory than she—to that sour, terrible little dance long ago, with her father driving them there in his car.

"At first it was fine—I mean that dance where the boys were trying to grow their hair long, toking outside behind the brick wall, being wise and blameless about drugs, their thin chests in thin opened shirts, wearing the Beatle boots that were the style, the gold-coloured bell-bottom pants of days long ago. All was fine until Orville went to get a Coke for her. On the way back he tripped over someone's feet. Were the feet put there on purpose by Junior Barker? Orville fell and spilled the drink over his new shirt. Brenda, sitting two tables away, pretended for his sake that she did not see. But she had seen. She flushed crimson against her soft, curly black hair. Two boys helped Orville to his feet—the cruel gesture was replaced by a gesture of kindness, as so much in life is, but Orville was humiliated, though he tried to laugh it off.

"So then, at that dance in our small high school auditorium, where so much hope and pain still is remembered, so it is as if the walls themselves could tell secrets of adolescent agony from 1950 onward, and all agony competing with each other, Junior Barker asked her, his girl, to dance. This was when Orville had gone to the washroom to wipe off his shirt. It was the nature of her youth to be unthinking. She jumped up as if on fire to get herself to the centre of the floor while Orville was gone. But she did not come back to Orville's table. She danced with Junior again. She held his hand and walked back to his table.

"Orville sat watching them, his shirt stained with Coke, his new tie looking ridiculous, for he had been the only student to wear one. The candle burning for no one but himself, and the crepe paper echoing in its crinkled shapes a final whimsical banality. I suppose this is what the beauty he had put his faith in had become.

"Suddenly Junior found himself lying on his back, his face bloodied. The disaster for Orville was the look of horror on her beautiful face. His outburst was to become known as the first sign. Brenda picked up her coat and went home. Secretly she had been mortified by his exclusion, and she had found an outlet for her emotional detachment in his attack.

"She ran home and remained in the house when he came to see her that night. 'I was supposed to walk you home, was I not?' he asked her politely, but a little sternly. And then the next day he got a drive to town with your aunt Betty, sitting in the middle of the back seat forlorn and mysterious. Jumping out at the Town Hill Street light and making his way toward her house.

"He asked her to accept his apology—promised her that he would never react like that again, he would never be jealous anymore, if only she would go out with him. Again he said this politely but sternly.

"The young girl, seventeen at the time, felt all the pressure to release him from his trance, telling him to go away. She told him she was Junior's girl.

"Orville was on one side of the porch door and she on the other. Sometimes he could hear her voice trailing off, which meant she was stepping backwards toward the big grandfather clock.

"'Go away,' she would whisper. 'I am Junior's girl.'

"'Pardon?' He seemed stunned, as if he had so convinced himself of his relationship with her he could not conceive of it not being continued. He remembered Junior in a blur—a kind of heavy presence on his right side as he tripped and skidded forward. Until that moment he had not known him.

"'I don't understand you,' he said. 'You went to the dance with me—you could be my girl, couldn't you? I think you might reassess who Junior is.'

"'Re-what?'

"'Reassess, and come to some other more equitable solution.'

"'Please listen to me.'

"'I am listening.'

"'Go away.'

"There was a pause, and then a kind of verbal asterisk:

"'You mean for a little while—I mean, what do you mean by go away, exactly?'

"'I mean go away.'

"'I will go away—I will go for a walk, and then, after a while, I will come back. I will then take you for a hamburger at Centre Snack Bar.'

"'That's not what I mean.'

"'Then what do you mean, exactly?'

"'Well, you know what *exactly* means?'

"'Yes.'

"'Then what I mean—exactly—is go away.'

"He walked off, hands in pockets, and then came around to the back door. Which startled her more than ever.

"'But okay—but do you know that clock?'

"'No, what clock?'

"'The clock you are hiding behind.'

"'I am standing in front of it—I am not hiding.'

"'Well, I can fix that clock—if you want me to. I have a preponderance of natural knowledge in that regard.'

"Silence.

"Silence.

"The sound of a little foot stamping.

"'Go away.'

"'But it doesn't gong right, you don't know what time it is.'

"'I do know what time it is.'

"'Okay, then—what time is it?'

"'It is time for you to go away!'

"Then, beyond the back door, from his side of it, he could hear a kind of sorrow, a gasp as if she was terrified. He walked to the end of the small two-storey house, looked through the rear window and saw her standing alone in the middle of the hall, looking first one way and then the other, as if she was terrified and wanted to run.

"'Ah, she is upset—I have upset her—I do not intend to upset anyone.'

"He was confused, and felt he would give it time.

"So he turned away, and made it to the gate, and then coming back to the front door this time, he knocked loudly and, his voice rather stern, said,

"'Well—when can I see you again?'

"For the next week or so her father would drive her to and from school, and her friends would meet her.

"'Drive around the back—drive around the back—there he is—drive around—no, stop here—I'll go in here.'

"Why did she accept his invitation, why did she go anywhere with him? she kept thinking. She kept looking out her bedroom window with the fear that he was standing under a tree."

"I wish he could have just left her alone," Cathy said impatiently.

"Yes. There might have been a lot less pain," John said. "But her friends egged her on as well, made her walk by him to see how he would react. And she did so, on occasion, just to prove something. I don't think she was thinking what pain it caused.

"And she found safety with Junior Barker. She found safety with a boy who owned his own truck, who, like her, had many good friends. Who liked only what others liked, and who wore that which made him so. Who all his life would, like many others, confuse crisp new pants with decency. The heady beauty of trucks and Ski-Doos, the refined emblems painted on doors and pinstriped gas tanks, the slogans on racing jackets and caps, that denoted the exquisite and falsified universe of the roar."

Then John added:

"But Orville came back, dressed in stovepipe jeans and a yellow shirt, obsessed with being able to prove what was inside."

"Inside?"

"Yes, that his inside was grander than his outside. Initially, his chronic devotion seemed to have dissipated in the lowering of the autumn sun. For a while he separated himself from everyone. But then people saw him standing alone one morning wearing a black coat in the mist and cold at the far end of the school lot, with flowers in his hand. He did not go to class, and stood there throughout. The girls went to him at noon, and told him Brenda wasn't there, that she was sick with nerves—and never to bother her again because she would soon have a nervous breakdown, and be nervous-breakdowned all the way to some hospital—so he'd better watch it. They said this, in fact, with the innocent caring that children have for one another, even for him, trying to be grown up and to make each other understand. But not all of them—there were varying degrees of distress mixed with lively taunts and sudden gleefulness.

"The next day he brought her a ring—a ring he took from your mother—and tried to hand it to her after class. A ring simple in its structure, in its size, with the pin-like diamond in its centre—crafted some sixty years before and kept in the oaken jewellery box at your house.

"It was as if he could not let go of some grand ideal, an imagined ideal of her. Of course she would not take it. He offered it to her like someone who did not know he had broken the rules, or even what proper etiquette was; thinking that if he could just utter the right words she would understand. But she continued to back away until she fell over a small brick ledge, scraping her hands as she broke her fall. She stood and rushed inside the building. Junior and two of Junior's friends came out and started toward him. Then Mr. Cameron came out and told them all to go home.

"Orville told himself then to ignore her, yet he was in a trance, unable to extricate himself from what he desperately wanted to ignore. Speaking to others from that time, I learned that certain girls loved the drama of it all. And he sat in class unable to breathe. He could not help himself. It was the first indication of his plight. So one day he waited for the break, and when Danny John left his seat behind her, Orville took it.

"'Please,' he said, 'please listen to me.'

"She got up and fled from the class while other girls shielded her.

"The very next morning he overheard, 'Here comes the Cyclops, Brenda—run!'

"A half-dozen girls began to laugh. For one split second, in the gaiety they all showed, Orville did not know they were speaking about him. He did not know girls do have the same trace of cruelty in them. Certainly Brenda herself could not have called him that? But he also believed it was all his fault.

"He went away and sat, alone, in the boiler room downstairs.

"But that night he was seen walking behind her by ten yards, his mouth opening and closing as if he wished to shout some remark that would hurt her as much as he had been hurt. But he could never manage to do that, with her.

"Eventually your father and mother heard about his infatuation from Brenda's parents. It was as if an unwritten contract had been called upon—that this child, Orville, needed special handling and his parents must now measure up and face it. Some unspoken law that parents knew, and could call upon if they had to.

"The boy had become aware of girls and was now a danger. That is how her father put it—and gave an embarrassed sigh when he said:

"'I think your young lad has discovered the ladies.'

"It was not just his eye of course, Cathy, but the disfigurement on that side of his face, which became more pronounced as he grew to manhood. It caused a certain terror, though he wished to terrify no one. And he made a mistake—a kind of mistake made by people overly sensitive to the affliction they inherited. At times he believed everyone was looking his way, when they were not. But now her parents had phoned your parents.

"Certainly there would be a woman for him, who would know he was kind and good, that is what Brenda's father maintained; certainly he was a nice youngster, that is what Brenda maintained—but the young woman who loved him would not be her.

"'She does not want to hurt the boy's feelings,' is what her father revealed, 'but she is frightened of him too. He tried to give her an expensive ring.'

"This was the very crux of the story, and perhaps of his early life—he had taken his mother's ring, which had first belonged to his grandmother, and which she kept in her jewellery box in her bedroom—and tried to give it to the girl. It spoke of a danger. He might do the girl injury. So her parents phoned your parents."

"Was it the ring I now wear?" Cathy asked.

"Yes. But what was so much worse was the fact that this man, her father, was your father's boss. This was the horrible position your father was now in; the embarrassment was palpable, for Brenda's father was speaking as a father to a father, but would be his boss the next day, would speak to him, order him, and at times not look his way. This was humiliation—endured, not spoken.

"So your parents came to town in the car your father had bought— the only new car he would ever have, drove it like he was somewhat unworthy of being behind the wheel, for he drove it so seldom that it being three years old still only had 2,300 miles upon its engine—and, stepping out into the bare October sunshine, your father said:

"'Orville, that is enough—stop this here.' He said it with an urgent entreaty that seemed to catch the boy in mid-stride. Orville had been walking behind her at that moment.

"Orville then caught on to the terrible crisis he had put his parents in. That his deformity had marked them as well, and they stood in triangular despair, silently looking at one another, while Brenda Townie escaped into the golden, leaf-strewn Thanksgiving sunshine. It was in a way, for others who might have witnessed this, strangely humorous.

"'Stop this now, boy—and get in the car,' his father implored. As if he was able to stop it like one was able to stop more pedestrian afflictions, clowning on a pit prop or jumping from a white snow-graced ice floe.

"Looking back at his father—his mother standing near the passenger door—he realized they believed they had a duty to protect this young girl from him—from a deformity she could not cope with or embrace. But he realized they were protecting him too, from a hopeless delusion of his own beauty. You see, it was his delusion—and not only that, but a terrible belief in his own ego.

The terrible hubris that he could be like other people, look like the young boys so attuned to the world. This is where he believed his crime lay—in a mirage. He would hate himself for many years, but would not know why. He would, from this moment on, hate God himself.

"The leaves blew away in the trees and his love quietly disappeared, her disappearance reaffirming—or finally affirming—for him that she hadn't wanted to hurt him by telling him how much she feared—and now loathed—his looks. He realized suddenly that it was conspiratorial—that is, her walk away from him was conspiratorial—as if she had been in on the planning of his humiliation, as if her father had told her his parents had been informed, and she was privy to grown-up knowledge that Orville was not. Her look demonstrated how conspiracy can be instantly gratifying and contagious—as if now she could act a part. He was to see this later, and later still among the university fellows in tawdry common rooms, among the professors and journalists, among committee members, among political operatives, among activists and advocates. And among this fevered, pitching group tossed up on the waves of opinion and sensation was Eunice. He wouldn't meet her for some years, of course—but her contagion to be part of who belonged and against those who did not he noticed first in his love's striding away. It would force him into accepting Christ on the cross, which would carry him to his death. But that was to come.

"What shame engulfed him then when he realized this, and how Brenda in that moment exploited it by a triumphant sway as she walked, an unconscious movement in the autumn air with the brilliance of leaves shimmering above them all, a cascade of immense dying beauty, and the sunlight on her small brown hat.

"He got into the back seat—remembering perhaps how proud he was of this car when his father purchased it after years without a vehicle—and was silently driven home, all the way downriver at thirty-five miles an hour, the scent of evening mingling with his solemn thoughts."

"So it should have been over, for Brenda Townie and my brother, Orville," Cathy said.

"It should have been. But at school the next day Brenda's girlfriends began to follow him about, their little figures swaying behind him, a flow of cookie-cutter replicas of each other's mischievous whimsy.

"'Where's my ring, Orv?' one asked, with the well-rehearsed middle-class gleam she had for a smile, the kind where you see her as a self-appointed conduit for others.

"He began to hide in the stairwells and washrooms. The famous 'Cyclops' poem was published in the school newspaper."

"I never heard of it," Cathy said.

So John picked up a scrap of paper:

There is a stupid country boy named Cyclops
Who in our great halls doth roam
He is a menace to all the pretty girls
But one he won't leave alone
He gave her a little ring
Just the other day
And his redneck ignorant daddy had to come and get him
To drive him far away.

John read the poem. Then quietly went over his notes again. In this, his going over notes, was a serenity, a counterbalance to the poem, that revealed all he referred to without blame or shame; and a conscious kindness to Cathy, the sudden unwitting victim. It came from him being an officer and having known these situations in many different ways, over many years. And Cathy was comfortable with this, though not blind to the reason behind his sudden perusal of his notes.

"Is that when the principal became involved?" she asked, as if remembering something spoken to her about it long ago.

He looked at her and continued:

"So the principal became involved—and so these pretty girls, with the remote sanctity a secretive group exhibits when confronted by the outside world, were brought into the office one by one, with their innocent complexions, pretty faces and disbelieving looks, and how incredulous those looks can be at times, saying they, in all their high-minded ethics, had intended no real offense in this. They were stunned that anyone might think this about, of all people, themselves. How could they be cruel? They belonged to the sorority, the one that needed a group and would always have a leader, who supported each other by mimicking. Nothing about how this sorority worked would ever change for them, for in effect it was twelve thousand years old. And Orville was the one to realize this.

"Still, they were told to face him one by one and apologize—and, as Jane said, they went through with it because they were Canadians. Yet he saw the rebuke in the glint of their eyes as they spoke, though their tone was impartial. Brenda did not have to apologize, for she had had no part in the poem's conception. But that Brenda turned her back now when she saw him made him realize she knew those who did.

"Afterward he did not speak; it seemed he had gone through trauma. For a month or more he was silent—which caused this next incident to be so spoken about. One day, disagreeing with a chemistry teacher about a certain compound, knowing that the compound was actually much simpler and more beautiful than the teacher seemed to understand, he threw a book at the man's head and shattered two Bunsen burners. His parents were once again called. They were asked to take him to a psychiatrist, who perhaps might find a way through to him. The word 'psychiatrist' was no less traumatic than the actual fact that they would have to take him to one. Of course, Cathy, you had been phoned and had taken the first plane home from Toronto. (That is when you fell in love with your husband, Al, for he paid your way—excuse me for saying.) And all of you, subdued and injured by something you did not understand, travelled along the old bumpy road to Moncton, to a doctor—Phyllis Prat.

"But I will now tell you something you did not know. The night before he was taken to Moncton, Orville had phoned Brenda, after two hours of staring at the phone, picking it up, dialing the number and hanging up. You might know that the phone, to him, black and heavy in the inside room, was like a lifeline, and a warning against his own rashness. Its inanimate form almost sweetly beckoned and repelled at the same time, in the small of the night, while the night got later. He finally made the call. And he said,

"'Would you like to go with me to Moncton?'

"'To Moncton?'

"'Yes—Moncton—I'll buy you a hamburger. Don't think I do not have my own money,' he said sternly.

"'Why are you going there?'

"'I have to see a psychiatrist—they think I might injure or kill you; silly of them—but I have money for a hamburger.'

"The phone went silent, and then he heard a click.

"So the psychiatrist prescribed pills but they made the boy sleepy and uncommunicative—and Maufat had to wrestle with him on the kitchen floor, trying to put into the boy's mouth something he did not really wish to give.

"Then one night Orville simply flushed the pills away. But then, I think, came his remarkable change. It came because he witnessed his mother with her back to him, crying, one afternoon, when she did not think he was there. She was sobbing out her love for him.

"So he simply left her and silently climbed the stairs. But then he applied himself in the small room he had. He stayed alone—and if there had been a way to slip food under the door it would have been done. At night, after the smell of dark entered the cold rooms with the scent of winter and left its deft fragrance in the darkest shadows of the house, he would be heard closing the back door, and his parents might hear, as they lay in bed upstairs, his boots on the solid moon-lighted white snow outside. He would walk at night under a moon, all the way down to the river, among the red-tipped wild alders, staring out over the quiet shelves of ice. How beautiful it was. Or, as flurries fell silently on the roadway so the tracks of cars would seem obliterated by a wet, sweet formlessness, he would walk in the shadows, his bootprints soundless in that falling snow.

"So the months passed in retreat and he was forgotten about. He no longer looked Brenda's way. He was nothing to anyone. He was ignored and forgotten. He began at that time to grow stronger and taller, and strode past those he had once sought affection from.

"But he was no longer 'fun' for his tormentors, and they needed 'fun' from him. He was looked upon as a failure, in all ways. But he no longer seemed to mind.

"'I will be someone great,' he said to your parents one night after supper, when the soft smell of mud was in the dooryard and the long evening let birds sing sweet and late.

"They thought—you thought—he might become a teacher. But that was not it at all. He would someday take on the entire world. He would dine with Governors General, meet prime ministers, converse with industrialists, strike up conversations with renowned academics, write essays on the theory and history of beauty, and be invited to deliver serious papers."

"Then he would be forgotten, accused, cursed, and die alone," Cathy said.

———

"The end of June came and Brenda was getting ready to go to the prom with Junior Barker when the first news of Orville became public: the first ever measure of him in print.

"He had collected a scholarship. And here, on this June evening, on the marble table at the entrance to his love's house, was the paper telling us this. *MacDurmot Boy Receives $12,000 Scholarship.* So the first line of the first article ever written about your brother stated.

"Brenda glanced at Orville's picture in the paper. She remembered her friends had skewered him in retaliation of his desire for her. She believed she had no part in it. But she believed her beauty did—and her beauty had a whispering effect now in her own ear.

"She was eighteen. She had run to the mirror to look at her corsage, laughing at the fact that it was not pinned right; that is where her beauty, elusive and immediate, whispered. Then for some reason she was suddenly glum as she turned back toward Junior and looked at him, in his happy importance, standing there. The glumness came because she felt her beauty should be worth more.

"Her smile came back, however, as she walked toward the front door again, saw his washed and finely waxed silver truck in the yard. And in her walk was all the youthful feminine seduction that is never calculated but always, and sometimes fatally, persistent.

"Junior, a fine-looking boy too, whose future was notable in that his father owned his own small fleet of gravel trucks, one of those men who look upon education as something odious, something to be dismissed and guffawed at, like a deformity, pretended he did not feel the slight turn of her face when he kissed her. He smelled of aftershave and a touch of hair tonic, and toothpaste, and she noticed this, and it would come back to her at variant times in her life—that is, that she noticed this. She glanced once more at your brother's picture.

"It would have been a picture, if not for Orville's brilliance, that would have been quickly forgotten; it could have been a black-and-white likeness of a young boy who had once upon a time merited some attention to a few people in a small town. But it would be the first notice. Orville himself was unsmiling in that picture, somewhat arrogant-looking, a look to try to diminish his adversary, that fellow who by now had wooed that incomparable girl. He seemed for a moment to be staring directly at her.

"Orville did not have a date for the prom. Nor could his parents convince him to go with anyone—even your friend Karen, who, home on a visit, said she would go with him, if he so wished. He sat at home, in the half-dark of the living room, watching the silent broken road."

3.

"HE WAS ALONE AND DID NOT WANT TO LEAVE, AND SAT in his room scared to death about how he would be viewed. He saw the world as absurd. Later he would see it as tragic. He saw himself as poor and unknowing. Later he would see himself as something quite extraordinary.

"He went away that fall with a new trunk—bought as a present by his proud father, who took the money from his wallet with that very sense of pride and relief that he could do so—and a brush for his new suit jacket, to the university half a province away over roads that had not been repaved in many years.

"His big new shoes made him walk so clumsily along those hallways. And though those hallways were on occasion superficial, he in his big clumsy shoes and his shyness was not so superficial or so glib. He worked alone and joined in no causes—even though some causes tried to seek him out—the rage against the war in Vietnam, the passion for equality for women, all left him numb in that so, so many of these people he had known in high school now acted exactly as they believed they were told they must.

"So most people distanced themselves from who Orville was. Even the professors—or, more to the point, especially those professors—seemed to scurry out of his way as he walked. His hands were so large he could cover their heads with his fingers. But he was silent. He saw in so many of them what he came to call *the vacancy*. Their search for beauty was a search for acceptance and security. This was his first disobedience—he had plowed fields, planted and brought in hay, worked in the woods, knew First Nations men and women. It would be as absurd for him to agree with those urban kids who spoke sophomorically about the joys of pastoral living, about their naive celebration of First Nations life or of the smell of goats and the birthing of calves, as it would be for him to start wearing beads and leather pants. So he was recused from their cabal."

"So you mean he was shunned?" Cathy asked.

"Yes. However, this shunning became fine for him—but a girl from high school kept some kind of a tab on him. For the sake of, she said Miramichi reputation. She could not get over the fact that he of all people had received an important scholarship. This was Cyclops, the one they were allowed to torment! And she would write home: *He is not at all polite, he gobbles his food—I don't even think he cares if it is cooked—and who are his friends?—he speaks to the janitor and the cook who wears her hairnet.*"

Cathy caught his meaning only in part but was vivacious and smart enough to within a few seconds understand it in full.

"Oh, of course he would, he was kind to all, respectful to those who deserved it; I know *they* would not understand," Cathy said, and she sounded like a young girl again.

John then mentioned the first part of the crux of the university story: that Orville had taken his required English literature course from a well-known professor, Milt Vale—known as a delightfully gregarious man—who required that his students must sign up to join *his new cause*, a yearly march called *March Against Violence Against Women*.

"Orville was asked about joining this march that first semester, and thought it over—or seemed to think it over—carefully. Finally he said he would go on the march. That those girls from Chatham, who promoted in sweet-smelling whispers the rumour that he was violent, might just be wrong. But halfway through the march, with those same young women shouting slogans and profanity, he wished he had not joined. So Orville let it be known that he would not walk with them again. He said he was embarrassed by it. All the shouting and slogans. And when one woman said, 'Everyone knows you wouldn't support us,' he added: 'You can go to hell.'"

"Orville believed that university was in some ways very bad for certain people. That they all acted in *uniform*, for things that were often contrived," Cathy stated.

"It was very bad for one Issup Farad, a Middle Eastern student on a visa, who drove a Lotus. He was Orville's friend, and asked Orville to help him with his labs. He too wished to be an archeologist and seemed to follow Orville's lead in this. But he cheated, more than once. Issup was always selling something, was always pleasant, always bragged about his family in Kuwait and how well-connected they were. Later on, in his thirties, Orville met him again; he had a French–Moroccan wife, and they had a villa somewhere in southern France. He drove a Mercedes and there was always an understanding that he could broker deals with a Russian colonel."

"Oh God—I never heard a thing about any of that," Cathy said.

"That has nothing to do with now—but later, you will see it has to do with an obsessive search for something, something that Orville caught in small doses, in various people. From Milt, Brenda and so many."

"Including Issup Farad?"

"He was the first to make Orville aware of the nakedness of this search. Issup had the respect of Milt and a girlfriend who believed him. Orville helped him, and did so gladly, seeing in Issup's dark curly hair and black eyes something of a narcissist, and therefore he became aware of the nakedness of this search."

"The nakedness of this search—for what?"

"Orville was utterly scrupulous. He never took a cent he didn't earn. He never in his life cheated anyone. But not so with Issup. There was a certain hilarity about how to make money—how to do things. His eyes shone whenever he had a new plan. Bringing in people from Kuwait to hunt moose or fish salmon, and doing deals with the government or DFO in order to cut corners about the number of people and what he might charge them. Renting camps along the river that he could then charge exorbitant prices for to Europeans willing to pay for a wilderness experience. Or smuggling in cases of Seagram's in order to bootleg to students at dances and carnivals, running for student council positions in order to facilitate the use of university funds. Within two years everyone on campus knew him. His years there were filled with a frantic energy.

"It was out of Orville's realm, and it made him reluctant. He had to tell Issup that he would not use people's camps or water in this way—he would not take moose or game in this spirit of money. Issup told him they could get up to five thousand dollars for a moose.

"Orville knew he had made a mistake. That is, he had told Issup when he first met him that he knew of a man who begged to get a camp on the water, just to the west of Arron Brook, only to sell it a year later to a German adventurer for a two hundred thousand dollar profit. Issup became convinced they could do the same thing.

"'I can't and I won't' Orville said.

"Issup simply said: 'Well you're the backwoods boy. Come, there's no shame in making money—my uncles make millions. I guarantee you and I can make a million in a year—I promise.'

"He smiled up at Orville, his big, one-eyed friend, in sardonic disbelief that this country boy, brilliant as he was, wouldn't want to make a million. There never seemed to be a thing out of place with Issup, never a curl in his hair that was wrong. And that curly head seemed to elicit a warning when Orville looked down upon it.

"'Okay—think about it, Orville—think about it—and let me know.'

"In the darkness of the bars in cold mid-winter, and nightspots with spotted carpets and stained white walls, you could catch Issup with a smile and a drink.

"Many of the pretty girls from the Miramichi chased him—they assumed Issup was exotic and international. He spoke to all of them of making millions, and how they could assist him in doing so. A few lost money—money was displaced and they never saw it again.

"Two had abortions because of him, one against her own will and integrity—and then suddenly he was gone; the pale smoke of his last cigarette still hanging suspended in the darkened air. Once Orville came upon him in the midst of a loud argument and a shouting match. Issup's hair was dishevelled and his eyes watered in the wind. He looked over at Orville and waved quickly, the expensive gold watch reflecting the sun. Later that day people came to Orville's apartment asking if he knew where Issup was.

"Yet Orville could not impress his professors like Issup Farad, who wore with comfort thousand-dollar leisure suits, and smoked French Gitanes-brand cigarettes and listened to jazz in his large apartment off York Street. Orville was far too rigid and ordinary— far too much a rural boy for the fillies of the university. But then a certain crisis happened and Issup Farad was abruptly hauled out of university and sent back home. His father took charge of him and he left one evening, his apartment left furnished with a waterbed and his pet boa, and even his cigarettes left beside the commode. There was a story. Of a scene and police at three in the morning. Beyond all of this was the fact that Issup had gambling debts of over

40,000 dollars, and the police were watching him. Issup was gone in Orville's third year. There was a story that he was hit over the back of the head with the flat of his uncle's hand, like a truculent boy. Orville remembered the sober, punitive look Issup's face wore, on that dark February afternoon, when he passed your brother hurriedly on the sidewalk, without speaking, for the last time.

"Orville missed him, and was depressed for weeks over his abrupt departure. For he hadn't any friends other than him.

"As the first years passed, as the red brick buildings of that unremarkable university became more known to Orville, and he to the very buildings he entered, he remained more solitary, an enigma and mystery. He appeared there as a grey shadow coming out of the snow and the wind, the snow blanching the buildings and his rough face. He wore CN rail gloves on his hands that his father once wore, and heavy black shoes, stovepipe pants and suddenly a bitten pipe in his pocket. He, it was said, rescued a man from suicide one night on Needham Street. But who knew, for he spoke seldom to anyone. He drank alone and no one sat with him at the Brown Derby. He was a regular there—and often would be at the door waiting, in the morning, still smelling of the night's stale beer.

"He did not attend class, yet his marks were pretty phenomenal. So much so that the suspicion of plagiarism plagued him. How could a young man know what he did, about subjects as diverse as chemistry, archeology, T.E. Lawrence's drive across the desert and Hitler's Eastern Campaign, of Spenser's *Faerie Queen*, or Pepin the Short and Charlemagne, without being obligated to the likes of themselves, who had studied in places like Iowa, Cambridge and Swansea? He was nothing more than a rural boy from the backwater of the Miramichi! It did require a certain daftness on their part to think that *un*critically by being that critical of a young rural man they themselves could not compete with. He passed in his essays, did his labs and was silent in their presence.

"So in his solitariness, his exclusion, came a search and a longing for something else. That's why he drank so much alone. In those moments, alone in a tavern, not bothered by those who would not come close to him, he imagined many great worlds on his own. The worlds of dragons and man, frantic and sublime, and the crimson tops of mountain ranges. And these worlds produced in him an ecstasy that he had experienced at times walking those bare, bleak highways in the middle of the night when he was a boy escaping from his house. He would find it somewhere—although as yet he did not know where. Nor did he really know what it was he was seeking.

"And one night he said to himself, sitting alone with two draft beers in front of him, the tavern empty except for him and the waiter, sitting at a table watching the black-and-white television:

"'Ah—that is where it would be. It will not be with dragons, it will be with those of ancient times who were said to have slain them!'

"The waiter looked at him, and said he remembered this huge man, with one side of his face seeming in torment, glaring at him in almost ecstasy with one piercing eye.

"'That's where it will be,' he said.

"'Where what will be?' The waiter asked.

"'Joy—boy—joy.'

"He tried to find it. And he drank his final drink and swept the table with his arm, and rose and walked solitary to the door, where he was greeted with a howl and a wind, and the blur of Fredericton darkness long ago.

"He tried to find it, in every moment of the day, on any day of the calendar—he searched for it as if he could take it home and plunk it down under the half-grainy moon in front of *her* and say, 'Aha!—now do you see, now do you understand?' But he did not quite know what it was he was looking for."

"He did not want the same as what's his name—Issup?"

"Oh, that is what propelled him forward initially. Still, he kept going back to his country sweaters, his worn jackets and boots. Perhaps it was his upbringing, perhaps he was too puritanical, but he believed he could find a greater beauty—he just was not sure where. He once brought home birchbark, the underside golden in the autumn sun, and told a fellow student that this was, as yet, the most striking thing he had ever seen."

"He wrote me a letter about that bark—I only forget what it said—it was a long time ago," Cathy said.

"He wrote quite a bit—in his desk, it was all there in a dozen scribblers. But he spent much of his time in those passages relating how he hunted, fished, threw a fly out at dusk against the brown current of Little Bartibog. In those quiet August evenings searching for brown trout in the pools that were a sacred part of his youth, he would toss a short line against the current, using a small bug with a brown hackle, and fill his basket before dark.

"But then I came across this. One night I saw his scribble: the ideal for man, he wrote, was a superimposed deity—the divine all men and women have searched for since Pericles. Because we had not found love, we turned to madness and burned to death little Joan of Arc. He himself did not quite know where a deity would be found. But you see, even back then, he was caught, because it ended—no matter how much he tried to dispel it—with *God*.

"When he came back from one of his trips up on the main Arron to fish fall salmon far above Glidden's Pool, he wrote about the fields beyond which men and women had settled in a community now gone. The twilight had come over old tombstones and the trees were shrouded, and late dark birds called, and the road held water and ochre mud, and he wrote this:

"*Sweet the Darkness That Comes in the Fall*

"So in my mind he was searching even then for the most noble of this beauty, and the greatest truth of all.

"He had a certain strictness about him also, which he wrote down, such as *Monday, Tuesday, Wednesday*, and reported back to himself—a bath in cold water, which he felt helped his face and skin; strong tea without sugar or milk; whole-grain bread, potatoes and white fish, with little meat, was his diet—almost no sweets. Now and then rabbits, because he had snared many when he was young and liked them."

"He lived like a monk," Cathy said, "while at that time cursing the monks who lived?"

"Yes, he did. He lived very much like his hero T.E. Lawrence, the soldier and archeologist. So like T.E. Lawrence he read both the Bible and the Koran, for archeological purpose. That kind of asceticism that might drive us nuts. How often that happens to certain esoteric fellows. He kept almost nothing in his small apartment, though for three months he had to keep Issup's boa constrictor, for no one else would.

"Still and all, his apartment and his choices were hardly a sign of a man searching for beauty. While at university he wrote that he saw in the dens of second-rate academic philosophers the sadness of many hundreds of grave, thoughtful intellectual conformists, their seeking in small groups their own idea of pyrite and emblems of splendour; in slight volumes of poetry and in the leaves of obscure and ambiguous knowledge. Often, he wrote, they lied to their students about what they had accomplished—a doctorate instead of a master's, for instance, and a book they would someday pen. But he wished to prove something different."

"Prove to Brenda that he was—"

"Much, much different," John said. "In a way, for difference's sake—show that he was his own man, no matter who disapproved. The stupidity, in a way, of youth. He quoted Socrates, and he quoted the New Testament, and he quoted the Koran, and he never explained to anyone what he was quoting. He would wait in silence wondering if others caught on.

"But always Brenda was on his mind. He was wondering if she had ever thought of him. You see, he was gifted in the extreme but she was extremely unaware of his gifts. If she only knew whom she had turned away from—but back then very few of us knew."

"Perhaps—I remember how embarrassed my mom was to have to sit in church on Sunday and listen to the priest talk about atheism and speak about the young man from here who was a wisecracker and tried to use Bible verse against God," Cathy said. "So the roadway dismissed him as much as the university did. No one spoke of him at the picnics; people pretended he didn't grow up here. They pretended he did not exist."

"And that, I think," John continued, "is what propelled him. But as we know, he learned that Brenda and Junior had married. It was a huge wedding, even the premier was invited, and pictures appeared in the paper. So one day he just packed up and went away. It took me time to discover where he went. He travelled to Mexico, spent time in Belize, settled in Costa Rica and lived in a village. There he worked in a small garage. He lived in a small adobe, on a back road of a village. He wrote two articles on archeological digs done by the government of Costa Rica, so even back then he was feeling himself into his vocation. Back then he was very straightlaced, and assumed a great dignity about himself. It was said he went a year without laughter.

"It was there he witnessed the murders of two American tourists. He had become friendly with them. They were both pacifists.

They were gentle and kind, and somewhat naive, believing that if they cared for others, others would care for them. They had him to their place for supper a few times. The woman was so hoping that her gallo pinto was authentic. She so hoped her Spanish lessons would allow her to do her shopping. They had him for gallo pinto one morning for breakfast. There they argued over the nature of pacifism. He said it was not in man's nature—and they were hoodwinking themselves.

"I think they were trying to hook him up with a woman they knew. One evening as he left their apartment they asked him to join them at noon. This man and woman, gentle and concerned about the world—worried about Catholicism, but from some town in Louisiana—their small bigotry seemed quaint. Orville was going to meet them on the beach that day and at the last moment was asked to check the starter coil of an old Ford. So doing that, he did not make it. If he had he would have come upon the butchery. He remembered the leather sandals the woman wore, strapped at her ankles, with a brass decoration of a starfish.

"He remembered the tattoo of *Peace be with you* on her sunburnt shoulder, faded with time, and the little medallion her husband had given her when they were at Woodstock. He remembered how tiny her husband was, with small arms and hands. They found them, the woman's arm extended, as if to ward off a blow, and the man's little fist clenched, in the end wanting to protect her whom he loved.

"The woman was stripped and the sandals stolen, and the stolen sandals sold for three dollars. It disturbed Orville for months. Secretly, it whispered in his ear that there was nothing man had that he really owned—that's what he was actually dealing with. This brutal attack told him man has nothing—and can offer only one thing to each other, seen in these two kindly people—compassion."

"So he came back to Canada," Cathy said.

"Yes, after staying for a month longer he came home and went back to university. He dedicated his master's to this couple—a little later."

"Oh—I saw that on the cover page—I wondered who they were. Bill and Helen Wyscroft?"

"Yes, that was them. The señorita they wanted Orville to befriend has somewhere been forgotten. Still, in the summer of his third year, working at an archeological site by himself along the Bay of Fundy— not bothering with any of the other students who'd been hired on— he found the mummified, five-hundred-year-old salmon spear and donated it to the provincial museum. Out of the blue, he was in the paper once more. And this was seen by everyone in his hometown, and laconically drifted to papers across the country."

"I know it made him popular—it was mentioned in *Maclean's*," Cathy said. "I remember I carried that magazine everywhere, kept three on my desk at work—I would say to customers, 'Oh, have you read *Maclean's* lately Well then, there is the best article I ever read about a boy on page thirty-three.'"

"Yes, it made him suddenly popular. It made him suddenly known. It made him suddenly—sudden, if you know what I am saying. Kids went outside and started to dig in their yards. 'Orville MacDurmot is a genius,' one of the quotes read, as you know, in *Maclean's*."

"It made him beautiful," Cathy whispered.

"After that your brother became popular. People sent him psyche-delic eye patches to wear, and he had appointments at the university to do research in the summer, looking for certain rocks and artifacts on the islands of the Saint John River and along the Bay of Fundy. He was better than most at doing so. He found a great many small things and donated them all to the Micmac and Maliseet reserves.

"So, Cathy, within a year your brother was recognized as someone unorthodox and brilliant. He was published when he was twenty-four.

He wrote a great essay—not as much about the artifacts as about their elaboration."

"Elaboration?"

"Yes a five-page essay, typed up and in his desk. With what sense of wonder the people who carved them made them, actually took the time to decorate them. This became his main fascination. That is, beyond the spear or a knife's target of fish and fowl—or even other men—was the consistent intellectual grasp that things must be beautiful in order to be treasured, to have a value that did not necessarily correspond to their use but often seemed to surpass, by intellectual embellishment, the very purpose they were used for. An embellishment created on the spear or other artifact that desired to please *the other*. For Orville the 'other' may have been a woman, a chieftain—but that the illustration always tried to climb the stairs to what was *undefined* made the supplication real—the supplication to an idea or a person by the creator of the image that tried to please something undefined by human speech. But, as Orville stated very early on, if the illustration was even a little too full of display, it would prove unworthy and be an act of self-idolatry."

"Like the exaggerated night march that he went on, a display instead of concern?" Cathy asked.

"Yes—that is probably true."

"Did Brenda know how well-known he was becoming?"

"Sure, she knew. His name was ethereal, in that it seemed to hover near her at moments in the day's sun, or at night as she walked the sidewalk home. She would hear it, and once from a car radio that passed her by. She ignored it most times, but always she realized it was there. That is, she could not ignore—could not *not* remember—those high school days.

"And about this time he became known to one Amos Paul, Chief of the Micmac band here—and this would become important, crucial to everything. Amos Paul wanted to meet him to discuss something. So Orville obliged him one evening when he was still quite young. They discussed, way back then—many years ago now—the dig that Orville started then, and was working on in the last week of his life; that is, just before he was arrested. Now this became a sore point for others in the Micmac band council, who wanted the land for something else, believed the dig was a complete waste of time and did not like the Elders telling them what to do."

"The Elders like Amos Paul?"

"Yes."

"You mean they wanted the casino?"

"Yes—"

"But the land was not theirs—or was it?"

"They had two band members research it. If the land was your brother's, they would never get to buy it; but if it was Eunice Wise's—"

"That changed the water on the beans. For on the east, they owned almost up to the waterfront they wanted," Cathy said. Then she added, "It was land that was long in dispute; the Wise family always said it was theirs."

"They approached Eunice one evening and hired a lawyer for her. Still, with Orville insisting he do a proper historical dig for Amos Paul, their idea of a casino was put on hold."

"It would seem crass of them to oppose a dig for a casino. But didn't they have a casino downriver?"

"Yes, though certain band members wanted this site. When Amos Paul died—if Eunice could claim the land, they could buy it—so they were the ones who paid for the lawyer."

"And as long as they were enthused, Eunice was too?"

"Yes."

"Yes—I see," Cathy said. "I do see—I see her—humanity—had something else attached to it. Maybe a suitcase full of loonies?"

"But that is much later on in the story," John continued. "Some years after his time at university. So now I want to mention how Orville came into contact with certain other people, and in a certain way entered politics for a short time when he was working on his master's. This was in the early eighties. You see, even the kindest of professors, stuck along those corridors having done their masters' on the very things, or with the hope of the very discoveries, that Orville seemed to step beyond, could at times not mask their resentment with enthusiastic smiles."

"The election!" Cathy supposed.

"Yes; and Orville had too long passed by an office door along one of the university's drab corridors that led down to his chemistry lab. In that office worked a biology professor who, along with eight or nine students, was preparing for a real *crusade*. Orville liked the professor, who wore horn-rimmed glasses, and fussed over amoebae, and had a grandchild named Zilo, and believed in New Deal politics. He was an old, slow man with loose-fitting false teeth, and the smell of ethanol and formaldehyde, and a look of an old socialist who had fought all the wars on the sidelines. Orville had taken two courses from him. So Orville grudgingly allowed himself to be talked into delivering pamphlets on behalf of the professor's campaign. He felt silly—and embarrassed, as he always did. And he looked at the pamphlets he was supposed to deliver with some hesitation. They had lines like:

"*No logging on provincial land (ever again)*

"*Environmental justice and a more inclusive society (from now on)*

"*Reproductive rights!!*

"In the stale basement room, the elongated shadows of evening, the smell of formaldehyde, the smell of dead reptiles, the smile of new young students who looked up to Orville now, in passive glee at their own participation in this historic event. They were girls and boys really, some only seventeen, and they set about making placards and signs with grave duty because their kindly professor had asked them to. They were led by a tall talkative boy named Scamper McVeigh who kept shouting to everyone that they were *dupes* of the system and they should end the monarchy.

"Yes, their politics demanded a kind of pastoral beauty without fossil fuels and without survival of the fittest—in fact, everyone would be allotted his or her small plot of land—the professor was certain of that. That is, labour and jobs, and good wages and work itself, seemed now to be beyond the point. In all his years with tenure, he never realized how many others, like Orville's father, scrapped and worked until their hands bled to make only one quarter as much as he. So, because of all this, late in August of that faraway time, Orville became very much aware of real political life and intrigue, and entered through the back door on a grimy, humid night, where he sat with men, some of whom had little education, but who knew what actually caused the wheels to turn.

"He found out quickly who they were, and what they wanted, and, moreover, who was to be taken seriously. He could talk to these men because he could relate to them. He knew exactly who they were. And by now they knew him. They had seen his picture in the paper, so they were sure he might be of some use to them. They were many times the behind-the-scenes men who picked the MPs and the MLAs—they would change their tack to any wind, blow hot and cold on any issue, revamp any idea, scorn or adopt any policy, look serene or outraged over the same mandate depending on the circumstance. These were men and women of back-room government. They would cheat as long as it was not apparent, and they would slander as long as they were not quoted. They could finesse a position in cabinet as well as any men in the country—they could pick a leader and set him up for failure just to get a leader they wanted. All of this shone that night in their glimmering faces.

"Orville had worked the woods like they had, had hunted, and fished, had hayed until his hands were scarred and blistered. No one from the professor's troupe of young radicals could he take seriously, but these men he did.

"So he was walking with his pamphlets proclaiming a new way one evening and saw a green-toned Monte Carlo parked in front of an old building on exhibition grounds. It belonged to a man from downriver whom he knew, and so he went over to say hello.

"And where did he find this man whom he'd gone to meet? At the racetrack, where Orville had an interest—not ownership—in a standard-bred mare called Lucky Luce. Orville went on occasion to that track to jog the mare—that is, exercise her, muck out the stall and feed her oats.

"All the talk that warm August night was of the federal election. The owner of Lucky Luce drove the Monte Carlo, and he and other men, and three women, were hoping to grab the Northumberland riding where Orville grew up. Orville listened to them, filled his pipe and heard what they said. He saw how old and new politics worked in the grime and heat of a racetrack of young standard-bred pacers. Not a professor he knew would divine to come down here."

"Lorne and Betty were there, I bet," Cathy said, speaking of her aunt and uncle, who had dealt in Conservative politics and haunted racetracks for years.

"Yes, they were. So Orville was welcome. All spoke of his riding, up north, and he knew even better than they did that two companies held the key to the entire region, and he knew too that one of these companies was Junior Barker's father's. It was strange to hear Barker spoken about with such animosity. One huge, round-faced man, with small eyes and a perpetual smile—looking like a rural Buddha as he sat on a metallic auditorium chair wearing a flashy shirt and dark pants, with heavy rubber-soled shoes on his feet—cursed and played incessantly with his carton of fries, flirted with Orville's aunt Betty, looked gleefully suspicious at anyone who entered the room, picking up his pop now and again to suck through a straw, and weakly shook Orville's hand when his uncle Lorne introduced him.

"Orville kept his pamphlets hidden in his pockets and sat down to listen. He discovered for the first time how deeply disliked, mistrusted, and what fodder for jokes this Barker family was. How people laughed at the old woman and her sons, and how the grandson Junior, with his truck and Ski-Doo, was looked upon. He was told that Junior had offered beer and money to one of the tough Godin boys in his dad's employ, asking this man to provoke a fight with him and then take a dive so the others would notice Junior's prowess. It would help him control the men in the future. Since the man refused, he was fired the next day, and then other men quit. Now these men had formed a small faction to oust the Barker trucks and graders and dozers and backhoes from any major job. This was what had been going on when Orville was living without friends and in solitude, or travelling in far-off Costa Rica.

"Someone also made a crude joke at Brenda's expense, and even the women laughed. His aunt Betty included. Then she quickly glanced his way, as if catching on to who this woman was. Orville flushed deeply. But he sat much as he always sat—his arms folded, his corduroy jacket buttoned, wearing a tie because he had been going from door to door. Since everyone knew who he was, he was invited to the back room, where chairs were assembled in a haphazard way and a fan flipped above them. So while in that room, knowing more than they did, he suddenly forgot his obligation to the New Socialist Party and told them this: if Mr. Barker bid on new road construction, replacing the very bumpy road Orville had travelled to university, he would show himself deep in Liberal favour; but the bid would be cancelled by a new government and Barker wouldn't get another chance at a federal contract if the Liberals were defeated.

"'So,' Orville said, 'Mr Barker is doomed—if he bids the bid will be rescinded; but if he does not bid he will lose his trucks. He is in debt of almost two million. He needs that contract. That is the ordnance you have to play with. You have to let people know that not only are jobs at stake but roadways, construction and a new economy—you have to let them know that Barker showed his greed, and mention how he did it on jobs where he excluded local men and kept half the river poor so Liberal fellows and cheaper labour from other provinces could work—and he did it as a political favour for jobs in another province. Go after him on who he hired out of Quebec—truckers and men from the Gaspé. Tell them this is the act of a traitor, no matter what he promises. Now that we are in a recession the seat will be yours.

"'Tell them he is not only their enemy,' Orville said, warming up, 'but the enemy of the people here, and he will make a bid to keep himself alive. He gave kickbacks to other Liberals in Quebec and else-where to keep himself afloat. But you see, he can't haul in any more favours with his party in turmoil. Tell them that. Tell them that he does not give a good damn for anyone but himself and has not since 1957. That Junior Barker, who wants to take over, is the very same or worse. And the woman he married—well, the woman he married—'

"'Who, the old man's wife? Doreen? Or Brenda?'

"'Brenda—yes, is that her name?—yes, the woman he married!' Orville said. Then he looked at Betty and flushed deeply and looked down at the floor.

"They looked at him, astonished.

"'I knew Leah,' the huge man with the comical grin said, speaking of Orville's sister. 'I knew her a long time ago.' And Orville's pres-ence was immediately gratifying to his aunt Betty, who longed to feel more important than she was previously allowed to. And now, as his aunt—even if she was a disapproving aunt—she was suddenly more attractive. So they spoke of Leah and his family, harangued and laughed and were solemn among each other as Orville spoke. So Orville spoke—and told them how Barker's downfall would help the Conservative cause enormously.

"'If you are smart, Conservative boys will replace Liberal ones in the road crews, and Barker, after thirty-five years of playing God, will be no more. Don't worry—he knows if his lowball bidding comes out now, people will resent it. So flog him on that,' Orville said. Barker now had no choice. He knew it, and so did Orville this night.

"'He now has a lot more enemies than friends,' Orville said.

"'Is that what you would do?' the jolly man asked.

"Orville suddenly felt a power over the whole Barker family.

"'Just detail how much control he has, and how miserable employment is on the river—how many jobs he could have given, and how many he did not give because he was seeking favour and cronyism elsewhere. How many men he kept out of work while bringing in outside labour because he owed people in other provinces. That will force him to bid. The Barkers will destroy themselves—your man will win,' Orville said.

"The jolly man said he and his cohorts knew all of this, but wondered how Orville did.

"'Oh—I've studied him for years,' Orville said, feeling a sudden terrible glee. And he added, 'Studied how he controlled so much. This is perhaps the one election you will be able to use what you and I have studied.'

"By the time your brother left this meeting, kissing his aunt and shaking Uncle Lorne's hand, Orville knew that Barker's Construction was in deep trouble. If he bid he would lose, if he did not bid he would lose. If he did lose, his company would crash because of the overhead of trucks and graders he had purchased over the last two years. (Orville had studied this too—how Junior had demanded partial control of the company and then ran up a grave debt.) Those glinting yellow machines in the great swept yard, where the gravel heaps shone light grey in the moonlight and sluice belts sat in vast, comfortable darkness, all measured out with a geometric hand. If his political rivals did what Orville said they should, Barker would be doomed.

"It was their destiny, now in woe. Yet by the time Orville left the meeting, Mr. Barker, 120 miles away, sat in somnolence and grave concern, looking out at his property as if apologizing to it, seeing something glint in the moonlight and after a time realizing it was the bumper of his son Junior's large, newly purchased half-ton truck. Junior, who had fired his two best men over nothing.

"Orville went to the tavern, drank eight draft beers, before going home, himself shaken by all of this nefarious venture. As if to get back at *her*—with a beautiful volley. And he was sickened with himself for having mentioned her name. All the time he had been speaking, the vision of her walking away from him that day his parents drove to town, and the poem 'Cyclops,' had played in his mind.

"'I don't care,' he said. But he did care, deeply.

"He now felt guilty. If, he decided, he was a noble man, he would try to correct it. But what could he do?

"The one thing he could do was phone the Barker family and tell them what was being planned for the bid he was to make. He did not know them, but he could phone Brenda. Tell her to announce that a union was to be formed, announce new jobs created, announce that men from other provinces would no longer be hired! He knew he could tell her that they might save their whole company by demanding an equitable bidding process with local workers. They still had time to hire men from all walks, with better conditions. They were still an important presence on the river. They still had time to bring a partner in, Little River Industries, a smaller, Conservative-leaning construction company that they, with powerful industry in Quebec, had frozen out before. That would give them credibility. That alone might gain them sympathy, and perhaps the very bid they sought, or part of the bid, which would allow them a subcontract and save them from Junior's extravagance. Orville knew he must make that phone call.

"But then he would be betraying a confidence he could not betray—people at the meeting who had trusted him—and he also felt no one at Barker's would listen to him. And further, if the shoe was on the other foot, would Junior Barker warn him? He did not phone.

"He never delivered another pamphlet. He stayed in his room for days on end as the weather turned cooler and the nights of fall came. He drank, and drank. And drank.

"On election night he did not go out, say anything to anyone, or even vote. His own candidate garnered 104 votes against the 6,549 votes of the eventual winner. So Orville sat alone watching on his small TV the results that swept the Conservatives into power, eventually taking over his own riding for the first time in forty-five years. He sat in solitude watching it, thinking of Brenda."

"But what had he done really?"

"Nothing—but maybe the sin of omission," John said. He paused.

"Yes—he did do that," Cathy said.

"Whenever he drove home after, he drove along the old Derby road in order to see their property. He was hoping they would stay in business. But after a winter and a half their gates were locked and their warehouses empty. The office where Mr. Barker had sat that night now had slivers of cracks in its windows. Within two years they were forced to sell off almost everything but two gravel trucks, one of which Junior drove for another company. For a while, as Orville's career began to blossom, he did not think of them. Then once, sometime later, he saw Brenda working at Stedmans. She was wearing a maternity smock with an arrow pointing to the word *baby* on her stomach. Now and again his name would appear in the paper about some observation he had made, quite succinctly and out of the blue, about something he had said.

"Over time Brenda began to collect these articles. She kept a number of articles about this man she had once run from.

"'Yes,' she once told a compatriot at Stedmans when a story about him was on the local television, 'I went out with him.' Then she said, almost in apology, 'Oh—well, it was so long ago.'

"That night she went into labour and her child, a little girl, was born."

John then told Cathy that it was time to introduce another one of his findings.

"That is, of a young man—younger then Orville by two years—who hitchhiked from the Miramichi with poems stuffed in his pockets to read on those cold February meetings to a literary group headed by Professor Milt Vale. There were some people at that writing group back then who were very fond of Milt—expatriate Americans who had come here just like he had, a woman named Flora, a professor named Burt, a man named George, and Scamper McVeigh—they came to read their poems and stories.

"I know very little about this group. It was a support group for local writers, I suppose. There are many local writers here—many are privately published, events happen at all times of the year. I know that Milt and Scamper McVeigh were quite demonstrative in their support of various writerly causes that all seemed attached to the university at the time. It was as if, at this moment, during that present time, with the lights shining on the green tablecloth of that small room, this was the one place the most shining examples of literary excellence would meet. They were academics, and believed fully in academia—in their place, which they jealously guarded. Though most of them never wrote well, they believed they should decide on how writing should be written well. It was they, they believed, who created the writers by doing dissertations upon the writer's work. It was they who if they didn't write great masterpieces could claim they knew too much to write them. But most of all it was they who did not wish to be singled out, and scapegoated—they did not wish to be left alone, they did not wish to suffer alone. So, jealously guarding each others' opinions and believing they were the most forward-thinking of people, there was a sullen hostility toward the boy who seemed to barge into the room one night. It happened I believe because of the belief that they were superior to the province they had come to, to teach. So to them this boy did not belong, even though he was from the province itself."

"Like the clubhouse?" Cathy asked. "That I wasn't allowed into?"

"Yes, quite like the clubhouse you were not allowed into. Most of them held doctorates, most of them dreamed of the day they would escape the university. I know Milt and Scamper were true friends, thought of as radical, and formed committees, held poetry readings and had story contests. And spoke to students in master's programs. Radical talk was all the rage, or the range wherein their work lay."

"And the Miramichi boy?"

"I am not sure about him at all. He dressed like a country boy. His shirt was torn, he wore work boots on his feet, his hair was cropped short. He had one or two charges against him for drinking, when he was younger. Spent a night or two in jail. Milt once asked another Miramichier—Eunice Wise, who did turn up irregularly to these meetings—why the boy even came. Milt actually feared people who were not like him. Eunice had decided that the group, the clean, orderly group of academics, was where she would like to be. That is where literary excellence was really decided.

"Later, to make everything about her position quite clear, Eunice whispered that the young man was no friend, and she had no connection at all to him. He was not progressive and he was not very liked over there.

"'Oh, I didn't think so,' Milt said. It was the first time he ever spoke to Eunice Wise—their forms making shadows in the dark against the opened doorway.

"'He's no friend of mine'—and she squeezed his hand. That was a poisonous touch, both to the other, unknown to each. For without the two of them in contact over the following years, no playbook could have been made. This was sometime in mid-February—a fleeting question, and nothing more, about this young man who had just left the small white building, with its ornate tables and chairs. The darkness enticed them, made them both conspirators, and the wind scuttled snow over their feet. The little feet and bigger feet making prints in the snow. Her hat had a bob at the top that wrestled with the wind, and only her eyes showed. So it transpired."

"What transpired?"

"Oh," John answered, "the connecting of their souls. He did not forget her name. An illicit grasp of some future they might have been vaguely aware of.

"Something bothered Milt about this fellow. He did not know why—he couldn't place it. But he knew this boy was dangerous to him. He felt this in his soul as well, from the very first time he saw him. He did not know why he was dangerous. Except that everything Milt wrote about was somehow undermined by this young river lad who seemed to write an opposing tract. He was outdone by his simple narrative. He hated to see him come in the door. Milt's work was so correct. And this boy's was clumsy—awkward, inelegant and untrained. And this was what Eunice noticed as well.

"So they began to ignore him. Once Milt said, with sudden annoyance:

"'You didn't steal that poem, did you?'

"'Oh no—where would I have?'

"'I don't know—but how do you know all of that?'

"'I lived it.'

"'You lived it—where did you live it? When did you write it?'

"'This morning—'

"Milt nodded and looked over at the others with a slight grimace and a shrug of his shoulders as if to question what the boy said. He didn't want to say he was a liar, but how did such a boy write anything well?"

"'He's got help with that—he can't even speak proper English—he's gotten help,' Milt said that night to Eunice, as he walked along with his scarf over his shoulders, and spoke into the gale wind, so his mouth felt raw.

"'You didn't help him, did you?' he asked the woman, which gave her a strange feeling of elation. They both gave a short burst of laughter, sparks from his pipe flew, and the cold air made them wince.

"'I wouldn't bother helping him,' Eunice answered. 'But,' she added, 'I did point out things to him—I have pointed many things out to him.'

"'I'm sure you did—I am sure—you have sophistication. He stole that, I know. He's coming over here to make fools of us—and we have important things to say.'

"'Well, *you* have important things to say.' Eunice said.

"Milt was enraged that this tragic little poem had the effect it had on him. This tragic little poem about a death in October had such an effect on him."

"This man from the Miramichi—was Orville a friend of his?" Cathy asked.

"Yes and no . . . "

"In what way 'yes and no'?"

"Orville knew him—and did not know who he was; that is, that he was this writer. But Orville did something quite out of the ordinary about the time he finished his master's. Orville felt obligated to read parts of Milt Vale's first novel as a favour to Professor Vale the summer of the election. Milt simply wanted to know if people 'spoke like this here.'

"So Orville read it, realized people did not speak or act at all like 'this'—here or anywhere else—but as far as I know made no comment about it. According to what I know now, he thought it was a very bad novel. However, your brother would not say this. He took Milt 's novel back and was relieved Vale was not in his office. So your brother left it in his box, with one word: *Thanks.*"

"What novel was it?"

"It is a novel no longer in print. Professor Vale had it self-published later that year. It was reviewed by a third-year English honours student for the student paper." So John fumbled about, found and read this notice. "The student called it a *delightfully whimsical novel filled with possibilities of sensual and amorous rebirth. And a true character study of today's modern woman, searching for sexual fulfillment and independence, unafraid to stand against all the harangues of the patriarchy of the Catholic Church. Professor Vale simply decries injustice and shows us a woman brave enough to overcome it. She overcomes the persecution by her husband, terminates an unwanted pregnancy, and with her wit and the help of an undaunted professor skewers the tyranny of old white males.*"

There was a sudden embarrassed pause.

"I came across this review in the archives, and read it about five weeks into the investigation. It was completely by accident. It was in December, before Christmas. The library I was in had a shelf of books that were published locally, and the notices about these books, from Michael Whelan right up to Fred Cogswell. But this review of Milt's book had been stuffed into the back of a copy of the book, perhaps by the student who wrote the review. It wasn't the only remnant of that time, but the one most interesting to me. All these local hardcover writers with their pictures fading away on the back, while the light through the window still came upon those aging words. I was puzzled about something. All these books, and none from this Miramichi writer who commanded attention for a while? So now," John said, "learning this, I read Milt Vale's first book. It took only three hours to read it. Then I decided I had to backtrack—and learn about this obscure Miramichi writer, who I myself had heard about only once or twice in my life."

"Why?"

"Because he too had gone to their group because of something I felt—a feeling I had as I went back one evening and sat in your brother's house. So I dug around, and found people who knew this Miramichi writer, or said they did. I asked about him, discovered what had happened to him, and realized that Orville, though he knew him, never knew him as 'the writer' he himself had once heard about. That is, he never put the two people together as one, in any way. That can happen in a land of dark and ice. You might pass people on a snow-covered lane for years and not know the artist within. And this I think would come back to haunt every one of them. The writer, you see, never spoke to anyone here about his writing. So no one knew.

"But then that night of the knives came, where they forced this writer out.

"'Unimportant,' I was told our man Milt argued vehemently one night, and even got up to show the mistakes on the chalkboard. 'Your story—if it *is* your story—is quite unimportant. There are great things happening in the world now, great events, people are looking for a better world, where is that in your work when you write about girls and boys in the backwoods drinking wine who still go to Mass on Sunday and get ashes at Lent? Come on—is that all the Maritimes are? Where is the real Miramichi? I bet I could take a trip up there and soon find the *real* Miramichi. Flora, you should do that—go to the Miramichi and write the real book! Put all this nonsense to rest once and for all.'

"Everyone laughed; the boy laughed too.

"But I heard from none other than Flora herself that he looked wounded, and in fact never came back. So hearing all of this as I researched him, I think now none had any idea what it was the boy was actually saying in his work."

"They were blind to it?"

"Oh, yes—yes, they were all quite blind. You see, it would strike Milt Vale one day, just as things would often strike him well after the fact, and he would never quite recover. No matter how much he had trained to be a writer, had done all the right things, gone to the right schools, he had missed it entirely. That day, the day he realized that he had missed it, he would turn ashen while looking in the ornate mirror in the bathroom of his home."

"Eunice—I imagine she had her say, as Milt's protegé—so what did she say?"

"Well—Eunice responded very harshly to his work too; she told him frankly that his work 'made fun of the Miramichi,' and that there was a true middle class and real thought on the river too. She addressed the people there. She said they must not take his stories very seriously because she came from the same area and had a wealth of knowledge about many things. And was a writer herself.

"'It's not all ignorance,' she maintained. So she cautioned this young writer, told him there was sophistication in the Miramichi, and an understanding of feminists seeking freedom and new race relations. And she patted him on the hand, and put him straight. She came to that green room, in the shadowy small building, for a number of weeks, sometimes only one of a few there—always diligently listening to Milt's advice. She was quite enamoured with Milt at that time. The boy hitchhiked home. It was his last time at the Tuesday night group.

"'I was harsh on him,' Milt said, 'but I had to be. I didn't want to—but I had to.'

"Then Milt's book was published, and he passed it around, and invited people to the launching. He did not invite that boy. And that boy—that writer had thought that Milt was his mentor. So he drank half the night in a tavern and showed up with a copy of the book, to have it signed. He wore a brown jacket and a big red tie, and the collar of his white shirt askew. His hair seemed straight on one side and curly on the other, and his ears poked out. He had the saddest, most gentle face.

"It was at that launch that the boy from the Miramichi ridiculed the book Orville had tried to read, the first novel of Professor Milt Vale. It was called *The Renter*.

"As he got Milt to sign it, the boy supposedly said, 'You know, sir, Mr. Sir, the book is god awful unfounded rubbish. Men don't act like that with women, women do not respond that way to men.' And he was drunk and said some other things very loudly and looked around winking—then he tried to grab Eunice and kiss her, saying: 'Hello, you darlin' from Oyster River!'

"Then he staggered over to the wine table and poured himself a glass of red and a glass of white. I subsequently learned of this from one of the wine servers that night. It took a great effort for them to get the boy to leave. They were in truth all frightened of him whenever he wanted them to be. The only thing was: like Orville himself, he didn't want them to be.

"The night after this book launch Orville met Professor Vale walking alone in the dark of March. There was wind from the north scowling down across the cement sidewalk, and slush froze once again to the steps of the library. The boy from the Miramichi had made light of this book the night before. So, fighting back emotion, Vale told Orville that he had helped the boy, had taught him how to write every line. The boy, Vale said, was jealous of him."

John paused, as if this was as far as he would go with this part of the investigation at the present moment. He walked to the window and stood there. The day was getting darker now, there was a sound of the wind coming up, and snow still fell.

"But Orville did not get to hear who this boy was?" Cathy asked.

And John turned back.

"Nor, and this might be considered somewhat a proud lack on his part, was he curious enough to ask. So he remembered it, if at all, as a distasteful event at the university. Then finally, some weeks later, Orville was invited to speak at his old high school, bringing with him certain arrowheads and a clay pot he had discovered. These came from those student digs in the early eighties.

"There in the corridors that now looked so ordinary he was surrounded by youngsters who asked for his autograph. At one point he stood beside the infamous locker where he had found the note from Brenda. And it all seemed to burden him. Though he tried to smile for the picture taken, he did not seem able to pull it off. They all stood next to him for this picture that was published in the *Miramichi Express. Well-known Graduate Drops By: Orville MacDurmot, now studying archeology, remembers his high school with fondness.*

"The principal was the same, Mr. Cameron the same, the English teacher the same. These were the people who wanted him expelled during the Brenda episode. These were the people who had ordered him to see a psychiatrist. They smiled at him—almost in apology— as they all stood for the picture, but behind that there was a slight feeling of reproach. The Miramichi writer was beginning his novel about your brother and the betrayal he would someday face. It was called *Darkness*. I do not think you know this."

"No—I mean, you did mention it last night—I saw the book last night, but I did not know of it before now."

"That night, your brother decided to finish his doctorate," John simply said. "He was actually being pressured by that biology professor to give up archeology, but found something in mankind that could not be extinguished, a search for true beauty. He also was questioning now what beauty was. And he would someday realize that all of us were born with this same beauty—and only ourselves alone destroyed it. Many did not take his doctorate seriously—or as seriously as they would have if they had thought of it themselves. It's amazing how certain academics can slough things off."

"So to them he was a loner, and in the end committed a horrible crime?"

John paused, looking through his notes, nodded tersely, and said:

"While working on his doctorate he spent a month at the Pitt Rivers Museum in Oxford, helping to catalogue and transcribe artifacts onto computer disks. He wanted to spend it at the British Museum because his hero, T.E. Lawrence, had supposedly worked there. But the Pitt Museum was quite a big thing for him. A huge, lumbering boy from the colonies invited to the centre of the world. A young British woman of four feet ten inches and Orville, jutting just over six foot four, were directed to catalogue artifacts from Canada. One day he came across a pair of young girl's moccasins that were over two hundred years old. They were called 'Post-European.'

"He thought often about these moccasins as he walked through damp London, and who it was who might have worn them. He could see they had been worn—walked on by this girl along the riverbanks in Quebec—and had ended here, in a dry, sterilized tank.

"Issup Farad was living in London then, and had an apartment there. Orville told him that he had had a dream about this young girl. She was walking to the river and had turned and smiled at him. But he said those moccasins were not on her feet but were encased in glass, and her feet were bare: *I need my moccasins. Help me, brother.*

"When he'd explained this dream to Issup over supper at the Hot Pot on Oxford Street, he knew he shouldn't have. Issup seemed unmoved; so Orville felt both ashamed and angry. He would not mention it again for twenty years.

"'You're lucky to be rid of Canada,' Issup said. 'It's nothing—not even a real country. We should have made money off the Germans; they love wilderness places. We could have made a million.' He shrugged when Orville said he would go back.

"'It's nothing,' Issup said, 'and the women aren't that great.'

"Issup was born in Iran to an Afghan father and a Parisian mother. They fled to Kuwait after the Shah. He had studied in Canada. He had already been in trouble in France. He knew worlds Orville did not. But Orville surprised him by knowing more about London, and in fact somewhat more about ancient Persia than he did. Issup asked him to his apartment, and for some silly reason tried to sell him a fake Afghan rug, at what Orville suspected was twice the price."

John paused, glanced Cathy's way for a moment, and turned his attention back to the river, and to one who lived there, who secretly hoped Orville would be back.

"By now Brenda had read about Orville six or seven times and during these times, when she read about him, she did wonder how he was. In a bit of her make-believe he had been her boyfriend for a while. For her own life was not going great and she did have time to daydream. She too, in saving his articles, was looking for some kind of exquisiteness, some magnificence in her day-to-day life. Her husband, Junior, yelled at her, told her she was stupid, and was furious at their new position. She was now without friends, and sat most of the time alone."

So John now told Cathy something more of this Ms. Brenda Townie.

"She saw Orville once after he'd come home from a trip to Princeton, some years ago now. One morning at the farmers' market. He did not notice her, or Junior standing beside her, or the tiny infant in the baby carriage. And she pretended not to look his way, but could not help it. That very same day—the day she saw him at the farmers' market—Brenda discovered that Orville had received a 100,000-dollar grant from the Canadian Anthropological Society to do research both in the north and here. That this grant had come about because of a benefactor who had insisted that Orville MacDurmot get this money or the largesse her family gave, of some 350,000 dollars a year, would not be so easily forthcoming. Like all such societies, this one was broke. They were professors who always needed funds. The person who demanded Orville get this money, who would remain anonymous for years, was Mary Fatima Cyr. She was younger than Orville by a good deal, but as she said, 'Yes, I am younger and not half as clever—but I have a good deal more money.'

"She, Ms. Cyr, had him receive this money because she had grown up beside him, or at least close enough to be considered beside him. She also had decided something. She was, as we know, exceedingly wealthy, and did not know if she believed in God, but she felt Orville would be someone to prove God's existence one way or the other—and having heard him speak one night at a gathering in Halifax about man's continuing search for the threads and gossamers of beauty, the hope for splendour in our lives (quite the same as the talk he had given in Princeton a few months before), she decided quite quixotically that she might help him on his way. For beauty must end, Mary Cyr believed, with God if there was one, or in disaster if there was not. For certainly it did not end with Orville's psychedelic eye patches. Now she may have been very naive to think he would find Him/Her; however, it was a noble thought that came her way. She would give Orville the money. He did not believe in God, but she felt he would or might come to believe. So she had come home to take stock of things and talk her family into it. She was thought of as frivolous to the extreme, and yet in a moment's breath could mention Dante or Proust, had read Faulkner, Brontë, Anaïs Nin and Henry James. She had read the poems of Milton Acorn and the poems of Nowlan. Now she was thinking of higher things. So she would give him the money. He would discover God and all would be well. She would not tell him to discover God, but she was certain he would fairly soon.

"Of course she told no one that she was relying on Orville to discover God, except me some years later. And we do know our own Mary Cyr made many mistakes but was no one's fool. She of course was one of the Cyrs—that family of industrialists and newspapermen and -women who controlled much of our east coast to the tune of some billions. They were not always fair-minded, and not always a benefit to us. She was the daughter of one of the fallen sons. I think the Cyrs in their own way helped and hurt our society in equal measure—and that Ms. Cyr helped and harmed herself to the same degree.

"But Brenda herself had become aware that this man was very different from the boy whom they'd all got together to protect her from. Princeton, which he had recently visited as well, was to her as ethereal as a distant isle she had read about as a child. So he was different than whom she had once known. And more importantly, in a substantive way he was very different from almost everyone else she had ever known. She was not quite sure if this was a good thing—it might not be, because she had not been told one way or the other. You see, our Brenda, like millions of others, had to be told who she was.

It was as if someone had a strange name, and you were not sure if you should like him or her; and then you discovered everyone liked him or her and so you should also. But she also realized Orville just may now have a poor opinion of her.

"In fact, though it took some time, she remembered her schoolgirl friends' protection as being self-infatuated, rapacious and hateful. It came over her in a wave of self-recrimination one sleepy afternoon. She suddenly stumbled to a chair and sat as still as she ever had. Yes, weren't they her protectors as long as it thrilled them to be so, and as long as her boyfriend had a new truck to drive them around? Weren't they her protectors when she cringed at his sight, and didn't she cringe at his sight, and within his sight, in order to have those protectors? And didn't all of them in some small parcel of their souls torment him on those days when he had done nothing to her? Didn't she walk by him with a slight sway of her hips? And didn't she once tell her girlfriends that he had to go to a psychiatrist because of her? And wasn't their sense of false duty thrilling and important? And the week before he brought the ring, didn't she say, 'Don't be mean, Orville—be nice to me, please' with a sweet, almost angelic smile, while those standing behind him giggled.

"She was now realizing she'd only pretended she did not lead him on so that everyone had a duty to protect her. In fact, this sense of duty was one of the crimes Orville's thesis explored: his blossoming belief that this collective hegemony was used to define people who searched for beauty by needing to belong to others they thought of as beautiful. That, he believed, was akin to worshipping a false God—the golden calf of modern life."

"That was harsh," Cathy stated.

"It was, in fact, apocalyptic."

"And Brenda was just a young girl at that time . . . she was just a child. And he did *lose* himself in her."

"I know. I do know. Still, Brenda knew she had been weakly seduced to go along with his tormentors because she had an energetic bevy of girlfriends that were 'protecting' her. Also the belief that the boys she hung around with were *real* boys because they had no ideas, and ideas frightened the Junior Barkers of the world. This is what tormented her the most over the months and years. Junior's guffaw when the boy tripped with the Coke he had bought her. Now, as she sat in her chair that afternoon, she was rendered immobile by this self-recrimination.

"And then something quite inexplicable happened. Junior, at about this same time, the time Orville was making news, was caught by a security guard tormenting a youngster at the rink. It came because under the mask of juvenile conceit was a certain lack of being. You see, Junior was alone now. He drove a gravel truck from their pit in Derby out to a construction site. His blue eyes shone with a kind of pale malevolence. He stood over her, calling her stupid. And then there was this eight-year-old at the rink watching his older brother play in a midget tournament. The boy was sitting by himself, cheering alone."

"Just, I suppose, as my brother had often done," Cathy said.

"One day Brenda was informed that Junior had been expelled from the rink. Junior himself refused to speak about it. Took a beer and went to the basement. It was strange how Brenda, sitting alone in the kitchen, in her new grey slacks and mauve blouse, could feel his presence far down that hallway, beyond those dark cellar stairs. Worse for her, the little boy was the son of a friend of hers—a friend of them both. He was considered slow. He had a lame arm. His name was Danny.

"Junior's being expelled from the arena occurred the exact week Brenda was preparing to have her first dinner party. She wanted everything relating to this party to have the kind of perfection she had grown up to understand. When she found out about Junior tormenting this child, she was holding one of her newly unwrapped crystal water glasses in her hand, seeing how pleasantly the sunlight slanted through the glass, when the phone suddenly rang. It was the parents of the boy. She tried to apologize, she stumbled over her words, and tears came to her eyes.

"The next day people began to cancel, or simply not return her calls. Until that moment she had never realized what it was like to be truly alone."

"That is so terrible for her," Cathy said.

"Yes. Terrible. And something in her heart was broken. She walked to and from work, and never planned a dinner party again; nor for some time did she accept an invitation to one. This was the exceptional shift in her fortune. Suddenly Junior was a less-loved presence when she thought of him, and their house on a side lane off Jane Street was silent, and almost unlighted, save for the porch light that shone on grey sidewalk gravel. Only a child's swing in the yard expressed by its very presence their condition. She felt people were always looking at her; she began to have trouble sleeping and there were now pills in her cabinet drawer.

"Then one night months later—one cold night when Brenda was waiting for a gale wind to stop so she could continue walking home from her job at Stedmans, Mary Cyr, one of the wealthiest women in Canada, seemed to appear out of nowhere. Her little car (she was driving a rental, and had come home only for a week or so before she was to go back to Toronto) rounded a turn and there she was. She stopped, rolled the window down and said: 'Well, my dear, you must get in before you blow away.' And drove Brenda home.

"At one point, stopping at an overhanging street light that tossed back and forth in the wind, Mary said, 'Oh—have you heard about Mr. Orville MacDurmot? He is certainly inspirational, don't you think? Well, maybe not—I am not quite sure yet. He does have major things to say about our world; about greed and beauty—or is it beauty and greed? I am not sure if he will get it right—but he will say them anyway, won't he? Or are there two kinds of beauty—the kind we seek and the kind we should seek? I am not sure. But he will finally figure it out. Then, when he does, watch out—our people are always alarmed at new ideas. The idea that all our lives we war with each other over the importance of false beauty—while the search for true beauty goes unrecognized . . . ?' She said this partly as a statement, partly as a question, smoking a cigarette and shifting gears.

"Brenda shrugged. She did not know how best to answer. She never seemed to know how best to answer.

"So Mary Cyr continued:

"'Well, maybe they are not new ideas at all. He would be the last to say they were. But I bet he will be the first to say something important about them. You know, I saw a picture of him meeting a group of officious officials of the Anthropological Society of New York because of the Bering Sea, or some bare sea, and his so-called vital knowledge of artifacts from James Bay; and an article from Franklin's dig, which he seemed to discover in one fell breath, and I said: "If he is going about digging at this and speaking at that—and finding five-hundred-year-old spears, and some sad artifact from Franklin's expedition, he could represent us with a better suit. And get his teeth fixed"—but I know he won't get his teeth fixed. It is his statement against the world, isn't it?'

"'What is his statement?'

"'He is determined to be ugly and to not take care of himself—to frighten the wits out of young people. Or old people. He is determined to make them see his other beauty. And he drinks too much—too much.'

"Then, thinking this too superior, she added,

"'Ah, but you know—I grew up beside them when I had time— sometimes I never had the time—I was here or there about the grave old world. But I know one thing—Orville is a genius—so he should be treated like one.'

"'A genius,' Brenda whispered strangely to herself.

"Then Mary Cyr asked, while shifting the gears of her small car (she preferred and almost insisted she drive standard, even if, when renting one, they had to send to a different lot to procure it): 'But how should a genius be treated? Well, in most ways, they are treated as poorly as my family treated my mother, who God bless her was not that much of one. Orville takes time to speak to people like Ida May Crump, he brings them vegetables from his garden—trout from Aggins Pool—he walks out in secret along the shore trying to find out what it is he is trying to find. He has become obsessed with finding the smallest mite of beauty—and our reason to seek it. That is what his interest is: why our obsession with what is beauty, when did it start, what trouble it causes us and how will it all end. So I thought: "beauty—yes, we all need something of that, don't we." You see, he had so little reason to celebrate it when he was young— all the beauties did was torment him. Still, he must have needed beauty—must have longed for it at night.'

"She looked at Brenda, and said:

"'Quite like your beauty, Ms. B—we girls have got to use our beauty right. But only in the right way, right? And you are quite beautiful, you know.'

"'No,' Brenda said. 'My ears are too big.'

"'Ears, schmears,' Mary said. 'You are gorgeous and you know it.'

"Then Mary Cyr said this:

"'I am not sure if that is the beauty he is now after, though. What do you think will happen to him? The dig he wishes to do here is already being protested by the Society he belongs to, as not being sensitive to Native traditions—ah, yes, he is the one not sensitive, even when it was Chief Amos Paul who asked him to do the dig in the first place! Can one imagine? In the last ten years we have suddenly had an overabundance of sensitivity toward people we didn't even recognize as people fifty years ago. How easily people change their targets without improving their aim. Those Irish professors who teach *Dubliners* would have burned it on the street near Trinity College in 1904.'

"Then, realizing Brenda wasn't in that loop, Mary said:

"'James Joyce?' Then she said, 'Those who write about the First Nations today as wood nymphs and river gods, talking about how terribly we English treated them, would have marched them to the bloody reserves themselves a century ago, the stinking little Prairie boys who took all the right poli sci courses—don't you think?'

"But Brenda again was at a loss.

"So then Mary paused and said:

"'But now all of a sudden we do consider people, people. And poor Orville will take the brunt of our newfound sensitivity, and if anything the dig will end up helping those Native claim traditions more than it helps Orville's dig. Because, you see, Orville has discovered something about beauty—one cannot "put on" sensitivity, or concern, or equality and make it be true. That is what he spoke about— and you know how he speaks—let me tell you, as he is accustomed to do, with his head down, not looking at the audience, as if he is somewhat too introverted to be seen.'

"'I see,' Brenda said, not really seeing.

"'But he has to prove something. Something happened here and he wants to explore it. And I am giving him money to do so. My family doesn't want me to, because they think he is somewhat unstable. That is the only thing they mentioned about it: "Don't you think, Mary dear, that he is somewhat unstable?" But if it was up to my family—well, enough said. I am doing it for Chief Amos Paul—a nice old man, who is on Orville's side, but who might not live to see what Orville finds. Still, some on the reserve will do everything they can to stop his dig, to be able to build their casino. That's just my theory. What do you think? Am I right?'

"'I don't know,' Brenda whispered. She whispered as if she had been suddenly hurt, or confused. She was somehow overwhelmed and clutched a Kleenex in her hand. Her raincoat was tied with a belt and her collar was up. She had looked for the last number of minutes terrified, as if she was being interrogated about something she had failed to do—worse, she did not know until now that anyone but she even realized she had ever failed to do it.

"Mary looked over at her kindly and gave a whimsical smile.

"'Oh, never mind me. I am never sure what I am spieling off about. You know something?'

"'No, what?'

"'He doesn't know it yet—but he is deeply spiritual, and it will cause him so much torment when he declares it! Because now he says he is an atheist. He will have to fight against so much—all the modern *isms* will be thrust against him like spikes. Atheism is the new theocracy—so they will go at him—hound him to death.'

"'You think that will happen?' Brenda said, still clutching the Kleenex.

"'Wait and see,' Mary said, warming up once more. 'Well, hopefully someone will help him. I do have a crystal ball—I got my grandfather Blair to buy me one in Morocco. And let me tell you something else before I forget—oh, never mind, I have forgotten . . .'

"Then Mary, seeing Brenda's fear, continued:

"'Oh, don't mind me—I just get carried away. I had to go to Professor Milt Vale's house for supper. That's why I'm home from Toronto. Milt Vale is so devoted to women's rights it makes me gag. He has marches where he protests "rape culture." But I don't believe him. No, no, I do not. I mean, any woman who has gone through that particular jest of God does not need Professor Vale. He is so squeamish around me I want to run to the bathroom and puke. Half of these concerns, ten years ago—none of them, especially Milt Vale, would have ever thought of. They would have been the first ones to tell little-bitty titty jokes.'

"'They would?' Brenda asked in a daze. 'They did?'

"'Am I being cynical, dear? Perhaps. Perhaps they are all okay. Anyway, as you know, my family is giving money for the new library over in Fredericton' (Brenda did not know) 'and Vale is on the library committee. He seems to be on every committee there is, something like a vampire, he only needs a cape, or a bat bite; and me being invited, blah blah blah, with the president of the university, oh blah, and his stone-faced wife, blah de blah blah—and I realized how seldom Orville's name came up last night until I brought it up, and mentioned his lecture at Princeton, and his article on James Bay, and on those artifacts at the Pitt—the moccasins in the little jar, like a specimen, and how it tormented him because she was a human being like he was—he did not say with the same soul as him, but someday he will, I am sure—and then at Milt's table I recognized their treachery, and how there was real hatred and utter jealousy of Orville—then they all did the hoochie coo when I spoke of him, preening and smiling, pissing themselves, "Oh, do you know him, how wonderful, yes, yes, yes, a fine student too"—but there was great envy over how such an uncouth man from the Miramichi could gain attention.'

"'I see,' Brenda said.

"Then, in a slightly elfin way, Mary continued:

"'You know—I just had a thought—it is too bad Orville did not have a girl to love him—you know, honour and cherish and all that jazz—it might have helped him through those old dark nights. He only had those high school rascals who tormented him because of his looks. Remember that awful poem "Cyclops"—well, I don't either, but some people I know have spoken as if they do. And who wrote it? Insipid, mean little sorority girls. What veneer of feminism they shellacked themselves with. You can't hate and malign and then say you are doing it for women. Were they once your friends?—I'm not sure—but girls like that have no friends, Brenda—only contacts!'

"And she turned to Brenda with her wise, delightful eyes and smiled. Then she said:

"'But that is what propelled him to heights. It was the tyranny of those who believe in peace and love—you know, against all the wars except the ones they start themselves. What is true is that—Orville is—quite beautiful, and shouldn't have to search for it. Don't you think that is true? Take a look at him now, his face is really remark- able—really extraordinary, isn't it? Don't you think he has already been betrayed? You see Orville and his dad, Maufat, took me fishing way up on the Bartibog, and there I caught my first trout on a fly.'

"Then she said:

"'Oh, what a lovely house you have—so...compact—I should be lucky enough to have a place like this. And Junior—how is he doing now?'

"Brenda, slow in determining how the world went, now knew she had misjudged and should not have. This was the terrible mask high school girls and boys were forced to wear. In the files somewhere in the New Brunswick archives, the sentiment she had displayed toward him long ago, the teasing and feigning terror, was embedded in thesis number 8908, on the subject of evolutionary design and the author's theory of a search for beauty.

"However," John continued, "Orville never used his doctorate to teach, never put his letters behind his name. In fact, half the time he forgot that he had received it, for he never did attend any graduation."

"And Brenda?" Cathy asked.

"She went home that night to a silent house, to a kitchen bathed in street light and an immaculately kept living room with a small clock ticking on the fireplace mantel. Brenda had married Junior because she was young and did not realize he was weak. But even more alarm- ing, as the sunlight on the crystal she was holding when she received that disastrous telephone call had told her, she did not realize that she herself was weak and had mistaken something important about the world. It was beautiful if things were nice, but not too exquisite. Things that were too superb frightened her and were laughed at by Junior. There was something that would always be beyond them as a couple. But if things were pretty, that was fine. Things should be respectable. She did not want anything too audacious or even too exquisite. But if Junior and she were married, and he was working in a large construction company, that was the something nice that compelled her when she was nineteen years old. For her parents had the same vision of what splendour was as she had—to them, her splendour seemed even more broadly focused, and ripe with greater possibilities than theirs was. There was to be much more than the railway station where her daddy worked for her. But soon an election came (how she remembered that night—and the panic in her home). And soon the company, which underbid others because of cheap labour, with its new trucks and graders, was bankrupt no matter that the old man fought valiantly to keep it afloat. She took a job at Stedmans. Her life moved on, and others moved away—some went to university and reported back to her about Orville—that he was something of a heroic figure, some great protracted figure rising out of the dust of his hobbled past; and some—a few—gave her the backhanded compliment, the damning faint praise of saying, 'Well, at least you married an ordinary man, never someone who will be too well-known.'

"She began to glimpse it—and to understand it now. She cringed at these memories. She placed sweet pink ribbons in her daughter's hair. Mary Cyr the great—if I might say, the *great* Mary Cyr—told Brenda only what she already suspected. All of this prophecy by Ms. Cyr was later to figure in the life and work of your brother. The tragedy is, he would outlive Mary Cyr by five months. Both would be martyrs in the end."

4.

"FOR SOME YEARS YOUR BROTHER WAS AT HIS HEIGHT, and it was then that Brenda was most unhappy. It was more than unhappy. She was at moments desperate, because their newborn was sick. The birth had not been difficult, and she had been proud and lucky to have such a beautiful child. But at nine months they discovered Kitty had a blood disease where her body was unable to balance itself to produce red blood cells. They tried steroids, and other methods, and then turned to blood transfusions when the child was two years of age.

"She read about this man, even though she might not have wanted to. At that same time, in South Africa, Orville was part of a dig at a site of early humans dating back well over a million years. It also allowed him a good deal of prestige. So now she heard that he lived for a while in Italy and Spain on that prestige, teaching part-time at the American universities there."

"So that made him talked-about?"

"It did—it did—our own paper *finally* did a feature article on his work."

John continued with this:

"Why was there a search for magnificence in the ochre-coloured past? Why would there be such a search when the rover travelled across the ochre-coloured landscape of Mars?"

"It is strange that when he was immune to it, people took him as ordinary."

"Yes, he became a fanatic only when finally, one bright morning a few years back, he linked much of this search to sin. And the Golden Calf as a replacement of God. Then he became a fanatic—and perhaps he was," John said. "I remember someone saying to me the day your brother was arrested: 'No wonder he murdered—look at what he talked about—sacrifices—and then he went to live in a monastery—that gave it all away.' I remember others at Jean's Restaurant exalting that they had caught him, I remember men in baseball caps, their faces middle-aged yet still youthful as boys, laughing at it all— saying they had always known he was deranged. Saying they had chased him away in high school because he bothered the girls."

"Yes—it seemed so likely even I believed it! Even I no longer believed him," Cathy said.

John paused and went downstairs for a cigarette. Then he went and bought Cathy a coffee and brought it back. He put down the paper napkins and the coffee and the donut with the peculiarity of a policeman treating a witness.

He smiled slightly, at how all of this looked, rubbed his eyes and sat down again.

"After Orville came home from Europe he bought himself that grand place here. It was old, but sound. And after a few months he began to do the research on the beach for Amos Paul. Sometimes Amos would arrive and walk down to the beach, sit on a log and speak to him. He would bat the deer flies away with his hat, and move his right hand over the little hair he had left on his head and smile as he spoke. Orville was doing something only he and Amos seemed to know about. Amos was old, and his legs teetered when he walked, and one day he walked into the woods to get a drink of water from the spring, and then went to his truck.

"'I don't think I will get back,' he said. 'My, my it is a beautiful place. But you are here—and as long as you are here I am certain things will get solved.'

"'I will solve it,' Orville stated. 'I intend to. It is along this two- or three-mile stretch—but I can only work on it now and again—now and again.' Then he added:

"'I make a solemn promise to you.'

"It was the last time he saw the man he admired more than almost any other, the old Micmac Chief, Amos Paul.

"So Orville started a project that would last until today. Now this caused a great problem for other members of the band. Not right away, not constantly either, but in the last few years. They wanted to claim the site—but, as Mary Cyr said, for a casino. To them it was the perfect setting. Yet if Orville discovered what he was searching for and the spot became a historical or sacred site, as Amos Paul and some of the Elders wanted, they would not get their casino built."

"So they wanted the dig stopped."

"Yes. But on he went. Looking for something Chief Amos Paul told him had happened years ago. But all of that began some time after he arrived home. At first there were months and months that passed in relative harmony."

"What changed it all?"

"One day, shortly after Orville came home from teaching in Europe, feeling the strange sensation of being back home again, he met the girl, Gaby May Crump. She was standing on the side of the road being teased by a group of children from her school. She simply stood there as they called her names. When she was pushed down he turned toward them and waved his arms and they scattered like little birds, all screeching and yelling that the boogeyman was back. He picked her up and brushed off her coat and asked who she was:

"'I'm Gaby,' she said.

"'Well, Gaby, you must come to my house and have a piece of pie.'

"'Can I have one for my brothers too?'

"'Yes, yes—your brothers too!' he said.

"The little children stood behind the trees watching him, and some of them yelled to her, 'He's going to kill you!' and then, all screaming again, they ran like hell down the dirt side road.

"He brought her to his house. He cleaned her jacket of mud. He gave her pie, and wrapped some for Gaby to take home to her brothers. He began to tutor her that winter in math and geography. He told her fairy tales, and read to her the Oscar Wilde story about the Prince and the Sparrow. She and he became friends. He then drove up to town, bringing her with him on Saturday afternoons. He bought her new dresses and other clothes, while people at the stores looked oddly and pensively on. It did not occur to him why. He then took her one early spring day to a sports store and bought her a fishing rod and a little pink bicycle. He had a love for her almost like she was his own child, and that would last as well—until his death. Or, if one believes his idea of love, forever. He brought things for her brothers, Pete and Tom, as well, and visited their house on many occasions. So many months went by where he cared much for this little child."

"But we do know how that love for her would look—today, also. Their concerned looks—that he ignored?"

"Yes—and now I believe, though I did not believe initially, that all of this was so innocent he did not even recognize why those looks came. He had come back to this great dark land after travelling alone across the world, so his work was mentioned in Singapore and

Cape Town. But he had always been alone, and he now had a little friend to love. You remember how few friends he'd had to love before. But yes, one must not seem to be that way with little girls in tow, even if one is not. He tried to get the mother, Ida, help with social services and gave her money. He took her to detox on two occasions, and stayed with the children when she was there."

Then, before Cathy could speak, John continued:

"When he first took possession of the house, he met Ms. Eunice Wise. Ms. Wise owned the property to his west. After a number of months Gaby May became a concern for her. Not at first, of course; at first she had no use whatsoever for the child or her brothers—the girl and the boys were nuisances because they had snuck into her back-yard and had stolen apples. Once Gaby and her brothers got into her pantry and took some peanut butter. Gaby had sat her brothers down at the pantry table and made them sandwiches. So Eunice was seen chasing them from the pantry with a big half-rotted stick, yelling. She telephoned the police on the children, said they were breaking and entering, and made it known with her first *No Trespassing* sign that she wanted nothing to do with the neighbours."

"But later?" Cathy asked.

"But later, of course, Gaby became her symbol of grievance. That is, after her and Orville's falling out. The concern seemed non-personal for a long time; just a straightforward concern of a good lady for a little underprivileged child, whom she believed, at any rate, that this man seemed to obsess over."

"Eunice was our early enemy—our next-door enemy," Cathy reiterated now, "and she always smelled so nice. Once I wanted to stand close to her because of how nice and soapy she smelled—but she shooed me away as if I was a fly. She looked upon us as hobos, I suppose—not unlike our Gaby. Orville must have known this in a second."

"But you see, after years of her thinking nothing of him, your brother's name appeared in the *Globe and Mail*—one bright and fine October day when all the birches outside her bay window shimmered and stirred with an autumnal burst—and she was a little upset about it. Why hadn't she noticed his brilliance before anyone else? I don't think she quite expected it."

"And then a few years later there he was, moving into the great old house across the long, high field of hay," Cathy whispered. "Right next to her."

"Yes, for two days she watched him move in from her upstairs window, looking across at him. Nothing is that calculated, but soon she was at his door, coming to help him paint and decorate. She carried her ideas of paint samples in a bright-green leather bag, and lay them on the kitchen table; stood beside him as he pondered them, pointing to her favourites with a brightly polished fingernail. Yet in a way there was a certain position of possessiveness over him, and strangely his house. Orville may have been flattered by all of this attention. That is what she initially wrote in her Moleskine notebook about him: *I have found a like-minded fellow here—and he is Orville MacDurmot, who spoke at Princeton with all the Princetonians, and of course you don't get there by accident. I knew him when he was a boy. He often came over to ask me questions about history and archeology. I think he wanted to find things buried in the earth. And he knew I would know all about it. So he still relies on me—he said just the other night when I was sitting beside him: You are the only friend I have.*"

"That's somewhat enthusiastic," Cathy replied.

"For a year or more after he bought the house next to her, Eunice was at his side, and very animated. It was as if they were dating. Or she might have supposed they were. I believe she was in some ways courting him—perhaps not in a certified way, but in a way that was clandestine. The idea of being clandestine works very well between men and women; a touch of the arm, or a glance across a room, a look of dismay when your object is leaving. Sitting beside your office-mate instead of your husband or wife and pretending it is innocent. This is the clandestine courting of beauty one to another that, because of previous obligation, can never be fulfilled—or when it is, often leads to a disaster of sorts."

"Why could it not be fulfilled with them?" Cathy asked.

"Because she misread him entirely, misread the world he was in, what he was trying to achieve, entirely—she was alive in her own fantastic fiction where she had placed him beside her. But it was his fault as well. So often he never told her why he believed in things. For instance, she began to mock the religious desperately when she was with him, in the pandering, fashionable way many have, and he was silent. Yes, religion was a bust, he knew that—men in cheap suits parading their virtues, holding their Bibles, priests who spoke with inflated piety, prissing and pretense—he understood it all—understood it at its very core—at its very shameful core—and you see he realized, by her ordinary trained slurs, that Eunice herself did not understand it. She only repeated what she assumed she had to understand. In fact, she was bigoted by cultural submission. But she had not really understood much about it at all."

"He wasn't what she thought?"

"He tried desperately to ignore her trained arrogance. He had not ignored anything like this since high school, and had promised himself he never would again. But he did try desperately to ignore her presumptions, the very standard affiliations her views put her in. She wanted to laugh, and have him laugh with her, at the people they grew up beside. It is what the American professor would do, the Upper Canadians would do—and she, progressive, wanted to do it too. This is what he caught in her quiet suggestions.

"He had to travel to Moncton once to appear on television to talk about certain things found along the Bay of Fundy. She went with him. They drove back at night through the Rogersville highway, along the dark road, and she sat close to him with her arm up on his shoulder as he drove, and spoke about joining marches for women's rights. That is: if he could forgo his nature—if he could just once not rely so much on his intuition—he could have someone, like other people did.

"'Don't you just hate this place?' she said one time. 'How the ignorant are so ungrateful and the sensitive, like you and me, have to put up with it?'

"Listening to these remarks, one day quite suddenly something struck him and he did ask her—though he regretted doing so—'Why did you break up with Calvin?'

"'My husband never understood my passion for justice,' she said, 'and for liberation.'

"He turned and looked at her in a strange way.

"'What passion for justice, exactly—and what liberation? Perhaps I don't understand.'

"'Well, your passions too,' she said lightly. 'The passion for freedom expressed by me over these last months!'

"He picked up a stick and walked along with it, tapping it before him, as if thinking.

"'Much like the young women I once knew in university?'

"'Well—yes, of course.'

"'And so do you think they are liberated—I mean actually liberated?'

"'Of course—they have taken all the right steps.' And she smiled at him as she marched along.

He was about to say, 'But I do not think so at all. I think they are mimics, many of them,' but held his tongue.

"'Besides,' she added, 'Calvin is nothing—just a fisherman!'

"It was turning cold, night was coming on. Suddenly he was sad. And looking down at her little multicoloured hat, with her tiny ears poking out, there might have been much to be sad about. He was distressed, and blamed himself. He went home. He started to tremble; for some reason he actually trembled. He felt he had lost a true friend, but in fact he had never had one. The worst of it was, she had called the police on little Gaby May Crump and her brothers, and had just told him so. There was glee in her voice when she explained to him why she had. He took a pint of rum and drank it slowly, staring at the fire in the wood stove.

"So that afternoon he did something that would become a trademark of his life—he closed all the drapes to his house and sat in the darkness. Yet when he went out late in the day she was standing beside him again. She took his arm and smiled up at him.

"'I brought you a bottle of pickles,' she said. 'And you did promise me a trip to Quebec City.'

"'Yes, I did say that—well, thank you,' he answered.

"But after this he determined to stay away from her. It was not that he felt he was better than she. He felt he had struggled against those in high school and university girls and saw in her the same measure against which he had struggled. He did not answer the door, and did not stir much from the rooms upstairs. One evening, about a week or so later, she saw him outside and ran toward him with a paper in her gloved right hand. She asked him to sign a petition for First Nations fishing rights. It was during the fishing dispute, which made the national news, when RCMP officers were positioned between white and First Nations lobstermen. Eunice's petition might have been a slight gambit to get back at her ex-husband—he was one of the white fishermen who had had his own traps pulled and destroyed by First Nations warriors. So she brought the petition to him."

"Oh—she made a pass—with her concern?"

"Yes. I think she was somewhat desperate to make a reconnection. But it may have been just a moment too soon, or too late. Perhaps she realized he was different than she had assumed, and needed a prop they both could lean upon. Yet the fantasy for companionship was about to dissolve. To have him she must show him how considerate she was willing to be on behalf of others. This is what she thought would be the best net."

"All this time she had misread him?"

"He wanted nothing to do with her petition. Like most people he didn't care who fished where, and agreed that the First Nations had a right to fish. He also believed the whites had rights as well, and they too must be protected. And he had his views on how the insular and silly Canadian media, knowing little or nothing of fishing, viewed it; that they, the media, so urbane and so sure of themselves, must always portray us as bigoted whites from the boonies. He reflected on what she had said about the people here during their walks. Shuddering at the position both of them were now faced with, he would not sign.

"Besides, he never forgot something that had happened here long ago. In 1967, two First Nations boys were hiking home in December. People on the roadway would not let these boys inside their homes because they were First Nations. He thought of this. This was truly one of the shameful events upon our river. As he thought of this, he realized they must have passed her family's door that night as well. He tried to be polite about the petition and simply said, 'No, thanks—it's not for me.' Three times. The First Nations boys died that night in the cold. And this is another thing—often, when Orville mentioned First Nations people, he said 'Indian'—because that is how he had learned to refer to them—each time he did so, she quickly and gently corrected him. 'First Nations,' she would whisper. There was a fury in him when angry and now this fury was about to come out.

"She came over for the third time in two days with her petition; he was in his yard, and as she spoke he continued to work. He had been trying to avoid her, and he was again drinking. Again rum, again there was a flat coldness in the air. Again he should not have spoken. He picked up a shovel and started digging along the side of the ditch, throwing snow and dirt across from her, which she looked at as she spoke."

"This was the start of the redoubt you spoke about?"

"Yes—it was. So he looked up at her and asked: 'Why?'

"'Why what, my dear?' she said.

"'Why do you love the Indians—excuse me—First Nations?' he asked.

"'That's a strange question—because they have suffered so much. You work for them as well.'

"He leaned on his shovel for a moment and looked at her.

"'No—I work for myself alone. Besides, many people have suffered here—many of us have suffered here—many more will—and people don't seem to care so much for them. Little Gaby May suffers a good deal. She is tiny and weak and brilliant, and lives only to be kind. She is partially deaf and made fun of in school. Yet you are not kind to her. I remember how you chased Gaby away with a stick. She was trying to get a few apples. You don't even eat the apples, Eunice—they could rot on your trees and you wouldn't care. You must know into what circumstances she was born. Be kind to her, and I will love you! Go to her now and ask for forgiveness from her mother, whom you ridicule, and I will hug you and take you to Quebec City.'

"'My my,' Eunice said. 'Have we been drinking, Mr. MacDurmot?'

"'Why take it out on children? Do you know that Gaby's brother Tom, the older boy, is First Nations—but that his father ignores him, yet goes to meetings speaking about injustices? Tom could die of injustice and his father, who ignores him, would still go to his meetings. I am just speaking the truth. Please, if you won't love her, leave Gaby May Crump alone.'

"Orville paused for a moment and then thought of something else, and his face flushed with rum:

"'Besides, you are often a little too quick to call the police. Years ago, when I was a boy snaring rabbits, you called the police because I snared at the back end of your field. You watched me coming out of the woods with two rabbits and went and phoned them. I remember that day in February as if it was yesterday. It was the day after the night I got lost. I needed those rabbits to sell so I could help Mom buy me a new pair of boots. Besides, I do remember the times you did make fun of me.'

"'I never in my life made fun of anyone.'

"'Oh, it doesn't matter. It never mattered. But so, so many did. You were just one. I don't care as much as people think. But I never forget—and I know our family had very little—I know all that—but you told me that day that I stank of rabbit. You yelled at me from the side of the barn and said: "Is that all your family eats? You're just like the Indians. My father says that people who eat wild game are just the stupid and ignorant ones like the MacDurmots—like the MacDurmots!" I remember how, that long-ago day, I came close to tears as I stood in the snow, because you looked so special and so nice, and even beautiful, and I did not look nice or beautiful at all. So your beauty made me think I was in the wrong. I thought that for a long time—that beauty like yours put me in the wrong.

"'But now that I had an idiotic article on me in *Maclean's* magazine or somewhere else, I don't stink—I probably stink now more than ever. Besides—you do not know why I was in Jordan.'

"'Pardon me?'

"'Well, you say I am your friend—you say, "Oh look, I can paint your cupboards in a colour that will pop"—but you don't know why I was in Jordan. And I won't tell you—I thought a week or so ago I might relate it all to you—what I do, why I read what I read, how I realize there are more good people than bad, but all races can be both good and bad, how the best parts of philosophy say the same thing—but you talked over everything I said and kept interrupting me. So why was I in Jordan? I began to mention it to you—but you didn't listen.'

"She reached to take his arm and then stopped. 'We have much in common—we both love art and culture and dislike hypocrisy.'

"He gave her a pained expression. He staggered a little, he felt the rum in his blood. 'I don't have anything in common with you. You are like the women that continually speak of being progressive and are trapped in their own rancour. That is what I know now. Yesterday I thought to myself: "Your father is greedy, your mother is greedy—your entire family is greedy—but worst of all, you're greedy." I think you wanted me to make love to you, but it would cost me too much.'

"'I never in my life—in my entire life. You are drunk, sir—you are drunk.'

"'I think this is what the last few months have been about,' he said, digging in the cold dirt again. 'I am drunk—and I see clearly.'

"'I now know you are a bad man,' she said; she was frustrated, and bright and clear tears gleamed in her eyes, along her small, whitened wrinkles, and her thin red lips closed tightly.

"'Absolutely—a very bad man. So get the hell off my land,' he said.

"'Let's get this straight,' Eunice said, 'I am not on your land. You are doing research on my land. I was allowing it out of the *goodness* of my heart. And the First Nations band knows that! But now—ha, now I see. You are a bigot.' And she laughed in hilarity through her tears.

"'Of course I am a bigot—a racist too.'

"'Yes—I see it now—yes, I see it. You are a degenerate racist! Wait until I tell people what a racist you are.'

"'Of course, run and tell, Eunice—if you were really seeking justice you would have seen beyond your nose years ago. Your nose is on my land. Your right foot is on my land!' he said, simply tossing some cold dirt over her black leather knee-high boot.

"She walked back to her beautiful country home filled with the decorative sadness of Canadiana, took off her new hat and soft suede gloves, walked on her nylon-covered feet into the back bedroom and, still wearing her pale-blue all-weather coat, lay on the bed and tucked her legs up under her, staring at the shelf of books, her little well-meaning petition in her hand.

"She was not so enthused about his dig anymore, and just after the fishing dispute she had a meeting with Chief Bedham. He sat behind his desk wearing a multicoloured vest, his face impassive, his hands folded in front of him.

"'Amos was senile,' Bedham said, 'an old goat—and spent tons of our money on this. But Amos is gone now—and we want the dig to stop. We always thought the Wises would come to some accommodation with the band over this land, since we know you yourself are progressive. Orville, however, thinks he owns it, and he is using our money and we want it back.'

"So Eunice sent a letter to Orville later that week, a cease and desist order. He paid no attention to it. Then a note came from a lawyer asking him to stop the dig immediately. Again he ignored it, and travelled away. A month or so later Orville came back home from Washington State. She saw his light go on in that bleak house across the field, saw him a few days later shingling the back porch wall—saw him running some electrical wire to his attic. Saw him walking along the top of his roof with that electrical wire on a spool behind him as if he didn't have a care in the world. She wrote all of this in her Moleskine notebook. How that terrible man had come home.

"Then, on a quiet night quite by accident, she saw, in the pinkish warm twilight, with the roadway covered in rosy spring mud, little Gaby May, degenerate Ida May's girl, run up to Orville's house—a house no one ever visited—and go inside, through the back porch door, wearing leggings and a thin dress, see-through in the last of the late-spring sunlight. Eunice slipped from her house, slipped too across the field and, hiding by a lumber cut, looked hard toward the kitchen window with the binoculars she used to watch birds.

"Gaby May was sitting at the kitchen table eating a bowl of ice cream. Orville was with this child, alone. She knew the house, of course—there was a small guest bedroom just off the kitchen. In fact, she had helped decorate that room.

"So—well, now she knew! He had bought Gaby clothes, bought her a fishing rod. Why hadn't Eunice noticed any of this before? What was wrong with her? And no one cared for children as much as she! There was something going on with that child—that is why Orville mentioned her. That is why he wanted Eunice to have nothing to do with the Crumps. He was afraid she would catch on. Now, it was her turn. So," John said, "she printed out a letter to the RCMP. It took her most of the evening. She kept an eye on his yard; she watched the child leave. She pressed the button as she pressed her lips, and the letter was printed, and that did seem to her to be a relief. This became the first of some thirty letters we were to receive about Orville MacDurmot from her over the next ten or twelve years. Add that to the visits we received from her brother about Orville, the complaints about the dig we received from the reserve—he had become a major grievance to the whole roadway. He did have Old Amos's contract, though, that allowed him to dig. This would meander through the courts over those years as well, and he would have to appear at various times.

"In this first letter Ms. Eunice Wise wrote that she had been concerned about the plight of the children who lived on the shore road. That she often felt misery over their plight. That she did have training in social work and had helped youngsters most of her life. That concerned people knew this. That she belonged to four organizations, including the Writers' Union of Canada. That showed her concern, she divulged. Toward girls especially. The ones like Autumn Henderson and Gaby May Crump. Now she believed Orville had enticed this young child from down on that road—a girl just beginning her menses (her word)—into the house. And he had taken her in his car—and in fact he let her sit on his lap and drive his car in the back field one day. That he felt he had licence because he was well-known and she was nothing but a little tragic ragamuffin."

"I see," Cathy said, trying to take it all in. "It would be an awful sight." But she wasn't sure what awful sight was being revealed to her—the one of Eunice in triumph mailing the letter or the one where huge, lumbering Orville sat a little child on his knee.

"Her brother did visit us to corroborate some of this, and he had words with Orville on a few occasions; but since her brother worked in Belledune, and lived with his wife there, the fight was mainly between Eunice and Orville."

"Is that her brother Lesley?"

"Yes."

"The first boy who ever kissed me, at the church picnic fish tank when I was twelve. I sometimes wondered where he went . . . "

"Well, you are much better off now." John smiled.

5.

"WHAT ABOUT GABY—THAT GIRL? TELL ME SOMETHING about her," Cathy asked.

"She was Ida May Crump's child—and you and I know about Ida May. She had a poverty that Eunice or we ourselves could not, did not know. We remember her when you and I were seventeen. Her blond Norwegian hair in the sun, her high boots with the silver eighteenth-century buckles and the red socks that came up over them, the blue eyes, her terribly pale face and a mouth that always had an eagerness in it. A kind of willingness or lasciviousness about it. She hiked to the dances in a woolen skirt and those high boots in the wintertime, and at times drank in the pit props with the men years ago. Her children were born without fathers. And the rumour started over the next while that your brother was taking advantage of Gaby because his looks were so horrid he could not have a real relationship. This is the rumour mill of rural Canada, the glut of Tim Hortons gossip. Those men who ride the buses from work and besmirch the secretaries. The gossip against Orville had the kind of hilarious beauty that gossip brings—it was soon all that was spoken about. But it was filled with darkness, as all gossip is. He received that letter from the other end of the world that I have already mentioned from Han Woo Lee, a kind man whom he used to take labs with back in university: *You wrote about a little girl, a little girl who is poor, and bright, and you are helping her—that is delightful—but you must not be alone in your house with her—I think it is bad policy. Remember she is a child of 11 years old. ICE CREAM, ORVILLE—LITTLE GIRL!!!! If you must tutor her in math, go to a neutral place; have another adult present. Your friend, Han Woo.*

"I am not even sure if Orville caught on," John said. "Still, our Mr. Han Woo Lee was to be proven right. A few days later the police visited to ask him about it. The young officer, well fit and smiling, during that bright spring day with his uniform impeccable, said in a kind of homey, well-intentioned way, after Orville explained that yes, Gaby May had been in his house after dark on numerous occasions because he had been tutoring her:

"'Is that what you call it, tutoring? You don't want to be called a dirty old man, do you, Orv, a well-known man like you written up in papers and everything?' And he slapped Orville on the side of the arm, to make him understand that this advice was friendly, but also needed. Then he frowned slightly to show that there was an import to his words that were not to be taken in jest. 'No more tutoring,' he said.

"Eunice was dressed in a blue skirt and tam when the police, a male and female officer, first came to speak with her, before the male officer drove over to speak with him. Just perhaps, she wanted to convey how dissimilar she was, how much more cultured, than the people she was valiantly trying to protect.

"'Yes,' she informed them, her eyes slightly deflected, looking at one of her blue painted birdhouses on the fence post beyond, 'You might be able to talk to him. There is something very odd about him—*his leanings are always toward the dead.* You do not notice it until you live beside him. Once a good person lives beside him, you begin to get a sensation of otherness—something wrong.'

"So the male police officer left her and drove toward his house on that glorious day in late spring. Orville could see Eunice standing on her porch steps looking his way, with the female officer beside her. He couldn't quite catch how much Eunice—a woman who almost always told people she had taken two courses at university, and an advanced writing course from Dr. Milt Vale—assumed him an enemy now.

"Now, however, the police told him not to bother Gaby or her family—that they did not want to hear any more complaints. They did not want him down near Ida May Crump's. There was no reason for him to hang around with a little girl. They said he was rich. Well, in a way he was. They said he was well-known, so if he wanted he could see to it that he was satisfied by buying from certain escorts what he needed. This was humiliating, of course. In fact, he had no idea there was a person called an *escort*. It was all strikingly new to him. And yet the young male police needed to caution him that there were no allowances for awkward male appetites. Orville was stunned, immobile, tragic and guilty.

"So Orville froze the next time he saw Gaby May. She approached his lane, and turned up his drive. He went inside and hid as she tapped on the door; he stood like Frankenstein's creature at the apex of his struggle. He would not see Gaby May again, he would not have a friend. Eunice, I suppose, did not know of the damage she had caused. Nor would she for many years to come.

"Gaby May stood at the door, saying:

"'Sir—sir—you were going to take me fishing?' Finally, in the way he did things, the way your brother always was, he came out and told her to go home and never come back into his yard—that he did not want to see her anymore. She looked at him, confused, then, sorrowful and frightened, she turned and ran down the lane, now and again stopping and looking behind her."

"He very rarely mentioned anything to me about her," Cathy said.

"He tried never to mention the child again. Not for ten years. Ms. Wise, until last week, believed impeccably in her frugal sense of justice. But she could never match one of his articles on the search for beauty in the earth. I suppose she knows that now."

"But is this what gave her an opportunity to be hired at the paper—to become one of the columnists?" Cathy asked.

"She was hired by the publisher, yes, who said he needed a progressive voice to fit the times we lived in."

"It takes me back to the clubhouse, with their select group."

"You do know it is still there—that little clubhouse? Tool shed, actually, now. You see, I had to go into it once to check the paint on a whim—and there on the back wall were the names of the members of her club, fading away in the sunlight coming through the side window."

"Ah, well," Cathy said. "It was not such a big thing, was it?"

"No, but to a child who was refused entrance like you were, it must have been terrible."

He told her that Orville began to drink at Dunn's, and slept in the back room of that place down near Ida May's. He had wrestling contests with the Dunn brothers, and usually won. They would knock each other around in the spring mud. For a while he did nothing but that. So other men from downriver would come to try to throw Orville, and bets were made. And Orville took on all comers. They went to the very shore where he was doing his digs, and he would toss men left and right. As if getting back at the world. But one night, some say he was picked up by a stranger and thrown against Old Face rock. That it created a small fissure in some shale rock that would be most important later.

"Then the stranger left, and they never discovered his name. But the mud on Orville's jacket from near the rock, and the broken tooth, said something—it may have been Mallory, the old man who lived far down on the Crockery—but no one believed that. He would have been too old.

"Like Jacob wrestling with an angel against the black midnight sky! Orville, old Mrs. Dunn said, had wrestled with someone who would later become Jesus Christ. And she told him so, and laughed when he got red in the face.

"He drank wine that night and, stripping off his clothes, swam from the shore to the island and back. It was in May, just after ice breakup, as if he was tempting God to kill him. He came back robust and half-crazed. (This was in fact not such a strange thing for many of the half-mad men from the Miramichi to do.) He built a fire on the shore, ten feet high, and was like a gargantuan shadow at dawn. No one went near him after this. But no one thought he was sane anymore. He was very capable of murder, that was sure. And already those he told to go to hell were piling up. People were frightened of him; Eunice was already being proven right.

"Then he went away for almost another year, and came home in the fall. He didn't work that year, and to this day no one knew where he was. He arrived on the train and walked the thirteen miles home.

"And this is when something else happened because of Orville's blood type," John said.

"Because of what?"

"Because he had type O—and was a universal blood donor. This is very important, especially for children. It was something that very few in town knew. However, some doctors here knew he was a universal. That is, when he came home after that extended time away, it seemed like a godsend to one family."

"What family?"

"One night late in October of that year, just the day after he arrived home, Dr. Sara Robb knocked on Orville's door. He had just returned and she was fortunate to have found him. She didn't enter his house, she simply asked: 'I hate to bother you, but I was told you were a universal. When did you last give? A child needs a transfusion—she has just come in—we had a power outage here, our blood bank is in short supply, so if you could possibly help—you don't have a phone?'

"'No,' he said, 'I had one for a year or two but no one phoned.'

"'And you don't often answer your door.'

"'Not often,' he said.

"'Why?'

"'I'm never sure I want to see who is there.'

"'So when is the last time you gave blood?'

"'Oh, a month ago or more.'"

"But that was not true, was it?" Cathy asked.

"In fact, he had wandered to a hospital in East Montreal and had given blood the night before. He was often doing this in strange places and in strange manners. If Sara had known this she would never have allowed him to give blood that night. But he did not tell her and she did not have time to check.

"Without another sound, without acknowledging anything, he took his coat and left with her into the wind and rain; the wind caused the rain to wash in silvery-white sheets along the river, and it seemed to explode along the surface of the road so that small shards of rainbows came up from the fumes of gas, and lights along the highway flickered off and on, and golden-coloured trees flailed against one another above them. Leaves, golden and orange, billowed and sank and rose in the wind, and crossed the hood of the bright little car. The lights of the hospital shimmered in the rain and the dark flumes of the great mill still swelled. When he entered he saw the child.

"The little blond-headed girl was sitting on a gurney in a bright-yellow rain jacket, red rain boots with a picture of Mickey Mouse on the front of each pretty boot and a yellow fisherman's rain cap. Her tiny fingernails were painted red. Her golden necklace held a golden cross. Her small earlobes were pierced and she wore silver earrings. She was adorned to be loved; and adorned too to be kept safe. But she was so pale and tiny when he saw her. There was an *otherworldliness* about her. And he noticed this otherworldliness in a flash of recognition. It was the recollection of dying children he had seen in other places at other times when he had tried to help.

"He himself was put into a service room behind a light-green curtain, and was there when Junior and Brenda arrived a few moments later. It was fortunate for Orville that they had been filling out forms. He saw them as they rushed to their little girl. Or not rushed, not both of them; Junior held back just a bit, not for lack of love but in deference to the child's mother, and in a way as a very subtle signal that he now needed to make something up to her. Orville, through the curtain, could see the beauty she still had, and how she held it over him like a spell. He had not known it was their little girl. He was weak with anguish; a feeling like an electric current flashed through him. He did not know if he could breathe. When the nurse asked if he wished to introduce himself, he said, 'No—I do not want them to know who I am, please.'

"He gave the blood using his right arm (he had used his left in Montreal). He then left without a word. He went home, sat at the table, stared around the kitchen at the flood of soft yellow light and the walnut cupboards, and suddenly collapsed on his kitchen floor, too weak to get to the stairs. The door was left open and wind howled about him; red leaves blew in through the kitchen and rested on him."

"Did Brenda discover who it was?"

"Yes—both of them did, a few weeks later. Both of them were stunned by this. So the teasing Junior did against him, the operations he enacted to shame those less than him, were now understood in a much graver light by Brenda herself.

"Yes, she could go to church, and so she did. She sat in the pew and stared at the altar, the bright sunlight streaming in across the marble floor, the statue of Madonna and child. All this silent beauty. She only hoped God knew why she was there. But now, after this, she said a prayer for your brother; she would say, 'Dear Mary, mother of God, make him believe in you—he is far too sorrowful not to—and I may have created some of that sorrow.'

"As far as Orville was concerned at that time, he had gone about as far away from penance from God as you might imagine. But in fact every investigation into the beauty of the past, of certain philosophers, ended without the ultimate answer he was searching for. And this answer always came to an end without the last door being opened. And beyond that door he knew—he felt he knew—was *goodness, kindness and simplicity*—and that's the beauty he was seeking; it was nothing else than that.

"He had prayed for God to change his looks during those days with Brenda Townie and God had not done so. He was by himself at the fort he had built. He demanded a miracle, and he said in a prayer that he would give God a chance.

"'Change what you can change. I am not asking for much—just make me like other people.'

"On the way out the next morning he passed Glidden's Pool at the narrows of Arron Brook. He was in trepidation. He thought he had felt something the night before; some change had come over him. He had felt it. He was hoping against hope, as they say. There at that pool, deep and clear, he slowly looked at his reflection. Alas, there was no change. In fact, in a startled way, he felt he looked more terrible. That day he began to dislike himself for praying, to see himself as a rube for doing so, for he realized he was far brighter than the priest or his parents. He went to Father Lacey one day before Father Lacey died and told him how useless he felt prayer was. The old priest said: 'But, Orv, your prayer has already been answered. God has answered it—in a short time you will recognize it all. He gave you that affliction to teach the world something the world needs to understand. That is the real miracle. You will see—and that girl whom you like—that girl will someday know who you are.' That was years before he saw her on the night he gave blood."

"And he did not speak to Brenda that night he gave blood?"

"He left that night without letting them know he was even there. However, Junior and Brenda were told about Orville donating blood. The nurse monitoring their child at a checkup a few weeks later, unaware of the relationship they had with the man, innocently and happily said: 'Well, she has the blood of a genius in her now—anyways that's what some says that he is—that man Orville MacDurmot—he was the lad that come up from his house to give her blood when all our power was out that night and we were on our generator, so she'll do well.'

"Junior said nothing. But he glanced at Brenda suddenly. He brought the child home and watched over her—for some sign. He did not know what sign. He bought her new clothes, new shoes and a new velvet dress. He watched Brenda as well—for a sign that she was disappointed in him. Then, out of the blue, Brenda was told something. It came on the day of her daughter's birthday. I had to go to the house because Junior had been accused of stealing from the accounts payable department of the company he and his father now worked for.

"This company where they worked was the leftover dregs of their old company, and Junior felt entitled to go in and out of the office and knew the combination of the safe. That surreptitious privilege died hard. He had wanted to buy a new car; he went for a loan and was turned down. They had accumulated far too much debt. So, as in years gone by, he took the money from the safe on a night in late April. Then he tried to say it was his money and still his father's firm.

"I was the one called to go to his house one evening in early May and speak to him. Brenda sat at the kitchen table in a new skirt and blouse, with a small red watch strap on her wrist and earrings that cast a shadow on her cheeks. The child was sitting in her high chair, her hair done in blond curls and her fingernails painted. Her luxurious hair lay to her shoulders.

"Brenda seemed overwhelmed at this news. It had come upon her so, so abruptly that her husband was weak, and a boy. Suddenly, when the house was most silent and I was taking my notes, I looked up.

"'It isn't your money, Junior,' she whispered. 'It is not our money anymore.'

"She raised a decorated Saint James china teacup to her mouth, her pale white hand shaking. He received a suspended sentence and community service.

"Later in the year, sometime in November, Orville came back home after being in France. He bought an Arabian horse that he rode up and down the lanes on quiet afternoons. But there was something even more significant that happened at that time. Some little thing."

He paused, saw that Cathy did not understand, and then quickly continued:

"Sometime after he came home, he got the first note—slim, to be sure—of recognition, and, yeah, of apology without saying so, from Brenda. It was a remarkable surprise to him, almost prophetic in some way. It came in the way of a little homemade card (Brenda was good with crafts), inserted into a small pink envelope: *Good job, thanks so much—do you remember me?—Brenda.*

"That was all. That was it. Unblemished but unremarkable, and a mistake to think it any more than what it might be."

"'Good job, thanks so much—do you remember me?'" Cathy said.

"Yes," John said. "The sadness of this moment should not be lost on those who have struggled so hard against so much. Looking at his reflection in the mirror, he smashed it with his fist. Blood and glass spattered everywhere. No wonder the boys and girls at Princeton laughed. He would have laughed too."

There was a pause. John saw Cathy looking at him, as the shadows lengthened and the bookcases behind her seemed muted. The snow fell still and he smiled gently at a woman he once loved.

"Was that the Christmas that the fire happened?" Cathy asked quickly, to deflect the stare.

"It was that Christmas," John answered, quickly too. "The small house just off the trail that led to both the beach and the Wises' property. It was Orville's house. He had lived there for a year or so before he bought his large house. So then he had rented it for next to nothing to a young man. The fire started in that small house down on his shore road at about five in the morning on December 24. It was a solid, crystal-clear night with a feeling that the dark would break into a glorious new day. Orville was not asleep but going over his maps in his study. He was searching for something down there—down on that shore. There was no tree in his house, no Christmas decorations, not one. The rest of the roadway, the villages and town, were asleep in the cold. He had been back home just a while, but seeing the smoke and flames, knew there were children inside—one was Gaby May. The children had gone to live with this man, an uncle, after Ida May Crump had died. Their uncle was someone else important to my investigation—he was the writer I mentioned earlier—the writer who had at one time hitchhiked to those meetings.

"The sky was clear and full of stars, but they were fading in the early hours, and snowbanks buckled along the side of the snowy lane; the old Jeep itself smelled of gas because Orville had rehooked the gas tank and it sat in the back seat. We know it was useless, of course. Fire like this is always so damned impertinent, like someone keeping a secret from you—and suddenly at the right moment he or she whom you trusted to be loyal breaks into a wild, shameless dance. That wild dance was suddenly pouring out of the roof. It had started from a hot plate that was left on in the back room, a curtain and an old pressboard wall.

"He broke open the door and climbed in—using the extinguisher he climbed the staircase, though it was burning—the children were all huddled in one room—but smoke was already overcoming them. Gaby May was on the bed, her face buried in a pillow; Tom and Pete, who'd already had one operation on his heart, were trying to smash open the back room's boarded-up window. Orville rushed in and picked them all up—Tom in his left arm, Gaby and Pete in his right. He came down the stairs with the beams burning above him, sparks falling onto his head and neck, and the spectre of flames, purple and blue, licking across the floor.

"Orville tried to go back in, but, though he had put some of the fire out, he did not manage to save the man; the man had managed to huddle the kids to the back room because he couldn't get them down the stairs. Then he'd gone out to the hall to retrieve his tin box and did not manage to get back. Orville did manage to haul him along the floor to the outside and administer CPR. But it was too late. The man was thin, and looked quite a bit older than his years. Orville's hair was singed, and his right arm was burned and required dressing.

"The young man was dead. But everyone knew Orville had helped save three children from a fire. The town whispered about doing something grand for him. However, Gaby May, the little girl who had come for ice cream, was one of the children he had saved. The idea that he had bought her a Christmas present and could not give it to her—the house was his, why was he awake when the fire started? So questions were bound to be asked. Everyone hesitated, and though he was commended in the news, his heroics were lessened by rumour of what might have happened."

"Damn it," Cathy said. "How does it all seem clearer to me now?"

"Clearer?"

"How gossip kills."

———

John shifted his focus to something else. Something he had been leading up to for the last two hours. It was a seismic shift, or a cosmic one—but one that sooner or later would close the gap.

"So now I will mention that boy from the Miramichi—" John said, "the one with his pockets stuffed with poems as he hitchhiked through the dark. The one who was the uncle of those children, and who became their stepdad after Ida died. He was writing a novel about downriver people, a novel about the world he had grown up in—he was writing a novel about you, your family, Gaby May and her family. But he wanted the last chapters to deal with Orville MacDurmot himself. He was fascinated by the publicity that often surrounded brave men and women in order to destroy them, and he must have felt Orville in some way fit."

"How so?"

"In his novel certain people strive to attain victimhood—and victimhood, such as Eunice's, allows for grand talk about 'reconciliation.' But the victims, many of them mimics, do not ever want reconciliation. They need revenge and retribution. So they find a *scapegoat* who they maintain is the cause of their victimhood, and try through rumour and insinuation to destroy him or her. Quite like they did with Mary Cyr in Mexico. So too with your brother, Orville. The book is a chronicle of how someone is singled out. Orville was violent, had been in fights, he drank alone and told people to go to blazes. But he also loved deeply. But over time the love he had for the world did not matter. Just as the rescue of Gaby and Pete and Tom did not matter.

"You see, he had pushed some girl at university who asked him if all the people from the Miramichi looked and walked like he did. Like an ape. She did it on a dare and thought others would laugh. He pushed her over a table.

"That was the second sign of his hatred. The rumour about him festered until Gaby May. Then the rumour eviscerates the scapegoat until the victim is sated and can pretend it is in the name of healing and reconciliation. That, Cathy my dear, is what this Miramichi writer knew and wrote; and in a strange way he too became the scapegoat, the victim of his own book."

"So it is about us?" Cathy said.

"Oh, yes. Now, for simplicity's sake I will use the names of the real people when I speak of his book's characters—it wasn't that hard to decipher who was who—the names in the book were slightly altered, of course; Orville's affliction too is slightly altered—but if I use the name Gaby May, I will use her name for herself and for the character who intrepidly represents her in this writer's pages.

"Now when Gaby visited Orville she lived as we know with her alcoholic mother, Ida. And Orville had clumsily tried to help. That, we know, was when the rumour against him was first initiated. The scar on his face in the sunlight as he stood beside her, his great arm over her shoulder as they walked, what else could it mean? We know now it meant gentle kindness and love—but to those soured in their own souls, what did it mean?

"Tom, the older brother, was bigger and surer, and tougher, and did not seem to covet attention from anyone. Pete, the younger, was sickly, with a very weak heart. We know that Gaby May and her brothers lived with their mother on the shore road, but after her mother died they went to live with this writer."

"You have found out all of this for us," Cathy whispered.

"Yes," John said, quickly and without ceremony. "Eunice owned the beautiful three-storey Brock home. She was alone, and the years had made her bitter, or more bitter than she had intended to become with the years. But your brother's house, a three-storey house as well, brooding with no one in it for weeks on end, a constant object of oppression, sat to her left. Winter storms would pummel it—great waves of drifting snow would lash up to its dark windows. All would be gloomy and hidden. She would see his figure walking knee-high in the snow, not even bothering to shovel. Then he would be gone, for a week, two, three or more. She kept watch, she kept vigil. Christmas of that year—the fire. Then all went dark and he was gone again. Eunice walked many times down the lane to witness the remnants of the burned house. She took photos of it from every possible angle. She wrote a column about it—where she spoke of the children, of the house being 'unsafe.'"

"So what happened?"

"We had an investigation. The police and the fire marshal came to the conclusion that it was an accident. The Christmas tree, a hot plate left close to it, and the back wall, all caught up in the disaster. The house was bulldozed away when Orville came back in the spring. And the effects of that young man who died in the fire were given to the children. The children were sent away. The boys to foster homes, Gaby May to a convent. Eunice silently watched all of this. Orville ignored her. Except one cold morning, when she came out to prune the naked branches of her grapevines, he was standing there.

"'There is something around here,' he said. 'I wouldn't travel alone to the beach—just for your safety!'

"'Why?'

"He shrugged.

"'Something—maybe a sick bear out of its den—I'm not sure—I think it is not a bear. Perhaps a large cat. I just saw it only for a second. And I saw tracks of a large cat before—and years ago. But just don't wander to the shore until I find out. And keep your dog in.'

"'Why not wander to the shore? Why keep my dog in?'

"'You do not want you or it to end up dead, do you?' Orville said.

"'That's a ploy. And you're drinking again. I can smell it. What is it you're up to, for my dog to sniff it out?' she said triumphantly.

"'Suit yourself,' he said.

"'What are you up to down there?' she asked again, walking boldly up to him.

"'If it was any of your business I would tell you.' He turned to leave her.

"'Well, at least Gaby was taken away from you. From what you wanted from her—thank God I got that done.'

"He turned back, looked at her, his face raw, his hands suddenly clenched into hard fists.

"'If you mention her again—if you dare mention her—'

"'You will what? What—say what you will do!'

"He turned away, into the wind, his face sideways against the cold.

"So three hours later she contacted the police. She told us she had been recently threatened.

"'Was it a verbal threat?'

"'I should say so!' she said.

"'Do you want to issue a complaint?'

"'Well, sir, why do you think I have phoned?'

"So they went and spoke to Orville again. The police officer told him if he could not get along with his neighbours—he used the plural—the police could not be sent forward every two days. The officer went away. Eunice wanted him to be taken to jail.

"So later that week she telephoned a lawyer in Chatham. Over the next few weeks he investigated how much land she should have actually gotten with the purchase of the Brock house. The next week she moved Orville's picket. She then moved the picket again when he put it back. She then sued him for that house that had burned. That went on for some time. Then she put a hammock between two of his trees. He took it down, folded it in two and placed it on her patio chair.

"She then, on Bedham's insistence, hired the First Nations man Danny John to put it up again. This was a signal to Orville about her concern for First Nations rights. Shortly after this the priest came to see him, having sucked up the gossip about the case.

"'You do not intend violence?' the priest asked, looking as startled as he was supposed to at something he, as a good man, found hard to fathom. For he too believed only in male violence and, like so many priests, believed the church now needed to conform to the new social-justice agenda. The day was suddenly freezing cold, but Orville stood outside in his shirtsleeves and spoke quite calmly.

"Orville knew a certain kind of bogusness had risen viciously against him.

"'You do not intend violence here?' the priest asked, shocked at the very question he was asking.

"'Why would anyone think so?' Orville answered. 'Why do you say I am violent?'

"'Because people say you are that type of man,' the priest said, and in spite of himself he smiled knowingly as he spoke. Orville reflected on where he had seen that type of smile and realized it was from the young police officer when he came to the house concerned over Gaby May.

"'Of course I am a man of violence; so are many you laud. You yourself seem to have taken up a very convenient and rather weight-less cross,' he said.

"Taken aback at this insult the priest drove back to the church, the small, dark car immaculately kept with the cross hanging from the inside mirror.

"The lawsuit over the burned house had its first court date. No real determination could be made about an 1874 land deed and a 1937 one. But Eunice owned something else by then."

Cathy looked up quickly at him.

"Oh—the empathy of the town. She suddenly became interested in archeology too. She would never be a 'white interloper,' she wrote. But she was an archeologist, she told people, and had a 'real feel for it.' 'I was the first to understand our First Nations brothers' archeo-logical finds,' she said. 'And they are mind-boggling.'

"It must have been excruciating for your brother, who deeply cared for First Nations men and women all his life, to have to listen to this, but he did listen to it without comment. The idea that she could usurp him, take over his very life, was indeed an obscenely pleasant one to her, as she went for her walks with her group called Wise Ears, picked up stones, pretending they were arrowheads, and recorded birds in spring, dressed in her calf-high boots and splendid rainwear. She had eight or nine devotees, and Orville was alone."

"She wanted to replace him?"

"Oh, so much so that when he left for Austria one day, she had a metal gate put across that lane where the burned house once stood. He would not be allowed to ever again dig along that shore. In fact, she wrote in the paper that it was her dig.

"'I will begin to dig away,' she wrote. 'And I have the conscience of the town on my side.'

"He was gone a fortnight. And two days after he came home, he took his horse and his rifle to go hunting. When he came to this new gate he turned the horse and started up toward her house. She was sitting out upon an Adirondack chair, looking down toward him. The air was thin, the leaves were almost gone—the sky was painfully blue.

"Suddenly he put the horse into a canter, coming right toward her porch. She stood as he raised his rifle and fired, and she screamed. It was done so quickly she had no chance to move. She was at his mercy."

"What in God's name—he tried to murder her over a lane?" Cathy asked.

"Everyone thought so. He was put in handcuffs outside his own house after he had put his horse away—he refused to stop brushing it and then phoned his father to take care of it. He was put in jail for the entire weekend—not let out until after the hearing. He sat in the cell without saying a word.

"Then Orville finally spoke. He told the hearing that there was a large cat on the porch behind her. When he'd turned the horse away from the gate to find another path down toward the shore, he saw it crouched down near the wooden table, and he acted. He was unsure himself that it was not a mirage. It was neither a bobcat nor a lynx. He believed it was an Eastern panther—an animal supposed to be extinct. It was a good head higher than a lynx and at least a foot longer. And it had what neither bobcat nor lynx had—a tail. It was also completely black.

"When Eunice stood, she had picked up her dog. And this is what he was certain the cat had followed onto the porch. In a split second he realized that if it lunged it would break Eunice's neck—she was, he said, such a wispy, uneventful little thing. He fired as it crouched ready to pounce, the bullet hitting above its head. It turned and jumped away and was gone. Nor did he wish to kill such a magnificent animal, and was glad it bounded away. Eunice fell backward and tipped the chair over. The little dog howled. It was the same creature he had warned her about. The mythical cat that, many people said, still existed here in New Brunswick.

"So that was his reasoning. And it seemed a desperate criminal ploy to evoke a mirage.

"They then called Bobby Beansworth—the chief forester, who had been at university the same time Orville was. He was delighted by this mismatch. Here was this famous man he could outshine in front of his own town. He stood and read, as if from a proclamation, and it was the New Brunswick proclamation of dissuasion about this mythical cat:

"'No such creature exists any longer in this province,' he told the court as loudly as he felt decorum allowed. He did not look at Orville as he spoke. 'The topography has changed,' he said. 'Our woodland species have altered.' He cleared his throat: 'No woodland caribou exists here now, nor does the wolverine any longer, nor the cougar and nor does the Eastern panther.' He then exclaimed, 'So if it was a cat— it may have been, well, anything from a small bobcat to a housecat.'"

"He smiled when he said 'housecat.' Orville himself said nothing. He simply sniffed and planted his feet more firmly where he stood.

"They took him back to his cell. The cops were very formal. But they could not help but warn him that he might get five years in jail. Maybe even six. Then some other police came to look at him. They spoke about the time he would get. Some said five, others said six. They told him no fame constituted a right to shoot people. Eunice was a Wise—a very popular family. She did not remember him warning her. Besides, people were saying he had used old Amos Paul to get money underhandedly. So what did he say to that? Hmm, what did he say? Hmm?

"He said nothing.

"But then Packet Terri from upriver, who had tramped the woods here for forty years, came to an additional hearing they decided to have the next morning. Packet told them he too had seen signs of this enormous cat on a half-dozen occasions. He told the court on Wednesday of that week that there were big cats like that, that both Daniel Ward and his grandfather Simon Terri had seen one, that no forester, especially Beansworth, would admit to anything that wasn't sanctioned by the province, but he, Packet Terri, was under no such stricture or obligation. That both the Eastern panther and cougar still existed here. And with that he placed a bag of scat on the table. It was frozen in time, scat dropped years before but collected by his grandfather, and placed in the freezer as evidence to wayward skeptics.

"'This comes from no bobcat, and no housecat—it comes, this scat, from a large cat—and if they were here in the sixties they are here now!'

"Orville repeated that it was a very large cat—larger than a bobcat or a lynx, both of which he had seen before. He said that when he fired it took a leap and was gone into the thicket behind Eunice's house. That he had no intention of harming the woman, only of protecting her.

"'There are no prints,' they said.

"'If it was a lynx or bobcat there would have been, because neither would have been able to leap so wide a distance,' Orville answered.

"'Certainly,' Packet said, 'doesn't it seem logical, if he wished to kill Eunice, he would have walked to the house and have taken better aim?'

"Orville was finally charged with unlawful and reckless discharge of a firearm. He was then sentenced to three months in jail. But the judge actually believed him. And so he was released after one. Still, they took his rifles away for fifteen months. He had to retake his safety course. He went back to work. He in fact (I believe this now) had saved her life. But to most, it was cut-and-dried—he was antagonistic to her because of her concern over Gaby May."

John lighted a cigarette and changed direction all of a sudden:

"Now Orville had a record as a bad man; it had crept up to this, and would never be relinquished until today. People from Blackville to Tabusintac spoke of him as a bad man. He drank alone, and people began to notice him as trouble. He was looked upon as wild and irrational. And people shied away from him on any street he walked. His attributes were strange, and his victories unusual, his ruthless nature understood. Your father and mother were harangued at times, when someone who had had a run-in with him decided to take umbrage. They did not deserve it, as you know."

"I know," Cathy said. "I know."

"So let us return to the man from Illinois, Professor Milt Vale. For maybe he holds the key to all of this—to the great valleys he and his friend Eunice entered together."

"What key is that?" Cathy asked. "And what valleys?"

"Envy, ambition, greed, covetousness and pettiness," John answered. "But envy most of all."

"Envy?"

"That's what this sin boils down to."

"And what sin is that?"

"Oh," John said, very softly, "murder. It all ended in murder."

"Murder?"

"Eunice had been hired on at the paper. She decided to do an exposé on the sexual abuse of young girls from poor families. She did not mention Gaby May by name. One day Orville, meeting her at the new communal mailboxes, blurted: 'You have cornered the market. But I do have a fear.'

"'Oh, what would that be, Mr. MacDurmot?' She glared boldly up at him. 'You stay away from me—people said one hundred feet—one hundred feet, remember, it's what people said. Get back—go, get back!'

"Orville shrugged, saying, 'If ever a young girl is raped or dies, it will be a sacred plum for you. And you will make sure it furthers your ambition in some way. You will not love her, will contort in your columns to use her, just like all your columns unjustly use people—use the First Nations, use women, and use children—all to seem brave without being so—anyway, that is my fear.'

"'You are an evil man—and often drunk.' She walked away. For now, at any rate, she still had the pen. And she was right about one thing. He had slipped and fallen away from what he wanted to be. He was often drunk."

"So after Orville's rebuke, our Eunice turned to Professor Milt Vale? Is that what she did?" Cathy asked.

John paused, looked at his notes:

"Yes, my dear, she did."

6.

SO JOHN THEN BEGAN THE STORY OF THE OUTSTANDING university professor Dr. Milt Vale and that regressive young writer from the Miramichi.

"The sadness of our Dr. Milt Vale over the years could have all been measured by the look he gave Orville MacDurmot that night he met him walking across the university grounds. The dark, grave look, almost accusatory, had come about because of that young writer from the Miramichi. The writer had said something very telling to Vale (or I do think it was telling) about his self-published book—a book Vale had been so proud of. It was a novel describing a rural woman liberated by an affair, and how she finally, with the help of a professor, was able to overcome the chains her husband had put upon her psyche.

"Vale liked the feel of the book, its white-and-black cover—its Fitzgeraldian 189 pages, slim but sure, and its picture of Milt on the back cover, sitting forward, looking quite austere, his goatee with a knowing touch of grey, and a pipe in his mouth. But the writer from our river thought the book was utterly silly; the sex, which was often and explicit, silly and boring.

"'Rubbish,' he said. 'Mindless rubbish.'

"Then this boy had gone away the morning after that remark and was not heard of for years. That is *years*. He was almost totally forgotten about. He lived in poverty and took care of his little niece and nephews after Ida May Crump died. It was not always easy. He had terrible fights with the older boy—one time they almost came to blows—so people might say they did not love. Like Rilke says, it is something irony will never have an answer for. That is, they loved each other deeply. Then one day this troublesome writer sent our professor Vale his novel, asking him to send it to a publisher—if he thought it 'good enough'—*if not, burn the bastard and I won't say a word. But you are the only one I can think of to send it to.*

"He wrote this last line in the letter (this was the age when letters were still written by men of the old world) with a flourish.

"But the Miramichi boy did not send the entire novel—he sent about eighty-five percent. (Nor, of course, did he send the final version.) That is what is so important in my investigation. The rest of the book he held back at the last minute to improve. He wanted the last pages to end the arc of the hero's life with an impact he felt he had not yet given. He decided that after the Christmas holiday he would send the very last chapters along, with the note he had composed in his head: *You thought it was finished, but here is the real ending.*"

"He wanted to impress?"

"Yes. I think he did. That is, the novel may have seemed finished on first reading, but the last pages now fully completed it, in a graver, more joyful way than was imagined. I believe he finished the very last pages two nights later. He had written the book here—but no one, least of all Orville, knew he was the writer from the Miramichi—the one Vale said he had mentored. Eunice knew—but for years she was allowed to tell herself she did not know him. She hated him because he had insulted Vale—and besides, he was no-account. Nothing of his had been published but one story. Some years before she had passed him by in the snow, when he was hiking to one of those literary meetings. He was stranded on the road with poems in his pocket. Afterward he worked in isolation, and only to Vale he sent this book: *My 'masterpiece,'* he wrote laughingly.

"It might or might not have been. Still, he was well aware of it being a fairly good book. If Vale liked the eighty-five percent, he would, the writer hoped, like the rest. The initial reaction would be important to him. It would give him courage to send the rest. If he had not sent this book Orville might still be alive—in fact, certainly would be; the child who was murdered would be as well—and there might never have been a moment where I began to wrestle with my past to seek a kind of absolution from your family."

"It is strange that all of this has taken place," Cathy said, her body suddenly shivering.

"The Miramichier was naive enough to think Vale actually might help him. He in fact had always been quite civil to Vale—except for that night he had made the remarks. The boy had ridiculed Vale's first novel, had done it at the very launch party for the book. What he had said was this: that the rural heroine who had the liberating affair with the professor was a dupe, a kind of mark that intellectual men for years pretended to understand, and was far more exploited by the concerned professor then by her husband, who once struck her.

"'The novel is perfumed, but it doesn't smell right!' the boy said.

"Women who stood beside Vale listened in silence, while some looked pale. Eunice Wise was one of these women. Hungover, his hand shaking, the boy sent a note of apology the next afternoon:

I am truly truly truly truly sorry—Truly!!
Yours truly

"Over time the book, the launch party, the boy were forgotten. But one valuable connection was made. Vale received a brilliant fan letter about this early novel from Ms. Eunice Wise. She saw herself as the book's heroine, for she had, she said, taken all the same steps in order to free herself from a disaster. Thank God she had done so.

"Then, after years of no one hearing from that writer, a manuscript arrived at the university's English department office. It was addressed to Professor Milt Vale.

"It arrived three days before Christmas, when there should be some jubilation about things arriving—that is, it arrived probably two days before that writer 'of some promise' (a statement I read about the only story he had ever published) was killed in that house fire where Orville had saved those children. By some fluke, the tin box with all the writer's work remained unscathed.

"I found out," John continued, "that after Ida went into the hospital, the writer took the children in. In fact, a local man—her last boyfriend, a man who lived with her while they drank her welfare cheque each month—brought them to him, holding Gaby by one hand and carrying their suitcases in the other—one under each arm, and one in his right fist. He waited a moment, thinking he would get a tremendous lecture for having sopped up so much of the welfare cheques in liquor, but received none at all. In his pocket was twenty dollars he had received from Ida for the children. He told himself that he had forgotten about it, told himself that he was in a desperate fog after he left the hospital, and did not remember that he had zipped it up carefully in his pocket. He spent it later that night at the tavern. Cursing later and getting into a fight out on the snowy white street, yelling that he would defend Ida's honour to the death.

"The writer brought the children in and sat them down at the table for lunch. There were times the writer had to scrape together enough to buy milk. And they did love him—all of this was in his book.

"Milt Vale would someday claim that book, and what is worse, by implication their adoption, without suffering a night of pain on their behalf. He would assume the reins of the book, and those children, and therefore take credit for what he had never done. Vale would never hunt moose—he would have been terrified to hear a bull moose grunt or a cow moose bellow—but in the book written about a wild world he did not know, he would claim to have hunted them down himself. Milt Vale would do all that. He would never hunt or fish with his boys, but in the book he did. I mean, he would *steal* all of that, he would filch compassion and love and sacrifice for those children from a writer who published one short story, wrote one true work of genius and died broke at thirty-five.

"It is certainly strange that if he had lived perhaps his work would not have come true," Cathy said, taking a guess.

"There is a scene in this novel that happened to the writer's adopted children early in their life, when Ida was still alive. One day at school, because of some bossy children, Gaby discovered who her biological father was. She decided to telephone him, and ask if he was going to buy her brothers and her a Christmas present. They had had no Christmas presents yet and it was December 24. She was told at school the day before that he would buy them one present because he was her dad. And she came home with this in mind. Not so much for her but for her brothers.

"When she had entered her house the previous day it was bare, except for a charity box delivered by Sydney Henderson, with a turkey and candy canes, and on the old table sat Ida's bottle of Hermit wine. Gaby knew all about Hermit wine and what it did. That night, Ida danced in the snowstorm with two strange men, who came into the house in their lumbering boots and told her, Gaby, that she was pretty. One said he could give her a beard burn—he would rub her face until it tingled with his beard. She could smell wine and mustard and some wood chips on his clothes. And the next day she had a red rash on her cheek, and remembered how the man had tried to touch her through her little thin dress. She'd wiggled away from him and run to the back of the next room and hid behind a couch, with an old newspaper over her, shivering and praying, and Ida and the man got into a fight in the kitchen. The torment and the night seemed to last forever.

"But she woke up early and helped the boys put up the tree. Then she decided she would telephone her dad—her real dad. At first he told her he wasn't, but when she said, 'But it's me—little Gaby May,' he finally started to sob.

"'Daddy—might you get us one Christmas present?' she whispered. But just then a woman came to the phone. And she said:

"'Youse all would have been better 'borted.'

"Then Gaby heard her father in the background saying:

"'Hang up—hang up—leave her alone, hang it up.'

"Gaby was about eight or nine years old at that time, about two years before she met Orville, four years before she went to live with that writer. This would be the harshest part of her life. Milt Vale had not adopted children, had not walked through the dark to get them medicine, had never struggled to buy them milk. He would never have to. He and Eunice would smugly claim them, and all those nights of happiness and sorrow, from Toronto to New York—"

John paused. He himself seemed quite emotional as he spoke. Not because this writer did walk through the snow to buy, with his last bit of money, medicine to help Tom with an earache on a dark February night—but that Milt Vale, who lived a life of disengaged privilege and smug, cherished certainty about all the proper values, would steal, claim and use it, as he said, from Toronto to New York.

"Ida Crump died; her small world included three rooms; her small victories included handmade cushions, a small flower garden, winning 203 dollars on a 50/50 draw. So the writer took her children in.

"Some years passed and then a strange event occurred. A novel arrived in a manila envelope addressed to Milt Vale. And a few days later Vale learned that this boy who had so frustrated and belittled his own life had died in a house fire down on the cold Miramichi Bay. But the novel had arrived.

"He thought it was all some drastic mistake. For a long time he could not believe it. For the first time in years he felt a weight off his back. Yes, there was no more boy from the terrible Miramichi to bother him—he was free.

"Such was Professor Milt Vale. The person we must now begin to view.

"He locked the manuscript away and got on with his life. He wore his suits, and lifts on his shoes.

"He was going to have a short story accepted in *Brick* magazine. Some famous Upper Canadian writer said she did enjoy his work. So the manuscript sat alone—long after that boy's funeral. And no one came to claim it or speak about it—and nothing was known of it. No one knew *he* had written it. It came as a bolt of lightning to Vale himself—that this boy whom he had never forgotten about had written a book, and no one knew but him!

"Certainly Ida May's children knew nothing much about it either. They were divvied up and parcelled out to the world—and now were living in different parts of the province. They would not hear of all the machinations of this novel until much later. Orville tried in vain to find out where Gaby May was, but would not be told because of what many thought had already transpired. But certainly he brooded and worried about her. That was certain.

"Vale told no one about the manuscript. He listened to broadcasts by the vast, sweeping CBC that he found so pleasurable to listen to, where so many of our broad-minded reporters live in like-minded cubby holes for thirty years. He read literary journals. He tried to start another story, about the plight of a professor always willing to do the right thing for women. He would forget about that boy, he decided. However, he knew something: the boy had died. He was buried in a small grave at the very end of an old graveyard, with a simple stone that gave his name.

"So Vale decided to learn more about him. He discovered that whoever this writer was, he was not thought of as being someone important. Still, Vale was the one who had studied; he was the one who took the Iowa writers' course, he had done his doctorate on John Updike. He was the one who had done all the right things, wrote in exactly the right way. So the talent was supposed to be his. It was supposed to be, but it wasn't."

John told Cathy he'd discovered that everything, in fact, was "supposed" to be Milt's. He had an ego that was at once charming and malicious. Once he followed a friend of his to Virginia, arrived there unannounced on the same day his friend did (this was after the Iowa writers' course).

He was there to try to get a job, because his friend had one. His friend was at first amused and then saddened by it all; heard Milt in his heavy shoes, his face all shiny, walking the hallways, slipping in to talk to professors, denouncing the very friend he had come to visit.

Milt, John told her, had met his wife there, in one of the small rooms, where she was reading Walt Whitman. To her, seven years younger, he was caring, gentlemanly and cultured. He'd had a poem accepted in *Midland Review*. She fell in love.

"So he came north, started a writer's group. And then this rude boy entered his life with a batch of poems written in pencil, with the sky gone slate grey in the night. Now the novel was in his possession.

"So," John continued, "finally, one December day almost a year after the fire, Milt wrote Orville MacDurmot a letter, the letter I found, asking simply how this boy was doing. Was he still okay, and if so, wish him well.

"But Professor Vale knew at this time that that boy had died?" Cathy said.

"Oh, yes—he knew he was wishing well to a ghost, and he needed to believe even to himself that he did not know this. Orville wrote Vale that very night. The man had died tragically and he was sorry. That there was a tin box with some things in it that was not destroyed in the fire, which he thought might have gone to the girl Gaby, and that the children had been separated across the province. Then he added: *It is strange that you would ask after him, for I think of him often—I believe he was a decent human being. Was he a student of yours?* He sent this by email to Milt's university office so Milt could then email him back.

"And our man Milt wrote back: *Thanks for the note. Yes, a student for a short time—but he was something of a drifter. I am sorry we couldn't have been more favourable, and helped him get his B.Ed. Do you know what was inside the tin box? Perhaps, if we look through it, we can know more about his last days?*

"Such was the answer he wrote to Orville MacDurmot some years ago, in an email, and such was the harried career of your brother that he really did not put two and two together. The written letter I discovered when I opened the desk; the emails I found when a tech I hired discovered your brother's password sometime later. Your poor brother's password was *123456*.

"*I do not know where the tin box is,* Orville wrote back. *I do think it might be with the girl Gaby May—but am not at all sure what would be in it. I liked him. One evening—and it seemed the only time—we found each other on a blowdown late on a November afternoon, with the last light of afternoon against the trees, and the roadway hushed and snow beginning to fall. We had both been hunting the same large buck, which had driven three does before him most of the day. We found each other watching the same rut mark, and he spoke to me of things of the earth, of wild places that I too knew so well in my heart.*

"Still, Orville was busy with his own obsessions, and did not connect what he might have. Therefore this novel, simply called *Darkness*, which no one seemed to know about, sat in limbo for almost two years after the young man's death. And each night Milt went to bed and wondered about that tin box.

"'Too bad he went back to save it,' he thought, thinking not that the man had lost his life doing so, but that he had done so—that is, saved it.

"'Ah—what a loss,' he blurted.

"He became concerned that Orville would know what was in this tin box. But he hesitated to ask again. And then all of a sudden one day, sitting in his home study, looking at one of his letter openers, he remembered that a very good friend of his lived beside Orville MacDurmot. So he telephoned Eunice and asked her if she had any poems for a small anthology of women's poetry he might be editing.

"So it was at this time that Eunice and Vale became closer. She began to send him her poems, and her photography. He would write her compliments about both. He did not wish to inquire about the tin box too, too much. He did, however, mention it to Eunice once or twice. Just in passing.

"'Do you think Orville might have it in his house?' he asked.

"'I am not sure what that man would or would not have,' she said.

"'I know—he's a liar, and a fraud,' he would say whenever she told him how much trouble Orville caused people, forgetting how kind Orville had been to him, how courteous he had been when he answered his emails.

"'He will be discovered for the lout he is,' she answered.

"'Yes—but I wonder about the tin box,' he said.

"'What is this all about?' she said one afternoon when he phoned her unexpectedly. The sharpness of tone showed she was no pushover.

"'Oh, nothing at all,' he said, and laughed. 'It's just when Orville was at university I was working on a book—and handed him some valuable papers in a tin box that my honour students helped me research—now I wonder about them. I'd like them back—they are a draft of a novel.'

"'Oh—well, if you want me to lower myself to ask him . . . ?'

"'No, no—don't ever ask him about it—promise me?'

"'Okay.'

"'Promise—I don't want him knowing what I do!' Milt said. When he was sure she wouldn't tell anyone, that this was another secret against Orville she could hold, he laughed, told a joke—a very bad joke—and hung up. But he was in anguish.

"He let it go and decided not to think of it for a time. For if he mentioned it too much it might give something away. Still, during all this time he pretended in that elusive way people have when we want to con ourselves that his motives were more ambiguous than they were. That is, he believed he had no idea why he was thinking so much about the tin box.

"Then suddenly, as if he could not help himself, he began to implore Eunice to help him locate it, and one day he got a phone call from her. She told him excitedly—and still out of breath—that she had snuck into Orville's house.

"'The bastard is away,' she said. Yes, she had become a spy. It seemed she was ecstatic over all of this. She explained what it was she'd worn—how her acumen of shading allowed her shaded entry into his domain.

"'Yes,' she said, 'I was in his house, I know it like the back of my hand—I found nothing, but the attic is locked—locked for now but it won't be always—what do you want me to do next? I could get my brother to do something if you want. He could break into that attic in a second. Orville is frightened of him. I taught him about so much he uses in archeology. I'd love to get into his desk too, get his notes to find out what he is doing on the shore down there—what would you like my brother to do?'

"Suddenly he trembled at her enthusiasm. His voice grew panicky.

"'Nothing—you have done what you can—this is just between us?'

"'Of course!'

"'I mean just between us!'

"'I said of course!'

"'Don't mention it to your brother—'

"'Oh—sure, no problem,' she said.

"But there was an uncomfortable silence for a long moment. Then she hung up.

"It was off-putting that he had taken her into his confidence. So he waited another month or so. He did not mention the tin box to her again, but spoke of her photography, and how sensitive her pictures were.

"'Beautiful and sensitive—with a real good knack,' he said.

"Then one day after two years of obsessing about it all, and after developing an ulcer, where at times he looked as pale as a vampire and had problems blinking, Vale unlocked the drawer and took the young man's novel out. He was conscious of a strange, sweet smell. It overcame him, as if he could feel and taste an actual physical aspect of greatness. Certain sounds seemed to swell in his ear and then dissipate. There was the entrapped scent of the lilac that had been in this young writer's desk, where the manuscript had sat. The manuscript seemed to meet one with a smell of oak and lavender, a sweet longing and timeless trace of an age that was fast passing into gentle obscurity; the unending beauty of a lonely summer road, of days in small houses with the ticking of an alarm clock somewhere upstairs. He remembered too what it was Orville wrote about sitting on the windfall late on a November afternoon, with the hushed dark along the trees and a snow beginning to fall.

"So then he opened it. He left it on an old desk in the basement and rushed upstairs. He sat alone in his living room until well after dark. He missed his class with his second-year students and didn't notice the time. The clock ticked and the night shadows passed gently over the room. Finally he got up and went for a long walk, down to the cathedral. A cat scurried across the road.

"'Someday I'll show you. You just wait and see,' he thought when he saw the cat.

"For some reason he began to run, with his galoshes flapping.

"The next day when he came downstairs to light a fire in the stove, he glanced at the first paragraph, clasping his hands together because they were cold, his tall, thin body making a kind of hooked shadow along the left wall; he was in a way a grey eminence.

"He began to read it, standing over it clasping his hands, his shoulders hunched—and discovering, though it was very poorly written, it was also something else. It was in some way a work of brilliance.

"Could or should he send it to a publisher? There were reasons to do so. One was to prove to people here, especially those who thought he was a fraud, like the writer-in-residence whom he detested almost as much as he detested this fellow, that he had discovered a rare talent. He would be able to say to that overbearing poet: 'Look at whom I have discovered!' He could say that and he would triumph in a way against all those who had shamed him. Still, he worried."

"So he procrastinated?" Cathy asked.

"So he procrastinated, telling himself he was always doing so for a good reason. The reason being, he told himself, he did not want to embarrass the memory of this young man after death by sending away such a bad novel. 'I will not embarrass his memory'—this is what he told himself, late in the day after classes were over and he was walking home in the snow. The snow that always fell in this terrible country, in this pitiless backward country, where one could see the treeline of desperate people.

"Finally, almost two years after he got the book, after he had written to Orville so he would be certain of the boy's death, after he had questioned Eunice a little, after she had searched Orville's house, and after he had heard nothing more about the tin box, he rashly put the manuscript into an envelope and sent the novel to an editor. *Take a look at this nonsense, Duffy—what do you think? I am not sure it has any merit whatsoever . . . ?*

"He attached no name to it, and no heading. For no particular reason—it simply happened that he had used the cover page to light a fire the first day he had started to read it, and so now simply placed a blank page over it. And though he tried to tag on a finish himself, he couldn't muster it. The subsequent pages had the title *DARKNESS* at the top.

"'It will never be taken,' he decided. He hoped it would not be considered much of anything. He prayed it would not be. But when he tried to sleep at night the beautifully haphazard structure, the defiant love in the words, troubled him. What troubled him is that the boy was able to write about murder and rape, and death, and the goodness of children, the tenderness, pettiness, sorrow and genius of women, the violent nature of men who were actually willing to die for a stranger—and all of it with love, without once needing to use popular progressive wisdom or social-justice theory.

"Still, Vale had almost forgotten it, as the days turned into weeks, when a phone call over four months later exhibited a greatly enthusiastic and humble response, and an offer of a contract, and a 35,000 dollar advance.

"'The little girl phoning to ask for a Christmas present for her brothers to a man she just learned was her father, a man who had passed her in the street a dozen times, my good God—good work, Milt. And her mother—her mother, how did you manage to write about her tragedy so well, the blond, thinning hair on the white pillow in the hospital at the last—and in the strands of long blond hair what do we see, her awful betrayal of herself for baubles—a beauty that is entirely false—but how the world betrayed her as well, while her eyes looked over at her child, the true beauty—expecting her child to hate her, and seeing her child's love. We remember then that mother at sixteen years old; her high knee socks and her mischievous grace and how so many men swam in that grace until she had nothing left to offer them. Now that's the real story of a poor rural woman, isn't it—it's nothing like *The Renter*! It towers over so much here.'

"'Well, yes,' Vale said, 'But what about my story—in *Brick*—you liked it too, did you?'

"'What—oh, well—compared to this?'

"'Yes—this is so much better,' Milt said.

"He said this in a daze—where he saw himself outside of his body saying it. He almost said he had not written it; almost. But he could not refute the idea that he had finally written a good book. Besides, the boy had come to him to learn how to write.

"When he saw himself outside of his body, he saw his posture, his slightness, his goatee, the patches on his elbows, and felt a kind of accusation coming to him from somewhere far beyond himself. In some way we must assume he did not know he would be assumed as the author of it until he was."

"So the book was published," Cathy said. "Affirmed."

"The book was published by Milt Vale fourteen months later. Cathy, he became a celebrity in literary circles. He earned a good deal of money—two producers wanted to make it into a movie. He would never be the same. The only question he was asked on those CBC programs he agreed to go on was: 'Do you think the ending needs something more? Doesn't it lead us toward a kind of final episode that was earlier touched on?'

"'No, I think I have finished with it,' he said.

"And people were silent because of his gravity. Besides, the book was already over four hundred pages. He must have taken years and exhausted himself writing it. And in secret too—for what he gave to magazines in those years was nothing like this."

"He had simply sprung it on the world?" Cathy smiled. "I mean, this is what they thought?"

"Yes. But there was something strangely absent in his soul—for, once, when they talked about Gaby, the little girl, born off a side road, who longed to be liked at school, who had crooked teeth and smiled as if she was ashamed, who, born deaf, went out tipping at Christmas to get enough to buy presents for her younger brothers and whose hands were rubbed raw by the boughs, he did not seem to know what tipping actually was. Nor did he, when asked, answer the question."

"'You mean what I give to my newspaper boy?' Milt had laughed. Then, realizing he must say something else, he countered caustically with:

"'She has her resources, little ragamuffins like that often do, but I always maintained that sometimes the Gabys are better off not being born—yes, not being born, that's why I put her in the book, you see—I wanted to show how hopeless her life actually was—why do we allow people like her mother to give birth?'

"'Really?' the interviewer said. 'I don't get that at all—not even a little bit—I think her mother in the end shows something of the greater tragedy of the human spirit. I think of you as writing about the Gabys of the world as if they are all precious—and, well, needed here with us now. That her life is not only important but magnificent. She breaks our hearts not because she was born in a shack on a side road to an alcoholic single mother, but because in spite of how she lives, she loves so deeply; and we realize she deserves our love—our commitment to love her no matter what.'

"Milt Vale should have been gracious and triumphant. But he was actually filled with a sudden spasm of hatred for some reason. This is not how he envisioned his greatest work—love of nothing more than what should have been an aborted child. What would all his friends think, also—he, who had once shaken Dr. Morgentaler's hand? Then he calmed himself. The spasms eased.

"'Yes,' he said. 'I did achieve something, though, by writing about her, didn't I?'

"'It reminds us of faith, really, and why we need it.'

"'Faith—what do you mean, faith?' Vale said.

"'Well—I am not a religious person—but no book has made me think more that perhaps I could be, or should be. You don't see the faith you have instilled in your own work?' the interviewer said. 'I see a grace in their world—a kind of celebratory greatness over which is the umbrella of human love—that whole chapter called "Pollen of Spring"—as if God's graciousness is spread irrespective of our wish to destroy it, or worse, to dismiss it again and again and again. And then that character Orville—who at first hates the world and all that is in it—feels hurt by women—it is Gaby May who makes him love again . . . What becomes of him—well, you do leave us hanging, don't you?'

"'Yes, of course—that is exactly what I was after,' he said, caustically. 'Glad you got it.'

"In the book, of course, the character's name is not Orville, Cathy—I just used it here—but it was Orville he wrote about, I am convinced; I am convinced he was whom the last chapters were about. The scene Orville himself wrote about, sitting on the wild windfall that late November, is there—that's what allowed me to know for certain.

"Still, there is something I realized over the last year. Milt had never realized the book existed on a far deeper level than he had comprehended or imagined. He had thought it was a book about the woods and backward people; that is why he had laughed so harshly at the Miramichi writer. That is why he had ridiculed him, made others ridicule him as well. Underneath it all—underneath all of this, was one thing."

"___?"

"*Rage*," John said. "Rage that he did not know and could not learn. For some reason he now began to hate the book terribly. He could not look at it in a bookstore window. He became wary of people. He did not want to talk about it. He did not wish to discuss it. It was not a book about desperate poverty and the lack of gender equivalence. It was a book about grace and beauty and love. I told you earlier he would be startled one day looking into the bathroom mirror. This is what startled him.

"What was actually amusing is that the trappers association of New Brunswick wanted to raffle off one of his books as a door prize and asked him to be on hand because of how well he had written about the deadly force of Conibear traps."

Cathy laughed. "I bet he didn't load his own bullets either."

"No." John smiled to know he could make her smile. "Nor could he dismiss little Gaby. People spoke about her. That was the problem. People asked him to explain her. What was he actually saying? And here is why he could not: you see, it was actually, and here is the real catch, a pro-life novel. The writer did not condemn pro-choice. But he did show where his own love of life existed. Milt, of course, had not known this. Could not realize it. *Abort her* was his only answer to the problems these children faced. He began to say that more and more in private. His hatred of Gaby seemed to know no bounds in private. He began to hate her as a character, and as a living entity. And many times he would not answer people when they began to speak to him about the book—and once, in a passion, he refused to sign a copy for a visiting couple from Oshawa who came to his side door.

"Milt Vale wanted to forget that the only book he had ever actually written he had had to self-publish. He wanted to forget that he had never worked with his hands. He had never died writing a book, he had never travelled along a road during a whiteout in winter with poems about snowfall filling his pockets. He had never adopted children no one else wanted, had never walked to town trying to buy them milk, had never had to marshal his energy to keep them warm, he never hunted or fished, never ran a rapid, never saw a bear turn to charge. Never spent a day on a flat hauling smelt nets. Never put a harness to a horse. All of this, however, was in the book he claimed as his own. He once spoke about that boy being frightened of him. He now realized that boy was frightened of no one.

"So he benefited from a boy who was dead, and he was assumed to be truthful and courageous by others exactly like himself. By his writers' group. And this misplaced sanctity he used much to his advantage with young women at the student rooming house he owned."

"I have not heard of any of this—but I do not know what any of it has to do with us," Cathy said.

"It will become clear. I recalled, about a month or so after I visited the library and saw the review of Vale's first book, that Milt was Eunice's friend. And I remembered she had invited Professor Vale to speak here once or twice. He bragged about knowing John Updike and meeting Timothy Leary when he was young. I knew now about the letter he wrote Orville. I pondered all of this for a while, not sure where it would lead me.

"Then I remembered what Mary Cyr told me once:

"'Eunice, I'm afraid, can be nothing more than Eunice; she is perfect at being Eunice but quite a failure at achieving anything else.

She wants desperately to achieve something—and that always assures she remains Eunice.'

"So I went to our bookstore to buy a copy of Milt's famous book. It is a rather gentrified little bookstore that has many quaint things in it—paintings and photos and pottery done by local First Nations women, dream catchers and handmade blankets. I went to look for the book Milt wrote—the second novel, the one called *Darkness*.

"But when I went to the bookstore to buy a copy of Vale's book I saw an exhibit of Eunice's photos as well. You know what one was of?"

"No—I mean anything, I suppose . . ."

"*OBA—OBA LGM* in splendour at sunset. It was one of her large photos. So she must have thought a lot of it. It was taken about three years before Orville's death."

"What is that?"

"The graffiti under the bridge, Cathy, that Elvis and I first saw that day."

"Oh—yes, of course."

"So, realizing this, I wanted to know."

"Know?"

"How far she could be led by her own willingness to be self-deceived. Discover the Eunice Wise that Mary Cyr once reflected upon."

"Discover her—Eunice? Discover what?" Cathy asked.

"Her participation in the mysteries I was trying to confront and unwrap in order to exonerate your brother. The paradoxes she must have had a glimpse at, through a kind of superb fog; and her need to prove Orville to be the person she said he was."

He paused, wondered if he was saying it the right way, and then continued:

"I at first thought she had made a classic mistake in championing Vale's first novel, *The Renter*, that she was a neophyte; but then I realized it could be no other way, for they existed within the same posture of sanitized middle-class propriety. The kind I saw in the bookstore—or in fact in most of today's bookstores; that gentrified wisdom in a multitude of books that tries to negate anything that is not agreeable or conventionally believed. And nothing, nothing, was scot-free."

"Nothing was scot-free?"

"Oh," John said, "Eunice actually disowned Gaby in the end. Just as Orville predicted she would at the mailboxes that day. In the last six years, when the dispute over the land became more acute, Orville worked totally alone—and had to fight to be allowed on this dis-puted land. He and Eunice were in court three times trying to settle the dispute. He was tired and angry and obsessed and did not seem to be quite right. While at the last she had First Nations lawyers on her side, saying that they no longer wanted him to dig there. That is why she had Danny John guarding it. But he and Danny got along, were seen laughing and talking. So Eunice called on other band mem-bers to come. Finally Eunice was given right-of-way and ownership. Shortly after, as we know, Orville discovered what he believed he was looking for—ancient bones. Everything should have been fine. He would make everything up to the Micmac band and to Eunice Wise."

"But—but it was different than he thought?"

"Yes—very much so."

———

"Did my brother know Mr. Vale—after he was at university?" Cathy asked.

"He did. He was in Fredericton giving a talk at the university about seven or eight years ago, and Vale came to his talk and met him later. This was a year or so after the book *Darkness* was published. Vale invited him to supper.

"He went over around dark that October night and rang the ornate bell, stepped into the front foyer, which was dark. A candle glowed on the ledge of a stained-glass window, a mahogany banister swept toward the upstairs hallway, the living room had a statue of a young naked African girl dancing, and on the mantel was a Fabergé egg—not one of the grand imperial eggs, but a Kelch, one with a clock set in diamonds and gold, designed by Fabergé for the great industrialist it was named for—bought when Vale was in Europe. It was certainly beautiful. Orville noticed it and said nothing. There were other guests there that night—a woman novelist who was Vale's protegé, a member of the board of governors who had dealt with Mary Cyr about the library, and a lecturer from the history department.

"Vale played the greatest of hosts, showed his penknives, his tapestry, his pewter cups, his two Bobak paintings, his Maud Lewis one, and then the Fabergé. He told its story—he had met someone in Florence when he was over there. It turned out that the man had a few things for sale. A golden Egyptian beetle, a spectacular ornate Afghan rug, an ancient jade Buddha worth millions—which Vale didn't get to see—and one thing in particular that caught Vale's eye.

"It was an authentic Fabergé egg. Twice Vale said no to it—but how uncouth he would be not to buy it when the price was so good. In fact, Vale suddenly convinced himself that it would show a kind of penny-saving pedestrianism if one did not buy it. Then, once he was determined to have it, he thought he had lost it because the fellow had left his hotel. But Vale met him again on the street by accident. At that point the man said he wouldn't sell it—it was a mistake to want to.

"'I knew him,' Vale said. 'His name was Issup Farad—a boy I had once taught—very clever—a bit of a showman—but I wasn't going to let it go.'

"Vale, fortunately enough, was able to talk Issup Farad into selling it, although he had to convince him to part with it—and they had an independent broker authenticate it—and, well, here you are. It was in Canada; people at the museum in Halifax wanted to look at it, and perhaps make an offer for it. So he would make a profit of some thousands of dollars if that happened. But that mightn't happen because he was now so taken with it.

"Orville said nothing. He kept his head down, ate his food, now and again looking up and nodding. At this time he looked bereft of intelligence, as if he was somewhere else—and when the pretty student novelist looked at him, he quickly put his head down again.

"Finally Vale sat back in his seat, looked at Orville curiously and said:

"'Orville, you know all about this stuff—but you haven't said anything about my Fabergé.'

"Orville had his head down, eating his peach cobbler.

"'Oh,' Orville said, not looking up. 'Well, it's a fake.'

"'A—fake?'

"'Of course,' he said. 'Of course—it's a complete fake. That particular Fabergé sits in a museum in Amsterdam. The broker must have been in on the swindle. I bet he was a Russian—it's a total fake. Issup Farad sells them by the dozen.' Orville said this callously because he did not know how else to say it.

"The young history lecturer suddenly coughed too loudly and then was silent. Orville looked at him curiously and put his head down again as if embarrassed.

"'It is definitely *not*—I will stake my life on that,' Vale said, looking about the table in confusion. The young female novelist smiled at him; the lecturer in history flushed, and then gave a 'Ha.'

"'But in a way you went along with it?' Orville said.

"The lecturer in history laughed, shaking his wild, dark head, and cut his fork into his crumble.

"'Went along with it,' he repeated mirthfully.

"Vale stood, went to the dining room cabinet, unlocked a bottom drawer and pulled out a document that authenticated the purchase—he showed it to Orville. Orville glanced at it, saw the heavy price he had paid, looked up at him quickly and said:

"'Oh, yes—that's a fake. Remember, I said it is in Amsterdam. I like Issup but I know Issup would lie to anyone. I told you before, this piece is at a museum.'

"'How can you be so sure it's a fake?' the young novelist asked.

"'It's far too heavy for Fabergé—it's a fake. It's not flaked with sleeves of gold—there is a touch of gold but only a tone—it is mostly sleeves of bronze. The hands of the clock aren't gold either. That's not a diamond inlay; that is glass. It's not the Imperial Blue—why, if you saw the 1895 Fabergé and compared it—or the 1903 Kelch,' Orville said, still looking down at his cobbler almost shamefully and quietly. 'It's not even a good fake—any kid could see it.'

"'Ha. Any kid could see it,' the young history lecturer laughed, as if this was part of the fun of having supper at Professor Vale's, and suddenly wiped tears of laugher from his eyes.

"Orville left the house that night. He realized that is why Vale had invited him there—to be shown the Fabergé. And look what it had come to! He walked down toward the water in the dark and saw the cathedral. He cursed and turned and walked away."

"He was self-pitying here?" Cathy asked.

"Oh, yes. Then to the other fellow. The fellow with the Kelch. Seven or eight years after Vale published *Darkness* to enormous recognition, he began to have problems with his son. His son loved him, was so proud of that big, important book he had written. He looked with awe at his father—once made him dinner and planned it from a great restaurant menu downtown. He would wait up late at night for his father to come home to that sweepingly large, sequestered house so he could eat supper with him, in that oaken dining room, and planned for a time when he and his dad would go on a trip, just by themselves. And then for some reason, one autumn afternoon his son took a bottle of pills and downed them with gin."

"What does his son have to do with my brother?"

"In a way, after Vale's son met little Gaby May Crump and fell in love, everything—everything in the world."

"Ah," Cathy said, almost stung by the revelation. "Ah, my good God."

7.

"THOSE FIRST WINTERS IN CANADA WERE VERY HARSH. His father was unhappy, and Aiden loved his father—but Aiden could see things his parents could not see. He could see they did not belong in what his father referred to as 'outer Siberia'—and he did not either, so much. His father hated it here—the weather, the slogging out into the snow—the coats and boots—but in a peculiar way; that is, Milt would not hate it if he could cause a sensation. He came here thinking it would be easy to emulate the success he'd seen others have in his home country. It seemed he did not have what it took down there. He did not blame himself. He blamed his countrymen. Professor Vale was one of these rare people—the kind of person who believes one knows poverty if they have taken a course and discuss it over fine wine and cheese. Not that they do this often, but it is the only way they have ever done it.

"Vale would sometimes phone Eunice late at night, just to tell her how much he hated it here. And to tell her that is why he wrote the big, important novel that took everyone by surprise.

"At first Aiden loved it here. Because he believed his mom, a professor of psychology at a small women's university in South Carolina, was going to soon be with them.

"When the snow came it whitened everything—washed over all the fields and buildings—so he could not see ten yards in front of him in any direction. It stuck to the side walls of houses, covered up the hedges. It lashed the windows and concealed whole sections in shades of white. But that was fine for Aiden. He loved the hidden quality, the secret gaiety in the joy of snow. But his father spoke so harshly against where they were that Aiden became influenced by his father's dislike.

"In another vein Vale believed he could find out things and write a grand novel, like no one had ever done, of all these backward people shackled to one or two great companies, working away in the hinterland, where for God's sake moose still roamed the highways.

"After phone calls between them, his parents enrolled Aiden in piano lessons far up the hill, and he was seen walking to and fro with his head down, his book bag on his back, silent and alone. I discovered that it would always be that way for Aiden Vale.

"His father was able to start a writers' group—where he believed as an American it was this group, *his* group—where he would teach and become well-known.

"And then one night—when everything was going well, and right in the middle of his loud, exuberant laugh—that boy arrived, in the cold, hiking with his poems in his jacket pocket.

"'Is this here the place where I'll learn how to write?' he said.

"The mean, scattered poems this boy read that very night showed so much intensity and passion and love for the land that Vale did not know, and had mocked, that Vale turned pale.

"'It can't be his work,' he told Eunice.

"Then, after Milt staying away from the very group he had formed because of his resentment over this boy, his wife travelled north to tell him she would not relocate. She had been offered the vice-presidency of the small university. And she wished to bring Aiden home with her after Christmas.

"Milt did not want her to accept the position. He accused her of manipulating him. They argued; he was bitter. He had avoided the draft and did not feel at all safe returning. He berated her, and she left on Christmas Eve and went for a walk.

"The city engulfed her in a strange, primitive way. Huge snow-drifts were piled at the corners where the streets met, and lights shone down with strange bleak yellow spots on the snow, while street lights on wet black wires waved in the wind. Outside Christmas trees beckoned far away, and lights from houses too looked yellow and warm but glowed so distant in the storm. It all seemed so primitive to her, this Southern girl whose family still owned a small portion of a tobacco farm, a girl who had had a coming-out dance at the local town hall when she was sixteen, filled with white dresses and crepe paper and punch bowls with red-coloured punch.

"She turned toward the university but was not sure which direction she should go until she saw a boy approaching along Beaverbrook Court, his hands thrust into his pockets. It was Aiden, coming home from his piano lesson. He looked so alone. She suddenly gave a cry at her own selfishness. She must take him back with her—she must. Her short, damp hair clung to the side of her round face. The rounded face of a Southern woman in a northern gale. She wore flat rubber shoes that slipped along as she walked. Her voice was lost in the wind when she called his name; it echoed away like a South Carolina bird caught up in a gale. Like a poor brown-and-yellow wren. It seemed, the wind, to batter his name into silence.

"*Aiden*—it was as if the name hung in the icy black wind about her. There was a sudden shard of blackness above and beyond her.

"So she turned to run after him—but it was snowing. The road was very slippery as well. She tried to cross in the traffic, not seeing the Don't Walk sign because of a snowbank, and suddenly the snow gave way and she felt herself sliding on the ice. She slid and fell right into the path of an oncoming car travelling down the hill. It could not stop in time. She put her hand up as if to say 'Halt,' as if she was shocked that a Canadian driver would want to hurt her. But no one had ever intended to hurt her.

"Aiden turned the corner because he hadn't seen it happen.

"In fact, he was going home to meet her, to tell her that he loved her, and wanted to return to South Carolina for good. He did not like it here with his dad. He was sad, and didn't like to disappoint people, but he did not like Canada anymore.

"He did not like his piano lessons given in that bare house with the snow falling and the naked white piano keys beckoning to him always from the same space in the large upstairs room's back corner. Nor had he learned to skate.

"He sat in the living room waiting for her to come home; at first nervous and excited to tell her what he wished. All the lights were off except the porch light and the Christmas tree. It was very late in the evening, that evening when the city police knocked on their door. It was, incidentally, the same Christmas that Gaby May had phoned her woebegone father to ask for a present for her brothers, with the hopeful delusion of a child.

———

"Time did pass. They healed, the world went on. And some years later the manuscript came to Vale's door. It was, if he thought about it, as if his wife was watching him at that moment, to see if he would do what was honourable, as an American gentleman whose navies and armies now ruled over half the world. He felt this in his very consciousness, and guilt plagued him. His life had been so utterly privileged compared to that Miramichi boy's. Still, for some reason he could not help himself." John paused a moment. "But there was a problem."

"What was the problem?" Cathy asked.

"The problem was—well, as I have already mentioned, not only did Milt not write the book, he could never think in the terms in which that writer thought. Philosophically, I mean—as well as every other way. And he actually believed his false refinement allowed his world view."

"The past was all a sham," Cathy said. "What was once believed was all false?"

"As I sat in your brother's house and listened to the rain end and felt the last of the diminishing sun on the bronze fire screen, something bothered me about everything to do with the case. I thought of Eunice coming to the police station and telling us she'd seen Orville carting something from the shore. That she had been for some time, almost four years, worried about Danny John. So could we go look? Of course we did—and she seemed so right at that moment we were at a loss for words. The theory, in the office where we gathered, was that she finally had won her case against him about the shoreline, and he had to remove the remains of two people he had murdered. He had removed the bodies and had taken them to his house to hide them in the attic—not a police officer in North America would think this not so. Yet a week after his death I realized how wrong everyone might be. As I sat in his house that night I became suspicious of her."

"Well, then, how did she know about the bones?"

"There was only one way she could have known about the bones. Either she saw them on the beach—which I doubted—or she had been in Orville's house searching for something else in the attic when he was out. That was the conclusion I came to."

"She couldn't have seen him from where she was?" Cathy asked.

"I walked through his rooms, and into the attic, and wondered aloud if she was in his house some of the times he was away.

"I then bought a copy of Milt Vale's novel *Darkness* and began to read it that night.

"It took me only an hour to realize that this novel would destroy Vale because he could never personally agree with it enough to have had the compulsion to ever really write it. The book in all its leanings and in its very essence was pro-life—the joy of Gaby and her brothers; the search for beauty by Orville. It was a strange and complete counterbalance to *The Renter* without ever stating it. It was, in fact, at war with most of modern literature—the kind Milt himself so valued."

"Do you know where the tin box was?"

"It was in three places in the last eight years. Gaby had taken the tin box with her to the convent, and it was in what the kids called 'the cloister room,' where all their superlative things were kept hidden from them as being temptations of the flesh. There it sat under a heap of fashion magazines for four or five years. If the nuns had looked at it, they might have destroyed it—however, perhaps not.

"'When you get out on your own,' her uncle had once told her, 'if my book is not yet published and I am gone, maybe show it to someone important; that is, someone who might know where to send it.'

"Seven years after Vale published the book *Darkness*, some three years after she left the convent for good, she took the *final* copy out, like a great treasure. It was almost lost many times over the years.

"She was now old enough to realize she had to do something with it. She thought of taking it to your brother, the man who had at one time been kind to her, who had tutored her in math. But he was on his travels, and she by some trick of fate moved to Fredericton to take a job and to go to school.

"There, within three weeks, she met Aiden Vale. So after she met Aiden—after they became boyfriend and girlfriend—she told him about a book her adopted father, who had died some years before, had written."

"How did they meet?" Cathy asked.

"Aiden met her one day in the rooming house that his father owned and rented out to young female students. Aiden went every few weeks to collect the rent, and to listen to any problems. On the very top floor, in the smallest of all the small rooms, a young woman with dark hair and brown eyes, with a small mole on her right chin and a comical grin, came that late August, with some books and a suitcase and an old tin box. She came to be one of Milt's tenants. Very different than the tenants in the book he had self-published. There, Aiden met her, and he said he would try to help her. They would take the manuscript to his father—and see what could be done."

"It is strange," Cathy said.

"She had started out for Moncton, but by the time she got to Newcastle the Moncton bus had departed (she had missed it by two minutes, no more), and she saw the Fredericton bus, loading passengers. She simply decided not to wait the seven long hours for another bus to Moncton, but to go to Fredericton instead. And how did she come to that rooming house, of all the thousand rooming houses? It was a complete accident as well. The rooming house across the street was the one she had been scheduled to visit by appointment, but she got the addresses mixed up. The top room in Professor Vale's building was available, and she was told she could have it for 89 dollars a week—so she never did get to Number 76 Graham—she found a room at Number 67."

"That is why Aiden took the bottle of pills?"

"Yes—later. So I had to see this room. While there I saw the other graffiti tag—the one I remembered, from when I had gone to that house some years previous. So it all came back to me. I bought a small disposable camera and took a picture of it. Yes, I had been there before, inquiring about Gaby May's brother Tom—before

Gaby May disappeared. Her brother had hauled a shotgun out against some men, and he had run. We needed to find him before he hurt himself or someone else. I thought Tom might have run to Gaby. But he had not. Of course, that was when everyone was still alive and well.

"Now, visiting that rooming house again a few months back, I was certain—certain for the very first time—what the graffiti was all about. I witnessed how young women were actually treated by Professor Milt Vale, living as students in cramped and neglected little rooms, sharing a communal bathroom. Aiden tried to work to make it livable for every one of them. He ran here and there, trying to find curtains, to get extra bedding, and now and again catching the mice that invaded the rooms in the fall. Once he came in and two girls were up on a chair clutching each other and screaming and Gaby May was standing in front of them with the little thing by the tail, saying: 'My goodness gracious, it's nothing but a mouse.'"

"You said you knew what the graffiti was about?"

"Oh, yes: love—it was about love. By accident she came and by accident she was, our bright, sweet Gaby May, who had seen more of life than Milt Vale could ever, ever, ever have imagined—and worse, Gaby had the terribly sweet provincial flaw where she innocently believed academic people like Milt Vale did no wrong. How could they do wrong if they read so many books? And now the two sets of bones we are speaking of, as I have learned over the last weeks, were not even of the same era—that is why Orville made a mistake when he discovered them in his dig on the shore. He just never took the time to decipher what he had found."

"Well, it is confusing . . . "

"I came to believe Eunice discovered the bones in the house when she snooped. There were enough signs that someone besides Orville was there when one took the time to look. But if you know Eunice, you know she had some good practice at it, a clandestine creep about her enemy's place."

"Bones that she believed he dug up when she won the civil suit over the property?" Cathy asked.

"Which did mean that," John said. "Still covered in the soil and clay of the shore."

8.

JOHN CLOSED HIS EYES FOR A BRIEF TIME; THEY FLUTTERED under the ancient light, the knob-and-tube wiring, and it was as if he was suddenly thinking of someone else—not Aiden, who had met Gaby and had fallen in love, but someone other, who was also caught up in this, in a way not of their own making—who lived in a kind of shadow world—whose own world had been swallowed whole, or if not whole, in part, and the vivaciousness of her own life had been stilled.

So he continued:

"We left Brenda Townie when Orville went away after giving blood. But she came to visit Orville after he came back. This was a remarkably daring thing for her, I suppose. She could never have imagined herself doing this just a few years previous. What peril it placed her reputation in—how daring and secretive her plan, how wise and splendid her decision to drive far around little Bartibog— that is, by the back way. And then to find herself by his door."

"Near the time when the bones were discovered?"

"No—long before the bones ever were discovered. By now he had become something unique in her mind. Finally he had. That is, he had always been unique. But now what made him so had changed from darkness to a kind of light—a little opaque but light nonetheless. She pictured him walking toward her through a half-solid smoke. So one day he was reading a report in *Archeology Today*, about a fake jade Buddha that had been sold to a middle-aged man in Valencia, Spain. While Orville was reading about this fake jade that had caused an uproar throughout the entire archeological community, there came a small red car driving up his lane, with mud along the sides, which showed the person driving had come perhaps by a circuitous route.

"The man who had sold the jade, who was captured a few months before in Iraq, was the same man who had sold the fake Fabergé to Milt Vale. Issup Farad.

"And so, now he was caught. The article was followed by an expansive list of Issup Farad's follies, stupidities, gambits, forged antiquities and major crimes, the stupidest having happened in Iraq: selling highly radioactive material to an Islamic general for a solid-gold commode.

"The commode was pictured. The radioactive material was not.

"Orville tossed the article aside when he heard a knock on his door. He had no idea who was there: 'Don't come in if I don't know you,' he said. And the door opened slowly."

"He must have been very startled?" Cathy asked.

"In a strange way too his heart must have leapt in joy. But from what I know she sat in a chair in the kitchen and he turned away and sat in the living room—alone, now and again rubbing the magazine pages he had been reading with his heavy black shoe.

"She came to him because it was her child she was thinking of. Still, she wanted him to notice her. Nor did she bring up the fact that the child had died; that she and Junior had struggled desperately to keep their child alive. So they sat in silence.

"'If you do want some tea, I can make you a pot,' he said.

"'Oh, no—I have just come to speak to you for a second,' she answered.

"'About what?'

"'You must have heard so many things about me—I often wonder,' she whispered.

"'It is awful what people will say,' Orville answered. (In fact, Orville had not heard anything. In fact, he thought she was quite happy.)

"There was a long silence. He could hear her fidgeting, wanting to break the silence that engulfed them.

"'Why don't you come out to the kitchen and see me? I won't bite.'

"'*No.* I am very much okay where I am, here and now,' Orville said.

"'What are you doing now?' she asked.

"'I am reading about a fake jade Buddha. A man in Spain spent 200,000 euros on it.'

"Then he paused, seemed to be shifting about in his chair.

"'But now—well, now all that is over for Issup. He was in Iraq when I was there. It seemed he did not mind that there was terror in Iraq if he could smuggle something out of it.'

"She was confused by his talk. So she said, after another moment, 'Still, it must be grand to be famous—did you really meet President Carter?'

"He paused for a moment, not knowing how to answer.

"'Yes—I did do so. He was at a conference.'

"'And he writes you letters?'

"'Two.'

"'Pardon?'

"'He wrote me two letters about a Biblical reference. Proverbs, I think.'

"So she said: 'And what did you do?'

"'Pardon?'

"'When he wrote you two letters—what did you do?'

"'I wrote him back.'

"He paused, thought, and said:

"'President Carter is a good man, but my father was every bit the man.'

"'I know,' she said. 'Daddy was his boss—remember?'

"Silence. Then she composed herself, and asked her next question slightly more sternly:

"'And did the president of France give you a medal for finding that place—where the Romans had that gladiatorial site?'

"'Yes—but that was a long while ago, when I was a kid, and others were there as well. It was something any schoolkid could have found. My last dig is here because I promised Amos Paul—once it is finished I will go away somewhere.'

"'But he gave you a medal,' she said, as if angrily trying to convince him of his own stature.

"'Goddamn,' he said, 'archeology is nothing. I would have been better as a dentist. I should have studied more. Besides, it was a medal foreign men or women get for service to France. You know yourself, as soon as you do anything in France they haul out the medals and kiss you on both cheeks.'"

"He was mean," Cathy said.

"I know. He was."

"'It must be grand to be famous,' Brenda said. 'Junior and I didn't make it to be famous.'

"Her worry about Junior was palpable; he had barely been kept out of jail. But she knew her husband's name allowed her coyness— and surprisingly, her charm. Saying: *Now we are alone—please know that I have come to you; you could have me and my husband would not know.*

"And he could hear that," Cathy said, more as a statement than a question.

"I am sure," John said, looking at her. "Of course. But something else was immense about Orville that she did not know."

"What was immense?" Cathy asked.

"He had intervened in the auction—with his first grant money. When her in-laws went bankrupt two years later. Your brother actually bought the two trucks to keep the business afloat. But instead of telling her this, he told her a story about what he was working on."

"Which was?"

"*Beauty*. He said he wanted to write a book on beauty, on man's search for beauty, on the *devastation* of beauty. On the *lie* of beauty. He himself had been gulled into searching for it, he told her. He callously mentioned how struck he had been by *her* beauty—and how it had changed his life. He told her it was she who made him think of himself as very ugly. He told her *he* had been exceedingly selfish. He shouldn't have got so enthused, he said. It was selfish to bother her. But if she thought he needed her now, she was sadly mistaken."

"That was unkind," Cathy said now.

"It made her cry. He heard her and revised what he said:

"'But you are still very beautiful,' he revised quickly. 'You have nice things—curves and things,' he said.

"Even Brenda had to laugh at this attempt. Then, before she could answer further, he told her about visiting the Taj Mahal three years previously—the beauty of the marble swimming in the moonlight, the feeling of coral under your feet, of gems and glory and the notes of paradise on the walls. He told her it was all a sham. He spoke about the Stone of Scone and the Sword in the Stone. They were shams as well, he said. She didn't understand him—they were separated by eons, it seemed.

"He told her about being with a group almost thirty years before and finding the mummified remains of a child in a vase that the parents had used after they had sacrificed this child to Moloch.

He accused her of being one of those who would follow any article of faith. That's what he now thought.

"He asked, did she know Mr. Moloch was one of the gods in Milton's *Paradise Lost*? He bragged that he knew more about the Bible than the priests who believed in it. He told her he might have believed if it wasn't for her. He accused her of being Salome. Then he was silent. Then he said God had warned everyone of every wicked deed in the world, and they still happened.

"He continued to ramble. He said the Old Testament warned the Israelites of this most profane god Moloch—did she know? Did she know? No, he said. And neither did Junior. He told her what was in the child's hair that day, so long ago: a red ribbon. He told her he often wondered what did her parents want on that day three thousand years ago—'a once-in-a-lifetime fashionable invitation to a princeling's home? Money?'

"'I don't know,' Brenda protested. 'I would never be like that, Orville.'

"He told her that was the first time she'd actually called him by his name. He told her he no longer dreamed about her, so why did she come now? She told him she was sorry. He then went back to Moloch.

"'Well then,' he continued, 'did you know that is why God stopped Abraham from slaying Isaac? To prove that *He* was the only God. But of course you did not know, you were too busy with Junior—well, you got him—how do you like him?'

"'Please,' she said.

"And then, with an almost crushed voice, the voice of a man who had been trodden upon, he continued:

"'Nothing will make me believe in God—I have almost proven God does not exist—I've just about proven it—one or two more weeks and it will all be proven!'

"'Don't say that, Orville, please,' she whispered, almost to herself.

"Then, after a silence of a minute of more, she heard:

"'You wanted *them*,' he said with a sudden indescribable sadness in his voice. 'You wanted them, Brenda. And now—what did *they* give you—if they gave you so much, why have you come here? They said I would have slapped you—those girls who wrote "Cyclops"—"Get away, Brenda, he will hit you!" I heard them say—maybe I would have, but they—they *destroyed* you!'

"'I am so sorry I hurt you,' she said.

"He tried to think. He picked up a magazine and flipped through its desperate pages.

"'Well, so am I—but what was this tiny child telling me? I was being told something—but what was I being told? *What was I being told?*'

"Then, before she could answer, he answered:

"'I was being told that it still happens—every day, in certain unspeakable clinics—and Abraham every day is told to stay his hand. And no one listens, because God is a fantasy and Moloch isn't. You see, I don't care, at all. Why should I be so moral—go ahead, get rid of them all in those unspeakable clinics, it's not my problem. We'd all be better off if little Gaby Crump wasn't even born!'

"'But—I couldn't do so,' she whispered.

"'Well—I hope your daughter will grow up to know what beauty is used for and how it can be used.'"

"He didn't know?" Cathy said.

"No, he did not know, and she said nothing—it is what haunted him about this later. That she said nothing! She then asked him who was Gaby Crump.

"'She was the light of my life,' he said. Then, almost tenderly, he repeated, 'The light of my life, and she is gone away and I don't know where she is gone, and I cannot find her.'

"Then he said, after a long silence:

"'Here's something else—if you think I have anything against women you are mistaken. I love them as much as anyone in the world. I always thought of you and I having a bottle of wine someday together—in Paris—and seeing Vermeer at the Louvre—but, well, Junior had a truck. So that stopped it. That and my being hideous, I guess. And Issup tried to buy a golden toilet—ha!'

"She tried to find the threads of connection in what he said, but there were tears in her eyes. There was a very long silence. She was silent, staring down at the kitchen table, small purse in her hand.

"Then his voice rose once more:

"'Anyway, the militants whom Issup so cavalierly traded radio-active material with, isotopes that came from the hinterland of some bleak Soviet backwater building, long dismantled, will someday use them to scorch the earth! Or *we* will scorch it all by ourselves—or Russia or China will demolish half the world—that's about the size of it: we will divvy up the destruction. We can't blame it on one race or ethnicity—for it takes the whole damn lot of us to do it!'

"He might not have known what he was saying. In fact, he did not remember half of what he said that afternoon.

"'So last year,' Orville said, 'the Iraqi and American governments asked me to help catalogue some of the artifacts found in Saddam's sons' houses. So like an idiot I went. An Iraqi colonel asked me if I wanted to meet someone. He took me past small, broken-up streets and bruised houses to a large detention centre, a Stalinist-like building surrounded by barbed wire. They had him—finally they had caught him—this little man named Issup Farad. He was caught trying to sneak a solid-gold toilet out of Iraq—he was caught, trying his hardest to get up a sand hill, in the late afternoon, with sweat drenching his white shirt, dragging a gold toilet by a strand of rope. I thought of his Mercedes sitting along a Saudi highway, abandoned, with the licence plate 5X760S, getting covered up in golden sand.

When I left him there was a very beautiful Islamic call to prayer—and all the rest of the building was eerily silent.'

"'That is sad,' Brenda said.

"'But I want to know one thing—how in God's name did Issup think he could smuggle a gold toilet out of Iraq?' He said this as if he was truly amazed by it. 'So he asked me to get in touch with his thirteen-year-old son, as if that poor, skinny child, who was waiting for his dad to come home, might be able to help him. The Yanks have poured billions of dollars into Iraq, and it is stolen. For my eight days' work I was paid 75,000 dollars.'

"So finally, after moments of silence, she said almost in a hush:

"'Seventy-five thousand dollars, Orville—for eight days, Orville. And you saw the Taj Mahal. My soul, Orville, you have seen the world—I must say.'

"He knew she had missed what he was trying to say but it was only because of her innocence. And he felt ashamed of himself.

"'It isn't so much,' Orville whispered.

"'But you have met the prime minister of Canada too,' Brenda continued, 'and people know your name.' She gave a slight, wonderful laugh, one that gave him her feeling of astonishment. 'I don't even know our MLA.'

"'Once I desperately wanted someone to know my name,' he said.

"'Oh,' she said, forgetting and laughing. 'Who, Orville—who?'

"'A girl I begged to take to a dance, a long time ago. Whose cute boyfriend had a nice truck.'

"'Oh!' she said, as if he had just struck her. She felt with his last statement a final brush-off, a final rebuke. She stood and waited near the kitchen door.

"Then she said something very peculiar, but almost harshly:

"'If you want—I will kiss you.' Then she almost whispered, 'I have been thinking of you. I have been for weeks, Orville. I have visited because I have been thinking of you. You are very special to me now.'

"This unexpected admission made him suddenly weak with desire, as strong as the hunger in autumn sunlight, and he stammered:

"'Why—why now?'

"'You never got your goodnight kiss!' she said cautiously. 'And I have never kissed anyone but Junior.'

"'I am sorry,' he answered. 'I am so, so sorry for it all!'

"He almost begged her not to leave. In his mind he begged her to go to that café in Paris and have a bottle of wine, and see Vermeer and be in his arms. He had the money to fly her there that night. The money to stay with her in Paris forever. But his pride did not allow him to be hurt again. She waited. She waited. It was agony. He let the door close—and the last bit of sunlight seemed to cast upon her face, making it shine in a bright, solid manner, as she walked by the window and disappeared."

"I feel profound grief for her," Cathy said.

"Yes, and I am sure—I am sure—so did he." John paused, and then, after a certain amount of time, continued solemnly:

"One cold November night some months after she had visited with him, with the wind sweeping along the empty streets a faint, wet smell of wintery gas, a woman rode her old bicycle with a small basket down toward the buildings off the town square. It was well over a year since their child had died.

"There at Number 129 ½ O'Connor Street, in the one big room on the ground floor, she made a small pottery bowl, with a design from the second century BC that was modelled after a photograph from an old magazine. The bowl would be taken home. It was an exact—or as exact as she could get it—replica of the bowl Orville had discovered on that dig in southern France some years before. It was pictured in an old article on him in an out-of-date magazine that she had kept

for a number of years. Now, Junior knew she had kept that magazine for a number of years, a silent reproach against who he, Junior,
was. Or at least, saying nothing, he believed that.

"Little Kitty, whose name she scratched into the bowl, was gone.
She thought often of that poor child sacrificed to Moloch, and wondered about her own need for beautiful things. Is this what Orville
thought? Had they done enough for Kitty, or did Orville think they
had sacrificed her? No, he could not think that of her—but did he
think it of him? Of Junior, and his need for money? God, it would be
horrible if Orville thought that. No, she realized; even more tragically, Orville was rebuking not them but himself. It was his lack of
resolve to come back to her that day, the day she called out to him in
his kitchen.

"Then she went home to her husband, hoping to make everything
right. What she was completely unaware of was that Junior's friends
had told him about her visit. People knew she had visited Orville, no
matter her circuitous route along the old highway. Worse, the auc-
tioneer's son told Junior that it was Orville's kindness that had kept
them in business.

"'So maybe she just went down on her knees to repay him,' the
man said. He smiled that utterly corrupt, cowardly smile that men
who break a secret about a woman always have, and with it destroyed
not only the secret but also the sanctity of Orville's act.

"The night she went to O'Connor Street, Junior, coming
home drunk, realized that she had taken the article about Orville
MacDurmot from the desk. To him, she had gone to him again.
He sat in the dark until he heard her bicycle coming up the hill.
The house was very still; all the objects were silhouetted with the
scent of autumn night and the light from the street. The interior
was bathed in a kind of glorious, half-grey elegance. Little vases and
jars sat quietly on the mantel and in the kitchen, and on the small

shelf between the living room and foyer. The brass front-door handle seemed to reflect the light from the street as she entered the house.

"He stood as she came toward him, scaring her so that she jumped back. Then, when she was in terror, seeing only his white arms and hands as she backed away, he grabbed her beautiful hair, the thing she took pride in more than anything else. He yelled at her that he had loved Kitty too. He beat her with his belt on her backside, tearing her clothes away, her blouse and her bra. The newly minted ancient bowl shattered; the magazine was torn, Orville's picture was crushed under her feet. She fled half-naked up the street and hid in a bush in Janet Tailor's yard. She sat on her knees staring out at the glum but perfectly lighted pavement. He had torn some of her hair away in his hand. After a while she began to shake. She made her way back down near midnight and crawled into the back seat of her car, now and again peeping out over the seat to see him at the kitchen table playing solitaire with their new deck of cards, the gold wedding ring that he had cut her nose with glinting on his finger.

9.

"AS FOR ORVILLE, HIS BELLIGERENCE WAS NOT GOOD FOR him. He now realized how much hell his search for beauty had cost. He was now left with no one in the world. So he closed up the house, left 40,000 dollars in your parents' account, gave the old horse to a friend and left everything behind.

"He was convinced after that day, speaking to her, that *the world's idea of beauty was awash with fear, awash with menace and hate.* So he pretended to himself that he was not going to Iraq to defend Issup. He pretended he was going to continue helping the British and Americans catalogue certain things from Uday Hussein. From the great palace, with its giant marble pillars and its enormous frescoes, its elaborate staircases, its grand pianos, its golden cherubim playing pennywhistles made of silver, its iron maiden still in use. He began to listen to the call to prayer, and became more opened to prayer. But then he realized that in some way he had been praying since he was three years old. He went down into the dungeon again to visit his friend, the one who had once worn white leisure suits in September and smoked Gitanes while playing backgammon for money. The memory of those university days still lingered in middle-aged Issup Farad's smile. But he was bald, and his face had lost its tone, and his eyes were dull, and in his lips there was the Dorian Gray lapse into balam.

"'Please,' Issup said hopefully, 'Tell them it was Dmitry. He is the real criminal. He supplied it. I bought it to sell but, you see, he supplied it. He deals too in human organ trafficking here and in Pakistan—hundreds die each year—there, I told you. I could tell you more—I mean, if they let me go. I'm done with it now—do they know who my father was?'

"He had no reason to want to help Issup. But in the end he did. From a possible death sentence Issup was given five years in an Iraqi prison. Issup's wife lost their beautiful villa; his son was removed from private school. Issup was released from jail after three years but could never go back to southern France. He was sent to the East, into Afghanistan, where his family had originated.

"Orville was alone on his way to the airport. He had stayed until the trial was over, and managed to find Issup a pair of boots, a thousand dollars and a carton of Gitanes—but that allowed him to be more on his own than he should, to slip through the cracks of those who would have handled him. People forgot that he was there. So the day after the trial he had taken a taxi when he left Baghdad. It was very simple. Men appeared, and just pushed him into a Jeep and drove away, while in sight of planes and the tower.

"His capturers travelled north with him to a village northwest of Mosul, and he spent two weeks with other people: young Yazidi children being sold into slavery; men, Christian and Yazidi. Major Abu Mohamed Ali Sin Bar was more concerned with a particular dark-eyed Yazidi girl than with your brother. She and Orville had been captured the same week and they had travelled together on a small truck with a tarp over them. And in the bleak village where they were brought there were stolen artifacts that Sin Bar was bartering—golden-winged calves, an actual jade Buddha, the very kind Issup had once pretended to have for sale. The girl had whispered to Orville in Arabic: 'Help me, brother.'

"But he had no way to do so. Yet he picked her up and left during a call to prayer, dragging legs chained together. They made it past the outside buildings of the village, but were seen by two teenaged guards. One, surprisingly enough, was a white boy from London. Orville was tossed to the ground, his arms burned with cigarettes. You see, he was not the victim here—he was the victimizer—the one they could scapegoat—the one who was guilty. This is what the London boy told him.

"As evening was approaching our major shot the girl's grandfather, who was in a white shirt and black trousers, and walked away, putting his pistol in its holster as he did so, concerned with snapping the safety strap.

"'Allah is merciful to all,' Orville said as he passed by. One lonely Yazidi girl who had spat at one of the captains was separated from the others. And, after a short trial, condemned to be burned. But the major spent a good amount of time unwrapping certain shards of gold he wanted Orville to examine. Where did they come from? Orville looked at them a second and took what he considered to be an educated guess:

"'From Tunisia,' Orville told him. 'And you already know that. And it's low-grade, and you know that as well.'

"The major smiled and looked over his shoulder at the Russian, said something, pointed at Orville's face and they both laughed.

"'One must tell the truth and not mix truth with falsehood,' Orville said, pointing at the gold as he quoted the Koran.

"Then, with the sky almost blue in its darkness and Venus shining brightly, Orville saw the Russian colonel, who had once been partnered with Issup, sit down at a table with the major and eat lamb and rice. But the Russian couldn't eat. He had a great deal of anxiety about the girl condemned to be burned, and when the Russian passed Orville later he glanced at him hastily and then looked off to the side. That is, he could do nothing, just as Orville could do nothing. He too was a prisoner here, and wanted to be gone.

"'Allah will give no one more than they can endure,' Orville said to him. The Yazidi girl who had whispered to him 'Help me, brother' was put into a cage with four other girls—the ones who had not been sentenced to death but were to be married. Boys and men sat about talking and laughing, and bartering for them. But later that night the girl was brought out and taken to the major's room by two young women. Then, after midnight, the captain and the major had an argument. The major looked distraught and he fired his gun into the dirt during the argument. The Russian laughed uneasily and said something in Arabic. After a while two women went into the room where the Yazidi girl had been taken, carrying a white sheet. Then the body was removed, along with some small shoes and a bloody towel and some underwear.

"The captain was very upset. The major shrugged and returned to prayer. Orville remembered when she had whispered 'Help me, brother' earlier that day. She was a beautiful child of fourteen. A year before, she had been in school.

"At dawn there was a call to prayer; the earth had the sour smell of blood. Food was being prepared, but he was not to have it. That day they caught the sight of Peshmerga troops. A Warthog fired at them from the sky. There was the *pit pit pit* sound of rifle fire between them and Kurdish fighters. A platoon of Peshmerga fighters entered the compound late that afternoon under the leadership of a Kurdish woman named Lieutenant Fara, and Orville was freed that night. So were three of the girls. Others had not been as lucky. There were two groups lined up to be shot as the Peshmerga were advancing toward them. Orville had been put into the second group—the group there was not time to execute.

"Orville was driven out over the dunes. The sky remained deep blue in its darkness and he saw the major's dead body. Lieutenant Fara had taken her World War Two pistol and right in the middle of his interrogation had shot him in the head. The Russian colonel had been captured and was standing in his underwear. His legs were thick. His chest hairy.

"Orville noticed a shooting star in the sky, and a small, yellow-backed donkey. Across the flat was a mountain rising up in the deep heaven, and down across the dunes the lights of a small village could be seen basking orange and purple in the night.

"A few months later Orville turned up in Canada. He started to look for Gaby May. He went everywhere, read every paper, went to every hostel, checked every restaurant and university from Halifax to Montreal.

"So in Montreal over two years ago he fell into depression. He carried little Gaby's picture, the one he had taken when she was a child. It was faded and creased, but he held onto it like it was the only thing of beauty he had ever had. He lived on the street and pushed a grocery cart. The same urge that had made him seek beauty now made him seek oblivion.

"One night over two years ago, he was sitting near a closed and vacant bakery at six in the evening. He was looking at the pale snow falling in front of him. An elderly woman walked by in a red coat and hat, a pair of high winter boots. The church bells up the street were pealing in the cold and she was on her way to Mass. Suddenly, she turned to him, bent toward his face and whispered: 'I am on my way to evening Mass. So I will say a Hail Mary for you.'

"She handed him five dollars and patted his shoulder:

"'Don't despair. Your life is in Christ's hands.'

"'I don't believe in him.'

"'But He believes in you.'

"'He never once said so.'

"'Then maybe He will give you a sign.'

"'A sign—sure, tell him to give me a sign. Tonight.'

"He said all of this jovially. He would never see her again. After a while he stood and went through the streets of East End Montreal, turning from one street to the next in the dark, pushing the cart and trying to find a place to sleep. At about one in the morning he entered a small dead-end back street called rue Tristesse."

"Rue Tristesse? 'Sorrow'?"

"He took out his sleeping bag, and his duffel bag, and lay down right beside a large opened garbage barrel. And after a time something in it caught his eye. It was the waving of a red ribbon that a gust of wind every so often caused to flutter above the barrel rim. It would disappear, and then again flutter in the breeze that came through the alley. As if it were beckoning him. So he stood, walked over and looked at the heap that was stuffed into the barrel near the door of an old locked garage. At first it was so startling he did not comprehend what he was seeing. It was a Native girl, probably a Mohawk or Iroquois child, of about fourteen. Her throat had been cut about an hour or so before. Now her eyes stared silently, dark, sad eyes that seemed to still be alive, or looking blankly in recrimination at the world she had lived in. The moon now appeared in the open sky and he could see the child very clearly.

"On her left hand she wore a small friendship ring. Her nails were painted purple, she wore dark eyeshadow, and her small tongue was pierced, with a stud too big. The barrel had filled up with a pool of her blood. She wore an almost-new black leather skirt and mesh stockings, and snow had fallen on her dark hair and slumped shoulders. She had no shoes on her feet. Her red blood had splashed over her painted mouth. Under her jacket was a white blouse, and on the jacket was a silver-coated emblem on the breast pocket. That was all he remembered, except that the sky seemed particularly silver-grey.

"She was a Native child from the reserve near Oka. She had run away from her home some months before. Orville stood there for many moments in silence—not knowing what he should do. The next hours were taken up with the police—at first suspecting him, and then realizing it was her male companion, high on meth, who had done this, and was hiding under a stairway just up the street, with the knife lying beside him.

"They ordered Orville to remain where he was because they needed to speak with him again. The body was removed from the barrel in the early morning, and the police cordoned off the lane; it was very cold, the snow began to fall, and a great blanket of white powder covered Montreal. So, after a lukewarm cup of coffee and a prolonged interview with a Constable LeBlanc, your brother went to a homeless shelter and slept on a cot. The next day Constable LeBlanc asked to see him again. He had phoned New Brunswick for some proof of what Orville had told him. The constable looked astonished, dejected and even angry:

"'You have 240,000 dollars in the bank,' he said, as if Orville would be surprised.

"'Yes,' Orville said, 'Some money—somewhere.'

"'And you worked collecting beautiful objects all over the world—and are quite well-known?' He placed a sheet of paper before Orville to show him the file he had collected, as if Orville might not know he was well-known. Orville glanced at it.

"'Yes—they say that.'

"'You didn't make it to either of your parents' funerals?'

"'No, and I am sorry for it.'

"'Well, why do you live like this?—It's not right,' he said sadly, as he had Orville sign his name to a witness report. 'Not right,' he murmured. He did look dejected and worried. But as Orville left he said '*Au revoir*' and the constable looked up and nodded.

"Later, after he was released, Orville remembered what emblem the Native child had on her jacket. Two small moccasins tied together. As he walked along Sherbrooke Street he thought of them. He had seen moccasins exactly like that at the Pitt Rivers Museum, laid obscurely in a box that a thousand vacationers passed by with an urbane glance. It was the first time in years he had thought of them. And hadn't Orville written on the glass case they were entombed in: *Moccasins, Post-European, Iroquois circa 1785*?

"Now they seemed peculiarly insistent, and important, and had been for years essential to his life. It was as if he was somehow directed to rue Tristesse.

"Two nights later, when he was on the bus travelling Highway 20 back to New Brunswick, it all washed over him. The inexorable truth that he had been seeking beauty in the wrong place. He clutched Gaby's picture, as that little ten-year-old girl who had wanted to go fishing.

"It was snowing and the bus engine hummed and people slept, and almost instantly, in the depth of sadness, he felt this question within him. It seemed to reverberate through his entire body, as if it came from another time and place: *You asked Josée for a sign. So I gave you a sign. Now do you see what Satan demands of the world? Now do you see?*

"And the bus hummed and the snow fell. And he heard: *Satan demands our children in garbage cans. And Abraham each day is told to stay his hand?*

"But he hadn't known the woman's name. Now for some reason he did. And now he remembered the red ribbon on those two children, three thousand years apart, and what he had said to Brenda about it.

For some time that night he tried to ignore this revelation as false. But he could not do so.

"So he impulsively decided then to visit what he had laughed at and ridiculed for years, the monastery in Rogersville."

"I see," Cathy said, for that is all she seemed able or willing to say. Then she added, "A pair of moccasins."

————

John waited ten minutes, and then, as the day receded—as the late afternoon had settled and evening was coming, he took a drink of water from the bottle he had brought, and looked up quickly at her:

"Years earlier your brother had picked up a book by René Girard. A book called *I See Satan Fall Like Lightning.* He despised the title, and bought this book in London intending to mock it. And he did mock it by relating the crimes of religion. Especially the Catholic religion—from the Inquisition to the Crusades, to Mount Cashel, Cape Breton, Montreal, the ignorance of certain local priests, the false piety of nuns. So he skewered the idea yet he did not read very much of the book.

"After he saw the young murdered First Nations girl and came home, the first thing he saw was the book lying on the floor in his study. I now suspect it had fallen when Eunice was in his study snooping. So he took it with him when he went to the monastery. He realized as he read it that he had witnessed most of what Girard wrote about."

"What?"

"That many millions of us felt we could become like Jesus himself by crushing belief, and in doing so, had in literature and art adopted the mask of Christianity in order to destroy Christ, to accuse our enemies and to scapegoat others in the name of social justice.

The notion of the ideal you emulate, then envy, then learn to hate, wish to destroy. Eunice had done it in her columns against him, and Milt had done it too. Eunice even more than Milt wanted to mimic and destroy the man she had once emulated. And all the while Armageddon was fast coming; Behemoth strode the streets once again. Seeing in this book an articulation of what he had known and seen in life made him realize he had made a desperate mistake about beauty, and about that book."

"That is a harsh vision," Cathy said. "Everyone would take him as completely deranged. They would exalt over his madness. And he would be called a hypocrite."

"Oh, he knew it—he knew how harsh it was. For three months he was silent, almost completely. He went to Mass, worked fixing computers and wiring for his keep. His one friend at that monastery was Brother Cortes. And when he began to speak he spoke for hours about the nature of beauty and how the earth had distorted it. How beauty had been taken out of the hands of little Gaby May and put into the soft leather gloves of Ms. Eunice Wise. How visionary insight had been taken from the soul of little Saint Bernadette and given to the souls of social-justice activists who desired to be exalted.

"Brother Cortes was a man from Wisconsin who had taken a vacation as a young entrepreneur and visited an old stone monastery in far-off New Brunswick as a curiosity some twenty-six years before. He had a job as a financial advisor. He had a great many things in his favour. He had a Mercedes and a pleasure boat. He gave it up. Your brother admired Cortes, and decided himself to become a monk."

"So, then—a monk," Cathy said, not without anger, "after all of this—all of this—all of this—but after all of this that he worried us about from the time he was fourteen, putting us through hell for years—he decides to be a monk. Is that in itself running away?"

"I have no idea if he would have become one. Cortes told him that first he should complete his dig on the Miramichi. He should do the dig for Amos Paul because that is who he promised.

"There was a letter awaiting him, saying that he had lost the civil suit. He ignored this, and the charge that he was destroying First Nations heritage. He found quite by accident the remains of those bodies. He was planning to go back to the monastery. He was done with his search. As he told Brother Cortes, God revealed Himself by revealing His enemy," John said.

"His enemy?"

"Satan."

"He believed in Satan?"

"After Iraq, he believed very much in Satan. Yes, so much so that he felt him almost physically. The entity who watches always from the sidelines as we perform for him. Satan, who fills the world with small, well-dressed splashes of menace."

"That's unrespectable. I mean, you become very unrespectable when you believe this."

"Unrespectable. To the respectable people like Milt and Eunice and the boys and girls they influence. Oh, yes—yes, Cathy, very much so."

————

Then John suddenly returned to someone else:

"The first day I visited with Ms. Wise last month, to ask some questions about her photographs under the bridge—the photo she took of *OBA*, which she did not seem to remember—she wore a bright new suit. I could see the tag she had torn from it in the ashtray. It was at that point I felt she was guilty: in the deep blueness of her suit, and the touch of rouge on her pale cheek. But she was initially so certain of herself that suddenly her fragility caught me up, and I was sad. I then thought of what Orville had said about the giant cat behind her, whose eyes shone green in the afternoon, whose pelt was shiny black, and I realized it was true. Because I realized, at that moment, that she had known all along that it was true. I think this was an ephemeral feeling—as if we were both seeing the same thing for a brief moment. That grand, exotic cat with the pulsating jade eyes that had sat on her doorstep like a vision. How could she not admit to that? It was actually a part of the beauty she sought. Her lips came together tightly, and we both unconsciously looked out toward the green veranda. Past the veranda where she had erected a giant fence to protect her property.

"Her sudden insentient expression made me realize, looking back at her, that the cat had in fact come quietly upon that porch. It had come not for her but for her little dog that she almost always carried about with her. I knew in an instant that she too had seen this cat and had pretended not to because he, Orville, would then be exonerated. She would have had to publicly thank him, and he might even have been commended. She could never have *him* exonerated—not then, not ever. Her desire for him had turned to rage against him. So then the story must be that he had *fired at her*—had tried to *kill her*. The reason being that she knew about his *relationship* with Gaby May.

"In a split second she decided that attempted murder of her is what had happened. She wrote Milt about it, and he was appalled. All *decent* people were. Nothing has to be true. This is what Eunice knew. She had known it since she was a child and had her little clubhouse. She had known how to use public opinion in order to make opinion grow in her favour.

"She knew how to capitalize on *his* infamy. She had devolved into the passionate side of war too briskly to see any truce with him.

She relished her right never to *really* care, but to *pretend to care.* *The Handmaid's Tale* would titillate and rule her life, but no real handmaid would she help. And she lived in the age when she was able to act this way without any consequence of pain. But look at what she had given up in order to malign him!"

"What?"

"She had given up the almost impossibly rare admission that she had seen such a beautiful animal—and on her porch. So with this discussion I had with her there was the realization that she was simply lying. I asked her again about *OBA.* Again she apologized and said she did not remember when she had taken the picture. It was at that moment I realized she felt she must lie. I knew Orville had actually fired his rifle to save her. She stood, went and picked up her dog and held it, as if for comfort. Then she came back and sat down and lighted a cigarette.

"'I don't remember *OBA*—where was it—under the bridge? I could have done it—I've done so many photographs now.'

"'What is more important is that it is now defaced,' I told her. 'It was quite beautiful—I am trying to find out who defaced it.'

"'One of the boys down there at any time?'

"'No—this was done, not at any time—it was done two weeks after Orville died. I am wondering—why?'

"She shrugged and looked away. Still, at this moment she began to understand she was implicated in something that she did not fully comprehend, or had intentionally wanted to misinterpret. I recognized by her expression, the sudden look of dampness on her face, that she was now aware she had been mixed up in something repellent. I began to realize at that time that our Ms. Wise was not as innocent of the tree of good and evil as she claimed. She had gorged on an apple or two. She had tasted some with her thin, chapped lips. But, on a more insidious note, she had no qualms about the apples she munched on.

It was, in fact, her subtle blackmailing of, at the time, her fiancé, Milt Vale."

"Over the book?"

"I had finished reading the famous book of Milt Vale's, *Darkness*, and I decided to mention it to her. I asked her if she had read it. She looked at me sharply—a little angrily—and nodded.

"'What a question! Of course,' she said.

"'A good book?' I asked.

"'A very good book—the best book written about us ever,' she answered, as if defending it against my impression of it. But she said nothing else. Nothing at all, and I could see she was trying to find an answer, some way to get around speaking of it. So I told her I thought it was a wonderful book.

"And I added, with some enthusiasm:

"'It is surprising, though, that he knew all about loading his own bullets, the best way to start a smudge in winter, Conibear traps, the best way to snare—how to call and hunt moose, bring the bull to him over the great chop-down just to the north. Surprising that a man who went to the Iowa writers' course by way of Illinois, and wore rather tightly defined three-piece tailored suits, his goatee ever trimmed, could possibly know all this so readily. I am wondering too, having read his first little book, *The Renter*—the book that idealized everything that made light of what he later seemed to cherish in *Darkness*. Rural backwardness is endemic in his first, and is quite sacred in the second. When he was here once, he spoke about books he loved—each one of them would disavow everything he said in this. I am left wondering too . . . '

"'What are you wondering?'

"'Well—I'm wondering if I could have him sign my copy,' I said.

"'But how on earth would I know?'

"'Oh—I think you would,' I said.

"So there was the sudden and surprising look of guilt in the deep blueness of her suit. She was a princess, but the pea of guilt could never be under enough mattresses to protect her from herself.

"I suddenly saw her as someone quite brutal. She had insinuated herself into Orville's life, trying to wrest his fame and celebrity, and had not ever let go. Now Milt *must* marry her because she knew something about the book *Darkness*."

"So then?" Cathy asked.

"So, thinking of Orville's innocence hidden in the lie of her fine manners, a week later—that is, a couple of weeks ago now—I confiscated her computer. And in her emails there was found the complicity both Milt and she partook in, without either of them divulging this complicity to each other."

"Eunice and Professor Vale plotted against each other?" Cathy questioned.

"Each of them had a scenario in their mind about whom the other might be, or perhaps what the other might accomplish for them. First, Eunice hated her ex-husband's common success. Over the last decade he had become quite successful. So now, angry with herself, she needed for her own self-respect to marry a very great man. And for his part, I now believed that once the bodies were found Professor Vale needed her, Eunice, to whitewash *OBA* away, for he had seen her photograph of that graf in the book-store as well. This subterfuge between the two would in the end cause Orville's death. But at least in part, what part she had really played would only be discovered by Eunice herself after she unceremoniously whitewashed the graffiti away. Then she would begin to realize."

"The forgery of the book *Darkness*?" Cathy said.

"She probably knew that—she would begin to discover the murder that it caused."

So John took out of his small leather pack the emails, which at first to Cathy's ears did not make sense. But as she listened to John read, after a time she became aware of something spellbinding:

"*Remember what I said on the phone,* Milt had suddenly written to her a week after Orville's death. *Their case is closed now, but if that graffiti is still there, Aiden will be questioned. He has had enough trouble in his life with the discovery of those bodies. Now that no one knows about that graffiti, let's get rid of it for good. So he will not be implicated.*

"*Of course—I completely understand,* she wrote back. *Are you sure it is his?*

"*I cannot assume it is not. In fact, it can't be anyone else's. You know he has one similar here—near my apartment in Fredericton. So if you could cover it over completely—paint it over or deface it.*

"So," John said, "Eunice Wise answered thus:

"*Okay, I will go down and see about it—as far as us travelling together to Tuscany next spring, all as I have to do is renew my passport.*

"Then later he wrote:

"*Is it done—did you paint it over?*

"But she did not answer him, so he wrote again and again; he wrote six more messages:

"*Is it done—Is it done?!*

"Finally, three days later, came her response:

"*Yes, it is done—I have sent for my passport.*"

10.

SO NOW JOHN TURNED HIS ATTENTION TO THE BONES.

"They were discovered by Orville—and, foolishly, brought to his house, at the time of a land dispute with his neighbor Eunice Wise. Worse, because Orville found them so suddenly after so many years and took them to his house, the bones were thought to have been 'hidden' on the land that was being disputed. He supposedly had also gone into hiding. That is, the police believed that after he had done the crime, he had lived hand-to-mouth in our cities and because of guilt was now atoning for his sin at a monastery."

Cathy said, "Even I thought that!"

"Yes, and what picture did he have in his wallet—that he had carried for a generation?"

"Yes—yes."

"The bones were hurriedly gathered by him and were laid in the very top room of his house, in the room above his study. He had removed them in the dark—he had no idea what he actually had—but worse, he thought he knew."

"So it was not Danny John?" Cathy asked.

John said:

"No, it was not Danny John. All of us made a terrible mistake. But you see, the mistake was Orville's as well as ours."

"So of course he had to be the murderer of who they believed was Danny John and the young woman?"

"Especially when the slight, fragile bones of the unborn child appeared," John said.

————

"When he returned from his retreat at that monastery he had to go to the store down the road. No one had seen him in years here, really. They were surprised that he was home; surprised by his appearance and the even more ragged clothes he wore. His face looked ashen and he was thin, his large hands dark and yet imprinted by red along the sides of his great fingers. There he saw old Mrs. Hubbard and old Mrs. King. He decided to go deer hunting the next afternoon. The meat was not for him but to be given away to those two widows. He had done this on a half-dozen occasions. You of course know that Micmac hunters do this for their Elders as well.

"Everything was scented of autumn and snow, and the pale sky sat above him in a way that was unmoving yet turbulent, static yet uncertain. He took his shotgun and four buckshot shells (for he was hunting deer in the marsh down near the overgrown swale that fronted the water and so he would be at close quarters) and made his way out in the brittle but still warmish afternoon. He had splashed doe urine on him, and wore a small orange vest.

"The day was filled with grey clouds. At certain moments, however, the sun did come out, and the ground was lighted in a pink gracefulness as if fairies were casting their sunlit wands over it, all the way along the shore. He saw a buck and followed it. He didn't shoot it."

"Perhaps he did not want to shoot it?"Cathy said.

"Perhaps," John said. "At any rate he was turning to go home. In his mind he had concocted a letter for you—in which he was to say that he would give up this life. He would have mentioned the little Yazidi girl, and the sleeves of gold the major had gloated over. He could not look at one more object that men and women desired after that day. The Yazidi girl and Mohawk child were worth everything he had ever seen. His past life in a way repulsed him. He was reading Thomas Merton."

"It was time to let go of the past."

"Yes."

"How is it not the strangest thing I have ever heard from a man who was once that little boy I played with? But who is Mr. Merton?"

"A Trappist monk—the book *The Seven Storey Mountain* is his auto-biography, published in 1948."

"But—the bones, those isolated bones—how did they get there if it was not Orville?"

"He had followed the six-point down the swale back toward the bay. Perhaps he couldn't get a clear shot, or perhaps he thought better of it. Anyway he lowered the gun and, turning away in the last of the pink twilight, he went out to the shore and walked by Old Face rock—that immense jagged stone carved by the weather into the face of God. The small fissures in it over the years, the petrified soil underneath, is where he had wrestled the Dunn brothers, and that stranger. He stopped suddenly to light his pipe, and he discovered a very small bone sticking out of the clay soil that would have been passed over by a thousand people."

"But not by him?" Cathy asked.

"Not by him who had studied them all over the world. It was the place he had wrestled many years before, against one whom Mrs. Dunn called 'the ghost'—the one person who had thrown him down when her own sons could not."

"It was at that spot?"

"Yes, very likely close to it—the Dunns' little house was gone— the one by the old brook—and the Dunn boys too had long moved away—but that was the spot."

"Strange."

"He was not in the least overcome by it. Kneeling down in the deep, cooling earth he believed he had discovered what he had been searching for at the dig he began so many years before. Remnants of a former age. Still, he was not sure exactly what he had found. Two bodies—actually three. (He did not know of the third—the unborn child.) He worked until his hands bled, and recklessly took the bones in his jacket back to his house. He didn't even have time to look at them and did not really ever get to. That night was cold and black. I doubt if he was seen doing so."

"And it was just three days after he had received a letter that *ordered* him to stop visiting that beach," Cathy said.

"Yes, it was the property of Ms. Eunice Dorothea Wise."

"Dorothea—that's what her middle name was; yes, that's what I was trying to remember. She used to say: 'You are a stinky, blinky, no good little rat-faced MacDurmot, but I myself am Miss Eunice Dorothea Wise,'" Cathy said, smiling and suddenly reaching over to take a drag off his cigarette.

"Yes, he brought what remains he could gather home (the tiny bones of the child were found by us later on), and left them upstairs in the attic. He thought he may have had parts of the remains of two bodies. He didn't know why he felt there was something strange about his find. And in fact, if he had done what he should have—which was study them closely and bring them to everyone's attention—he might have been saved. The bones were covered in dirt and clay soil. It would take time for him to decipher what he had, and he had promised to travel to Saint John's L'Arche community the next day to give a talk.

"So he went to L'Arche. There among them he said:

"'My life changed because of the murder of a child. More than one child.'"

"He was thinking of the child in Montreal and the little Yazidi girl?"

"Of course he was. The next time we see your brother he is hand-cuffed through waist chains, emerging from the back of an RCMP SUV with multiple cameras on him. They brought Orville in, and one of our police officers—the very same fellow who told him once that he wouldn't want to be called a dirty old man for bothering Gaby—came into the room to talk to him. Years had passed and he was angry at himself for not stopping this Orville MacDurmot years before.

"'Do you know what you are being charged with?' he asked.

"'Of course—but you are all mistaken.' Orville even laughed at this, for he felt it was preposterous.

"'Mistaken! Mistaken! What do you have to say about it?'

"'Say? I've nothing to say—except let me go back to my business and leave me alone. I must give my life for someone now.'

"'Who?'

"'Just someone—a young girl, whom I couldn't help.'

"'Do you wish to make a phone call?'

"'To whom?'

"'A friend?'

"'I have none.'

"'A family member?'

"'No, thank you.'

"'A lawyer?'

"'Why in God's name would I ever need one for this?' Orville smiled.

"The officer told me later that he was almost ready to mention Gaby May, to yell at him for impregnating a young girl and then killing her, but instead he shrugged, grabbed his pen and notebook and left the room."

"Because he thought Orville knew whom he was being charged with killing?" Cathy asked.

"Yes. Of course. Every one of us did."

"So Eunice, our Eastern panther, must have celebrated!" Cathy said blithely.

11.

SO JOHN BEGAN TO RELATE TO HER THE CONCLUSION OF his investigation.

"There were two incidents of murder on that beach. So I will go back five whole years to just before the second murders—that is, the murder of the mother and the unborn child. The first murder is an entirely different story."

"They did not happen at the same time?"

"My love, they did not happen in the same century," John cautioned, then smiled, realizing he had just called her "my love" and in some way meant it.

"So the other body was not Danny John!" Cathy said again.

"No, it was not. So I will go back five years. At that time young Aiden was happy; he had just painted the graffiti under the bridge. He had left directions to where he was in a sketch so his father wouldn't worry, and he and Gaby had hitchhiked to the Miramichi for the weekend. On the very day the graffiti was painted, Orville was not even in Canada—he was in Iraq."

"Which would have cleared him?" Cathy asked, almost in trepidation.

"Completely," John said. "Completely—but we were blind to everything. We had become blind—the entire river, as if a great infection, had spate at us." John stopped for some moments, so that the whole building was deathly still. "But your brother did not know it was important. That is, until his last moment he believed it was simply a mistake that would be recognized as a mistake."

"Hubris," she said.

And she had gotten the word right—*hubris* was the word she was trying to remember. It lighted up the mornings in summer from years gone by when the young boy turned to his sister and she saw in his one useful eye the damning gleam of utter brilliance that she was the first to recognize. That brilliance matched with his own Achilles heel.

"Of course," John said. "Hubris it was—but the kind that makes one weep."

———

"Now," John continued after a moment or so, "the idea I wish to impart is the look of sheepish horror that passed over Milt Vale's face that moment, about five years ago now, when he realized there really and truly was another manuscript of this novel—and that it was in the possession of a young child—this flimsy waif of a child, Gaby May—a female child of nineteen, who was sitting across from him with an expectant look on her face. Hoping against hope for the manuscript that she was finally showing him. The expectant look came because she was aware of some sudden transfiguration in his disposition—he looked strange all of a sudden as he began to read her uncle's book.

"Professor Vale kept his head down for the longest time, with the bald spot on his head getting red. He flipped the edge of the paper with his fingers and finally, turning the pages over to page 52, looked up at her with an ashen look—a smile played, if you can use that term anymore, on his lips, but he said nothing. It was as if he was waiting for her to tell him something dire. To laugh and say he was caught.

"She didn't say anything, however—she glanced at him quite curiously, her head cocked to one side, because he seemed so utterly astonished by her. Then she looked over at the Fabergé piece that he had placed on a back shelf in his office, thinking how beautiful it was and wondering why was it hidden in such an obscure place.

"'My dear, this is quite the little book—'

"'It is?' Gaby May asked.

"'Well, I am not sure—I am not saying it is bad—but I need to look at it more closely.'

"He knew a little bit about her life—not much. She was the girl who his son had met one night when he went to collect rent. Yes, she lived on the top floor, in the smallest of all the rooms, and worked the night shift at Walmart stocking shelves. So she couldn't have been very bright, he thought. His son was very shy and Vale had tried to get him to make friends. But he had never been able to do so. But half of this was Vale's own fault. He was convinced—or he had convinced himself, though this was not spoken of—that it was Aiden's fault that his wife had died. And Aiden knew as much, without saying anything or anything being said.

"But now, Aiden had met this girl. Gaby May made him happy—he spoke more, he talked about things. He realized he could do things, and she told him he could, all with the innocence of a child who views the world as open and uncomplicated. She was now in the midst of helping her brother, but soon, she told Aiden, they would be together. He wanted, Aiden did, someday to be a painter. She bought him paints—Bombay blue, reds, pale green, bright yellows, in small bottles and tubes, and hid them in his pockets. He would come home from visiting her and there would be a tube of deep-orange paint in his jacket pocket.

"*For your first masterpiece painting, our autumn leaves falling into the brook*, she would have written. *Someday we will live on the Miramichi and you will become a great painter.*

"But how strange all of this was to Professor Vale—that she met and protected his son; that was the thing—she protected his son, with fury, and made him feel loved. No one who had ever met her could not succumb to her treasure of gifts. And what, then, was her treasure of gifts? Vale tried to understand. Not money or fame, of course. She had none of that. But her gentle humanity, courage and love. That is the beauty transcribed in wisdom and flowing down from the rock, to put all other beauty to shame.

"How incomparable the harshness of her upbringing—her mother a chronic alcoholic, bringing various men home, while Gaby May had a mother's job taking care of her brothers, working to make Christmas boughs to sell so she could buy them presents—her hands bleeding—and then to hike down in wintertime to visit her dying mother, who breathed oxygen and bled through the nose, while little Gaby sat beside her and spoke to her of heaven while tears ran down her cheeks—all of this was seemingly gothic to Vale—he could not comprehend it, not the way it should have been comprehended. And then her brothers, a hard lot after their stepdad died in the fire— there was no one they had loved more. But Tom, who had warred with everyone, even his stepfather, whom he loved, was in jail now— the other brother had died a while before.

"Milt had learned this other brother, Pete, had been crossing the river while working. They said he had gotten a cold hiking to see his brother and that over the last days his cough had gotten worse. He believed he needed to save a thousand dollars and the three of them would be able to live together in an apartment. They would get Tom help. Oh yes, Tom was the strongest, the toughest, the meanest on the river. As tough as Packet Terri, Harold Dew or Jerry Bines. But he was lonely and sad, and like so many on the great river, needed kindness.

"That is why Pete and Gaby knew they needed to help him. On weekends Pete and she would hitchhike down to the jail to see him. Pete sitting in the visitors' room, with his small hands scarred by work. Gaby, as always, would be seated beside him. And what did their coming to see him inspire in Tom? At first he was querulous and blamed them for something undefined. He blamed them for his mother, his life, because it was he who could not forgive himself for not going to his mother's funeral. He blamed the writer too, he blamed him until he could not blame any more and, crying, said:

"'No, he loved me.'

"Tom did not consider how hard these trips were for his smaller brother or for little Gaby May, how often they were stranded on the road, how they had been left at times in the middle of nowhere. How Gaby always carried Kleenex and cough medicine in her pocket for Pete's cough, and how one cold evening, if anyone had been watching, they would have seen a strange sight on the side of the empty highway: Gaby, trying faithfully to get the last of the cough medicine onto an old crooked spoon to give her childlike brother, because he coughed whenever he drank from the bottle, as sleet pelted down on their faces.

"But one late-autumn day Gaby got a call saying that Pete had fallen in the river trying to cross it with a chainsaw in his hand. The day he died he had forgotten his piece of blueberry cake that she had made him, along with his cough medicine on the counter. Then for a long time she could not bring herself to tell Tom why Pete didn't come with her anymore and why she hitchhiked alone.

"'Tell Pete to come too—I miss him, Gaby—tell him to come see me too—he don't write me now, he used to—I made him upset with me?'

"Poor Gaby one day had to admit to why Pete no longer came.

"Now she had one brother left. She visited Tom whenever she could—she tried to get him help. She attended all of the court cases involving her brother. She pleaded with the judge, and sat on the courthouse steps, and never once gave up hope.

"When Milt Vale first heard of these exploits he said to himself, I must really do something for her. Then he said, Perhaps I should write a novel about her. Yet the more he learned about her, the more he realized, trembling all over, that he had already written this novel—or had claimed to.

"That she was the *one*—she was the *chosen one*, whom that writer from the Miramichi had cherished for so long—to write about. She was what beauty was about: *Sir, you said you would take me fishing—*those words still seemed to sing in the trees above them, to lilt and measure out of some deep reservoir of humility and love. He who was sitting at his grave desk with all his grave books could never catch that purity in a bottle.

"She in fact was the antithesis of those very secure and arresting women our good man Vale pretended to know—she was so very different that in so many ways he could not begin to be able to write about her—but supposedly had. She was the young girl in his novel who had phoned her father and had asked him to buy them a Christmas present. But her father said he couldn't do so. And so at nine years old, she tried to get money by herself. How sentimental all of that was, what maudlin, lowbrow Victorian rubbish. No one would believe it, would they? No sophisticated writer would clutter up their life with her. Yet he had claimed her very life in two dozen interviews. Yet he too must have known—even he must have known—the exquisite gift of God she was, and now, seated before him, how she proved what God intended for us?

"But was it her? He disliked Eunice Wise as a complete fraud, truly self-pitying and vulgar, yet he was sited to be with her. He found Gaby May almost perfect in a strange imperfect way—yet he was terrified of her. So one day after meeting her (this was before she gave him the manuscript), almost out of the blue, she said:

"'Aiden says you are a very famous writer. I am so honoured and proud to meet you, sir!'

"'I've travelled—I've been to the Louvre,' he said, for some reason he didn't at all understand. He looked at the simple cross around her neck, her mischievous grin and the fake Fabergé behind her head. Her mischievous grin came only because of the way he said *Louvre*.

"But her voice came as the sound of waves on the beach—suddenly he felt all of this was being watched, and was preordained in some mysterious way; that he was in the presence of someone *holy*. She was the one, he had heard from Eunice, whom Orville had wanted to take fishing, and was warned not to see. He knew at this moment that Orville had never hurt her—he knew it like the sound of those imagined waves that Orville must have loved her only as a child. But both of them had used this lie to try to destroy him. Vale's lips trembled slightly when he thought of this. Eunice, who had in her own life never loved a child, never in her life, but had written about them in her columns to prove to herself she cared.

"He was startled and for a long time could not look at her.

"'Yes, I am famous,' he said, inspecting the wood on a cabinet in his study and rubbing his hand along it. 'You didn't read my book, did you?' he added. But he did not look her way—he kept his eyes on the edge of the cabinet.

"'Oh, no, I am not so bright as to read many books—but my step-father wrote a book one day and I was wondering if you might look at it—it was long ago—but I have a copy. Aiden said you might take a look. My dad—I called him my dad—was a real writer—but he didn't have much luck and when I heard about you I said to myself, Boy, I wish my dad had met someone kind like Professor Vale.'

"'Oh, of course—bring it along,' he said. His voice was weak, almost stifled, at that moment; he had stopped rubbing his hands along the cabinet.

"The first thing he thought was, it couldn't be *the* book. Then he thought she must be *tricking* him—she knew and must have been after money. So he must talk her out of it—he must trick *her*—because, well, because his very security depended upon it. For he never could call Eunice greedy, but verily he could say it about her, this child. Still, there was something else—something mysterious: it seemed she had spent her whole life in a part of the world he had known nothing about, in leafed-over valleys with rushing, dark, fertile water, wind blowdowns crisscrossing forlorn wood roads, and animals like muskrats—that her presence at this moment, in his very comfortable Fredericton home, with the ratty sweater and the old stockings she wore, the cross around her neck, did not detract from her but gave her a wondrous magnificence—and that magnificence was found in her innocence. If he had been more humble he would have called it grace. He may even have taken her hand, and said:

"'Help me, Gaby May—I have done a silly and incautious sin, and I need your help—please.' And if he had said this, if he had, and had told her, she would have taken his hand and forgiven him. But that moment did pass, and he could not. What was worse, she was staring at him, at this moment, almost with love.

"Milt remembered how she spoke about going out in the winter on snowshoes, falling over every ten feet, with the grey, gloomy wind so strong it kept her in one place for moments on end—walking through fields with her brothers, chopping holes in the ice for water and taking it back on her old toboggan, two buckets at a time, up the long slippery hills in half-desolate spaces. She described it almost verbatim to what was in his book. His face was white, and he was petrified. But he was petrified for a peculiar reason that should be seen by us with pity—with actual pity. His terror was because she was not duplicitous. If she had been, he could have been conniving, underhanded and angry. If that were the case he might have been able to be more underhanded than she.

"Yet this was awful in another way. This was the kind of person his son loved? She was not the kind of person, the kind of girl, he had dreamed of for his son. The daughter of a doctor or a lawyer—there were plenty of those, and they were fashionably entrenched in the idea of progress, just as he was. And how horrible it was that his son had no interest in them. He did not know it was horrible, mind you, until later, when she had left his presence and he felt he had not impressed her, and she had made him talk too much—so she must have caught on to him. That is, he felt agitated that his soul was small compared to hers. And not only his soul—but Eunice's soul as well.

"Then the next day, when she brought the manuscript, he discovered for certain whom it was his son loved. And he had no idea what to do. This would lead them into a somewhat dangerous liaison, and he knew he had to hide secrets from her."

"From her—you mean, from Eunice?" Cathy said.

"Yes. So Gaby left the manuscript with him. It was as if the tattered yellowed pages scalded him when he felt them. And then she came back four days later.

"'Is it any good?' she asked; she was a little out of breath, hoping against hope.

"'I am not sure,' he said, and he waved his hand, as if the question annoyed him. 'Where is this grand author now?' he asked.

"'Oh—he died in a fire,' she whispered. 'Well, he wasn't my dad—but we thought of him like he was. He took care of us as if he was—in fact he was—he was our mommy's brother or cousin, I think.'

"Milt laughed at the 'I think.' Then he looked serious once more.

"'So your uncle?'

"'Yes—an uncle! We called him our stepfather too.'

"'And your brothers?'

"'Well, you heard of Tom, and my brother Pete died crossing a river. He slipped and his heart gave out—he was trying to get money so we could all live together.' She said simply, 'But he had rheumatic fever as a child. And you can see I have a bulb in my ear—because I am partially deaf—but your son, you see—you see, sir, your son does not mind my infirmity.'

"'Infirmity, does not mind. How terrible—I mean for your brother,' Milt said, sitting back and lighting his pipe and looking down at the bowl. 'But please, dear, don't get your hopes up! Like I say, this is quite the little book. But I am very, very busy, you know—many people want me for many things! Many people want me to read too, too many books. So I can only get to it when I can get to it.' He was pleased that she was so innocent—so trusting of him—that was his plus.

"He smiled and patted her shoulder. She nodded, sighed, left him and went downstairs.

"The more Milt thought about this, the more he realized that if any of this came to light, in any way, his life would be ruined. He would be so shamed; the public shaming is what he could not take. That is, all of his life he had done what was considered radical—he had *taken on the system*—how easy a phrase that was. Especially to activists, who said they were 'taking on the system' while they used the system so completely, had burrowed themselves in standard orthodoxy so wonderfully. And then to be outed by this—this mistake that he had made (for he had convinced himself he must have given this Miramichi writer all the ideas for the book, so the book was, as he said privately, a 'shared responsibility').

"He immediately thought of destroying the manuscript, and then saying he had mislaid it, telling the little one that it was not a very good book. But perhaps she had already shown it to someone else who had read the book—i.e.: *his* book. And so he hesitated at this moment, realizing the horrible position he was in—that *she* had placed him in. Also she had given him something more with this copy—the last two and a half chapters—and he could not read them. Now that they were there in front of him—now that they were before him, he felt unable to look at those pages. He felt very tired—so tired of it all.

"Yes, he had better handle it himself. He would say the book was not worth publishing, and he would be tolerant but also stern. She wouldn't be able to see past his awareness, and he would outshine the manuscript by convincing her that he was the authority on it. Then he would say, 'Just leave it with me, dear' and she would never see it again.

"But I will stop with Milt in the study with the manuscript on his desk. I want to return to the emails for a second. In those emails there is a certain blasé feel about this great book of his. Eunice, of course, wrote and congratulated him: *You are getting some fine reviews, I must say*. But it seemed she never really wanted to talk about his second book, his masterpiece. Then, about two years before Milt met Gaby May, he accidentally met Eunice at, of all places, a small campground near Woodstock, where they had both stopped one hot day. He was travelling back from Toronto, which he liked visiting (he could shine there with certain people he knew), and she was travelling back from shopping in the States.

"They spoke standing in the parking lot in the glaring heat and it became apparent by the way she looked at him that she knew. It was the only time she had looked at him with such a daunting glance. She had read the book *Darkness* and knew it to be someone else's, and she knew whose it was. Yet he knew by her look she would not tell anyone. Still, the imposing glance told him, Milt, that no lie could be hidden under a fine tweed jacket, especially from one who secretly commiserated with the lie itself.

"So about three weeks after meeting him at that campground, three weeks after giving him that daunting glance, she emailed Milt and declared that she needed a 'compatible spirit' in her life. That her life had been tragic on the Miramichi. Did he feel a connection to her, as she did to him?

"*Yes, I have felt so too*, Milt emailed her.

"*So, so glad to hear from you*, she had emailed back.

"So," John said, "that was the beginning of their more serious relationship, which by the time Milt met Gaby had gone on for a while. He helped Eunice place her photographs at an exhibit, helped her get hired by the *Miramichi Express*. But she helped him as well. She had already searched fruitlessly for the tin box. She had not spoken a word about what she suspected.

"Now back to Gaby. After Gaby left him that day he went and lay down on the big, bright-yellow couch in his study and stared at a small volume of Japanese poetry and stories from the Middle Ages, and the book *Confessions of a Mask* by Yukio Mishima. He then drifted off to sleep. He dreamed he had to step over a huge windfall and kept catching his new trousers on a sharp twig.

"When he woke later that evening the entire house was quiet. A stillness that was oppressive seemed to surround the greying room. Everything in it appeared fossilized and distant. The light was almost absent in the sky except for a pale blemish; his book spines looked ornate and secretive. He stood abruptly and became dizzy. He clutched the bookshelf nearest him to steady himself. For a moment he was at a loss as to how he came to be in his study. Then, realizing how he came to be there, he went toward the desk to take the manuscript and destroy it; only then did he believe he could live in peace. Yet the manuscript no longer sat on the impressive oaken desk. It was—gone. He called Aiden to him.

"'Where is the manuscript!'

"'Oh—Gaby asked me to get it. You were sound asleep, Dad, so I didn't wake you.'

"'Why did she want it back?'

"'She didn't want to bother you with it—she felt bad that she had bothered you. It was an imposition.'

"'But is that any reason!' he screamed—at the door, when the air was turning dark. 'That you would just walk into my study!'

"Professor Vale had stopped his reading of this tattered old manuscript at the point where the little girl was hauling water up the long hill at twilight on her old toboggan, both her mittens soaking and a small wisp of smoke coming from their tarpapered little house. He stopped reading at that point because he remembered she, Gaby, had told him that story the very first time he met her—and that story was not only in the manuscript written by her stepfather years before but on page 52 of his bestselling book. You know, the one Milt always said he had written about desperate poverty and lack of women's rights in the Maritimes?

"Again he was sure she had caught on and had gone to see a lawyer in order to start a cataclysmic lawsuit against him. He did not know she had gone to pray for her brothers at the church of Saint Francis, kneeling with her head lowered and speaking to her best friend, the Virgin Mary.

"He also did not know she was pregnant with his grandchild. And she'd had an ultrasound, and the child would be a girl. But she did not wish to tell anyone yet. She had another doctor's appointment in a few weeks and after that she would tell Aiden. It was her greatest hope that Professor Vale would like her. She tried to do what it was she thought he would like. So today she took the manuscript back. She didn't want to bother him because—perhaps, she thought, it was not at all a very good book, and it would embarrass him to read it. She did feel that a sensation had come over him when he had looked at it. And after she left the house she went to Westminster Books and bought Milt Vale's book. She would read it, and then when they were alone—or perhaps when she was with Aiden and him, she would ask a brave question about it—try to ask a question he would smile at as naive—she knew how to do so. (She had done it already with him by telling him the little story of her childhood.) Then she would produce his book from under her coat or sweater and ask him to sign it—and she hoped all three of them would laugh. For she wanted him to like her, for she loved his son.

"But now there was the ultrasound and it made her feel very special.

"It was a sacred moment to her—there was something about Milt that lacked that feeling of sacredness; it was as if he was in hiding from himself and the real world. Sometimes she would see him rushing about his large house as if he was being chased by a bat, and he would look up startled at nothing at all.

"She knew something was bothering him when she spoke to him, but did not know how to describe it. She felt the presence of his body—and not his spirit. She noticed his shoes and his tweed cap jauntily on his head before she noticed his soul. That Orville would begin to describe the sacredness of life because of the fluttering ribbon on the head of a murdered child would not have surprised her at all. Milt would have missed it completely.

"But Milt realized something about Gaby as well. He realized he had missed most things about women and men that were real. That *The Handmaid's Tale* was not at all close to being true when it came to the Gaby Mays of the world. He did not know quite how to say this to anyone, though. It seemed to impact him now and again—a certain moment in the sunshine, a certain look on the street. And the worst of it was, when she gave him the manuscript he saw the last chapters—but couldn't yet bring himself to read a line. And now the manuscript was gone. Well, he had to get it back! Then he could say it was his copy—he could even say the Miramichi writer had stolen it—yes. And he'd had to rework it from scratch, yes, and only Eunice Wise knew this. Yes. That's the ticket.

"But we could ask, had Gaby read the manuscript of her uncle's book herself? Of course. She had read it twice. Her father had rewritten and reworked the last thirty pages two days before his death. It was about a man very much like Orville coming to terms with beauty—and what beauty actually was—and finding it in the gentleness of a girl, Gaby May. Yes, maudlin rubbish—but as deep as oceans are deep.

"So this particular night Gaby had asked Aiden to help her gather the manuscript back, because she did not want to bother a man as important as Milt Vale. And so Aiden snuck into the room on his tiptoes and little Gaby hustled it away.

"You see, Milt's hubris always betrayed him. He was inordinately proud and wanted to let her know the kind of favour she was asking. If he had not made her feel unworthy to ask, she would never have taken it back. She put it back in the tin box. The book her stepdad wrote had made her laugh and it had made her cry. It made her laugh and cry. Now she would see if Milt Vale's great book did the same.

"She went home, to her room at the very top of the house. There she snapped on the light and looked out the dirty window toward the bottom of town. She took off her shoes and socks and worried and prayed about her brother Pete, whose heart had given way, and Tom, who had not had many chances in life and was now in jail. He had been angry that they had sent him to that foster home in Saint John and started his life of running away. It did not seem that she could help him. Then she quietly got into bed with the big book Professor Milt Vale had written. It had cost her a lot of money, but she did not mind. She was in happy trepidation when she read the inscription: *For you, Aiden, my son.*

"How great life would be, she thought tenderly at that moment. She knew Aiden had given up almost everything to please his dad. That is some of the reason why she loved him and encouraged him to take up his paintbrushes again. In fact, he had just tagged a cement abutment near her old home on the Miramichi. It was beautifully done, and if one looked very closely—but one had to look closely—intertwined with *OBA*, which meant 'Our Boy Aiden' (the last words his mom had ever spoken about him), was a secret message, just behind, in slightly more opaque yellow and tan colours: *LGM*. Together, *OBA LGM*: 'Our Boy Aiden Loves Gaby May.' Recently Gaby had bought him a blank canvas—for the time when he would stop tagging and start painting in earnest, paintings of rivers and lakes and Gaby May herself. He said that someday he would paint her in the nude and they would sell it for 95 million dollars, and they both laughed greatly:

"'As long as your dad doesn't see it—what would he think my soul?'

"The canvas was in her room at the top of the stairs, hidden in the closet. She was too dreamy to read tonight. She put the book down and went to sleep. Early the next morning she left for the Miramichi with both the tin box, housing her father's manuscript, and Mr. Vale's big, important book. She had to go straighten out her deceased brother's affairs. He did not have many affairs, but like all people, he had a few. She had to see about some kind of stone in the graveyard, near where her stepfather and mother lay."

—————

"If"—John spoke solemnly now—"you are amoral, or have tendencies toward it, you do not believe you are—and I am quite certain you do not know you are. For in some way amorality has no sense of itself. It is not attuned to wickedness or sinfulness, for it does not believe in either—it is in some ways unaffiliated with what is unmentionable. Your life works on the premise that all things could be true; therefore, if they help you, they must be true."

"Unaffiliated with what is unmentionable?"

"Unaffiliated with sin itself—because to you and your comrades, sin does not really exist—so no behaviour is really scandalous, save for the fact that you always blame others for scandal and not yourselves. To Milt it would never have mattered if Aiden lied, cheated on his exams or in a game of golf. These things were fine if they advanced some promise or some career. Very often Milt lied about whom he knew and how well he knew them. That he had dinner with John Updike and spoke often to Norman Mailer. And this was so usual it was taken as the proper form. Except that Aiden himself could not lie—and did not use lies or the scandal others found themselves in."

"And neither did Orville?" Cathy asked.

John paused, said:

"No. Neither did Orville. When Orville and Mary Cyr went to visit Amos Paul, who wanted him to help discover if a Micmac myth about great warriors was true or not, Amos, sitting at his little kitchen table, said:

"'Two wolves war in us. One is evil, the other is good. One is envy, cruelty, deceit and hatred. The other is humility, kindness, honesty and love.'

"'Who wins?' Mary Cyr asked him.

"'The one we feed,' Amos told them.

"For many years Orville did not think much of this. And then he could not stop thinking of it in relation to people he had known. So he came home determined to finish the dig for Amos Paul. He began to visit the monastery in Rogersville. He went there and remained silent for a long time. A day after he had discovered the remains, he visited L'Arche in Saint John. They asked him why he had gone to the monastery:

"'The murder of a child, I suppose. Yes, more than one child.'

"'Do you believe in Satan in the wilderness?'

"'I have been in the wilderness and I have seen Satan.'"

"Bad timing," Cathy said, partly seriously and half in morbid jest.

"Just as the bodies were being discovered in his house by the police," John concurred.

"But our Eunice and Milt—they had the proper form?"

"Yes. The date of their wedding was set before it all imploded."

"But it did implode?"

"So let us return to that terrible time five years ago now. A time when Orville was in Iraq dealing with his own soul and had in many ways forgotten Milt and Eunice, and thought he would never deal with them again.

"Milt asked Aiden one day, about three weeks after Gaby May had taken the manuscript back, where this little Gaby May was. When had Aiden last spoken to her? Aiden said he had not heard a word from her for over two weeks or more. He thought she had gone back to the Miramichi to settle things about her deceased brother. He had expected her back some days ago. Aiden was now very worried. Her cellphone went to message almost instantly.

"'Message . . .' Milt said, almost imperceptibly. It seemed that he was agitated; it seemed he was trying to think of something. 'Cellphone . . .' he said, '. . . cellphone?'

"'Yes, her cell?'

"'You didn't tell me she had a cell,' he said.

"'Of course—why shouldn't she?'

"Aiden realized his father's superficiality and said nothing further. He often said nothing now. For he had failed his father by not getting accepted into McGill, and the thing his father confronted him with whenever he tried to break free was the death of his mother. Why had he not been home? She had gone out to look for him, she didn't know the streets—it was awful, but she had left to find her son.

"'I am going out to find our boy Aiden,' she had said.

"Milt would bring this up every time he became upset over something. And Aiden said nothing now because he was frightened his father would explode and bring it up again today. The first time Milt mentioned it was the night Aiden had made his father the special supper from a restaurant menu downtown. He wanted to celebrate with his dad. But finally his dad turned to him and said:

"'Why weren't you home like you were supposed to be?'

"And Aiden, standing at the stove (every time he got up he put his chef's hat on), had no idea what to say. He was about thirteen at this time. His face turned heavy and tears ran down his cheeks as his father started to berate him. How dare he not be home, his father said, why had he not come home? The piano lesson had ended—it had been held earlier in the day because it was Christmas Eve.

"Aiden did not tell his dad he had run down to the university bookstore to try to find a book of poems his father said he liked. It was going to be his Christmas present to his dad, that book by Pablo Neruda; but he'd stayed too long searching for it—he was sure it had been on the shelf the week before—and finally they told him the store was closing. Why hadn't he asked them to put the book on hold for him? But his father never knew about this. He'd finally picked up another book for his father, quite at random. It was *Paradise Lost*.

He had just grabbed it in a hurry, to get it to the cashier in time. But he never gave it to Milt. He kept it in his room, and had not opened it.

"'You know she wouldn't have gone out if you had been home.'

"So the special dinner did not come off. Aiden sat at the table alone and the candle burned down, and his father went to his study. That was four years before Aiden met Gaby May. From the first his father did not want Gaby May around. Milt found her too coarse. He found her uneducated, and unsophisticated. She was the kind of white girl who might have come from a trailer park on the side of some awful highway, he had initially thought.

"'There are lots of other girls.' He had said this a dozen times, because he thought of his son as entering a different door into the adult world. He actually had a girl picked out—a Harriet O'Hara. Her grandfather was a retired professor, the family was quite wealthy, and Milt had ingratiated himself with them. Milt laughed raucously when he laughed; he spoke obsequiously when he spoke. He bought the girl a present—and had asked her to dinner on two occasions to meet Aiden. But all his plans were thwarted. Then that girl, Gaby May, to whom he had rented the smallest, tiniest room on the top floor, came to his house one day. But *who* she was was even more startling. Almost—preordained.

"And then Milt said one night, in something of a conciliatory tone, after Aiden had not heard from Gaby in over three weeks:

"'I don't think she cared a damn for you, son. I am sorry for it, I really am—I wish I could say or do something to make it better for you—but from now on I will try to look at things from your point of view, I will try not to harm you—no, she never cared for you!'

"'Yes, she does,' Aiden said, punching his small fist on his knee. 'Yes, she does care for me, she told me she cared for me—she told me, she told me she loved me—she told me, okay, Dad?—she did!' His face was shining with tears.

"'No. Girls like that—born like she was—can't be trusted. She said she was going to move out—I told her I would decrease her rent—but she simply shrugged at that.' Milt, in fact, had just thought of saying this. And he nodded as he spoke, as if verifying what he was saying. 'When you are brought up lying like she was—you hurt so many people.'

"But Milt had to tell Aiden she did not care for him, because he knew Gaby would not be back. It had all started because of a remark Aiden had made on a Monday evening three weeks before.

"'Guess what, Dad?' Aiden had said. 'Gaby May is reading your book—she is taking it with her to the Miramichi—she wants to ask you all the right questions about it because she wants you to like her. So don't let on you know.'

"'What about her father's manuscript—what will she do with it?'

"'Oh, she has it with her too—she is going to look at the differences between them because she wants to see what a *real* good writer is like; because I told her how good a writer you are. I think she might give it to that man—that fellow who visited you one night, Orville MacDurmot—to see what he will be able to do. See, Dad, she doesn't want to bother you about it. So she said Mr. MacDurmot might be able to help her. But she doesn't think he is home—he has been away for a while now—I don't think anyone knows where he is.'

"'All Vale could think of at that moment was the scandal. His face flushed beet red and he smiled a kind of soft, crooked smile that parted his lips as his eyes became glazed. In his glazed eyes was malice, and fear. Beyond that there was the smallest of feelings within his psyche, hidden almost from himself, about the terrible reputation the Miramichi had for murder. It became more and more pronounced as the day wore on. It affected him like microbes. That is, the idea of murder. It intrigued him, in some hard and diabolical way. For he had gotten away with other things—why not this thing? And he had convinced himself, like so many of our social activists, that there was no evil—only progress or its lack.

"'How could this have happened to me?' he thought as he left the house that night."

"This was five years ago now?" Cathy said.

"Five years," John said. "Five years have passed since that moment. Four years before Orville appeared in our court, charged with murder. Since that moment a whole investment in what one wants the world to be was played out by Eunice and Milt Vale. Neither of them knew how much the other knew the narrative was false—both pressed each other to see where the limits of this falseness was, both of them believing the other one thought the narrative was true; or, more to the point, believing the other one thought *they* thought the narrative was true. They dined, went to the Playhouse, had dear friends who painted rock coves and bushes, spoke of the environment and socially advanced political change, but something was always between them that was not spoken about.

"Yet once the bones of the young woman were found last year in his house, and she was found to have been pregnant, and Orville was charged, and died, then something else took over."

"What took over?"

"The terrible forgeries and blemishes of Milt's and Eunice's lives began to overshadow who they were. They began to make a series of mistakes—here and there. We must be comforted by the fact that we will never be sure how much Eunice Wise really knew. Yet it is true enough that she did not want to know. She had to prove to her ex-husband that she was exceptional. For after he, Calvin Simms, went away after so many trials in his life—after he had married her as a young woman of twenty who was once in love with him, after she and her family tried for many years to intimidate him—Calvin built up his own small empire, his crab fleet of seven boats and twenty-six men working for him. He was known all over as 'Calvin the crab man,' and had become a millionaire. So she needed Vale to expunge the scent of crab legs and the smell of the sea; the sea an anathema to Eunice except, of course, in paintings of coves and boats, in small rural coastal villages that had become gentrified, like those along the South Shore of Nova Scotia, where her painter friends were. There she could pretend to be a tourist from Vermont if she so chose. There she could pretend lighthouses were quaint, like they were supposed to be, and fishermen didn't really exist except in pieces of art, and crafts. So all of that was compelling, all eight feet of it showed that, as far as their interests, in art, life and companionship, they lived in a world disassociated from the truth they continually believed they sought."

"But Gaby? Tell me about her."

"I will go back to the horrible event itself—if you need to know . . . ?"

"I should, I think, know."

"It is not pleasant. It is horrible—as bad as it gets."

"Yes—I mean, I should know!"

"Then I will tell you. The day Aiden told Milt that Gaby had purchased his book, and was taking it to the Miramichi along with the manuscript from her late uncle, Vale told his son he had to go out for the night, to a literary function. It was a function for Irish writers at St. Thomas, and they were showing a movie about O'Casey. Professor O'Hara would be there, he said. So he might be late. He sounded upset by this function but told his son he could not escape it—O'Hara, he said, needed him there.

"He went to his study and picked up one of the beautiful pen-knives he had bought in France one year—one that sat on his desk to open his mail. He took the penknife with him. In the afternoon, he travelled toward the great river using the route Aiden had drawn out so well for him some weeks before, when Aiden and Gaby went there for the weekend, when Aiden, unknown to Milt at the time, had tagged the abutment of the bridge with *OBA LGM*.

"'Where are you going exactly?' Milt had asked before they left that day, because he was beginning to suspect that Gaby was the very girl who was written about in his book. Aiden had drawn him a map on a piece of heavy paper, for his son, already a brilliant illustrator, wanted to show his father how capable he was. That is, he drew it so Milt would be proud of him. Now the diagram Aiden had given him would help him find her.

"Drifting now and again over the centre line, his eyes bleary, our man Milt tried to think, over the two-hour drive, of a way out—a diplomatic solution to his tricky problem. For a while he thought of buying the manuscript, even welcoming Gaby into the family. It took him wholly two hours extra to find the road down into what people called the Crockery, amid a series of wild woods and streams, fronted by the great wild bay. In fact, this is where Orville often hunted. Here Vale saw rocks and cliffs and darkness all, all around. Finally, thanking God, he found it. It was so unusual—it finally appeared right before him, with a small light on in the window—perhaps two or three miles from where that man he had heard of, Sydney Henderson, had lived. This was the place Gaby had been born. Her father had left her when she was three, her mother had died when she was eleven. But Ida's old house still stood. So he went to the little home that Gaby had inherited from Ida May to talk to her.

"The fact was, she knew. Once he came in, she knew—and almost instantaneously. His body—his physical appearance—is what made her understand. There was a sudden coarse sense about him. His thin lips curled up, his eyes looked from one spot in the room to another. And she was struck dumb by why he was there, and knew she *must leave*. That is, suddenly, like an innocent, she became aware of how horrendous this was. The room was illuminated in a pinkish hue by light, and the stove was on like a comfort from the past. If she had not tried to leave he never would have struck her—that is how he mitigated his culpability.

"All he had wanted was the manuscript that she had taken back with her. He said he wanted to reread it. When he said she was part of the family, he said it so insincerely she smiled kindly. She looked at him strangely; her beautiful eyes were startlingly bright. His lips were thin and purple, his eyes glazed over; he had a strange hilarity in his face, but his face was utterly pale. He glanced at his copy of *Darkness*, which was opened to page 52. She had gotten that far before she had truly caught on (of course, she had known from the first page, but had flipped to that page to confirm it). The only person who could have written this famous book was her own uncle. Milt realized, glancing at the book, that she knew. So he asked again about the manuscript.

"'It is in a safe location,' she said, her eyes kindly upon him, as if to say—as some women do about someone's abused spouse, 'She is in a safe location.'

"'But I need it back,' he said. 'I will pay you—I will pay you 25,000 dollars—tonight.' He took out his chequebook and waved it at her, as if to convince her to be the person he already thought she was.

"Her lips moved slightly in such a subtle way, as if she was ashamed by him, and she lowered her eyes but did not answer. She had just gotten up from the table when he came to the door, and she had said, 'Aiden?' thinking it was he. But it was not the boy she so dearly loved. The boy who was actually so much more like his mother than his dad.

"Milt raised the ante. 'Yes,' he said, '50,000—it's our book—and you too are part of the family. You will always be a part of our family. Who did you give it to—did you give it to Orville? Tell me and I'll give you 100,000.'

"They stared at each other in silence. He had his soft doeskin gloves in his left hand—he liked them so—and something in his coat pocket.

"'My dear brother, help me,' she whispered, which is what she used to say to Tom when she had to lift the water bucket onto the sled. Tom, the tough one who stood up to the world.

"But Tom could not," said John. "Because I had put him in jail. That is what I will not be able to forget.

"'Brother, help me,' she whispered again, and tried to leave. But the door was blocked by a man who had read all of Spinoza once."

"He did not know she was pregnant?" Cathy asked, her hands suddenly trembling.

"No, he did not know she was pregnant with his grandchild when he struck her with the penknife. She finally reached the door and then fell back with a sigh, and her legs trembled, and then she lay still, her eyes open, and blood came down her cheek. It was as if she was sleeping. The hearing aid that was still in her ear gave him a strange feeling of dread. He kept muttering to himself—much like many murderers anywhere. He searched for the manuscript for an hour, could not find it, and was of the opinion that he must turn himself in. But then, no one would ever know he had been there. He was filled with nausea too, and went outside near a tree and vomited."

"Damn," Cathy said. She spoke quite simply, quite clearly.

"But people not knowing where he was did not matter in the end—for everything worked to Milt's advantage. He was on the lower part of Orville's land. The very land that was being disputed in the courts. The land that Eunice wished to claim, that would someday be hers—the land where she had Danny John build a sweat lodge before he disappeared one winter morning.

"At this time Orville was away; at this moment no one knew where he was. But we know now that he was in Iraq. That did not come out until a few days ago."

"So Vale was safe," Cathy said, as a statement of fact.

"So here was a secret place—and Vale could hide the body. Perhaps she would never be found. The wind was blowing so the very trees seemed alive—and asking him questions about what he was doing. He carried her down to where six ancient rocks jutted out—one was called Old Face, where you and your brother used to go swimming, but Milt did not know this—and there, between those ancient rocks, he buried the child—the two children, really, though he did not know that either. He took off her clothes—all of them, he felt he had to—and bundled them together.

"Nor did he know that her cellphone fell to the ground when he picked up her jeans, and lay there in the very hole he covered up. As he stood to leave he heard the sound of waves crashing against the shore—exactly as he had imagined hearing them that day, a short while before, when she spoke to him. He removed her hearing aid, throwing it into those wild waves, the sound of which made her laugh in joy the first time she wore it.

"But something else happened later. He wandered out of where he was and found himself at Eunice's place. He had turned up a long lane, thinking it was the way back to the highway, and mistakenly came upon her house. Worse, before he could turn around, she recognized his car. So he parked in her driveway and walked to the door. There, where every well-varnished board in her living room floor was a plank of years of small plots and ploys against a variety of her lowbrow neighbours, from moving picket signs to blocking roads to writing columns, she spoke about how harshly she was judged for the great things she was trying to accomplish. She spoke of the need for feminism. She spoke of women's rights, and intolerance. Even Vale himself couldn't digest her broad-minded vigour tonight.

"But when she said almost out of the blue—so suddenly, without warning—that Ida May's children should not have been born, one dead and one in jail—and that poor little girl abused and raped by Orville MacDurmot—he gave a slight quizzical look, and he was worried she would see into his soul.

"'What—whatever do you mean?' he asked.

"'Abort them. Like Gloria Steinem did,' she said fiercely, like a hen with a dying chick. 'I said this to Orville once when I knew he had abused the child—he fired a rifle at my head.'

"'Why—why would he?'

"'Because everyone knows he's never had relations, you see, with any real woman. Not a grown woman like me, at any rate. But a child—a child he used. Don't worry, he was screwing her cute little ass off,' she said, but then, realizing some hidden voyeuristic and erotic delight in the image these words produced, she smiled vaguely at it all, seeming for a tiny moment to appreciate her own deft enthusiasm.

"As she talked on, he was conscious of trying to concentrate on the prettiness of her living room, the heat in the house, the smell of varnish and some kind of perfume. But Milt could not concentrate for long. He kept thinking of something strange. That is, something had just entered his mind so forcefully it seemed to come straight at him as if from another dimension; a dimension that unexpectedly was entirely *real*—that is, flashes of shredded hair and small pieces of skull would explode in front of his face. He would think of the girl's white, naked body, quite remarkably beautiful, the little mole under her right breast, the hearing aid still in her ear, think suddenly of Aiden, and how the two loved each other desperately, and begin to tremble. Then a small piece of skull would land on his chin. Oh, he had cleaned it all up—so why was this happening?

"'No one fools with a Wise,' Eunice was now saying, 'or they soon know what they're in for! Why, look at my husband—we almost ran him off the river. I will always win in the end. Mess with my family. Just try it on!'

"He nodded almost catatonically.

"Then she put out her cigarette and straightened in her chair, pleased she had given him that kind of information about her awful pedigree. She kept staring out the window with a solemn, dark look, knowing her words had had their desired effect. Her sudden brazenness really concerned him—he hadn't expected it—but it was so sudden after all this time of thinking he knew her, her audacity impressed him. He knew she suspected the book, and he now knew how formidable her enemies found her. And how formidable he would find her if she ever thought he had crossed her. So he was caught in the web that until this moment neither of them had realized she had so expertly designed.

"'You think he will end up hurting someone—that Orville fellow?' He was dying to say more, to give more of an indication of what he meant, but he became uneasy, trying to decide whether or not he should. Another bit of the child's brain seemed to hover in the air just before his head, moving toward him so that he physically shuddered. And then he noticed Gaby, just for a moment, standing behind Eunice, with her back turned, and a hole in her head.

"'I am certain of it,' Eunice said.

"'Well, we should stop him before he does!' he protested, and seemed to raise his hand weakly to brush his face. Eunice watched him do this, as if he was wiping some lint or something away, something in front of his eyes. Then she smiled kindly and asked Professor Milt Vale how in the world had he bruised his fingers. He smiled and shook his head and said he was helping an old friend move, but became evasive when she asked for a name. But then he said, with sudden inspiration, that he had taken the trip because he'd wanted to see her, to make sure Orville was not bothering her again. Both of them knew this was a lie.

"'Me! How kind of you—to visit an out-of-the-way old woman like me—my—where did you say your friend lives?'

"He tried to think which way was upriver and which way was down. So he stood and, being just as evasive, he suddenly kissed her, and put his hand under her blouse and over her left breast.

"In his mind he was calling Eunice a name. He couldn't help it, the name just came to him as if seared into his brain. And he saw one in front of him, on the floor crawling toward him: *Viper*. It took every ounce of strength not to say it.

"'You're way too mysterious and charming, I must say,' she said, her head falling back as he undid her blouse. 'Look at the hold you have over me.' Then she whispered, 'Putty in your hands,' as she led him to the grand, cold couch where they could vouchsafe their love. She lifted up and kissed him with her tongue.

"He drove home, both his legs shaking, and one of his arms, and one of his fingers bent a little sideways. For some silly reason he could not get out of his mind how little Gaby May had walked toward the door with the penknife sticking out of the top of her head, and how she'd kept feeling for it with her hand, and how he, Milt, had watched her fumble for it in a kind of startled terror."

———

"So now," John said, "I wish to talk about Aiden for a moment. Aiden had just heard that the girl had told his father that she was moving—that she had thought it over and did not wish to see him again, and it was better that she just go. When he went up to her room on Graham Street, however, her clothes hadn't been touched, and a slip of paper said she had another doctor's appointment on the 29th of the month.

"So Aiden went to the doctor she had the appointment with and waited. He waited the entire day. All day there was heat shining through the large bay window of the sterile office, and he sat in the corner staring at the flat glass door. Then, in a trance, he walked back down to the bed-sitting room. This time, however, the clothes were gone, except for one sweater, and the chair that she liked to sit in had been moved down the hallway for another student.

"After this he became morose and silent—too silent. He began to hang around with the group. They were called 'the group,' and they had their own little room in a shed at the back of Scamper McVeigh's yard. Scamper had been a long-time member of Milt's writing group. Once he had believed he was going to have a book published. And he was a great fan of Milt's—because they both had ridiculed real writers for having *artifice* since the two of them were so full of it themselves. Therefore writers who had bought and paid for their own experiences and were actually filled with artifice were deeply lauded. Falsehood never cared if it was false.

"Since then Scamper had done yardwork, and lived with his parents. He smoked pot and called the police 'pigs,' and had his own small car that his mother paid for. He went on protest marches. He wrote a masterpiece or two, went to poetry readings, where he always asked unusually insulting questions. As he grew older he got fatter only in one place, the stomach, and his hair fell out all except for his ponytail, which hung in two strands down his back. So in some ways he felt time slipping and wanted to do some grand thing to prove himself.

"His mother, however, no matter how many times he landed in trouble, or was obnoxious and overbearing, thought he was brilliant. He would argue all night long on some exceptionally esoteric matter while inspecting his wineglass, and she would still say, 'That's why Trevor can argue so well—because his father and I taught him.'

Trevor was his Christian name—or first name, since the family wisely had so little to do with Christianity. They had given that up as well.

"It was here 'the group' spoke about revolution and counter-revolution and changing the system. For a long time poor Aiden believed in changing the system, for it certainly needed change. Milt couldn't reach him at this time, would leave him money on the marble table in the foyer. The clink of money on that beautiful marble top sometimes woke Aiden as Milt left the house. More often, though, Aiden was the sole occupant of the large house, as Milt spent time in one of the ground apartments in his rooming house courting a young student he had met. More often Aiden was alone on summer nights, walking the streets well after midnight, smelling the flowers in many gorgeous yards.

"He became vice-president for the group—and he helped the treasurer collect the dues. This was to get money to have parties after the meetings in which they were going to change the world. Most of the group were the displaced sons and daughters of high-end provincial civil servants and professors. They had come of age in the sweet city—the comfortable city of elms and brick buildings and glorious older heritage homes. The city with backyard cottages where lights were turned on and night birds darted against the shrubs.

"On those lazy, hazy days of summer, in the little clubhouse behind the three-storey wooden house of Scamper McVeigh's parents, a clubhouse painted red and green where the group toked hash and smoked marijuana, Scamper McVeigh told them he was hatching a plan to kidnap someone and demand First Nations rights. He smiled as if this was so startling and justified no one would be able to dispute it. He had come up with the plan all of a sudden. He said it was better than roadblocks or burning things. It just came over him. He told them he'd decided to kidnap a professor of history who had said in a lecture that some First Nations problems were created by the First Nations themselves, and that apologies sometimes fell on deaf ears. Scamper wanted to hold this professor for one million dollars. One of the group said he did not want to do it.

"'Why not?' Scamper asked.

"'It should be two million,' he answered with a little smile.

"There was also a dispute over where they would take him and hold him. Near this house off Churchill Row, or to some other location. It became more serious when Scamper began to follow this professor to and from his home on Montgomery Street. To wait on the sidewalk for him while Scamper's friend, the one who wanted to demand two million (which was voted down), followed the man's wife home twice, and erratically yelled at her once from across the street.

"'Hi, you dog,' he roared. And then, 'Woof, woof, woof!'

"The group was ordered by Scamper to dress in black, with black sneakers and black socks. So some did, and others refused to. The talk went on all summer, with Aiden saying very little because he believed it was a joke. Scamper had given them all plans. The plans really made no sense, drawings of the bicycle trails and little X's of places that the saucy fellow who wanted to demand two million wanted to show them.

"I do not think Aiden had much to do with it. He just went there to drink beer and listen to people who were going to change the world. There he could forget that Gaby May had gone. Then one night the history professor's son, home from his summer football camp, saw Scamper standing on a garbage pail and looking into his parents' bedroom window, holding a map, a knapsack and a heavy mallet in his hand. The professor's son asked him what he was doing. Scamper had become so enthralled by his mission, he simply believed everyone would approve of it.

"'Setting the world free, man—setting the world free. And anyway, what's it to you?'

"'You are staring in my parents' window, for one thing,' the boy said.

"Scamper, his face in war paint, jumped down and began screeching and swinging the mallet. The son, who played for the Saint Mary's Huskies of the Atlantic conference, grabbed Scamper by the neck and shook him half-silly, and dragged him to the police. That was the end of their plans for the million-dollar ransom, and the end of their clubhouse. The group of disaffected youth broke up.

"The sons of civil servants and professors who wanted to change the world, and ended up with their leader standing on a garbage pail and looking into the bedroom window of a fifty-five-year-old history professor and his wife.

"How strange it was, who Aiden went to in order to be saved. How he wore dark army jackets and boots, and had his head shaved. He went to Scamper, who, years before, had attended the literary meetings, wrote about female transmutant sex aliens, and at thirty-seven still lived in the loft in his mom and dad's garden house. His mom was a psychologist and his dad a retired high-ranking civil servant. Aiden carried Gaby's picture in his leather wallet," John said. "And a picture of his mom."

"How lonely he must have been," Cathy said.

"Then, about a year after Gaby's body was finally discovered—that is, about three or four weeks ago—Aiden acquired and took a bottle of pills. He took them in late afternoon in a back upstairs room of his father's garden house, an almost-empty, unattended room overlooking the back fence of his father's large, private house. He left a note saying: *I am sorry, Dad.*

"He had laid forty sleeping pills on the table and took them one at a time with drinks of gin and Kool-Aid. His father was fortunate enough to have called his name and found him slumped over and hardly breathing, and took him to the hospital.

"A few days later our Ms. Wise visited Aiden in the hospital; that is about a month ago now. Ms. Wise sat in the chair near the bed, and his father looked cautiously out the third-floor window. Ms. Wise explained to Aiden that Orville was the man who had terribly abused little Gaby.

"'For *years*—we know that now,' Ms. Wise confirmed. 'It was what I desperately tried to prevent. The police know how I tried to prevent it.' She was now demure, her neck was thin, her hands slightly yellowish. She asked if he remembered her, always a great friend of her father's. Aiden tried to remember but was not quite sure.

"Ms. Wise told him that Gaby hid this abuse from everyone and had moved to Fredericton to rid herself of him. But he had a hold over her. Eunice said this to comfort him. She smiled and told him that in a few weeks she and his father would be married. Then she reached out and took his hand.

"So she continued by telling Aiden that Orville had killed the girl he had continued to abuse—because she wanted to get rid of an unwanted child Orville had given her and was ashamed of. She spoke of Orville killing her in a rage. That he disliked the First Nations boy Danny John, who had once protected a girl named Brenda Townie from him when they were in high school. She said she had hired Danny John to help protect not only her shoreline, but little Gaby May. So it all came together nicely for her.

"'I just wish your father had been able to rescue her—that night you came over,' she said, looking at Milt.

"'Over—when?' Aiden asked, his thin body trembling.

"'Oh, it's not important, son—I just had to take some boxes of books over to a friend—nothing important.' Then he said, 'But if

I had known—if only I had!' And suddenly he began to cry. He had just heard that Gaby was pregnant with his grandchild.

"Then, after Ms. Wise took his hand, Aiden wanted to tell them a story.

"He spoke of Gaby May walking beside him in the cold, telling him she had a surprise, and suddenly pulling out a whole bunch of paints for him. To her it was the grandest thing in the world, something that had cost her dearly, and she had had them hidden in her pockets. Those were the paints he had used to tag the wall beneath the bridge. When he mentioned the canvas she had bought for him, and how he had found it the day he went to see her room, his father looked shaken and Aiden sensed this, and realized it was too upsetting for his father, who had not had time to get to know her well."

12.

SO JOHN CONTINUED BY SUDDENLY INTRODUCING ANOTHER man:

"But Milt did not know one other rather important thing. That a man brought up in foster homes, thrown to the wolves at a young age, anti-social and having no fear of people like professor Milt Vale, would come into play some months after Orville's death. That although Milt himself had the graffiti erased, in caution, it was luckily not before I saw it once, and Elvis, who saw it as well, mentioned it to this young man.

"Now this man heard Gaby had been pregnant. So his niece too was killed. And this person was old-fashioned enough to think of this little girl never as a foetus, but as a child. This man was Gaby May's brother Tom. He happened to be in jail when Elvis was.

"So one afternoon when Elvis spoke to Tom, he spoke to him about the court scene when Orville died. They were in the small library together, with a few books, a few puzzles that the prisoners did, and some small birdhouses they were allowed to paint.

"'Tell me about it exactly,' Tom Crump said, holding one of the birdhouses in his hand and moving it about intently, as if trying to find its brightest spot or its darkest flaw.

"'Something was not right in his head with how he reacted,' Elvis said. 'It was as if Orville was just discovering Gaby May had been killed—and was dazed by that. It was as if he believed she had gone to Montreal, just as everyone believed. Just as you believed. And he had gone there to search for her. His look did say that!'

"Tom said nothing for a long while. At first he wasn't moved by this. Except in a strange, melancholy way. He put the birdhouse aside carefully and kept mashing his hands together, looking at the floor between them in a dead, heavy gaze.

"Tom had been planning not to take his parole but to assault a guard so he would be put into Renous with Orville. That plan had changed now. Now he must get out, and he must discover for himself what had happened. Something had happened to his little sister, which might not have had anything to do with Orville. And slowly he got Elvis to relate everything he could about what he remembered about the tag, so they sat together at supper:

"'It was dazzling, it was all the colours of the rainbow—red, yellow, green, orange and blue—splendid as love,' Elvis said softly. 'LGM was intertwined with it.'

"'LGM—is that so? What do you think that means?'

"'I do not know,' Elvis offered.

"After they went back to their cell, Elvis composed a letter to his mom. It would be transcribed on the computer and sent by email from the office the next day. He told his mother he was done breaking into houses, and he only had thirteen more months to go.

"Much later Elvis woke. It was the middle of the night—one light on in the corridor—and the large man was standing over him in a grey shadow, his face puzzled because it had taken Elvis so long to awaken.

"'I do,' Tom said.

"'You do what? What do you do?'

"'Know what it means. *LGM*: Loves Gaby May,' Tom said. He said this and he sat down on the edge of the cot, and looked blankly at the sink and the pale green wall.

"'Yes—that might be true,' Elvis said, sitting up slightly—which revealed, by the refracted moonlight from a window across the corridor, a portion of his twenty-four tattoos, many of them scratched out by himself over the lonely years. 'That might be true.'

"Tom looked at him, shrugged, offered Elvis a stick of gum and went back to his cot and lay down."

———

"So Tom would get out of jail about the same time Aiden took the pills in despair. And after a while, Tom would make his way to Fredericton. By this time Vale had done all the work—he believed he was as safe as any man could be. Orville was now dead and the tin box was missing—nothing whatever could refute Vale's ownership."

"If only Vale had confided in her," Cathy said now, "admitted to her his mistake. I feel she would have forgiven him. He could have said it was a mistake."

"But by the time he struck her in the head in terror, it was too late," John said. "He must ask forgiveness—and, as a sophisticated man, an urbane fellow, he no longer knew how. Oh, there are many who do—ask forgiveness, and know the world as well as you and I—many men in university, and women as well, who would have done the right thing in a second. But Vale wasn't one. To his mind, there was no evil. I came to think over the last two months that we all have a choice."

"What choice?"

"It comes down to which form of beauty we follow. Which form we obey."

There was a moment when he, John, suddenly reflected on hell—and what Orville had said about it; that, as Christopher Marlowe had said, hell was never anyplace special, but could be anyplace at any time.

"Just maybe, where those who whitewashed *OBA* were—where they were, hell was also?" Cathy asked.

So John said:

"Yes, those who whitewashed *OBA* away—and knew that the Savage boys had left the whitewash under their skiff."

"In what way?"

"It is how I knew who it was who painted over the tag. I realized the moment I looked around on the day I discovered it was rubbed out that it could not have been Aiden—it had to be someone else."

"Why?"

"It had to be someone who knew this side of the river, knew that the flat-bottom boat was there and, more importantly, that a bucket of whitewash paint had been left under it. Someone had used the paint, and put the lid back on haphazardly. Somebody who knew the Savage boys, and the skiff, and that the paint had recently been left there."

"Couldn't Aiden have found the paint and have done it himself?"

"He would have brought his own paints to do the job, those Bombay blues and reds and yellows that Gaby bought him. Looking at how beautifully the tag was done, I realized that Aiden was an artist. This was art frozen on a concrete wall. But it was besmirched and destroyed by someone who forgot they supposedly cared about art. So I focused on the person in those houses nearest the bridge who may have defaced this shrine to Gaby May—Aiden's Taj Mahal. So looking at the houses along this stretch of road, I realized that one house was your brother's, who was now dead."

"One is the priest's."

"One, the one that belonged to your grandmother, is vacant. One belongs to your parents, who are also gone."

"One belongs to Eunice," Cathy whispered.

"I knew within ten minutes that it had to be her. And within a half hour, what I did find in that old toolshed was the gloves she had used, lying on the shelf near the names of the clubhouse members."

"But why did she—what did it matter if it was there?"

"It was perhaps the final link back to Milt Vale himself. So he sent her down to do what she did. She could not chance carrying the paint—someone might see her do so. She had to go under cover of dark, knowing paint was already there. Her photographs from that position were hanging on the bookstore walls. Doing this for Vale was the price she paid to be accepted by him forever. Milt found her useful—in a way, she was his most useful conduit—but in the stillness of her den, she too plotted against Milt for complete acceptance from him. How far into the heavens she rose. It was, in a way, blackmail. I realized, reading all the letters she had written to the police, that she had been too much of a major player against Orville's humanity not to continue to gain from it after his death. She could do nothing now but continue to blame him. It must have all been desperate for her, that night in the wind, in the dark and the rain, with the whitewash paint flailing back against her face and dripping on her suede gloves."

"How do you know—the dark and the wind?"

"Because of the way the paint splatter happened, as if wind had taken it off the brush itself—dark because she would not do it in daylight. Splashed on her suede gloves because I found them in the old toolshed, once used as her clubhouse, and we have taken them as evidence now."

"That they were forced into a terrible partnership so not to destroy each other?"

John said, "When we went back and excavated where Gaby had lain, the cellphone was found—but it was not put with her remains, but with the boy's. That is whom we thought the phone belonged to. We believed it was Danny John's body and his phone; since Eunice told us she had phoned his cell a hundred times, it stood to reason that it was his remains and his phone."

"But it was not Danny John's phone?"

"No—a rather big mistake—it was not even Danny John. All this held up the investigation. That is, we believed Eunice's scenario almost completely—that Orville had gone down to the shore, killed the girl he had impregnated in a rage because she was going to get rid of the child, and then killed Danny because he tried to intervene. If it wasn't for a man named Tom Crump, Gaby May's connection to the great book *Darkness* would never have been discovered."

13.

JOHN NOW PAUSED A WHILE. IT WAS GROWING DARKER TOO.
The lamplight spread out with greater intensity and illumination
against the wall, the books took on a heaviness—a mystery too, from
words written with human longing some centuries ago, still awaiting the one who would open them up with love—while the window
looked out onto a black curtain, like night out a window in winter
when they were both children. Cathy sat before him, her face dusky
and her eyes vivid, the top two buttons of her spotless white blouse
undone in almost an official way, her neck held point by a tiny silver
cross. He looked at her in sudden longing—as old as the ages passing;
older than all those romantic, tragic books surrounding them, many
bound in supple leather, depicting scenes of love and death.

She looked at him and he at her. And both thought the same
thought; both suddenly thought of making fierce love in the sudden
quiet of a neutral room. Yet because of some sad reasoning, they hesitated at that crucial moment, and it passed into eternity undone, both
of them at times regretting that they hadn't for as long as they lived.

"And Tom? What about him?" she said after a long time.

"Tom . . ." John said, as if coming out of a daze. "Tom Crump
did not know what any of this was about, but he needed to find out.

Tom decided to go to Fredericton and meet Aiden Vale. He visited Aiden in the hospital about two weeks ago. Tom had his own ideal of beauty. He displayed his well-constructed tattoos, the one of a golden maple leaf between the thumb and forefinger of his left hand, bordered by silver ink, the one of a red broken heart on a blue background hewed onto the side of his thick neck that he had done in honour of his brother. His cut-off jean jacket exposing an affiliation to powerful Harley motorcycles, his leather boots dusty and embossed with silver straps. *John 15:13* tattooed on his left arm. His hair long and braided to honour his First Nations status. And he sat down and stared at this forlorn and broken-hearted child of privilege. He leaned forward, rubbed his hands together and asked Aiden why he had erased something he had drawn so well when she was standing beside him.

"'Which tag is that—that tag under the Bartibog Bridge?—that tag—no—I would never erase that—I could never do it—someone else did, not me.'

"Tom looked at Aiden's face. No, perhaps he had not done it."

"You mentioned John 15:13," Cathy said. "I was trying to think of it . . ."

"It was a tattoo on his arm in honour of his brother, who died crossing the river: 'No greater love has a man than to lay down his life for a friend.'"

John now related that Tom had been sent the manuscript. Gaby had sent it to him the very afternoon of the day she had died. Although, of course, he did not know this then. He had believed she had left for Montreal, because of their brother's death.

"But she had gotten the manuscript out of the house before Professor Vale came to see her. She had walked up to the road and flagged down the Tracadie bus, and had put the tin box on it, with the address of Tom's apartment, his phone number and a note: *Keep this with you. Someone might have even stole it,* she had written. The tin box was sent to him by bus—it sat with other packages, and was sitting in the luggage compartment of that bus when Milt pulled into the service station beside it in Boiestown. He was at that moment two feet from it on his journey. And of course he did not know."

"So the tin box went to Fredericton?"

"It arrived at Tom's apartment house outside of Fredericton two nights after we arrested him. He had been on his way back to the river to see Gaby earlier that day, to see about his brother Pete's stone. We pulled him over in Doaktown. And if we hadn't, Gaby would have lived. The book ended up in Tom's storage locker, taken there by a friend who worked at the bus depot. Tom simply thought this was a parting gift by her. The manuscript was still after all these years in the tin box, sitting in the basement locker of Pigmont's Apartments.

"To him there were many scribbling people on the Miramichi who wrote many things—nothing was surprising about his odd stepfather having written something as well. But Gaby's note propelled him to see about it. So visiting Aiden, he asked if Gaby ever mentioned a book to him, written by his stepdad."

"'A book . . . yes—what would that have to do with Orville MacDurmot?'

"Tom looked at him with anticipation, his arms folded and the tattoos on his forearms speaking of an undeniable kind of dramatic response to the world.

"'Orville—I don't think it had nothing to do with Orville,' Tom said. 'It must have to do with other people—people who my stepdad knew long ago. Some who believed they knew a good deal. But none of them knew my stepdad's world. That is why he wrote it. He told me once he really thought it was a good book, but I never read it.'

"'Yes,' Aiden said. But he knew exactly who these people were, and now he was beginning to see what utter dread might have loomed under a tweedy jacket for the last eight or nine years. Suddenly a great unexplainable concern came over his face—'concern' was the word—over what a terrible secret his little Gaby May might have discovered on those last few moments of her happy life.

"'A book,' he said. 'Her stepdad—your stepdad—did write a book . . . but—'

"'But?'

"'I don't know,' Aiden said.

"Tom looked at him curiously. 'Did you like my sister?' he asked.

"'Loved her.'

"'You didn't kill her?'

"'I would have given my life for her, ten times over,' Aiden said calmly and softly.

"'And do you really think it was Orville's baby—and he killed her? That's what people said about it.'

"'The child was mine—Gaby never was with Orville.'

"'You are sure?'

"'I am sure,' Aiden said.

"Tom nodded. They were silent.

"'Well,' Tom said, 'why would she ever be upset about a book?'

"'I am not sure why.'

"Then Tom asked:

"'So can you read my stepdad's book for me?'

"'Okay,' Aiden said. 'I will.'"

"But by this time," Cathy said, "as you mentioned last night, the whole thing—"

"Yes, it was to be solved. I still had no idea there was another manuscript of the book. So Tom was the key. Two days later he visited Aiden again, with that manuscript. He sat down with the famous tin box—there it was, rusted and bent, showing signs it had come through a fire. He flicked the latch and took out the old, yellowed paper. Aiden began to read. He looked confused.

"'What is it?' Tom asked him.

"But Aiden, not looking at him, continuing to read, said, waving his hand:

"'Please go away.'

"He said it so forcefully that Tom nodded and left. And then Aiden left," John said. "He walked home in his jeans and hospital gown, and the streets were vast and empty, the trees towered above him, and lights glowed resplendent from great Victorian houses in the soft, mercurial evening, with traffic moving slowly along the lanes near the beautiful river. And then arriving home, he appeared at Milt's upstairs study door. It was night and the study window was half-opened (Milt the master of fresh air); the books had been taken from Milt's shelves and were being dusted off by Milt himself. There on the floor, a library of a thousand books sat disembodied from the man standing in the midst of it all, as if in the end he knew nothing in their pages. He only wanted safety, the safety the middle-class white world wanted, the kind that allowed escape from the darkness, a safety that didn't have to share, or really be compassionate, or ever face danger. A people who needed to live within the bounds of contrived concern, and an engineered social anxiety. For years and years our man Milt had been a true and sophisticated master of all of that pleasant, civic-minded conceit. He had taken boxing lessons, and knew how to mention all the various tendons and bones in the body, and left all his characters without a soul.

"At first Milt thought Aiden had escaped to do himself harm. That was his first feeling of shock when he turned and saw him. He was holding Yukio Mishima's *Confessions of a Mask* in his hand.

"'What—' he said, flinching, 'what's wrong, Aiden—what is it, boy, what is going on here?'

"'I have the last chapters of your book,' Aiden said. Amidst all those other volumes, Aiden took out the last forty pages of the book and placed them on the desk. 'You should read them.'

"'I will call Dr. Faun,' Milt said.

"Then for some reason Milt turned off the desk lamp and sat down in the corner with his head in his hands. Milt's idea of beauty was the marvellous golden and silver and bronze letter openers he had collected in his travels. How he had prided himself on them. One he managed to buy in Paris, the time he told Gaby he had visited the Louvre. Milt could not bear to part with them. Even the one he had used that night—the special one from boulevard du Montparnasse. The lovely Fabergé, though deemed a fake by many more people than Orville, sat on a perch above him. It was valued at 232 dollars in the end. He had spent almost fifteen thousand on it.

"Aiden sat in a chair staring at his father's books.

"'Ah well,' Milt said, and he rose finally and went out, into the upstairs hallway, and leaned against the banister. It was nice to look down the stairs to the living room and the fine white carpet, and the bronze statue of the naked dancing girl he bought with his first royalty cheque. But the tragedy—the main tragedy—was the young man sitting in the study; that was his life's greatest tragedy. They were separated by a gulf of time and space, almost impossible to ever make up. The stars themselves were now beginning to come out.

"When Orville was away in Saint John, giving his very last talk at L'Arche, Eunice had been in his house. She had walked his stairs many times over the years, sat in his rooms, looked at his papers, his articles and his clothes. That was one thing the terrible Orville MacDurmot had never reckoned on—her finely tuned deceit. She pocketed at least a half-dozen things over the years that have now been recovered.

"Milt had asked her to look for this box many times—even before *Darkness* was published. So she knew he couldn't have been asking her for a good reason, but she slowly convinced herself that it could not be for a bad one. So she lighted a cigarette and waited until dark.

"She could see Mars in the night sky, the Little Dipper way above. She dressed in a scarf and tight black leotards. She wore a hat that hid her face. She snuck across the field, and entered through the back door, and tiptoed on her soft-soled sneakers. Looking for that old tin box that Vale said belonged to him and contained some papers for his next novel. So she went into your brother's house—two days after the bones were exhumed and taken to his attic. Another day or two later, the bones would have been transferred to Moncton or Montreal. She did not know she would ever make such a coup. Some months before, when she'd gone through his bookshelves, she had accidently knocked *I See Satan Fall Like Lightning* to the floor. That in fact is what changed Orville's life. The hatch to the attic was most often locked and she did not try it this night. She pocketed a small silver tray for good luck and was on the stairs coming down from his office when she heard Orville open the back door and walk in. A real terror entered her spine. She turned and moved upstairs again, to hide. She tried the attic latch just as he was climbing the stairs, and for the first time found it open. She escaped up there. Suddenly she discovered she was crouching beside the remains of bodies. She quickly realized, because of the dirt and clay, that they must have come from her beach. So her victory in the civil suit had caused him to remove murder victims.

"She looked at the bones and almost screamed. She was terrified he would come up and cut her throat. But that night he lay down on his bed and he drifted into deep sleep. The light of the moon came in through the skylight, and she was kneeling in the wan dark beside two skulls. When the house became silent she fled, without finding the tin box and not caring for it ever again. Darkness, darkness all around."

14.

"WHEN SHE CAME IN TO THE POLICE HEADQUARTERS LAST year, she was genuinely frightened of something she had seen. She wanted to talk to me and no one else. At first I thought these skulls had to do with Orville's research. Of course they must have. We all were convinced it was nothing. She of course did not say she had entered his house, but told us she had seen him carting them from the beach. So over the next two days, checking the beach, we actually discovered the graves, or what was used as graves. We found the cellphone, and pieces of a woman's pink sock. So we had no choice, really. We were compelled to speak to him."

"Why did she want to see *you*? You were a visiting officer there."

"I am unsure why she asked for me."

"No—I think you dated her . . . ?" Cathy said slowly, catching on to what he had mentioned hours before about Orville and himself—Orville having far too few loves, and he, John, having far too many. He blushed—it was strange to see him do so—and said:

"Yes. Once, many years ago, just after she had divorced Calvin, when I was covering an accident on the bridge, I approached a woman using binoculars and looking at starlings, to see if she had seen anything else. She was so prim and proper, I wondered who she was.

"Later that year when I was asked to speak at a criminology course, I saw this slender lady eagerly staring at me, dressed in some flawless fashion. But after a while her concerns became too confused for me. I realized a police officer was not for her; perhaps a professor was. She was a receptacle of all that grave knowledge of what the police do wrong. So I think this coup of hers was part of a triumph against me as well. The night she reported the bones, she stood before me as if totally vindicated for some supposed injury I was unaware of. So I thanked her for informing us of all of this and her eyes became pale-blue darts.

"'Where did you see these bones?' I asked.

"'He was carting them to his house,' she said. And she looked at me with a kind of hilarity—a sudden hidden glee.

"In the following days, with the signs of the small graves being disturbed, the old cellphone discovered, a girl's pink sock and more bones—of a young man, and an unborn child—a warrant was issued. I took the cellphone and showed it to her. She was visibly upset—terribly so. She told me it was Danny John's. The whole river was sickened and inflamed by it all, as you know."

"And so what happened to make it all change—to make her a suspect?" Cathy asked.

"It was the day I visited your brother's house, almost a year ago now. At that very moment I knew something was wrong. That day, when the last of the sunlight flared against the brass rims of the fireplace screen, I sat for an hour or more, disturbed by the letter from Milt Vale to Orville MacDurmot about an obscure young man. I wanted to know more about this man, whom I discovered to be something of a writer. And about the trust fund Orville had set up; the instructions meticulously given to his lawyer, Tom Prince.

The well-known searches he had orchestrated for this girl. And then there was Eunice. Her literary group was named Wise Ears—they met in her home every Wednesday night. She had her own little collection of protegés who doted on her. She'd told us that Orville had brought the bones up to his house on Wednesday, because he went to L'Arche on Thursday—so why did no one else from the Wednesday group see him, or why did she not tell them she'd seen them?"

Then he said:

"Do you read the papers?"

"Not since they condemned my brother."

"Well, if you read them yesterday you would find out they do not condemn your brother anymore. Last night I went to visit Eunice— to tell her what my investigation had slowly uncovered. She was staring at something in her living room, a painting she had bought on her last trip to the South Shore, where they had rented a cottage at Mahone Bay. I don't know if it is a good painting, but she seems to like it. I went through the porch and looked inside—her hardwood floor was immaculately polished, and a fire burned—there was a sweet scent of roasting wood. She turned and looked at me, surprised—or, not surprised, shocked—or with deliberation, as if she was ready to answer something."

"Why—I mean . . . ?"

"The papers you do not read reported that the identity of the man would be revealed but that it was not Danny John; and, on the bottom fold of the same page, that Orville had been in Iraq doing work, and had later gone to Ottawa and Montreal. That he had from there, after months of solitude, entered a monastery, but for a very different reason than the one Eunice and others excoriated him for.

"So the papers you do not read were rehabilitating your brother in front of her eyes. Even the paper she now edited was doing so. Eunice was finally seeing Orville for the first time. Finally, a year after his death, it became certain that he wasn't even in the country the day Gaby May was killed.

"So I went to speak to Eunice about what may have actually happened to the girl Gaby May. She lighted a cigarette with a certain clever aptitude and sat down on a fine black rocker against her white wall backdrop and stared at me, as if waiting for a reprimand.

"I began by telling her it was not Danny John's phone. That it took some time to discover this, for the phone was damaged. But Orville was dead and buried and many still thought of him as a murderer. I said this was as much her wish—to have him thought of as a murderer—as anyone's. I told her we'd discovered it was Gaby May Crump's phone. I told her that Orville was not in the country. I told her Gaby's skull was pierced by what the forensic pathologist concluded was a long, narrow object—perhaps a penknife. 'So what; you found the bones I told you about at his place,' she said.

"'Yes—and he was certain he had found what he had been looking for.'

"Then, showing her both the written and emailed letters to Orville from Milt, I asked her why in the world would Milt Vale be interested in Gaby May's uncle years ago.

"'The man who became their stepdad, and died in a house fire?'

"'Why was he interested in this unknown Miramichi writer?' I asked.

"'I have no idea,' she said, and took a drag of her cigarette and looked out the window at the night. The smoke of her cigarette curled up luxuriously against those well-framed paintings.

"I said I did not believe her. I then asked her if she knew of the startlingly beautiful graffiti on the old bridge's pillar. I reminded her again of the photograph she had taken of it. I then told her that Danny John was alive—not buried in the sand, as six of her columns on racism since the time Orville died had maintained.

"I told her there was racism still in the world, but it was a disgrace to use it for your own self-aggrandizement. That identity politics was a sham—and that her fine, luxurious coating of feminism was also.

"That she had been the receptacle of the pliable and modern self-deception for her own sake. That I was beginning to think *Darkness* was not Milt Vale's book. It had never been in his soul to write it.

"It took her a while to catch on to the house of cards she had invented about the death of her protegé Danny John. It stung the skin of her face as she looked up at me.

"He was the hero who had died protecting both her land and the girl Orville had killed. It was in essence a flight of fancy that buoyed her, a whimsical madness that sustained her plans for the future. How could it not be true? Its perfection was self-evident.

"She stood and walked away, shaking and weak, and sat down on a finely crafted white chair at the other end of the hallway. Her now-ancient dog nuzzled her drooping left hand. Her whole sad little body trembled. The illusion she had created over the last twenty years had shattered. She had stepped out of it and must now contact the law."

"But then, the other person—the other remains—who were they? It was not Danny's phone, so who was he? Did he have a phone—where was his cellphone?" Cathy asked.

John suddenly trembled, for he was not well himself—and he remembered his long search for Danny John, how Eunice had berated him for doing nothing because Danny John was a Native boy, and how he had to become involved in band politics—how debilitating that was for him, a white officer, so easily scored the enemy in these matters, so easily suspect most of his life—and how he'd had to give this side of the case over to Markus Paul, who interviewed Elvis in jail—and how they discovered from that interview that Danny John had stolen band funds one winter afternoon and slipped out of the reserve for good, crossing the great bay ice toward Pointe-Sapin, and disappearing into the mist of cold.

"It was funds that two principal members of the band council, Bedham and Versace, had stolen from a huge transfer payment the band had received from the federal government. Danny simply decided to steal the funds back, ostensibly for the people, and then decided these funds, the 200,000 dollars, might be better used to help Danny John himself. For he had asked himself, Who had helped him before? Well, not so many. So he had stuffed the money into an old leather book bag and headed away.

"It was amazing too; first he was dead, then alive again, now he was missing—and maybe dead, for no one had heard a breath from him in years. And then one afternoon a week ago Markus Paul went for a drive toward Campbellton, wondering to himself how long it would take to ever discover where Danny was, and saw Danny John hitchhiking home—lonesome and broke.

"'Oh, hello, Markus,' he said, 'How are you, Markus?'

"Markus asked him if he would like a bit of a drive back to the reserve.

"'Oh, of course, Markus—thanks, buddy.'

"'Everyone said you were dead and buried.'

"'I did not know that,' Danny said.

"It was what Elvis tried to tell people when he said Danny was six foot one," John now said. "The memory of Elvis saying that produced more than ever the sensation that the right people are so often not listened to, and sometimes the most accurate theories are not heeded by those who harp about accuracy. This robbery by Danny John was supposed to include Elvis—but Elvis couldn't begin to imagine doing something so grand. So he simply said, and said it more than once, the only tidbit of information he was about to divulge: 'Danny was six foot one.'"

"The theft was never reported," Cathy said.

"The money was supposed to be used for band affairs, but it was taken by band members, Bedham and others, and hidden in a wall. Danny stole it about three hours after the people who initially stole it put it in the back wall of the band office," John said.

"But now he was on his way home to face the consequences—"

"Yes, with a coupon for a Burger King burger and three dollars in his pocket. Feeling the worse for wear—and hoping the boys had forgotten what he had done."

"So then—who was this other boy, whose cellphone they thought they had?"

"If Gaby May had not been buried beside him—if a small fragment of her foot was not showing that afternoon when Orville walked east toward the bay, those remains might never have been found. Gaby helped Orville find *him*, and find her. But to discover who that boy was, we needed to solve an incident that Chief Amos Paul had called on Orville to help him with twenty-some years ago."

"One evening in summer—twenty-some years ago—that's the time this other boy died?"

"No—no—that is when Amos asked Orville to help solve the mystery that had puzzled him from the time his own grandfather had told him the story. That is when he gave Orville the maps of the river from the Scotsman who had drawn them—with the outline of great white pine beaches and islands, and five or six staggered rocks jutting out. Very much like that map hanging just outside this room"—and John pointed to that map quickly. "Orville realized those rocks might be the ones near Old Face, very near the place you swam as children."

"So it happened sometime earlier?" Cathy asked.

"Yes—it happened two hundred years ago."

"Two hundred years ago?"

"Yes," John said. "It was not only the unborn child's DNA, which finally pointed to someone other than Orville being the father. It was the few artifacts we, over the last eight months, discovered with the remains of that male skeleton.

"They were discovered during a dig that we ordered near the Old Face rock. With these, I went to the museum here and then I travelled to Toronto and talked to a forensic anthropologist we hired to look at the bones. We knew within three weeks of Orville's death that they were much too old to be those of Danny John. This boy's history was suggested by anecdotes and stories but never proven until now."

The lamplight fell on books in French, the huge door was three-quarters shut, and a light beamed down on the faded hallway carpet and the polished banister, and on the ink map of the Miramichi drawn by a Scottish settler in 1812. John looked over at that map for a long moment, envisioning life and events from flashes in time. Then he continued:

"It was a shadowy instance on an obscure river, as far as the great British Empire was concerned, with its Hudson's Bay and East India companies, its soldiers in red tunics and its war at that time on two, maybe three fronts. For years Orville searched on behalf of Chief Amos Paul, gave up, decried his luck, was silent in the face of opposition and criticism and went back to his books, trying to discover what no one else seemed to know. They arrested him a few days too soon, and he would never live to know that he was right."

So John said he waited impatiently for the forensic report, and everything he discovered about the crime against the young woman led him backward in time to a young man and his novel.

Ms. Wise had written columns about Danny John since the terrible discovery. She spoke about residential schools, about the loss of dignity of First Nations peoples. She now asserted that she was part First Nations. That is, she insisted on her significance—that of knowing Danny better than all others. In fact, she never knew him half as well as Orville did.

"The real story was much different. Danny John had left years before because he was sick of Ms. Wise, he wanted to get away from her, so much so that he used to tell people, 'If Eunice phones today tell her I'm dead—I can't listen to her anymore. Besides, I do not like her wiener dog.' He was also tired of the band politics over the casino—how money was being taken by men who were in charge of money; something police officers were not allowed to investigate. They might have built the casino ten years sooner without this well-constructed larceny. So Danny John decided to do something about it himself. It was in some ways heroic."

John, who had been reading his notes, looked up suddenly and waited to speak again. He waited because Cathy was now weeping—like a child, a little girl, tears flowing. She had begun to see something—the idea that he, John, might clear her brother's name completely. She realized that he could return the name Orville MacDurmot to its proper place. She knew, she said, she could never repay him. He did not answer, he simply waited.

"I can't ever repay you—you went to Europe?"

"Yes . . ."

"To the Middle East—to help us?"

"Yes."

"How can I begin to repay you?"

"You have repaid me already," he said.

"No," she whispered.

"One thousand times. When you came to me, asking me to help—frightened that I would not—my God—you gave it all back to me. You allowed me to help you," he said. "To help us get over how I hurt you years ago."

John told her he was now impatient with the Ms. Wises of the world. That millions of Eunices insisted on their priority and damaged the world. Perhaps he did not want to blame them for being so self-deceived; at the same time, he realized they were far from blameless. Eunice, he felt, had lied, stolen, cheated and manipulated to create a space for herself, and this had created immense suffering for the people she had targeted.

"Justice will come," he said. "Justice will come."

Cathy simply looked at him as she dried her eyes, in a kind of hope mixed with sudden dread.

"Did you ever hear of the five Chiefs during the War of 1812?" he asked now.

"No," Cathy said. "No, I did not."

"Orville did not mention them?"

"No."

"No one—almost no one—knows of it. Amos Paul, when he was Chief, wanted to know if it was a legend or was true. He contacted your brother, and had a meeting with him at the little band office in Burnt Church some years and years ago. He told Orville of his theory about where this incident had happened, and what might have happened, and hoped Orville could help him. Orville already had heard of this, and so decided to discover if it was true. Mary Cyr became involved, and gave funds—the ones she mentioned to Brenda that night in the car. The ones certain band council members thought should go to them; which became a catalyst in a few stealing some of the transfer payments some years later.

"Orville began his work in solitude. That is what he was doing up, the night of the fire, studying old hand-drawn maps that Amos Paul had left him; that is what he was doing when he told Eunice to get off his land. That was when he saw the panther on their disputed land, and warned her. The panther is significant as a symbol—for it certainly did exist at the time this First Nations boy was alive. Perhaps that too spurred Orville on."

"To what?"

"Well," John said, snapping his fingers quickly as if to erase twenty decades in an instant, "let us go back a ways—to when our whole forest here was deeper and larger and much greener and darker, and the river was pristine and moved like a quiet god. Back to the War of 1812."

So John picked up a document he had researched, and read slowly, deliberately and in some wonder, amazed that this was actually what her brother had been searching for.

"Here five men lived. And these men were the five most powerful Micmac Chiefs, living in a world now controlled by the British. The Americans wanted to work with the Micmac once the war started— hoping to start a rebellion along the coast to help American clipper ships moving against Quebec, and promising great territorial gains. The Chiefs remembered who they had been, and what power the British had taken from them. The British at this time were not harassed in the south of the province; in fact, gunpowder was loaned to the Americans in July of 1813 to celebrate their Fourth of July. But there were also spies and movement along the Miramichi and Northumberland Strait— Baltimore clippers moving toward our bay . . . I know this does sound like a history lesson from a bygone time.

"The large regiment at the time, the 104th, was preparing to travel overland into Upper Canada to stop American forces coming up from Detroit. What was available was a small regiment of a few British soldiers and some volunteers. This troop of men was sent along the King's Road to protect the valley at all costs—the lumber and fishery and the shire town of Newcastle—from a raid by American and Micmac rebels who might be arriving.

"The Brits waited out bad weather and made it to Gray Rapids in mid-June of 1813. It was to the men something like a forced march over uninhabitable places, some of the boys having been here in this country but a short while, some sick with dysentery. Most, except the Loyalists who had just enlisted and some Acadian volunteers, had never seen the animals they were to come in contact with. Their captain was Ezra Ahearn, a small, angular Scotsman as loyal to the British Crown as the most British Loyalist. He is the Scotsman who drew those maps—" and John pointed to the map in the hallway. "So at this moment—"

"He is standing here too," Cathy said.

John nodded.

"So this undermanned regiment met with a British gunship near Middle Island. And what came of it within the week was a decision to refit this ship into one resembling a clipper, ambush and stop the rebellion—"

"How?"

"The Chiefs expected to meet with American officers from the thirteen colonies. British men of war had driven the Americans from the bay mouth and had sunk that clipper sometime before—but the Chiefs were not aware of this. They were waiting for the clipper to come in."

"He—the boy was a Chief?"

"No—he was the son of the Chief from Esgenoôpetitj—what we now think of as Burnt Church. The Chief was talked into this clandestine meeting. And his fourteen-year-old boy came along to this meeting with him because he wanted to see the beauty of the great ship. He begged his father to let him come, to see and stand upon it.

"But," John continued, "it is what happened earlier in May of that year—what was reported to Ezra Ahearn about what that young Micmac boy wore—that started everything. The boy had come up to the Bartibog River mouth with a sheath made of doe hide to do business in bartering for eggs and a sow pig at MacDonald Farm."

"Doe hide—was unusual?"

"In 1813 it was very unusual—the first white-tailed deer shot in the province was not shot until the autumn of 1884 by a hunter who thought it was a caribou. It was an animal that lived at that time much farther south. That is, there were cougars in the woods then, and Eastern panthers, moose and caribou, but no white-tailed deer. So this doeskin sheath could not have been from here. It had to have come from some foreign presence. If the boy's father caught on that this had given them away, we do not know. But most probably it was overlooked. The boy had been given that knife and sheath as a present, most likely by an American who might have been working for an uprising. A short four nights later, Ahearn heard from people at MacDonald Farm of this strange sheath. He sat in his room at the barracks in Fredericton and thought it was perhaps nothing. But then he rose to the challenge, moved as many of his men as he could spare along the dusty King's Road from Fredericton, moving them by night and hoping not to be detected."

"All because of doe hide."

"So this was when the plot to counter the American plot started. It started with a message to the barracks in Fredericton about a strange sheath, and then the march north, while at the same time the five Chiefs were themselves plotting to meet the Americans on a clipper on a night in August off Sheldrake. They were promised a free hand to the territory—of course, we know that would never have happened.

"The Chiefs made camp here, near your brother's land, and canoed out to the clipper—whose fast, sleek body they saw in portentous silhouette in the evening sun, flying the American colony flag. If they had been circumspect about the sight of great ships they might have known it was a more cumbersome British vessel that awaited them in silence—a broader hull and less sleek than it should have been, with its guns housed and not naked, as the clipper's would have been. The five Chiefs—all grand men in their own right—and the boy had never been on such a ship before—here they were dressed in soft leather jackets and moccasins, wearing fine braids, their hair long and sleek and down their back, and carrying on their persons only bone-handled knives, with white beads they wore on their necks. They all climbed up onto the ship, eagerly succumbing to its beauty, to the scent of rope and tar, the sound of lowered sails still fluttering above them in the twilight. It would have been warm, the sun just going down, catching like fire on the teak wood and brass. But they had been betrayed so fully that when the last man clambered up the net rope the trap had already begun to be sprung. Betrayed not only by the sheath, but also by other Chiefs who would not join the insurrection. Too late they saw the British flag rise and turned to see the ten British soldiers in scarlet tunics, their buttons glinting in the last moment of sunshine.

"At the same moment they heard, in a cackling kind of self-virtuous voice:

"'*Fire* Mr. Covney—Fire, sir!'

"It was the voice of Lieutenant Ezra Ahearn, who may have said this in a voice searching for order and British propriety.

"Gorwithsha stood in front of his son as the first volley broke from the barrels, and hit him down in his mid-chest. He moved toward the soldiers as he was fired on again. Four musket balls hit him in the chest and face as he protected the boy. Four musket balls struck him before he fell—as the other Chiefs fell around him. The boy tried to charge them with his knife drawn. But he was wounded also. His father picked him up and threw him from the ship. The boy lost his precious sheath and knife, the sheath falling loose when he drew his knife to protect his father, and he probably died of shock when he hit the water. He was cast up here, taken by the current—for a time he lay in the open, and then slowly his body was interred by the mud and soil. Days passed, the ship slipped anchor and moved away. Then weeks passed, then months, and the war ended; years—and then almost two hundred years later, what fell near this boy but another body from another age—from a time so much in the future the young man lying beside this young girl, or actually some feet to the side and below her, would have been astounded, frightened out of his wits; now and again the buzz of her cellphone sounded in the small mud and rock crevice between the bodies, its eerie light illuminating and dimming, illuminating with each message and dimming down to nothing, six inches from where the boy's hand bones lay. It was as if the boy, who had been so proud of that deerskin sheath, the last thing he'd held two hundred years before, could have answered that cellphone, could have said hello to young Aiden Vale. So it kept ringing, its light coming on, and fading, and fading away.

"They lay beside each other as if destiny provoked them to be together in the end. Above them at that time Orville was searching for any sign of the remains of the five Chiefs—not knowing that, when he found it, it would allow him only days to live."

"Terrible—terrible what happened to those men—that boy. But it was—also—the war of 1812 to '14," Cathy said.

"It was," John said. "It was the march from Fredericton, the clandestine meetings, the refitting of the ship—it was war in all its messy commerce. The plot and counterplot were both thought of as stunning. Both plots carried beauty in the genome of man—both ideas of what was beautiful, used to betray."

"Because of a boy's attraction of a doeskin sheath."

"Yes—because of beauty—he carried the doeskin sheath on him like Milt carried his doeskin gloves or Eunice her Moleskine notebook. His bones were almost petrified when found, but again we did not realize this in time. If Orville had lived a few weeks more, we may have."

15.

VALE WAS PROVEN RIGHT—HIS ANIMOSITY TOWARD
Orville, his predicting a terrible crime, never once hidden in the last
four years, was now some splendid insight into the nature of man.

"My God, you called it," the head of the department said to him.
"I am so, so glad we did not hire him years ago. The girls were right
about him—whatdaya think?"

"Yes—awful business," Milt said. "Awful for that child—you
know I was tutoring her—I wanted to help her—and then Gaby
wanted to do the right thing, you know, about her pregnancy; I knew
she had been molested, you can always tell—though she spoke not
of it—I thought she had gone to Montreal to have the abortion. I
would have paid for it—but he caught her somewhere down near
that terrible place she grew up—she finally confronted him, told him
she would reveal what had happened. He would be destroyed. So he
went insane—Catholics, you know. There's enough of them to last a
lifetime. Then he went running to the monastery. I had no idea there
were monasteries left to go to, but there you go. I guess they have
them up in that place."

"So you knew all of it?"

"All of it—no," Milt said, sadly, shaking his head in humility, with his eyes turned upward, "not all of it—but I did know much of it—I often said I was glad the university never hired him—great moral concerns—there is no place for morality in learning—well, is there? I travelled up there, you see—went there just to try to find out for myself—the place needs fewer Orville MacDurmots and more Eunice Wises."

This was all said earlier in the afternoon; that last afternoon. The afternoon John met Cathy in the library to tell her arrests would soon come. Then John and Cathy left the library and it was night, and John went to a judge to prepare a warrant.

Milt walked jauntily back to his home, went upstairs and in a fit of energy decided to clean his bookshelves. The beauty of the lie exquisitely beamed out on his shiny face.

Only Aiden, his son, was the blemish—the blemish that brought back a certain memory of a bit of brain flying up and hitting his cheek. The tiny hand of Gaby fumbling for the knife, as if taking it out would save her. That was the blemish. Sometimes the sight of hair and blood would seem to glide upward to him when he closed his eyes during a lecture on Jane Austen. So he worked at polishing his shelves and dusting his books. That always seemed to take his mind off things. He was planning a full two weeks in Mahone Bay with Eunice—but if he could slip out, he knew of a young lady there as well; a poet he knew from one of the small villages. She wrote what was true about exploitation. Her poem "Marriage Is Rape" was a wonderful commentary. What seemed so true about the relationship between Orville and Gaby was for Milt true in its purest form. That is, for Milt at this moment, it was the purest of all truths. *And, what was best, no one could say it was not.*

It was just after six in the afternoon. The day was almost dark when he heard someone on the stairs, and then Aiden was there—and what took place initially has already been mentioned.

"You discovered her dad's book and stole it and she found out," Aiden said.

"That was my book and he stole it—don't you see, son?" Milt said. He was so forceful at lying. He walked back into the study and picked up his pipe. He blew through the stem while looking at the youngster. He asked why Aiden had ever gotten mixed up with some ignorant tramp like Gaby May—some little fool. "I will simply burn the manuscript and that will be that! That will be that!"

Milt dragged on his pipe, the sweet, glorious scent of rich tobacco mingling with the polish he had used on his bookshelves. There was the shadow of a man in the doorway just as Aiden said, "I will not let you burn it. You will have to kill me first. The last chapters prove you could never have written it—the whole book proves it as well."

Tom Crump, who had carried a shotgun out toward men who had come to attack him, had been in jail, and was staring at the man he had just heard call his sister an ignorant tramp. But for a while, over a minute, not a thing was spoken. Nothing. And then Professor Milt Vale spoke, earnestly and nervously, his eyes darting from one to the other.

"We need to get my son help—he killed Gaby May and the unborn child—I went up to the river to stop him—I had the tag erased so no one would know—but I can't hide it any longer. I am ashamed I hid it—quite ashamed, but anyone would protect his or her child—any decent human being. I am sorry I cannot protect him anymore."

And he put his hand on Aiden's shoulder, as if once again begging him for the lie that would free him. Aiden sat in the chair staring straight ahead. Momentarily it was as if all three of them inhabited their own vacuum, each processing their own information.

"Why did you want to burn my uncle's book?" Tom asked.

Milt flushed his pipe and smoke softened the air before them like a veil.

"Why did you?"

"Because—it's simply a copy of my book."

"Of your book?" Tom asked. "No, no—that's a mistake, it is my dad's book. I was there when he wrote it—"

"No—a copy of my book," Milt said. He smiled ruefully at all of this, held Aiden's shoulder again and squeezed it.

"Is that right?" Tom asked Aiden. "Is that why you were upset—why you wanted me to leave you alone?"

Aiden stared at the piece of Fabergé—the false, gold-plated decorative leaves shining dully—that Milt had first seen in a small hotel in Florence years before. Sold to him by a former student who loved jazz, tried to imitate Chet Baker's songs, and was this day, his last day, under a section of bridge in Kabul, the pillars filled with graffiti anointments and emblems of curses and love: Issup Farad, all his dreams now contained in a spoon, a heroin addict left alone by the world to die. Aiden stared at that false piece of art as he spoke, while his father still held *Confessions of a Mask* in his hand.

"My father stole your dad's book—he stole the book and published it as his. I know he was sent it just after your dad died—I too was here—Gaby found it out—he killed her because she was going to tell me, we were going to have a child—my dad killed my child, his grandchild—and for the last year he's blamed Orville MacDurmot."

Then he said:

"I brought him the last forty pages to show what the book was missing at the end of it all. Now he wants to run away."

And then he added:

"And if I were him, I would want to run away too."

Tom was incredulous. He was still in shadow, the day was ending, there was a smell of polish, and the marble end tables were darkening moment by moment. The nice leatherbound nineteenth-century man's travelling case with letter holders and silver shaving kit sat up on one end with its weak brass snaps broken and its aged and spotted red-cloth interior just visible. Tom stood there, his face flushed, his hair falling down to his coat collar, his jean jacket with letter tags, his eyes piercing the night. He then walked over and picked up Milt with one hand by the throat. Milt tried to scratch his hands away.

"Bully!" Milt screeched. "You are a bully, young man!!" His small fingers tried to pry Tom's hands away. He dropped Yukio Mishima's book.

"Leave him alone," Aiden said, with such force that Tom simply dropped his victim and Professor Milt Vale fell down on his knees. Then Tom said:

"Why would anyone ever want to steal a book?"

16.

TOM DID NOT KNOW WHAT IT WAS ABOUT—HOW ANYONE would simply do this. And so, put into shock, he left the man on the carpet, left Aiden sitting in the chair, turned and went back down the great mahogany stairs and out into the dark, closing the door quietly, his face refracted by the door window's flecked cut glass; then, with the last of last summer's leaves red and gold and poised to fall, and a hundred thousand golden leaves blowing down the wide, white cul-de-sac, the elms high over his head, he walked away. And just to the north, a bitter snow still fell.

But far from becoming the end of his life, as he felt it was, in five years this man, this Thomas Dollard Crump, would be seen at Saint Mary's University doing research. His was a fascinating story—the man who was born again by trafficking in a tragedy. He, Thomas Crump, would wrestle himself up all the way to his master's in English because he had to discover what books were about, and then in 2014 he would begin to teach at the university in Cape Breton. His past would be remembered in the sweet light shades of a leather-bound book that would be dedicated to Gaby May. He would marry and have two children—Gaby May and Peter Orville.

Tom would become an authority on what happened to his stepfather, to what happened in and to the literary world. He would become his stepfather's executor. *Darkness* would be republished in 2012 with the right author's name, and an introduction by Tom himself. It would be bound in leather and reintroduced to the public, having the missing pages that completed the tome.

Because of John Delano's warrant, Milt was taken into custody a day later trying to flee to the States. He was dressed in his three-piece suit, his brown leather gloves and what he always called in his own stories his "galoshes." There is a picture of him being taken out of the car in St. Stephen. He was trying to cross into Calais, Maine. He hired a very good lawyer, who came with fine credentials and had once led the Conservative Party. It was widely believed that Milt had stolen the book. But as far as the murder of Gaby May went, it looked as if he would get off. He was granted bail, and was on paid leave from the university. The grand house on that cul-de-sac sat under the awning of spacious trees, beyond the lights of the porch. He wrestled over every tidbit of evidence—the receipt for gas he bought in Boiestown on the very date little Gaby May had sent the manuscript to her brother was a sticking point. Milt complained, and in a way justifiably, that he couldn't be expected to remember exactly why he was in Boiestown five or so years before. Except one might counter that he had rarely been that far out of Fredericton in that direction, and only twice before to the Miramichi.

The prosecution was looked upon as young and outclassed—until they convinced Eunice Wise to testify against him. It was at this point when one realized that Ms. Wise could change her opinion of a person, or her own part in someone else's life, in the flickering of a second. Her profile now, especially around the neck and throat, was shaded and wrinkled. She wore multicoloured scarfs to hide this and she now looked her age of sixty-three.

Suddenly, Milt's defence was given warning that she was meeting with the young prosecutor and her team in Newcastle.

She met with the prosecutor on a number of occasions. She had to decide how she would fare. It would not be fair to actually accuse her. She knew this—that the erasing of the graffiti actually worked in her favour. It showed her to be deliberate in her naivety. She told the prosecutor, though, in a backroom meeting, that it might be much better for her if she said nothing at all. For as perverse as it was, the position she had cultivated, of helping both poor and Indigenous women, seemed more plausible if she said nothing about Gaby May's horrendous murder by Eunice's own boyfriend. If she did not speak, he might go free. But if she was content to let the murderer of this child go free, it might actually be better for her status as a tremendous advocate of justice. That is, by her not testifying, people might still be convinced it was Orville's crime. This, in fact, is what certain of the public thought as well—and she did have her supporters, brave, candid women and men from Halifax and Toronto universities, women committed to change, who told her this trial was a male ploy to damage her reputation. Certain radical advocates were against her saying anything at all.

However, if she and her group of supporters continued to blame Orville, the same righteous assessment of who Eunice was could be fully maintained. Orville would continue to be the one true suspect she had fought against valiantly for years; Gaby May, whom she had tried to save, his childlike victim. This was the prevalent view for so long, and she was looked upon as being so brave in combating him, why not continue it?

"You had nothing to do with it, so do not get involved," one woman advised.

It made almost perfect sense in our modern world. And there was a reason to continue with this scenario. After all, she must think of her own best interests, and the interests of women that she knew, who had stood beside her, hated Orville most of their lives and were stalwarts of truth and honesty and justice. So at a certain moment, seeing an advantage, Eunice became coy, granted no interviews and retired to her grand house.

But the police did not want that, so to accommodate her, Eunice was courted and feted. She became the most important object of attention on our river. The prosecutor met with her five or six times. And this did seem to flatter her. The prosecutor, a woman who secretly loathed her, knew and loathed her protegés Sharon and Jane, loathed her insipid group called Wise Ears, loathed their smugness, nonetheless sang Eunice's praises, boasted about Eunice's dedication to the truth. So in order to facilitate her ambition, Eunice became as much a victim in the public eye as Gaby May—in fact, almost a co-victim: she gave an impact statement, and how she had been treated seemed very harsh. Her family gathered about her, the well-known Wise clan, certain someone had hoodwinked their kind, gullible sister. The prosecutor, understanding how she must smile and nod at these deplorable, grasping people, detested them all.

So poor Milt was left on his own. Yes, her testimony revealed that he had a hold over her. And then, when Danny John disappeared, it was life-shattering. Her work with the First Nations was chronicled in fine detail and so too was her building a sweat lodge on her property. The disappearance of Danny John caused her an extended nervous collapse, heightened by feelings of failure; failure because she didn't do enough. She just didn't do enough. So she had a psychological dependency on Milt Vale. But as the trial went on Eunice's freshness and vivaciousness returned. She had escaped Milt Vale's mendacious spell. She looked startlingly able to make a fresh start. It seemed this was what was most important, for everyone involved. Gaby May's horrific murder was secondary.

————

The defence, however, showed Milt as a man who had led an exemplary life—a life of seeking wisdom, of collecting artifacts, of having great conversations on these, of devoting his time to his students—some of whom testified on his behalf. Of helping the Miramichi writer with his work—and of being the victim of someone else's misunderstanding—that is, Duffy's misunderstanding—the publisher who thought Milt had sent him his own book. Milt was as shocked as anyone that his name had appeared on the cover when it was published, and he had planned in his retirement to set it all straight. (The royalties he received, he said, had been put in trust until he could find the author's children—then why, he argued, would he strike Gaby?—and besides, he'd had no idea who she actually was.)

But the worst was this: he had gone to protect Gaby not from Orville, but from Aiden, his son, who had murdered the young woman because he wanted to protect his father in an act of extreme devotion. Gaby became Aiden's girlfriend for one reason only, to accuse Milt of stealing the book, and to blackmail them both. It was not Aiden's fault, this misplaced idea of love—but it was Aiden who took the bottle of sleeping pills because he could not live with himself any longer. Milt at that time became convinced of what he had suspected Aiden had done. But it was not the first time he had suspected Aiden, he said, wiping his eyes and then blowing his nose; no, he had suspected Aiden in the death of Aiden's own mother. He was sure she had been pushed into oncoming traffic fourteen years before. It seemed Milt was telling the truth; for how could a father lie so deliberately about his own child?

"I could have straightened it all out with Gaby if Aiden had only given me time."

He did love Eunice; he had planned to marry her. They kept putting it off until he retired. He did not blame her for what she thought—but she did not have to live, as he did, with the ghost of his wife, or the memories of trying to help his son, a sad, thin loner who wrote on walls and was under a psychiatrist's care.

"And that," the defence asked, "is why you had Ms. Wise white-wash the bridge graffiti?"

"That is exactly why," Milt said, in a tone bordering on surprise. "Yes. That is it exactly."

Aiden himself was not asked to testify because he was still under Dr. Faun's care. But the prosecution never charged him, either, for they at least knew he had done nothing.

Milt, after the jury was initially deadlocked, was declared not guilty. His face shone with a kind of primeval exultation. This look, which he wore whenever he met someone, lasted for months. He went back to teaching his favourite book, *The Scarlet Letter*. A book that had all the right benchmarks, against the right things. Though his classes were now much smaller and other younger, more energetic professors were trying to push him along to retirement, he met a young woman, a devotee of his. He invited her to his grand house, and showed her his collection of carvings and paintings and, with a look of triumph, his beautiful Fabergé egg.

He often waited for, and expected, Aiden to come home. He wondered if he could make it all up to him in some way. It had been bad to use him that way, but there had been no alternative. Once in a while he would actually see Aiden on the street; he would see him walking away, up the hill, with his thin legs moving as quickly as they could. Aiden, he learned, lived in a shelter, but he did not know where.

"Aiden, my son," Milt would call out. "Aiden—Aiden, my dear son," he would call, hoarsely at the end.

———

Then one night some two years after the trial, when this young woman from Chatham had left his house and the downstairs lights were on, Milt Vale received a phone call from the Department of Foreign Affairs in Ottawa. No, he had not known where his son had gone. His son had left a year and a half before. There was no word from him at all—

"Yes, I understand, that's the name—Aiden, yes, what is it? He was where? Where?"

Aiden had been killed fighting alongside the Kurds against Islamic fighters, in the small, unknown town of Kobani. He was trying to help rescue a Yazidi girl when he was killed. "Help me, brother," she had called out, and he had bravely run back to get her. He was under Lieutenant Fara's command, in a regiment in the Peshmerga's 17th Brigade. But as he came from behind a smokescreen and a broken wall, he took two bursts from an AK-47. It was all over in a second, all his pain. He was buried at a small gravesite. He was twenty-six years old.

Why did he do that? Why had he gone there? No one seemed to know.

Later that same year the girl from Chatham found a young boyfriend, and Milt after this was mostly alone. He began to get rickety on his feet, though, and once the poor old man fell while climbing the stairs. That was the night he took to sleeping in Aiden's room, and found in Aiden's back closet the Christmas present from all those years and years ago. It was, strangely enough, a copy of *Paradise Lost*. Milt picked it up; there was a tag on the wrapping: *To my dad, the best dad, Love, Aiden.*

He trembled when he saw that. And opening the book finally, he read about Satan, Beelzebub and Moloch, and all those great evil spirits, principalities and dominions he had once refused to believe in.

―――

That year the land Eunice claimed went to arbitration, and into court once more. The First Nations band demanded it all, and set about to prove it was theirs, because of the very discovery the late Orville MacDurmot had made.

It was awarded them, and a plaque was set up to honour the boy and the Chiefs. Just beyond that there is now a First Nations–owned casino situated where the body of the young warrior from the War of 1812 was found. There is a beautiful road to it, and spacious oak trees line this road, and an ancient square-rigger is situated off the shore as a major tourist attraction. The place is called the Forgotten Warrior. People visit from as far away as Saskatchewan.

But all the Wises were involved in trying to sue the First Nations band, and the lost money became a terrible sore point—especially since the patriarch still ran the family from his wheelchair. Now bitter, no one in her family speaks to Eunice. She still takes photos. She herself has not spoken to Milt since before the trial.

―――

The night Cathy left the library after listening to the tributes to her dear late friend John Delano and his solving of seventeen major cases, she passed Brenda Townie going home from somewhere. Brenda crossed the street to speak to her. It seemed Brenda needed to ask about him, to tell his sister she had made a terrible mistake about Orville, in some way.

"We all made a mistake," Cathy said, "about each other, and what our lives should have been."

Brenda walked home alone. All of it was over, and she could never go back even if she tried. She could never be that beautiful young girl again. Her parents were dead, and her in-laws saw to it that certain young men that Junior was known to become excited by, to follow about in his Mustang, and sometimes take for drives back along the Tower Road, were paid money to keep quiet. No one wanted that to get out. Still, it was known.

That night the light was on in the basement when Brenda got home, and she sat in the back bedroom drinking from her bottle of wine, feeling Junior's lonely presence far away down the stairs. The day Orville was in court Junior would not let her out of the house. She tried to go, to support her friend, the one who had loved her. But Junior was furious about what people might think. He blocked the door and refused to let her go. She begged him for an hour, for this one favour—but though tears welled in his eyes, he said no. Then he tied her arms and feet with Kitty's little skipping rope, and carried her to the bed.

Later that evening, when the darkness came in like silk, he came into the small bedroom, untied her and said in a soft, even compassionate voice, while looking out the window and holding the bright-red skipping rope with the blue handles in his left hand:

"He is gone—he jumped to his death a few hours ago. That is why I didn't want you to go—you can thank me for not allowing you to see it."

She sat up on the bed and stared at a point on the floor for hours. She didn't even cry. What was the use of tears?

But now she had a friend—he was an older man, the only friend she had. She had met him, strangely enough, the long-ago day she had left Orville's house. She had taken the back route through the woods, and had hit the gravel on a turn and gone off the road. A man happened to pass by in the opposite direction a few minutes later, and stopped to help her. He was coming from fishing Glidden's Pool. She certainly was a beautiful woman, and dressed provocatively—adorned, really, in the middle of this sun-clouded day.

Before she drove away he gave her his name and telephone number on a printed card. She put it into her purse and forgot all about it.

Then one day a few weeks after Orville's death she telephoned him.

"You mightn't remember me," she said.

"Remember you—of course—Brenda—of course!"

"I might take a drive—do you mind if I visit?" she asked.

His name was Calvin Simms. He had done well in the crab indus-try, and he liked to buy certain things—he had bought many things of beauty for her over the past year.

His house was far downriver, on the bay; very large and inter-connected with rooms and stairs. It was built on top of an old seventeenth-century fort, and the great ancient stones that were part of the basement foundation still held prisoner shackles—and Calvin's wine cellar. When you walked through the wine cellar, with stones laid by men from seventeenth-century France, you came to a great arbour that had a crystal swimming pool, with sunlight flush-ing down from an opening in the ceiling. He bought wine from a vineyard in France, the vineyard owned by those people who had given Orville the commendation. She drank that wine often. It was nice to go and be with Calvin once a week, and then to go place flowers on Orville's grave. It was scandalous. People were talking about her all over town. Of her being the crab man's whore. Junior might have suspected but Brenda no longer cared.

———

Mr. Covney was the last to leave Beaverbrook House that night they were honouring John Delano. He shut off the lights—all was in darkness—all the books and emblems and trinkets and medal-lions, mementoes from certain Canadian men of history—and he walked down the blocks to his back bedroom. Mr. Covney was a good man, old though, and should really retire. There was nothing much he could say about anything that was spoken about that day—he had shovelled the walkway and made sure the furnace was on. He had nodded to certain neighbours and listened to the tributes to John Delano, and smiled when Cathy MacDurmot, one of John's great loves, was pointed out to him.

He had no idea—and who would?—that he had seen the "extinct" Eastern panther on the same day Orville MacDurmot had shot at it. That was the day he and a friend went deer hunting down along the swale. The panther walked right in front of them half an hour after Orville had fired at it. But they were so startled they did not know what to do. Then it bounded and was gone into the deep spruce woods to the north before they could actually even say they saw it. Six months later it was seen far up along the Bathurst highway by a trucker, whom no one believed either.

Mr. Covney, who never before in his life had hunted deer, was excited to show his friend the bone-handled knife and old deerskin sheath his great-great-great-granddad had taken from a wild First Nations man, whom he had fought valiantly to the death. Or so Mr. Covney had heard. It was the only time he had hunted deer, and he didn't much like it. It was the only time he had ever taken the knife from the house, and he returned it to its glass case. He wasn't much of a hunter—and as far as the old knife went, he had no idea what in hell it was worth.

———

Danny John was back home, and had become a band councillor, but Eunice would not speak to him either. She did once try to reunite with her husband. She wore all the appropriate clothes, a sparkling red riding vest and a small bunt cap, and walked into his house with a smile, thinking, "He will know I am back." That terrible woman Brenda Townie was sitting in the large white living room dressed in a black vest with small pearl buttons and pleated slacks. When Eunice left she started to cry—harshly, bitterly, for a great many reasons.

Scamper McVeigh became head of the Kinsmen in Lower Lincoln, New Brunswick. He also ran for MLA, unsuccessfully.

———

Orville MacDurmot received the Order of Canada posthumously. His sister, Cathy MacDurmot, accepted it.

She went to the reception and dinner at Rideau Hall, and sat at a very nice dinner with people she did not know. Later she took the train back to Toronto. On the trip she took the note Orville had sent her just before the trial and read it for the last time:

You see, Cathy, they have made a mistake—believe me. For once they figure out what it is I was doing on the beach, I will be released to great acclaim. They will finally love me. Oh, yes—I often wanted to be loved. There will be abundant apologies coming my way. But I do not need apologies. I will simply ignore the apologies. What I need now is to find where Gaby May went, so I can award her the trust fund, and bend down and kiss her on the cheek and apologize for not taking her fishing. I will take her fishing someday. If you ever do see Brenda Townie, tell her I am so very sorry—so very sorry I did not go into the kitchen that long-ago day, and put my arm around her once. Just one time for us both. But I was too afraid of rejection all over again. I have had that often enough. So I am sure she will understand. If you ever speak to Eunice, tell her the reason I was in Jordan was to help excavate a site in Petra. She will understand. Tell her I am very sorry for a great many reasons.

It is with his papers now, buried somewhere in the archives in a university that once refused to hire him.

John did not take the cheque she offered him. She had enough money from Orville's estate to give it to charity.

———

In 2014 Junior asked Brenda to renew their vows, and so she did, in the church in Newcastle. There were few people in the small alcove at one end of the church, so few that their presence made the church seem deserted. Brenda wore a fine, glittering diamond pin that Calvin Simms had bought her, and since it was November, high black leather boots that came to the top of her soft, rose-coloured skirt.

———

Shortly before Milt Vale died in 2014 he heard the name Kobani on television and he looked up, startled. There he saw a burned-out street, heroic fighters and a grave on a hill, black smoke rising over the world, making it all so dark. In the distance he saw the terrible black flag where those who had just beheaded and tortured eighteen Christian men and women were selling Yazidi girls.

So frightened of what he was seeing, Professor Milt Vale closed his eyes; he shut them like he did when he was a little boy. But when they closed, he witnessed a setting with trees and leaves and beauty all around, his boy, Aiden, and sweet Gaby May walking with a young blond-headed girl between them, and he heard laughter in the air. They were walking away from him toward a silver river in the sun. He didn't know if it was the Miramichi, but it may have been. He couldn't imagine how much love there seemed to be in that child's laughter. He whispered for them to turn and face him. He found him-self falling to his knees. He pleaded with God to allow him to see their faces—to see their faces once again so he could beg forgive-ness from them both; that he would give up everything—everything he had ever had, had ever achieved—just to see their faces one more time.

But for some reason he was not allowed.

Acknowledgements

I wish to thank Lynn Henry, Amy Black, Anne McDermid, Liz Mitchell, my sisters, Mary Jane Richards and Susan Marshall, and my wife Peggy. In fact, for most of my life I have had too many women to thank for standing by my work and career, for the road has often been mined with too many obstacles.

I have not forgotten this in the female characters I have managed to create over these many years, from Leah to Lois, from Elly and Autumn Henderson to tough irascible Janie McCleary (modelled after my own grandmother. In fact she didn't need to be modelled after anyone else). Of all the female characters I have created, Mary Cyr and Gaby May Crump, so different and yet so much the same in their humanity, are among my favourites. And of them all, Cathy MacDurmot, who I first wrote about when I was twenty-three, in a book about her and Orville called *Blood Ties*, has stuck with me, along with her first love John Delano. She, Cathy, was and is still modelled after my sister-in-law Mary McIntyre, who I met when she was a beautiful young girl of fifteen. I realized she and John must meet again, and come to terms with their past love. I realized Orville's deformity would cast him out, and make him a scapegoat, for people would fear what he said and criticize what he did, and find in him an easy target to mock. But one is always mocked by lesser men.

One must not mistake religion with searching, as Orville did, for spiritual greatness. Unattainable for sure, cast out as ironic, yes. But the search in itself is fine.

That is what Mary Cyr and Gaby May Crump, and Autumn and Elly, would know.

DAR
December 2020

DAVID ADAMS RICHARDS is a Giller Prize and two-time Governor General's Literary Award recipient and one of Canada's pre-eminent writers. His recent novels include *The Tragedy of Eva Mott*, *Mary Cyr* and *Principles to Live By*, as well as *Crimes Against My Brother* and *Incidents in the Life of Markus Paul*, both of which were longlisted for the Giller Prize. Among his other novels, *The Lost Highway* was shortlisted for the Governor General's Literary Award and nominated for the Giller Prize; *The Friends of Meager Fortune* won the Commonwealth Writers' Prize for Best Book and was longlisted for the Giller Prize; *Mercy Among the Children* won the Giller Prize and was shortlisted for the Governor General's Literary Award and the Trillium Award. Richards is also the author of the celebrated Miramichi Trilogy and has written four bestselling books of nonfiction, *Lines on the Water*, *God Is*, *Facing the Hunter* and *Hockey Dreams*, and most recently the collection of essays *Murder*. In 2017, he was appointed to the Senate of Canada on the advice of Prime Minister Justin Trudeau.

ALSO BY DAVID ADAMS RICHARDS

FICTION

The Coming of Winter
Blood Ties
Dancers at Night: Stories
Lives of Short Duration
Road to the Stilt House
Nights Below Station Street
Evening Snow Will Bring Such Peace
For Those Who Hunt the Wounded Down
Hope in the Desperate Hour
The Bay of Love and Sorrows
Mercy Among the Children
River of the Brokenhearted
The Friends of Meager Fortune
The Lost Highway
Incidents in the Life of Markus Paul
Crimes Against My Brother
Principles to Live By
Mary Cyr
The Tragedy of Eva Mott

NONFICTION

Hockey Dreams
Lines on the Water
Extraordinary Canadians: Lord Beaverbrook
God Is.
Facing the Hunter
Murder and Other Essays

POETRY

Small Heroics
Wild Green Light (with Margo Wheaton)